LIFE AND DEATH

'Belinda Bauer is one of the best British
crime writers out there right now'
Simon Kernick

'Bauer at her best . . .
the true heir to the great Ruth Rendell'
Mail on Sunday

'Belinda Bauer's thrillers are always compelling,
always original, always brilliant. I will rush
to read anything she writes'
Mark Billingham

'Our most inventive crime writer'
Metro

She writes so beautifully, plots so cleverly and exhibits
a razor-sharp understanding of people and places'
Literary Review

'This gripping, unsettling tale blends a murder
mystery with a blackly comic look at the
gradual erosion of "normal" family life.
You won't want to put it down'
Bella

'Gripping and original'
Sunday Times

'Lingers in the mind like an unwelcome guest,
albeit one with a dark sense of humour . . .
powerful, compelling reading'
Spectator

'Belinda Bauer is the most interesting crime
writer in England today'
Val McDermid

BLACKLANDS

Winner of the CWA GOLD DAGGER FOR
CRIME NOVEL OF THE YEAR

DARKSIDE

FINDERS KEEPERS

'Surprise, of course, is the most potent aspect of suspense.
And Belinda Bauer knows exactly how to manipulate that element,
right until the very end. What's more, she's shown, not just how
to keep surprise bubbling explosively away, but to do it with
extraordinary dexterity, maturity and feeling'
Daily Mirror

'Belinda Bauer's third book represents a remarkable achievement:
almost a return to the good old Victorian triple-decker novel of suspense,
but created with a deftness that allows each book to stand alone'
Independent

'Bauer is not occupied by writing a "crime story"
– although there is a crime at the heart of it –
she is more interested in writing a novel'
Karin Fossum

'*Finders Keepers* has an enjoyably creepy premise . . .
But it's the book's humour that really shines. Bauer reveals
her Gold Dagger-winning writing credentials in her neat
skewering of everyday pomposities and her wry asides'
Observer

'Belinda Bauer hit the big time with the excellent *Blacklands* and
continues to explore her theme of West Country cruelty and corruption,
balancing the procedural and psychological aspects of crime. Once again
she nails the petty grievances, prejudices and loyalties of village life, and
shows how some law enforcers operate at the outer edge of competence'
Financial Times

'Compelling...Bauer blends a psychological crime story with
a darkly humorous narrative . . . I can't wait for the next one!'
Bookseller (Booksellers' Choice)

'One of the leading names in crime fiction'
Stylist

RUBBERNECKER

Winner of the Theakstons Old Peculier Crime Novel of the Year Award

Belinda Bauer grew up in England and South Africa and now lives in Wales. She worked as a journalist and a screenwriter before finally writing a book to appease her nagging mother.

With her debut, *Blacklands*, Belinda was awarded the CWA Gold Dagger for Crime Novel of the Year. She went on to win the CWA Dagger in the Library for her body of work in 2013. Her fourth novel, *Rubbernecker*, was voted 2014 Theakstons Old Peculier Crime Novel of the Year. Her books have been translated into twenty-one languages.

Belinda's latest novel is *The Shut Eye*.

For more information, visit **belindabauer.co.uk** or ⬛ **BelindaBauerBooks**

THE FACTS OF
LIFE AND DEATH

Belinda Bauer

BLACK SWAN

TRANSWORLD PUBLISHERS
61–63 Uxbridge Road, London W5 5SA
www.transworldbooks.co.uk

Transworld is part of the Penguin Random House group of companies
whose addresses can be found at global.penguinrandomhouse.com

Penguin
Random House
UK

First published in Great Britain in 2014 by Bantam Press
an imprint of Transworld Publishers
Black Swan edition published 2015

A CIP catalogue record for this book
is available from the British Library.

ISBN
9780552779654

Typeset in 11/14pt Caslon 540 by Falcon Oast Graphic Art Ltd.
Printed and bound by CPI Group (UK) Ltd, Croydon, CR0 4YY.

Penguin Random House is committed to a sustainable
future for our business, our readers and our planet. This book
is made from Forest Stewardship Council® certified paper.

1 3 5 7 9 10 8 6 4 2

To all my sisters and my secret brother

1

IT HADN'T STOPPED raining all summer, and the narrow stream that divided Limeburn ran deeper than Ruby Trick had seen it in all of the ten years she'd been alive.

The ditch that marked the crease in the gorge usually held a foot of tumbling, tuneful water. Enough to wet your knees but not your knickers.

But this summer was different. This summer, the sun had only shone apologetically through short gaps in the dirty Devonshire clouds, and the stream was fast and deep and dark. And although Adam Braund could still jump from one mossy bank to the other if he had a run up, the children all gathered to watch him now because if he fell in, it was just possible that he might drown.

The lane that rose a steep, curling mile through the forest to the main road was always mirrored with wet, while the cobbles between the cottages closest to the slipway had never lost their green winter sheen. The trees that threatened to push Limeburn's twenty-odd houses into the greedy sea below never dried out. Leaves dripped even when the sky did not; the stream spewed from the cliff face like a fire hose, and the steep dirt footpaths that escaped Limeburn through the woods were nothing but lethal slides.

Not that that stopped anyone, of course.

There were only five children in the village so they were forced to be playmates, just as they were forced to live in this dank place that smelled of kelp.

Chris Braund was the eldest at thirteen. His brother Adam was a year younger, but a year taller. The Braunds were descended from Armada sailors washed ashore, and they all looked like gypsies. Then there was Ruby with her shock of red hair. After her came seven-year-old Maggie Beer and her two-year-old sister, Em, who slowed them all down. Both were stick thin and see-through pale. Maggie had to linger for Em, the boys went on ahead, while Ruby was always left somewhere in the middle.

To the west they were allowed to climb the path through the forest to the stone stile. In a small clearing there, a bench on the cliff looked out through a leafy frame and over the black pebble beach to the Gore. The Gore was a slim, flat spit that jutted a hundred yards into the waves before turning abruptly and stopping. It was said that the Devil had tried to build a bridge across to Lundy Island, but had been thwarted when his shovel broke.

Ruby didn't like the Gore or the story.

They made her wonder where the Devil was now.

Hanging from an ancient oak beside the bench was a loop of fraying rope where they could swing – if they wanted to burn their palms and fall in the mud. Still, they did swing more often than not, because that was all there was to do.

Sometimes Chris and Adam climbed over the stile and went on up the pathway. 'All the way to Clovelly!' Chris had boasted on several occasions, but when Ruby had asked him to bring her back a toy donkey from the visitor centre, he said they'd run out.

Ruby never went past the stile. 'That far and no further,' her mother had warned her. That was partly why. The other part was that, even on a sunny day, the woods beyond the stile were too dark and too quiet – a tunnel of green with the threat of the unseen drop on one side, and tangled undergrowth rising on the other. The pixies in the woods would lead you in circles – even right off the cliff – if they could. You'd have to turn your coat inside out to keep them away.

At the foot of the Clovelly path was a small stone beehive-shaped hut. They didn't know what the hut was supposed to be for, but they called it the Bear Den because even in the dry it smelled like bears. The children took turns to squeeze through the tiny door and sit in the dark with their knees tucked under their chins for as long as they could stand it.

Adam held the record, which was ages.

To the east, the Peppercombe path was even steeper – a switchback of mud and wooden planking in a makeshift staircase between clinging brambles.

Halfway up was the haunted house where they weren't allowed to go. They spent much of their time there, picking among the cinders in the fireplaces and knocking glass from the empty windows at low tide, to hear it tinkle on the wet pebbles a hundred feet below. Each year the worm-chewed floor jutted out further and further over the disintegrating drop. There was one place where Ruby could lie with her eye to a knothole in the floor, where there was nothing between her and the dark grey sea.

It was like flying.

Or falling.

Ruby Trick lived in a tiny two-bedroomed cottage called The Retreat. It was owned by a family in London who had bought it and named it and then found it was too distant, too dreary, too damp to retreat to – even just once a summer – and had rented it out until they could sell at a profit.

That was never going to happen. The Retreat would cost less to demolish and rebuild than it would to repair. Ruby's father, John Trick, hammered bits of scrap wood into draughty window frames, and slapped filler at the widening cracks in the walls, but each year The Retreat fought a losing battle against nature.

The forest didn't want them there – that was plain to Ruby. While Clovelly kept it at bay with size and industry – and, ultimately, brute tourism – Limeburn was just in its way. The stream and the road and the thin line of houses were never going to be enough to keep the trees on *this* side of the coombe joining the trees on *that* side. It was only a matter of time. The advance party was already established. Ferns sprouted from stone walls like little green starfish, while rhododendrons and hydrangeas crowded back doors and shrouded rear windows. And, even as the trees surrendered their branches to loppers and chainsaws, so they tunnelled sly roots under enemy lines, breaking through pipes, loosening foundations and shifting walls out of true. In Rock Cottage the living-room floor had bulged and finally splintered to reveal a root of oak as thick as a man's leg. They'd all been in to look, and to help old Mrs Vanstone rearrange the furniture around it.

John Trick always said there were some things you just couldn't stop. Already the houses further up the hill had been swallowed by the forest, their stone hearths now washed with rain, and home only to spiders and bloated toads, while the houses that were left had nowhere to go but the sea, which gouged relentlessly at the cliff beneath them.

The long, curved slipway tempted the water up into the village, and sometimes it came. During spring tides and storms, sandbags were packed tight behind wooden slides in the doorways, and people took their heirlooms and TVs up to bed with them, just in case.

By day, it was easy to forget that the trees and the ocean were lying in wait. By day the children played in the woods and stepped gingerly across the giant pebbles on the beach to paddle in the rockpools.

But by night Ruby could feel the tides tugging at her belly, while the forest tested The Retreat, squealing against the glass and tapping on the tiles.

And she wondered what it would be like – when the outside finally broke in.

2

JOHN TRICK DROVE them up to the main road to get the bus – Ruby to Bideford, her mother only as far as the hotel, from where she brought home leftovers so good that Ruby would sometimes get up in the middle of the night to finish them off.

Their car, once white, was now frilled with rust. The car seemed to hate them as much as the forest did, and sometimes wouldn't start. When it did, it coughed and jerked all the way up the winding mile.

The hill from Limeburn to the main road was like a ride. Ruby had been to the fair once in Bideford. The rollercoaster had been small, but big enough to frighten her, and it had started like this – with a grindingly slow pull up an incline that had looked like nothing from the queue, but which had felt so steep once she was in the little cart that she'd thought she might flip over backwards.

They were always tense in the car – waiting for it to fail. Her father hunched over the wheel, her mother gripped her bag in her lap, while Ruby's fingers ached, she clutched the headrest so tight. They all leaned forward, as if it would help, as the car lurched in bad gears around hairpins, under the murky canopy of green.

Halfway up was a stable made from an old railway carriage, and a tiny paddock of mud. There was never anything in there, but Ruby always looked.

'That's where I'll keep my horse,' she said five times a week.

'What will you call it?' her father always asked.

'Depends,' Ruby idled, 'on its colour and nature.'

'What if it has a name already?' asked her mother. 'You can't change it.'

Ruby frowned. She hadn't thought of that.

'She can call it anything she likes, can't you, Rubes?' said her father in the mirror. Then he shook his head and murmured, 'Spoilsport.'

Ruby liked it when Daddy told Mummy off. Mummy was too big for her boots, with her fancy job at the hotel and her fancy chef's uniform. Showing off – that's what Daddy called it.

They passed the stone chapel where thick ivy knitted the graves together, then surfaced from the cover of trees into daylight, next to the little shop where Ruby spent her pocket money. There was a sign that promised ice cream – although the freezer was always full of fish fingers and frozen peas – and a wire cage by the door that held a local newspaper headline to the wall. It changed once a week, or whenever Mr Preece remembered to do it. Today there was a FLOOD THREAT TO 1000 HOMES.

The car juddered to a halt and they clambered out. Ruby had to wait for Mummy to get out because there were only two doors. She could see a small knot of children already at the stop. They were divided between above-the-hills, who came from the clifftop farms and hamlets, and below-the-hills, from the beaches and the forest. Aboves had wifi and ponies; belows piled sandbags in their doorways against high tides, and their hair was always matted with salt.

Before she closed the door, Mummy bent down to look back into the car. 'Could you try to see about the bathroom window, John?'

Ruby rolled her eyes. Mummy was always going *on* and *on* about the window! Why didn't she fix it herself if she was so bothered?

'If I get time,' said Daddy.

'What else do you have to do?' said Mummy, and Daddy leaned over and pulled the door shut. Then he turned the car round in a jerky circle, and sank beneath the trees.

The above-the-hill kids waited for her mother to get off the bus before they called Ruby 'fat bitch' and 'ginger minger', and stepped on her black shoes and white socks until they were good and muddy.

John Trick was twenty-nine and had not worked for three years.

He used to do welding at the shipyard, and when there was no welding he'd done scaffolding, and when there was no scaffolding he'd done labouring, and when there was no labouring, he'd started to do nothing at all.

Then he had done nothing at all for so long that he'd gradually adjusted, until nothing had become the new something.

The new something was the drive up the hill and back and breakfast in front of the TV. It was combing the beach for driftwood, and surprising limpets for bait. It was a six-pack of Strongbow cooling in a rockpool, and pissing in the sea like a castaway.

After a while, he wondered how he'd ever found time for a job.

And on days like this, that suited him just fine. The morning rain had stopped and the cloud had thinned so that it only diluted the sunshine, rather than blocking it out completely – a reminder that, somewhere up there, summer was as it should be. The sheltered cove was always warmer than the clifftops, and the moisture was already leaving the land for the sky again in steamy wisps.

Through cheap earpieces, Johnny Cash and Willie Nelson sang to him of real men and the women who'd wronged them. Sometimes – when the wind was up – he'd join in.

Short snatches of songs carried off on the spume.

He had collected half a dozen limpets and now dug one out of its shell with his penknife and put it on the hook. The outer flesh was tough, and the creature pulsed in his fingers as he threaded it over the barbs.

He cast and felt the weight touch the bottom, then he took up the tension on the line, and settled back into his old nylon camping chair.

John fished mostly at the Gut – a squareish wound

blown out of the rock with gunpowder two hundred years before, so that ships could land their cargoes of lime and anthracite. The kilns where the lime had been burned were still there, built into the sea wall either side of the slipway – fortress-like stone ovens forty feet high that were now occupied by rats and by gulls, and so acrid with the shit of both that not even the children played there.

Mackerel was his most common catch, with whiting a close second. Both were good enough eating, and if he bothered to pick his slippery way to the end of the Gore, he could catch eels as long as his arm, and dogfish. Rock salmon, they were called in fancy restaurants, and sometimes Alison rang Mr Littlejohn at the hotel and he'd say yes or no. If he said yes, he gave Trick a tenner a fish. Then cut them into eight thick steaks that he sold for twenty quid a time.

John snorted around his roll-up. A hundred and sixty quid for a fish *he* caught and his *wife* cooked. He failed to see how Mr Littlejohn could sleep at night, for the thieving old bastard he was.

He could have sold the dogfish to the Red Lion in Clovelly, of course, but he never went to Clovelly, even though he could see it from here, across the shallow curve of the bay. Clovelly was the favoured brother to Limeburn's runt, and nobody in either village ever forgot it.

The fluorescent end of the fishing rod shivered, and he tensed, ready for action. But the tip pinged back into position, pointing skywards with a trembling finger.

John subsided.

Bloody crabs.

Sometimes he would reel in and check the bait and cast again somewhere else, but it seemed like a lot of work when the air was so warm and the cider so cool.

He closed his eyes and waited.

He slept.

That night the window row began again. First the window, then how much the new tyre on the car had cost, then the mess Daddy had made cleaning the fish in the sink. Ruby went into the other room before it could get to the job.

Wherever the row started, it always ended up at the job.

It got there without her.

3

M ISS SHARPE WROTE two words on the whiteboard
and Ruby copied them carefully on to the cover of
a brand-new blue exercise book.

My Dairy.

'You should write in your diaries every day,' said Miss
Sharpe, to groans from the boys. She put down the
marker pen and walked up and down between the desks.
Ruby liked it when Miss Sharpe walked about, because
it made it harder for Essie Littlejohn to poke her with a
pencil. Essie's daddy owned the hotel where Mummy
worked and Ruby hated her, with her big ears and her
good crayons and her fancy mains gas.

'All the things you do, and the thoughts you have,'
Miss Sharpe continued. 'All your secret dreams and plans
for the future.'

Ruby noticed that she had pale pearl varnish on her
short nails. Ruby wasn't allowed to paint her nails
because only slags painted their nails, but Miss Sharpe
didn't look like a slag. She had ugly brown hair and no
make-up, and her only jewellery was a bracelet that
tinkled with charms, including a little silver horseshoe.
Ruby liked the horseshoe, and – by extension – Miss

Sharpe, so she didn't see how Miss Sharpe could be a slag. Maybe nail polish was only slaggy if it was a French manicure, like the girls from the college, who smoked on the bus.

Miss Sharpe saw Ruby looking at the charms and smiled her lopsided smile. She had only been here since the beginning of term, so she hadn't had time to get miserable yet.

David Leather put up his hand and asked if he could write about his milk-bottle collection and Shawn Loosemore asked if he could write about smashing up David Leather's milk-bottle collection, and everyone laughed – apart from David and Miss Sharpe, who had to clap her hands to make them all be quiet.

'Of course, David. Hobbies, or what you did at the weekend, or what you want for your birthday, or your pets. It will be like Facebook, but just for 5B. Then,' she said, 'those who want to can read their diaries out in class, and we'll be able learn about each other's—'

The bell rang and Miss Sharpe had to raise her voice over the scraping chairs.

'—everyday lives! Have a lovely weekend everybody!'

Ruby stuffed *My Dairy* into her plush pony-shaped backpack, then trailed out of the classroom behind the others.

The other kids had no interest in her *or* her everyday life.

Writing it down wouldn't make any difference.

Monday, Tuesday, Wednesday, Thursday, Cowboy.

Cowboy Night was the best night of the week.

On Cowboy afternoons, Ruby would get off the bus and go into the shop to spend her pocket money under the suspicious eye of Mr Preece. She didn't like Mr Preece, who had hair curling from his ears, and eyes that looked too big behind thick glasses. She took an age every Friday to buy the same two things: a Mars bar and a copy of *Pony & Rider*, which were her treats for the week.

By the time she reached the little chapel, she'd always eaten the Mars bar.

Pony & Rider lasted longer, and Ruby ambled down the hill, envying the pretty girls with their long legs wrapped around immaculate ponies, and looking for good pictures to cut out and stick over her bed, until it became difficult to see by the miserly light that the forest allowed. Then she hurried the rest of the way to Limeburn, letting gravity speed her home.

Daddy sucked spaghetti into his mouth in long strings that were still attached to his plate, and Ruby did the same, but Mummy said 'Ruby!' and made her stop. *She* wound her spaghetti around her fork so that it was like putting a knot of wet wool in your mouth. It wasn't half the fun.

'Mmm,' said Daddy, 'that was great, thanks.' He leaned back and played the drums on his tummy. Sometimes Ruby had to guess what song.

'More?' asked Mummy.

'Please.' He made the most of a burp and Ruby

giggled. Daddy could say 'Bulawayo' before finishing a burp. He laughed too; Daddy was always in a good mood on Cowboy Nights.

Mummy got up and crossed to the stove. Daddy watched her all the way. When she got back with the second plateful, he said, 'What's the occasion?'

'What?'

'New shoes.'

Mummy looked down as if they were a surprise to her too.

'Oh,' she said, pushing her hair behind her ear.

Ruby leaned off her chair to see the shoes. Mummy always wore flat ones because she was too tall. These were far from flat, and had lots of thin straps. They looked like the shoes models wore in magazines.

'Mum gave me some money for my birthday,' said Mummy. 'You remember.'

'That was months ago.'

'I haven't had time to go shoe shopping.'

'Bit high, aren't they?' said Daddy.

Mummy looked under the table at her feet. 'They *are* a bit higher than they felt in the shop. I just thought it would be nice to have one good pair just in case . . .' She tailed off.

'In case of what?' said Ruby.

'Just in case we went out somewhere,' she shrugged.

Daddy sucked up the new spaghetti.

'Can I have some more spaghetti too?' said Ruby.

'What's the magic word?' said Mummy.

'*Please.*'

25

'Are you still hungry?' said Mummy. 'That was a big bowl for a little girl.'

'Let her eat if she's hungry,' said Daddy.

'I *am* hungry,' said Ruby.

'See?'

Mummy pursed her lips and Ruby felt cross, because faces like that made her remember that she was fat. Not fat like David Leather, whose legs rubbed together so hard that there were threadbare patches on his school trousers, but fat enough to hate a waistband and a mirror. Daddy said it was puppy fat and it was cute, but Ruby knew it wasn't.

Mummy got up and brought the pan over and draped a little more spaghetti into Ruby's bowl. She didn't sit down again; she stood, watching the clock.

'So,' said Daddy, glancing at the clock. 'What's the occasion?'

'No occasion,' said Mummy. 'Just thought I'd wear them tonight to show Mum what her money bought, that's all.'

Ruby wound the spaghetti around her fork against the bottom of her bowl. 'They're too high, Mummy,' she said. 'You'll fall over on the cobbles.'

'Break an ankle,' agreed Daddy.

Mummy stared at her feet and bit her thumbnail. The nail was already ragged, and when she went to work every day she put a fresh blue plaster on it.

Daddy pushed his chair back from the table and Ruby sucked up her last mouthful of spaghetti, then rushed upstairs after him, to watch him change.

Ruby loved Daddy every day, but on Cowboy Night she loved him even more, with his black clothes and black hat and the fake brass bullets glinting at his waist.

Cowboys was the best game she played in the woods, even though she didn't have a hat or boots or a gunbelt. She had sticks that were shaped like guns, stuck into the pockets of her jeans as if they were in holsters.

Daddy adjusted his black Stetson so that it was low over his eyes, then opened the bottom drawer. Ruby craned to see what was coming out of it, because she wasn't allowed to open the drawer herself. She wasn't allowed to mess with Daddy's cowboy things.

It was the Texas string tie, with a blue stone cattle skull and pointed silver tips to the laces. Daddy stood in front of the pitted mirror that hung on the back of the bedroom door, and looped it over his head, then replaced his hat – making sure it was just right in the mirror.

'Wow!' said Ruby.

He grinned and tipped his brim in her direction.

'Why, thank you, Miss Ruby,' he drawled, making her giggle.

He sat on the bed and pulled on his cowboy boots. Black with fancy white stitching. Mummy had found them in a charity shop, but they fitted like gloves.

'You need spurs,' Ruby said.

'You think so?'

Of course she did; she'd heard *him* say so often enough.

'Mummy has new shoes,' she pointed out.

'Well,' shrugged Daddy, but didn't go on.

Her father never said it in so many words, but they both understood that if her mother's work weren't so *seasonal* they would all have things that they wanted. In the season she worked almost every night and some days. In the winter she only did weekends, and they ate so much fish that Ruby could smell it on her pillow.

Daddy pulled open the drawer once again and took out the black leather gunbelt. He hitched it loosely, so that the holster hung low on his hip.

'Can I tie the string?' said Ruby, kneeling up beside his leg.

The leather thong was difficult to wrestle into a knot and turned into a loose half a bow.

'Nice tyin', young 'un.'

Ruby beamed at up him. 'Sure, JT.' She tried the accent, but it wound itself around her tongue like a cat and came out in a miaow.

Daddy used to have a gun in his gunbelt. Not a real one, but that didn't matter – the government had made all the Gunslingers hand in their guns just because one stupid man shot some people miles away. And the man wasn't even a cowboy, so it was really unfair.

But even without a gun, something about Daddy's hat and his cowboy voice and his unshaven jaw always excited Ruby in a way she couldn't put into words. He looked like a film star. Even the pale scars that curved through his eyebrow and across his right cheek looked good on Cowboy Night. In Ruby's eyes they almost made him better. More *dangerous*.

'John?' her mother called up the stairs. 'It's quarter past.'

Daddy rolled his eyes at Ruby, and Ruby rolled them back. Nanna and Granpa came at half past. Granpa made her sit on his lap, and Nanna's idea of sweets was fruit.

'Can I come with you?' It burst out of Ruby. She'd learned not to ask often, but she hadn't asked for *ages*.

Daddy stopped adjusting his belt, and made a face in the mirror that looked like consideration. She held her breath.

'Not this time, Rubes,' he said.

'When?' she said, emboldened by the pause.

'When you're older.' He always said the same thing.

'I'm older *now*. I'm getting older all the *time*.'

There was a silent moment when Ruby thought she'd gone too far. But then he turned towards her and grinned.

'No, you're not!' he said, and started to tickle her. 'You're not getting older!'

She giggled and rolled. He'd forgotten his cowboy accent, and the only burr in his voice was a West Country one, as he made her suffer with joy.

'You're my little cowboy,' he said as she shrieked. 'You'll *always* be my little cowboy.'

'John? They'll be here any minute.'

Daddy stopped tickling and sighed, and Ruby flopped on to the bed, wheezing and still giggling on the out-breaths.

'Big Nose and Ping Pong are on the warpath,' Daddy whispered, and Ruby laughed. They called them that – just between themselves – because Granpa's nose *was* big, and Nanna's eyes were as poppy as ping-pong balls.

He straightened up. 'I guess I'll be headin' out then,' he said, back in character. 'You have fun now, y'hear?'

Ruby made a face. '*How* old must I be before I can come with you?'

Daddy adjusted his belt for a long time, and when he spoke, it wasn't in his cowboy voice.

'Don't rush to grow up, Rubes,' he said. 'There's nothing good waiting for you there.'

He tilted his hat so it was low over his eyes. Then he got his accent back. 'You stay home, Miss Ruby. Stay out of trouble.'

At the door, Daddy spun on his heel like a gunslinger, and drew on Ruby.

'Pow! Pow-pow!'

Instead of a six-shooter he pulled a Mars bar from his holster and lobbed it gently to her. She gasped with delight – then shushed as he raised a secretive finger to his lips.

'Don't tell Mummy,' he said.

Then he tipped his hat to her one last time and jig-jogged down the stairs, whistling 'Red River Valley', because it was her favourite song.

Ruby's smile faded with the tune.

How could Daddy say she shouldn't rush to grow up? It was all right for *him* to say! He'd probably forgotten what it was even *like* to be little, with all the fatness and the bullies and the homework.

She thought of all the good stuff waiting for her when she got older. The first thing she would do was buy a pony so that when she got a job she could ride it to work and to the shops and hitch it up outside so she could see it from the window. And with the money she made from doing . . . *something* . . . she'd buy her own custard creams and not have to search every time for where Mummy had hidden theirs. She'd live in a warm house in a sunny field, miles from trees, where mould didn't blacken the walls and where the wind never squealed through the windows.

Daddy must be wrong about growing up.

She couldn't *wait* to get there.

4

LEGEND HAS IT that in AD 878, Vikings under the leadership of Hubba the Dane landed thirty-three ships right here, at the broad mouth of the River Torridge, and headed up the steep hill to launch an assault on Kenwith Castle. They barely got a mile before they met the English defenders coming the other way. The king's men had the high ground and the raiders were repelled, but not before the battle claimed the lives of thousands of winners and losers alike.

The dead victors were carried back to Kenwith under the first Eagle standard ever captured, while the Danes were buried where they fell – in mass graves dug easily in earth so softened by carnage that it is known to this day as Bloody Corner.

Since then, not much had happened in Appledore.

For nearly twelve hundred years, the little village serried its way up that same hill like a much slower, more respectful invasion. The first row of cottages rose straight from the muddy estuary, and the tide lapped against painted walls and seeped into basements on a twice-daily basis.

Appledore had a post office, three churches and six

pubs: the usual ratio. In summer, little galleries and gift shops opened in people's front rooms, selling handmade and home-made gifts, although the hands and homes were mostly Chinese. Not like the Hocking's ice cream, which was made right here in the village from great golden mountains of real butter, and sold from a fleet of vanilla vans.

And not like the ships.

Appledore folk had been building boats for gener-ations, and at its peak Appledore Shipbuilders had employed over two thousand men: so many that one village alone could not satisfy the demand, and men had come from miles around, working shifts around the clock, and riding to the yard on cheap old step-through scooters that cut through sleep like 4am buzz-saws. For half a century the huge iron shed had dominated the river and made bonsais of the trees. Great warships slid from it and into the river, causing passing yachts to bob and pitch like toys. The dry dock had once been the biggest in Europe, and it had seemed that the good times would never end.

But everything ends – especially good times.

And when they ended in Appledore, fifteen hundred men lost their jobs.

Overnight.

Fifteen hundred breadwinners. Fifteen hundred skilled welders and fitters and carpenters and machinists, suddenly unemployed in a place where the job centre only regularly offered bar work, labouring and babysitting.

Many of the men never worked again. Not legally,

anyway. They missed the work and the money, of course, but more than that, they missed their mates and the way men could be when they were with other men – which was not the same way they had to be when they were with women.

So they found other places to meet. Some of them met in the bookmaker's, some in the pubs, some in the snooker halls.

And some of them joined the Gunslingers.

The Gunslingers were a loose group of maybe twenty men who, once a week, dressed up as cowboys and met at the George in Appledore – just as the Shootists did at the Bell in Parkham and the Outlaws did at the Coach and Horses in Barnstaple.

North Devon had its fair share of cowboys, that was for sure. All week they worked in banks or did odd jobs, but Cowboy Nights transported them for just a few hours to the Wild West, where men were men, women were buxom, and jails were made of wood.

When the Gunslingers had first appeared, the residents of Appledore had been a little nervous of the men in boots and black hats who swaggered down the narrow canyon of Irsha Street every Friday night. But after a while the net curtains stopped twitching every time a cowpoke passed through the little fishing village on his way to the pub, and it was left only to small gangs of teenaged boys to laugh and shout insults.

From a safe distance.

Once at the George, the Gunslingers got drunk and showed off and flirted with the barmaids, and talked in a cowboy way about cowboy things.

Like fashion.

They fell on any new item of cowboy clothing or equipment like Beverly Hills housewives – poring over it for style and authenticity. Funds and geography dictated that items usually failed on both counts. Nellie Wilson's holster was from army surplus, Scratch Mumford's poncho had been crocheted by his mother, and Blacky Blackmore's cowboy hat had a Pixar logo under the brim.

The Gunslingers' most authentic asset came when Frank 'Whippy' Hocking would ride his hairy skewbald, Tonto, through the village and tie him up outside the George. There, tourists took pictures, and small children fed him sugar and ketchup and any other pub condiments that were free. 'No mustard,' Whippy always told them. When he left, the worse for wear, the other Gunslingers would come outside and help to push Whippy up into the tooled leather saddle. It always took at least three of them to heave him upright, because Whippy was one of the ice-cream clan, and quality control was his life.

When they weren't peacocking, the Gunslingers played a casual game of poker for pennies and bickered back and forth about old TV Westerns – wavering between *Bonanza* and *The High Chaparral* and *The Virginian*. Between them they had pirated all the box sets. In the films they were split between Clint Eastwood or Gary Cooper; John Wayne or Jimmy Stewart. Their jury was always out on Kevin Costner, who promised so much and so often – then somehow always managed to ruin things with gills or a bad haircut.

If a man joined the Gunslingers – and if he were not

thoroughly unpopular – he'd be given a cowboy name. Whether he liked it or not. Mostly these names were bestowed for low reasons that barely troubled the imagination. Blacky Blackmore delivered coal, Hick Trick lived in the sticks, while Daisy Yeo mooed loudly and randomly, in a sort of agricultural Tourette's; in the supermarket you could hear him aisles away.

Some men tried to join up with their cowboy name all ready to go, but the Gunslingers had no truck with that. Indeed, they were apt to punish such presumption, which was why Len 'Pussy' Willows' membership had been short and fractious, ending in a brawl that had memorably spilled out of the George and all the way down Irsha Street.

Just like real cowboys.

It had happened six months ago, and they still worked it into at least one conversation a week.

As the night and the beer ran down, the Gunslingers would get reflective on how much better life would be if only North Devon were open of range and filled with cattle – preferably ones which needed driving from one end of the county to the other on a regular basis. They'd put Willie and Johnny on the jukebox in a mournful loop, and sigh into their empty glasses and empty holsters, and long for the good old days before varmints started shooting small children and everyone got so damned jumpy – even about replicas.

5

THE NAKED GIRL sat on the empty beach.

The tide was so far out that its edge had disappeared in the low grey cloud, and the sand was hard and wet in the persistent drizzle.

She sat cross-legged and hunched over. Cold and snivelling, with her back to the invisible sea, and her hands trapped under her icy buttocks.

'Call your mother,' the man said.

Fresh sobs burst from the girl and the man looked at his watch. He prodded her again with the phone. It was an iPhone. Better than any phone *he*'d ever had. And the girl was what? Sixteen? Seventeen? Ridiculous.

'Call your mother,' he repeated slowly.

The girl was crying so hard now that when she tried to say something, he couldn't understand it.

'What?' he said. He frowned in concentration, but her words couldn't get past her weeping.

'Oh, for fuck's *sake*! Stop crying and speak clearly!'

'You're going to kill me!'

'Yes, I am,' he agreed. 'Call your mother.'

She only wailed loudly.

'Don't you want to say goodbye?' he asked, almost kindly.

The girl raised her snot-stained face defiantly.

'Shut *up!*' she shrieked, and lunged at his legs. She didn't get her hands from under her bottom fast enough, and toppled forward on to her shoulder and her face.

He righted her roughly with the toe of his boot. The left side of her face was coated in a gritty tan mask, and she blinked and gasped as though she'd risen from the sea, not the sand.

He held up the phone so he could take a picture.

'Eight megapixels,' he observed. 'On a bloody phone.' He showed her the photo. 'Maybe I'll send that to your mates. What do you think? I've got all their numbers in here.'

Her face slackened in misery.

'Please don't,' she whispered. 'Please don't send that to anyone.'

'Then call your mother.'

The girl started to cry again – hard and steady. She shifted her weight to release one of her hands from under her buttock, and took the phone from him. She was shaking so hard that she took three goes to hit the right number. On the screen a picture of an old-fashioned telephone vibrated in time to the ringtone. Under the buzzing picture were the words *Calling Mum*.

'It's ringing,' she wept.

'Really?' he said sarcastically.

'What do I say?'

'Say goodbye.'

'Can I tell her I love her?'

'If you do.'

'I do love her!' cried the girl. 'Can I speak to my dad too?'

'This isn't *Who Wants To Be A Millionaire*.'

The ringing stopped and a face appeared on the screen.

'Mum?' said the girl.

'Do I look like Mum, peabrain?'

'Ricky, get Mum.' The girl was suddenly calm.

'What am I? Your slave?'

'Just get her, Ricky! It's an emergency.'

The boy had a stud through his eyebrow. Spoilt brats, the both of them.

'What's the magic word?'

'The magic word is *fucking please you fucking arsehole*.'

'I'm gonna tell Mum you said that. You're in deep shit.'

'I know,' said the girl, and started to cry again. 'I know.'

Ricky turned his head to one side and yelled, 'Mum! Kelly's on the phone!' Then there were some random ceiling shots before a woman's cheerful face appeared.

'Hi, Kells.'

'Mummy?' That was all the girl could get out before the crying overtook her completely.

The woman's face was instantly washed with panic.

'Kelly, what's wrong? Where are you?'

'MummyMummyMummyMummy . . .' The girl's snot and spit looped from her lips and on to the phone.

'Say goodbye,' the man reminded her sharply.

'Kelly, who's that? Who's with you? Where are you?'

'He's going to kill me, Mummy. He made me call you to say goodbye.'

The woman's face went loose with horror.

This was more like it.

'I love you, Mummy!'

'KELLY! Brian! Call the police! BRIAN! Kelly, baby – wait! Who's there? Who's with you?'

The girl tilted the phone towards the man and he grinned and waved.

'Hello,' he said. 'I'm going to kill your little girl now, while you watch.'

'NO!' she shrieked. 'No! Wait! Wait! Stop! Brian! BRIAN! Someone's got Kelly! BRIAN!'

He started to laugh. Her hysteria was so tinny and tiny; it was like watching a sea-monkey throw a tantrum in a little glass bowl.

The woman babbled, 'Don't hurt her. Please don't hurt her. What do you want? I'll give you *anything*. What do you want? Money? Please just talk to me and tell me what you want. Anything you want. PLEASE!'

He didn't want anything else, but he couldn't answer, he was laughing so hard. He doubled over, choked with mirth.

The girl saw her chance; she got up and ran away.

Away from the pile of clothes and towards Westward Ho! Back to the slipway, the bingo hall and the Hocking's ice-cream van.

The man straightened up and ran a few loose paces after her, but then stopped and just watched her go – arse jiggling, phone waving, and a high, reedy 'Help!' squirting from her every few strides.

It was one of the funniest things he'd ever seen.

He pulled off the balaclava and laughed until he finally wound down into long sighs of amusement – then he wiped his eyes and looked across the flat brown sand, where he was the tallest thing for miles. It made him think of *Gulliver's Travels*. He'd had the book as a child and had never read it – but he'd looked at the pictures again and again and again.

Now *he* felt like Gulliver, stomping all over those little people, flicking them off cliffs and picking them up by their heels between his giant thumb and forefinger.

Making them do whatever he wanted them to.

It made him feel *mighty*.

6

IT WAS SATURDAY, so Ruby lay on the floor and watched the sea as it swirled far below the overhanging room in the haunted house. The water was slate-grey with white veins, and when it withdrew it hissed and made a deep clicking sound as the big round stones rolled about the beach under the waves.

It was hypnotic.

She didn't know how long she'd been here. Maybe an hour. It was getting dark and she was getting cold, but she kept waiting for one more wave, one more retreat.

One more.

One more.

Ruby shifted a little against the musty floor. Her chest hurt.

Again.

She'd first noticed the pain when she'd been reading *Pony & Rider* on the old rug that was the same colour as the big spiders that marched into The Retreat in the first week of every September, as if they'd booked a room. It was a sharp ache, like lying on a hair bobble. But when she looked there was nothing there.

Now, as then, Ruby drew her forearms under her sides a bit, to relieve the pressure on her chest.

Just one more wave.

'Can I look?'

Ruby took her face from the hole in the floor to see Adam Braund standing beside her.

He laughed. 'You have a red ring round your whole eye.'

She blushed and touched her face, but felt nothing.

'It's not bad,' he said. 'It'll go.'

She shifted over, and Adam lay down and put his eye to the hole. Ruby was on her tummy beside him, propped on her elbows, staring at the wall. There had been paper on it once – yellow daffodils and purple crocuses. Now the flowers were faded to brown, just like real ones, and speckled with black damp.

'We should make another hole,' said Adam. His voice was muffled, because he was speaking into the floorboards. 'Then we can both watch.'

'OK,' said Ruby.

He got to his feet and Ruby trailed around the house behind him, while he picked up scraps and tested window frames. There wasn't much left that the children hadn't already dropped into the ocean.

'Shit!' Adam sucked his thumb, and when he took it out of his mouth blood welled quickly, then leaked away through the tiny canals of his skin. It made Ruby feel a bit sick to see it.

'Does it hurt?'

'No,' said Adam. He wiped the blood on his jeans, and started to tug at a banister spindle. It came free with a surprising jerk, and they both laughed. Then Ruby followed him back through to the overhanging room.

Adam chose a place twelve inches from the knothole, where two floorboards were parting and daylight already showed through. He inserted the spindle and twisted and levered until the rotting board split and opened into a new hole a few inches wide, then he picked at the edges until the worst of the splinters were gone.

'There,' he said, and lowered the spindle through the new hole. 'Let's watch this.'

They both got on to their tummies again – their elbows tucked in and their hands in fists next to their ears – and counted down together.

'Three.

'Two.

'One!'

Adam let go of the spindle and it speared the next wave and disappeared. Then they saw it again, briefly, tumbled in the froth, before it was sucked out to sea for ever.

'Cool,' said Ruby.

'Yeah,' said Adam. He shifted to get more comfortable and his leg nudged Ruby's. She nudged back, and he held firm. Without taking their eyes from their spy-holes, they giggled as they pressed their calves and ankles against each other in a fake tussle, then gave up and subsided into silence.

They watched the sea for another five minutes, then Ruby remembered how cold she was. She was about to get up and go home when Adam spoke. His lips were so close to the floor that Ruby had to ask him to repeat it, so he lifted his head and looked at her.

'Do you know why this house is haunted?'

'No.'

He turned his head and looked at her. 'Do you *want* to know?'

Ruby pursed her lips and thought about it. She'd thought *Haunted House* was just a name they called the dilapidated old building. Sure, it was run-down and creepy and had cobwebs and draughts and drips and weird noises, but until this moment she had never truly considered that it might actually *be* haunted by real *ghosts*. That idea was both awful and thrilling. She could already feel the back of her neck prickling just at the thought of it, and it was on the tip of her tongue to say no, when she realized that Adam Braund *wanted* to tell her, so she said yes instead.

He rolled on to his side to face her, with his elbow under his ear, so Ruby did the same. Their knees touched, but this time they both ignored it.

'My dad told me this,' Adam started, thus establishing the truth of it right up front. 'It was a hundred years ago and there was this pedlar—'

'What's a pedlar?' said Ruby.

'Like a sales rep. But in the olden days. He came down the hill with all his stuff that he was selling on the back of a donkey.'

'He can't have had much stuff.'

'Nobody did in those days,' said Adam, and Ruby nodded because that was true.

'What kind of stuff?' she asked.

'I dunno,' said Adam. 'Toilet roll and Pledge and things. Just stuff for the house.'

'OK.'

'So he came down the hill to sell stuff and there were these two old sisters who lived in this house, and they offered to let him stay over for the night.'

'In this house?'

'Yes,' said Adam.

'Why?'

''Cos it was night and it was raining outside.'

'OK.'

Ruby wanted to glance around the room, but was starting to feel too nervous to do that, in case she saw something frightening. This was nowhere near a ghost story yet, but she was primed . . .

'So he tied his donkey up on the cobbles and spent the night here.'

'OK,' said Ruby warily.

Adam lowered his voice. 'And nobody . . . *ever* . . . saw him again.'

The words hung in the salt air between them.

'Where did he go?' whispered Ruby.

'Nobody knows,' Adam whispered back. 'His donkey was still there in the morning, but all the pedlar's stuff was gone, and his money too. Someone stole it *all*.'

'Who?' said Ruby.

Adam shrugged mysteriously, then went on. 'This is the good bit. Like fifty years later, when the old sisters died, another man bought this house and was going to fix it up, but he started to hear noises from upstairs, when there was nobody there.'

Ruby glanced nervously at what was left of the ceiling. 'What kind of noises?'

'Banging. Moaning. *Ghost* noises, y'know?' said Adam breezily. 'And one night he went up to see what was going on, and the bedroom door slammed shut behind him, even though he was alone in the house, and he couldn't open the door, even though the key was on the *inside*.'

Ruby stared at Adam, her mouth suddenly dry.

'And then something in the room attacked him.'

'What thing?' she breathed.

'Nobody knows,' said Adam solemnly. 'He was a grown man, but he screamed so loud that people ran up from the village to see what was happening, but none of them could open the bedroom door, and all they could do was stand there and listen to him screaming and crying until morning.'

'What happened then?' said Ruby, her voice cracking with dread.

'In the morning the door suddenly swung open all by itself, and they found the man inside, all bloody and stuff, shaking under the bed. He'd been beaten up, but there was nobody else in the room with him.'

'Sssshhh-it,' Ruby said, even though she wasn't allowed to.

'He'd screamed so hard he couldn't even speak any more. And *then*,' said Adam, propping himself up to better effect, 'and then he *runs* out of the room past them, and down the stairs, and starts digging in the fire-place with his bare hands, all through the ashes that were still hot from the night before, but he didn't care and he dug until his hands were all bloody and his nails fell off.'

Ruby was cold with fear. She couldn't encourage Adam any more; she only stared, unable to look away from his sombre face.

'And under the ashes and the flagstones he found a hiding place dug out of the earth, and in there was the skeleton of the pedlar.'

Adam left room for her to gasp, and Ruby did.

'Those old ladies had murdered him and stolen all his money and stuff, and it was *his* ghost that was so angry that he, like, *lured* the man up there and sort of put it into his head where to look for his bones, so that his body could be found and given a Christian burial.'

Ruby shivered and Adam did too, even though he knew the story already.

'Wicked, hey?' He grinned.

But Ruby only looked over his shoulder and said slowly, '*That* fireplace?'

Adam rolled over to follow her gaze.

The fireplace stared silently back at them, squat and square and grey, with ashes in its middle, and blackened all around by centuries of scorching.

All cold now.

The waves crashed and hissed below, and the stones rumbled, and Ruby was suddenly very aware that the only thing between them and the sea was an inch of rotten wood and a one-hundred-foot drop.

She scrambled to her feet. 'I want to go home.'

'Don't be scared,' said Adam. 'It's only a story.'

'I know that,' said Ruby. 'I'm not scared. I have to do my homework.'

'Me too,' said Adam, and got up.

Both of them avoided looking at the fireplace, and Ruby knew for sure that if they *weren't* scared, they would even now be sifting through the ashes and lifting the flagstones to find the secret hiding place that was big enough to hold the body of a murdered man.

'You're shivering,' said Adam.

'I'm cold,' said Ruby.

'Do you want to wear my hoodie?' It was thick and red with BIDEFORD COLLEGE on the back.

Ruby nodded, and Adam took it off and Ruby put it on. She didn't try to zip it up in case it wouldn't fit and Adam saw how fat she was. Still, its fleece lining was cosy, and it smelled like detergent and warm boy.

They went less cautiously than usual down the brambly, muddy steps into the village. At the steepest part, Adam reached up and took her hand.

When they got to the gate of The Retreat, she gave his top back to him and said thank you.

'No problem,' he said. He didn't turn and leave though. He lingered.

'Don't tell anyone I told you that story, OK?'

'OK,' she agreed. 'Bye then.'

'Bye,' he said.

When she shut the door, Ruby noticed he was still standing at the gate.

7

MUMMY HAD GONE to work and left a chicken pie and a note about how to heat it up. Ruby looked up at a noise from her parents' room. She'd thought Daddy was fishing, but when she went upstairs, there he was.

'What are you doing?'

'Cleaning the house,' he said. 'Want to help?'

'OK,' said Ruby, and went in and sat on the bed and watched him take stuff out of the wardrobe, look at it, then put it back exactly where he found it. He only threw away about three things, and that was all make-up that Mummy didn't need.

Ruby saw a little book with 'Diary' on it.

'Oh,' she said, 'I have a diary!' She opened the diary to see what kinds of things Mummy wrote in hers, but there was only boring stuff like 'School, 4.40. Double shift Thurs/Fri. Knickers for R.'

She was R. She remembered getting the knickers from the market in Bideford – they had the days of the week on them and Friday was spelled 'Fiday'. She always hoped she didn't get hit by a bus on a Friday.

'Let's see,' said Daddy.

She gave him the diary and he flicked through it while she carried on cleaning. There was a first-aid box with some old plasters, a bottle of Calpol from when she was little and a box of Paracetamol.

'Can I put a plaster on?'

'Sure, Rubes.'

She chose a cute round one from the box and stuck it on her face so it looked as if she'd been shot with an arrow.

There was a crumpled plastic bag that held a few old boxes containing necklaces and things. Mummy didn't wear jewellery because it made her look cheap, and she didn't have any good stuff anyway. Not like Maggie's mother, who dripped with jangling gold and wore a big ring on every finger. All Mummy had was one pair of small diamond earrings in a blue velvet box with a crown on the inside and the word *Garrards*, and a matching necklace in another box, except oblong this time, not square. The diamonds were tiny and the inside of the lid was covered with white silk and someone had written on it with felt-tip: *Think of me when you wear this, baby girl.* Ruby frowned. She hoped the necklace wasn't for *her*. Sometimes Mummy tried to girlify her by buying her a pink top or a flowery clip for her hair. Christmas was coming in a few months and she didn't want a boring old necklace.

Inside the third box was a brooch. It was shaped like a fish, covered with diamonds for scales and with rubies for eyes. It was cute, but it wasn't even Mummy's; on the box it said it belonged to someone called Tiffany. Ruby stuffed the bag back where she had found it and opened a shoebox filled with loose photographs of people she didn't know.

'Who's this?' She held up a photo of a pretty young woman with dark hair. She was wearing a white summer dress, and was holding the hand of a little boy in a cowboy outfit.

Daddy took it from her. 'That's me,' he said. 'And my mother.'

'Ha!' laughed Ruby. 'You were a cowboy then too!' She peered up underneath the photo in his hand. 'It says *Johnny and me* on the back.'

He turned it over and touched the writing with his fingers.

'Your mummy was sooooo pretty,' said Ruby. 'Not like Nanna.'

'Yeah, she was,' said Daddy, and winked. 'That's why I'm so good-looking!'

Ruby giggled, then sighed. 'I wish I had a cowboy outfit.'

Daddy ignored the hint. Everybody ignored her hints. Sometimes she wondered why she bothered *giving* hints. She'd been hinting about a pony for years.

Daddy was still looking at the picture, so Ruby sidled up alongside him so she could look at it too.

'Was your daddy taking the photo?'

'I can't remember.' Daddy put the photo in his pocket and looked around him. 'There's nothing here.'

They put almost everything back exactly where they'd found it, then they ate the pie cold, and straight out of the dish, because Daddy said it was nicer that way.

* * *

Later, while Daddy watched TV, Ruby took her diary out of her pony backpack. She opened it on the first blue-lined page, which was always so encouraging.

She wrote: MONDAY.

It didn't look quite the way she'd wanted it to – the D was a bit like a P and she had to go over it twice – but so far, so good.

She gazed at the window and chewed the top of her pen. Then she bent over the book again and underlined 'Monday'.

It was wonky. She should have done it with a ruler.

She chewed the pen some more, until the little plug came out of the end of it, then she sucked on that so it stuck to the tip of her tongue like a big blue pimple. If she waggled it about, she could see it at the bottom of the slope of her own cheek.

Then she underlined 'Monday' again.

Then she went and got a glass of milk to help her think.

Finally she wrote:

MONDAY. _No horses in the paddick. Drew maps for school._
TUESDAY. _Maggie fell off the swing on the cliffs and it bled in her sock._
WEDNESDAY. _Played in the woods. Found a good stick for a gun._
THURSDAY. _No horses in the paddick again._
FRIDAY. _My Mummy got new shoes and my Daddy said they are to high then Daddy went to cowboy club and I tied his holdster on his leg._

SATURDAY. *Me and Daddy cleaned the house.*

Ruby put down her pen and sighed deeply at the nice blank page she'd ruined with her boring life.

8

'CALL YOUR MOTHER.'
      The woman sat in the woods. Cross-legged on her hands and a bed of red-brown pine needles, soft and prickly under her naked thighs.

She squinted up at the man.

'What?'

He waggled the phone at her again. 'Call your mother.'

He didn't know it, but her name was Katie Squire. She was twenty-six and she'd been walking the South-West coastal path alone for twenty-four days without experiencing anything worse than a blister between Fowey and Kingsands. Completely preventable; she'd forgotten to wear two pairs of socks.

She was wearing them now though – two pairs of red hiking socks, and nothing else.

She stared at the hand holding her phone. Apart from his lips and eyes, it was the only part of the man Katie could see, and the fingernails were bitten and dirty around the cuticles. The thought of those fingers touching her skin made her feel hot and shivery.

'Call your mother.'

'No,' she told him. She hadn't called her mother for months; she wasn't going to start now with this.

Whatever *this* was.

She was shocked by how calm she was. It was too bizarre to take seriously, she supposed. She'd been walking through an unexpectedly lovely tunnel of trees, with the sea sighing softly somewhere to her left. The only warning she'd had was a loud rustling in the undergrowth – and the time between *that* and *this* (whatever *this* was, she thought again) was an iron grip on her arm and a surreal blur of stumbling and shaking and standing on one leg, trying to unlace her walking boots, while her skin raced with goosebumps and her teeth chattered like a joke skull.

But now she was calm.

Numb, possibly.

He'd said he had a gun but she didn't see one, and it was too late now.

Above them, it was raining, but here on the forest floor it was dry. Only the sound of the drops on the canopy overhead gave the rain away. Katie had been to a spa once and they had played the sound of raindrops while she'd had a massage. This was a bit like that – apart from there was no massage.

And she was naked in the woods with a pervert.

Apart from that.

The man fiddled with her phone and then held it up. She heard the fake shutter noise and blinked in the flash, then he turned the phone so that she could see her own stark image – as pale as a frightened ghost on the bed of terracotta needles.

'I'll send that to your mother. Then she can see.'

Katie said nothing.

He looked at the photo and his teeth grinned through the hole in the black wool. 'For a young maid you've got right floppy old tits.'

It wasn't true but it stung. This, *of all things*, brought tears to her eyes. Katie fought them. She wasn't a crier. She hadn't cried when he'd forced her to walk off the path. She hadn't cried when he'd forced her to strip. And what did she care what this weirdo thought of her breasts?

But she did care. It made no sense, but she *did*.

And then the wrongness of that caring made her angry. She shook her straight dark hair out of her eyes defiantly and glared up at him. 'How would you know? I bet you never even *touched* a breast. Is that why you force women to strip off in the woods? To get your jollies?'

'Shut up.'

'*You* shut up.' Katie had three brothers, so 'Shut up' was home turf to her, and she drew strength from a row that suddenly seemed very familiar, despite her nakedness and his balaclava.

'I want my clothes back. I'm freezing.'

'*I* want you to call your *mother*.'

'Why?' she said suspiciously. 'Do you know her?'

He hesitated. 'Yes, I know her.'

'Bollocks,' she decided. 'You don't know my mother. And anyway, she wouldn't want to talk to anyone who'd do such a pathetic, cowardly thing.'

It was true, Katie realized with a surge of emotion. Her mother might be an interfering old cow, but she had principles. *Why* hadn't she called her in months? There was no real reason. And suddenly Katie was impatient to speak to her. To hear the gossip. To tell her she loved her.

But she wasn't doing it in front of this bastard.

She glared at her attacker. 'Look,' she said, 'either hurry up and rape me or bloody well let me go.'

He made a sound that was halfway between a gasp and a cry.

'*Filthy!*' he said. 'Filthy little *whore*.'

'*You're* filthy,' she spat back. 'Making a total stranger take her clothes off. Taking pictures of it. *That*'s filthy. That's *sick*.'

He angrily pressed the phone against her face, squashing her nose, pushing her off balance. 'Call your fucking *mother*.'

Katie slapped the phone away, sending it spinning off a tree.

'Call *yours*, arsehole!'

He swung at her so hard that when he missed, he almost fell.

Katie got up and ran, and he went after her.

This time he didn't stop after a few strides. Instead, her running ignited some deep chase instinct in him. Like a hound after a hare, he wanted to catch her. Wanted to bring her down.

But the girl was quick – even in socks – and nimble through the slender trees that were close-knit and had thin, stiff branches that jabbed at head and hands.

With every stride his anger grew. Once, he got close enough to touch her shoulder with his outstretched fingers, and she shrieked and ducked backwards under his arm and ran off at a new angle. He turned too fast and fell on to needles so thick they were like a prickly mattress. It didn't hurt, but it did harm: by the time he got up she had broken the dark cover of the trees and was on the main road, crying and shouting and waving down cars – naked but for her tattered red socks.

Shameless.

He watched from behind a tree as she got into a little silver car and disappeared, then yanked off the balaclava, his blood pounding with the fury of losing her – of losing *control*.

He'd blown it. Both times, he now realized. It was all over too fast and brought him no satisfaction. This time hadn't even been funny – only frustrating. And the girl had given him a load of cheek too, which made him feel like a stupid little boy instead of like a man in charge of the situation.

He scratched his head all over; it was hot and itchy from the wool.

He went back through the trees and found her clothes and her rucksack and the broken phone. There was a thick wad of money in a beaded purse, and shop-bought cheese and pickle sandwiches, which he ate as he drove out to Abbotsham cliffs. Pretty much everything else he threw into the hungry sea.

He watched her T-shirts and knickers and cotton trousers spread-eagle over the waves and felt cheated.

This time he hadn't wanted it to end.

9

GIRL, 17, IN BEACH ASSAULT.

Mr Preece was changing the headlines in the little wire cage as Ruby got off the bus.

Ruby wondered what assault was. She had a mental image of a girl rolling about in the salt that the sea had left behind on the sand. The new headline was MASKED MAN STRIKES AGAIN. But then Ruby saw the poster for the Leper Parade.

The Leper Parade in Taddiport was an annual orgy of running sores and fake blood, hunchbacks, crutches, and people with their arms hidden in their jumpers. Every year there was a prize for the best leper adult and the best leper under fourteen. Daddy had entered last year, but that man from the King's Arms always won the adult prize because he really *didn't* have a leg, and that meant nobody else was in with a chance. But Ruby always imagined that one day she might be the best leper under fourteen. She'd dress in rags and put ash and dirt on her face, with tomato sauce and Rice Krispies for scabs. That's what the other children did. Last year's winner also had black stuff coming out of his eyes, which was amazing. She wasn't sure she could compete with that, but she would certainly try. She must remember to ask Mummy to get Rice Krispies, because usually they only had boring old fake Weetabix.

Ruby was in for another treat inside the shop. *Pony & Rider* this week had a free LED safety light in a little plastic bag stuck on to the front of the magazine with a blob of clear gum. She couldn't wait, and bought the magazine and a Mars bar without even browsing.

'That was quick,' said Mr Preece.

Ruby said nothing.

Outside the shop she peeled the bag off the magazine cover, then tore it open with her teeth and took out the light. It was small and round and had a clip, and a button on the back that, when pressed, started it flashing red.

'Wow!' she said out loud, even though she was alone.

She wriggled out of her backpack and clipped the light to the plush pony's ear, like a rosette. Then she set off down the hill.

As the light grew dim under the trees, she wondered what the LED looked like on her back. Just past the chapel, she balanced her backpack on the tarmac and trudged back up the hill a-ways before turning around to look at it.

'Wow!' she said again. The tiny little light was like a beacon – flashing brilliantly, even in what passed for daylight in this miserable summer.

She hurried to pick up her backpack before it could soak up the rain from the road.

There were no ponies in the paddock, but Ruby hung on the gate anyway, reluctant to walk away in case one suddenly appeared.

Starlight would be a good name. Or Pegasus if it was white. *Grey*, she corrected herself. *Pony & Rider* said there was no such thing as a white horse.

A car pulled up behind her. She turned and saw Mrs Braund.

'Jump in out of the rain, Ruby!'

Limeburn people never passed someone on the hill without offering a lift, whether they knew them or not. The road was so steep that it was a difficult walk up *or* down. Mummy often got a ride down the hill from the bus stop on Thursday nights with Mr Braund, because that was when he was on his way home for the weekend from his fancy job in London.

Ruby opened the door of the big 4x4 and climbed in beside Adam in the back seat; Chris was in the front because he was the eldest.

'Hi,' she said.

'Hi,' they said.

Adam and Chris didn't go to her school. They went to a private school and they never caught the bus. They wore striped ties, and grey blazers with red shields on the pockets. She looked at Adam's knees. Usually they were covered by denim, or bare and tanned in khaki shorts, but today they were in black school trousers. They made his legs look like a man's.

The back of Chris's head looked more grown up than the front.

In the cage behind Ruby, the dogs whined because they were close to home. They weren't Jack Russells or collies like normal people had, they were matching brown Labradoodles called Tony (blue collar) and Cleo (red), and their birthday was celebrated in the Braund house just like the boys' birthdays were, with balloons around the front door and a cake. April the twenty-ninth. Even Ruby knew the date, although she wasn't sure any of the Braunds knew the date of *her* birthday.

Mrs Braund smiled at her in the mirror. 'That light's a good idea, Ruby. Makes you easy to see in the shadows.'

'I just got it free on my magazine,' she said.

'That's nice,' said Mrs Braund.

She was a pretty woman, Ruby thought, with hair so blonde it was almost white, except for that curious dark bit down the middle, like a reverse badger, and she wore lots of make-up and jewellery. Ruby had never seen Mrs Braund in dirty old jeans or a bad jumper. Even the welly boots she wore when she walked the dogs were fancy brown leather things with laces at the top. Chris had told her once that they cost £200 but he was a liar because nobody would pay that for wellies.

'What's your magazine?' said Adam.

'*Pony & Rider.*' She showed it to him.

'Do you have a pony?'

'No.'

'Do you ride?'

She hesitated. 'No.'

Chris laughed without turning round, and Ruby felt herself going red.

'So what?' said Adam at the back of Chris's head. 'You read *FourFourTwo* but you don't play for Arsenal, last I heard.'

'Yeah, but—'

'Now, boys,' said Mrs Braund, and Chris shut up and they drove on in silence.

Slowly, Ruby pushed her feet as far under the driver's seat as they would go, so that Adam wouldn't see her muddy socks.

~

The Retreat was unlocked, which meant that Daddy was home.

Ruby stood with her back to the front door and listened for the familiar sounds her father always made before her mother came in from a shift – the scraping of fish scales, slide guitars on the CD player – but there was nothing. Only the usual background noises of the wind keening through the bathroom window, and the trees testing the bowed roof.

'Daddy?'

She fumbled for the switch and turned on the light.

'Daddy?' She wanted to be the first to tell him about the leper parade. And to show him her light.

And then Ruby froze at a sound she'd never heard before.

Ching.

It was a high, metallic ring. Like someone dropping a five-pence piece into the bathtub.

She only heard it for a second and then it stopped.

Ruby felt the silence thud against her eardrums.

Nothing. There was nothing.

'Da—'

Ching. Ching.

She sucked the word back into her mouth and held it there.

Ching. Ching. Ching. Ching.

Ruby felt a little black worm of fear twist across her belly. The sound was like the ring of a loose shoe on a horse.

Or on a pedlar's donkey . . .

She quietly turned off the light, and looked up at the ceiling.

Ching. Ching.

It was coming from Mummy and Daddy's bedroom.

'Daddy?' she said carefully, but there was no answer, and suddenly the sound of her voice all alone in the damp air made her resolve not to speak again.

Ching. Ching. Ching across the floor. *Ching. Ching. Ching* back in the other direction.

Luring her up there.

The thought made Ruby's bladder loosen a little, and she clenched her thighs to keep the piddle from running down her leg.

She wouldn't go up there. She *couldn't*. Couldn't open the bedroom door and get trapped by a crazed ghost until morning. She thought of her mother tugging at the unlocked door, screaming for help, she thought of her father hammering on the yellowing paint, and of Adam Braund shouting her name, while all the while a dead man in chains terrified the rest of the wee out of her – and worse.

Ruby's face crumpled in self-pity. She wasn't going to go upstairs to be got by a ghost!

But she didn't have to . . .

Ching. Ching. Ching. Her breath caught once more and she watched the ceiling all the way across the bedroom to the door. And then she gasped at the unmistakeable transition: *Ching-creak. Ching-creak.*

The ghost was coming downstairs to get her.

Ruby's back flattened against the front door, which snapped shut under her shoulders. Her eyes fixed on the narrow white door that shut off the winding stairwell from the front room.

Ching-creak. Ching-creak. Ching.

The sound stopped behind the little door and her breath stayed in her bumping chest. Then, in a rare show of athleticism, she darted to the sofa and tumbled over the back of it, dropping into the dark triangle of space that was filled with dust bunnies and lost things – a glove, a pen lid, the back off the remote control. A red light pulsed to the same crazy rhythm as her heart and with a jolt Ruby realized that it was the LED. She fumbled behind her and pressed the button, then knelt there, shivering, her eyes only just above the velour back, staring so hard at the little white door that they stung.

The door creaked slowly open.

'Daddy!' Relief was like a sugar rush. Ruby jumped up.

'Why's it so dark in here?' he said, flicking on the lights. He was already in his cowboy gear.

'Didn't you hear me shouting?' said Ruby.

'I wanted to surprise you.'

'Why?'

By way of an answer, Daddy swaggered across the room towards her.

Ching. Ching. Ching.

Ruby frowned at his feet, and then gasped. 'Spurs!'

'Not just any old spurs,' he grinned. 'Jingle Bobs.' He lifted his heel to show her, spinning the spiked wheel that jingled like sleigh bells. 'Those little metal bits? That's the clappers. That's what makes the noise, you see?'

He put his foot down and did a little dance to make them ring.

'Wo-ow!' Ruby climbed back over the sofa and bent to have a closer look. Now that she could see how it was made, the sound wasn't scary at all, only pretty. She felt like a fool.

He put his boot up on the coffee table. 'Look at that workmanship,' he said, running a finger across the silver shanks. Horseshoes and tumbling dice were hammered into the metal in little dots. 'They're the real thing, Rubes. All the way from Wyoming.'

'Wyoming,' she breathed. 'Like a real cowboy.'

He grinned. 'You should see the stuff you can buy, Rubes. Real genuine cowboy things.'

'I bet they cost *loads*,' she said.

Daddy said nothing and picked lint off his knee.

Ruby's awed expression flickered. 'Does Mummy know?'

He frowned and took his boot off the table with a clink. 'She isn't the only one around here who can buy things, you know.'

Now she'd upset him.

'I know.'

He jingled into the kitchen and back out again with a bunch of red roses. 'See?'

Ruby's eyes popped. 'Are they for Mummy? They're *beautiful*.'

'They should be. They cost enough.'

'She'll *love* them.'

'Yeah, I know.' Daddy smiled at the roses and everything was fine.

Ruby plumped down on the sofa. 'Make them go again!'

Happy to oblige, he jingled around the room in his spurs. He kicked up his heels and tapped his toes, and Ruby laughed and clapped in delight.

And the fun only stopped when Mummy opened the front door.

10

THE ROW WENT on longer than any row Ruby could remember. The job and the shoes and the car and the job and the window and the spurs, and the job and the job and the job.

Ruby bit her thumbnail. It wasn't Daddy's fault he lost his job. It was the recession. He caught fish for them, didn't he? He cleaned the house and he made her dippy eggs and baked beans for tea. But all Mummy ever did was be mean to him and yell. She never *used* to yell – neither of them *used* to yell. They used to laugh and show each other things on the telly, and go for bus rides to the beach. Not *this* beach with its rocks and pebbles, but a *real* beach with sand.

They used to love each other.

Ruby turned up the TV, but she could hear the ebb and flow behind the kitchen door. Finally it flew open and her father strode past the TV, the Jingle Bobs quiet in his fist.

'Where are you going, Daddy?' said Ruby.

'To cool off!' he said, then looked at the kitchen and shouted, 'Before I do something I regret!'

Mummy appeared in the doorway, tea towel in one

hand, a plate dripping in the other. 'Something *you* regret? What about *my* regrets? Living in this dingy little *hole*. Working all hours while you go fishing and dress up with your friends and buy stupid *toys* instead of taking care of your family! *That*'s what *I* regret!'

'If you think you can do better, then leave me and Rubes here!' yelled Daddy. 'And you go off with your fancy man!'

Ruby gasped.

Daddy yanked the front door open and slammed it so hard behind him that the little china dog trembled on the window sill.

'Fuck *you*!' Mummy hurled the tea towel after him, but it flopped on to the rug halfway across the room.

Ruby got up and went after Daddy.

'You stay *right here*, Ruby Trick!'

Ruby hesitated, then pulled open the door – her heart thumping at her own disobedience – and ran down the hill, tripping and slipping across the green cobbles in her white school socks.

Daddy was already in the car.

'Can I come with you?'

'No,' he said. He turned the key and the car started.

Her face crumpled. 'Please, Daddy! I don't want to stay with *her*.'

His jaw clenched.

'All right then.'

She climbed in beside him.

'Put your belt on.'

Ruby did.

* * *

They drove in silence. First towards Bideford, and then away from the sea through the unlit lanes, where the lights of oncoming cars could be seen from miles off, lighting up the sky over the high hedges.

Ruby didn't know where they were and she didn't care. Daddy and Mummy had argued before, but they'd never thrown things; never walked out, never said the F word. She didn't even think that grown-ups *knew* the F word. She thought about Mummy kissing a fancy man and tears welled up in her eyes and made the night into coal-coloured cobwebs.

'I *hate* Mummy!' she said, and burst into tears against his arm. 'She didn't even say thank you for the *flowers*.' And another wave of weeping broke over her.

Daddy put his arm around her. 'Women want a man who can take care of them, Rubes.'

'But you *do* take care of us!'

Daddy just squeezed her against him while she cried.

She looked up when he stopped the car in a narrow lane between two high hedges.

'Where are we?' said Ruby, wiping her eyes.

'Here,' said Daddy and nodded at a gap in the hedge. 'I ever show you this?'

Ruby looked across the road at a little white box of a guardhouse beside a red and white barrier. There was a light on in the hut, and Ruby could see an old man inside, drinking from a mug. His uniform collar was too big for his neck, which made him look like a tortoise.

'What is it?'

'This is where I used to work.'

She was confused. The hut was only big enough for one person. 'Where?'

'There.' Daddy pointed.

Ruby looked beyond the hut. For a moment she thought she was looking into the black sky. Then she realized it was an enormous corrugated-iron shed – bigger than fifty houses – looming over the landscape.

'Wo-ow!' she said. 'It's *huge*.'

He said, 'Got to be big, see? We built proper big ships inside. Ships big enough to go all over the world. South America. Africa. Brazil. Places like that. Proper big ships.'

'Bigger than the ones on the Quay?'

'Some of 'em, yeah. Fifty thousand tonnes, some of 'em.'

'Wo-ow!' said Ruby again, although she had no idea what a tonne was. But fifty thousand of them was a lot.

The shed was gigantic, and being out here in the countryside made it look even bigger – towering over the high hedges, next to the narrow lanes and with no other buildings around it.

Ruby pointed down the lane. 'How do they get the ships to the sea when they're finished?'

Daddy laughed and told her they slid straight out of the shed and down into the river on the other side, dripping with champagne.

'Wow!' she said. 'I wish I could see that!'

'Me too,' said Daddy sadly. He stared at the shed. 'We used to have a right laugh here. I remember we used to send the new boys down to the stores for a long stand, or to get a bubble for the spirit level.'

'Why?'

'It was just a joke, see? Just a bit of fun.'

'Ohhh,' said Ruby, but she didn't get it.

He wound the window down. The rain had stopped and the night smelled like green and river, and the hedges rustled with small, secret night things.

'Daddy?' said Ruby carefully.

'Hmm?'

'Are you and Mummy getting . . . *divorced*?' The word was so hard for Ruby to say that it ended in a tearful squeak.

'No,' he said. 'Never.' He flicked his cigarette out of the window, and the night was so quiet that Ruby could hear it sizzle as it hit the ground.

'Don't you worry, Rubes,' he said. 'I'll always take care of you. I just wish Mummy didn't have to work. I wish I could keep her safe at home in a glass box.'

'Like Snow White?' said Ruby.

'Yeah,' said Daddy. 'Like Snow White.'

Ruby imagined Mummy lying in a box on the kitchen table, with her hair all brushed and a little bunch of flowers on her chest.

It was so romantic that Ruby's lip wobbled.

They drove back up to the main road and soon Ruby recognized the outskirts of Bideford.

Daddy stopped outside a shop and bought a six-pack of Strongbow for him and a Twix for her. He opened one of the cans and took a few gulps, then wiped his mouth on the back of his hand.

'Now eat your Twix, and we'll go home and have hot milk.'

'With sugar?'

'Yes.'

Ruby opened her Twix and took a bite. It wasn't her favourite, but it would definitely do.

'Better?' said Daddy.

She nodded.

'Good. Hold that,' he said, and handed her the can and pulled back on to the road towards home.

As they drove, he held out his hand now and then, and Ruby gave him the can. It emptied quickly and she put it in the well behind his seat.

As they left Bideford, they passed a woman standing at a bus stop.

'That's Miss Sharpe!'

'Who's Miss Sharpe?'

'My teacher. Can we give her a lift?'

'Maybe she doesn't want a lift, Rubes. Women can be a bit funny about taking lifts.'

'But it's raining. *Please*, Daddy!'

Daddy trod on the brakes and peered in his rear-view mirror. 'All right,' he said. 'Get in the back.'

The car didn't have back doors so Ruby scrambled between the seats as he reversed up the road to the bus stop. When he was level with it, Daddy leaned over and wound down the window a few inches.

'Want a lift?' he said.

Miss Sharpe peered at him from under her umbrella with a suspicious look on her face. 'No, thank you,' she said. 'I'm waiting for the bus.'

'Hello, Miss,' said Ruby, leaning forward between the seats.

Miss Sharpe's face cleared. 'Oh, hello, Ruby! I didn't see you there!'

'We can take you home, Miss,' said Ruby eagerly.

'It's all the way in Fairy Cross,' said Miss Sharpe. 'I don't like to put you to any trouble.'

'It's on our way,' said John Trick.

Miss Sharpe still seemed uncertain. She looked back up the road towards Bideford, as if she might see the bus coming, but it wasn't.

'Well, OK then . . .' She got into the front seat and shook her umbrella into the gutter. She also had a gym bag and a badminton racquet.

'Thank you,' she said. 'You're very kind.'

'No problem.'

They drove for a bit, with only the sound of the wipers clicking back and forth on the windscreen. Ruby hung between the front seats so she could smile at Miss Sharpe whenever she looked around.

'Did you like my diary, Miss?'

'Yes, Ruby, it was very good.'

Ruby looked at Daddy eagerly, but he didn't give any indication of having heard her.

'Is that a tennis bat, Miss?'

'No, it's for playing badminton,' said Miss Sharpe.

'What's bammington?'

'Well, it's a bit like tennis, but you don't play with a ball, you play with a thing called a shuttlecock.'

'What's a shuttlecock?'

'It's like a little cone made out of feathers.'

'Does it fly?' said Ruby, and Miss Sharpe laughed.

'Only when you hit it.'

'Oh,' said Ruby. She found it difficult to picture that. Hitting one of those with a bat must be like swiping a cartoon bird – with all the little feathers floating down to earth afterwards.

They passed the sign that said FAIRY CROSS AND FORD. From the other direction, Ruby knew it said FORD AND FAIRY CROSS, just to be fair.

Miss Sharpe said, 'You can drop me just past the pub. Thank you.'

'But it's raining,' said Ruby.

And her father added, 'It's no problem to take you to the door.'

'You're very kind,' said Miss Sharpe again.

John Trick followed two more brief instructions, and then stopped the car outside a short terrace of white-washed cottages.

'Thank you very much, Mr Trick,' said Miss Sharpe, getting out. 'And I'll see you on Monday, Ruby, bright and early.'

'Bye, Miss.'

Miss Sharpe put up her umbrella and waved back into the car with her racquet, and they set off again.

Ruby hung between the front seats and told Daddy about the diary.

'Miss Sharpe said it was excellent,' she lied, but it was wasted anyway, because Daddy had gone quiet again, so Ruby went quiet too, because she realized that things couldn't be all better just because they'd been for a drive.

Daddy sipped from another can of cider, so Ruby got back in the front and dozed the rest of the way. She knew the route so well from her bus ride to and from school that even in her semi-sleep she could map the road home. Dimly she felt the swings through the S-bends at the Hoops Inn, and slid forward a little as the car nose-dived down the hill to Limeburn.

When they finally pulled up in the tiny cobbled square just feet from the drop to the beach, she stretched and yawned.

Daddy sat without getting out, finishing the second can of Strongbow.

Ruby was getting cold, but she was nervous of going into the house alone and seeing Mummy again.

Maybe Daddy was too, because he drank a third can, looking up at the light in the bedroom window of The Retreat while the ocean breathed in and out in the darkness.

'You know,' said Daddy suddenly, 'when we first got married, your mum used to call me her hero. She used to say I'd rescued her.'

'Like Snow White's prince!'

'Yeah, like that.'

'Did you have a horse?'

'No.'

'Oh.' That was disappointing. 'What did you rescue her from?'

He shrugged. 'Just, you know, I come along like a prince and swept her off her feet.'

His smile faded. 'She needed me then, see. When I had a job.'

'Can't you just get another job?'

Daddy shook his head and gave a bitter little laugh. 'Not in this economy.'

Ruby nodded. Her socks were still wet from the cobbles, and her feet were like ice, but she could hear Daddy thinking, so she didn't want to whine like a girl.

Finally – without taking his eyes from The Retreat – Daddy sighed deeply. 'Women can't help it, you know, Rubes.'

'Can't help what?' she asked through chattering teeth.

But Daddy went on staring up at the bedroom window, while Ruby sat and shivered beside him.

'Can't help *what*?'

11

WHEN SHE GOT home, Miss Sharpe realized that getting a lift had gifted her an extra half-hour with which to do whatever she liked.

So she put her badminton gear in the washing machine and cleaned out Harvey's litter tray, while the big grey rabbit rocked gently around the kitchen behind her. Then she got out her marking for the evening and poured herself half a glass of white wine.

Any more would be stupid, and she didn't *do* stupid.

She was sensible far beyond her twenty-six years, and had been that way for most of her life.

Georgia Sharpe had realized quite young that she was not pretty enough to catch a boy with her looks. She had believed her mirror when it told her that her wiry hair fizzed and spat like brown sparks around her head, that her eyes were small and pale, and that she had a mouth that turned down at one corner, making her look a little disappointed. But the truth had never daunted her, and by the time she was sixteen she was glad not to have been burdened by beauty. By then she'd watched her prettier friends dumbing down their lives to accommodate idiot boyfriends, and made up her mind that that was not for her; that she would get by on her brains and her good nature, even if it meant being single her whole life long. An old maid, her father said, but young Georgia thought that being single sounded rather exciting – and a lot less complicated than having to worry about the hopes and dreams of what she always referred to as 'some random man'.

So, instead of succumbing to panic-led convention, Miss Sharpe had upped sticks from flat Norfolk and moved to sinuous Devon, where she joined the badminton club for exercise, bought a house rabbit for cuddles, and – until she could have her own children – enjoyed those belonging to other people in class 5B at Bideford's Westmead Junior School.

She wasn't stupid, so she'd never expected *all* children to be enjoyable – and so it proved. For every Jamie Starke with her A in English, there was a Jordan Whitefield, with his essays punctuated only by bogeys. And for every sweet-natured David Leather, there was a Shawn Loosemore, who gave smaller children Chinese burns when he thought no one was looking.

Children lied, too. Miss Sharpe had expected a bit of exaggeration, but she had been surprised by just how tall their tales could be. In the first week's diaries alone, Shawn had tamed 'a wild stallyon' and Connor Nuttall had done a triple somersault in gym – which he'd then painfully failed to repeat for a rapt crowd of children on the hard tarmac of the playground.

Miss Sharpe still had a pile of this week's books to go through, but already Noah Jones had swum all the way from Appledore to Instow, and Essie Littlejohn had found an adder. It was half dead this week, but Miss Sharpe suspected that next week it could well be fully alive and – if nothing was said – the week after that Essie might be charming it out of a basket with a flute.

She understood why they did it. The more outlandish the lies, the more attention the children seemed to glean from their classmates.

Miss Sharpe knew that it was probably her duty to caution the children against embellishments, but she was reluctant to be too dictatorial because the lies were so much more entertaining than reality. Most of the diaries were plain boring. There were endless Playstation sessions, karate clubs, homework, and doing each other's hair. David Leather seemed to practise the violin every spare minute of the day, and if Miss Sharpe heard one more time about there being no ponies in Ruby Trick's paddock, she'd scream. Even Jordan had said *'Again?'* and made a loud snoring sound, which had made the other children laugh.

She thought of how Ruby had tried to show off to her father in the car tonight. She understood that little-girl need to have her daddy's approval – even about something as mundane as a diary. She'd spent her own formative years trying to catch her father's eye.

But after her mother had died, nothing had ever really caught his eye again.

Miss Sharpe wondered where the scars on Mr Trick's face had come from – ugly, pale arcs that distorted his eye and his dark brow. He wasn't what she'd have expected for the father of Ruby Trick, with her red hair and freckles. For her own amusement, she'd started to give herself points out of ten for predicting what the parents of each child in her class would look like. She hadn't met them all yet, and wasn't terribly good at the game. She'd only have given herself a two for Mr Trick. Unlike David Leather's parents, who were perfect tens. *They* had come to school about David being bullied, and could barely fit through the classroom door. They were nice people, but as the parents of a victimized child they were ineffectual – too kind and too comfortable with their own girths to understand that what their enormous son needed to survive school was boot camp, not violin lessons.

Children were sponges – sucking up whatever was around them without any effort or intention, be it prejudices or food. They thought what their parents thought, said what they said, did what they did.

Ate what they ate.

By that reckoning, David Leather was doomed.

But Ruby Trick wasn't. Not yet. Her red hair and dirty socks made her an outsider, but Miss Sharpe understood *that* only too well.

Miss Sharpe finished her wine. Maybe she could give Ruby the support and encouragement *she*'d missed out on? Maybe she could make a difference to her life. Be remembered fondly. Get a card when she was sixty saying *I owe it all to you.*

Wasn't that what being a teacher was all about?

Miss Sharpe sighed and scooped Harvey on to her lap. His ears were so soft they were almost imaginary, and she murmured gently against his silken head, 'Clever boy, Harvey.'

She giggled at her own tipsy foolishness. Harvey was a

rabbit. All he did all day was hop, eat and poo – none of which really required a motivational speech from her!

Ruby Trick, on the other hand, was an isolated child without discernible talents, assets or friends.

That chubby little sponge needed all the help she could get.

12

ALL WEEK LONG, Ruby watched her father like a dog watches a man with a tin opener. She knew from school that it was always the daddies that left, and her tummy squeezed like a fist every time he reached for his keys.

Sometimes he took his fishing rod, but he didn't bring home any fish, and when they drove up the hill in the morning, empty cider cans rolled backwards from under the driver's seat.

At school Ruby huddled on the dry strip under the overhanging roof and watched the other children mob Shawn Loosemore, who had stroked a seal on Westward Ho! beach, and Paul Powers, whose father had bought him a brand-new motocross bike. Ruby knew Paul from the bus. He often smelled mouldy and Ruby noticed that his school shoes were still as scuffed and peeling as ever. His dad must have spent all the money they had on that bike.

If *she* had exciting things to write about, the other kids would be nice to her the way they were to Paul. Nobody had liked him either before he got his motorbike. Now he had lots of best friends hanging off his shoulders, giving him things and begging for a playdate.

She didn't have a motocross bike or a pony, only a cross Mummy and a silent Daddy, and who wanted to come all the way to Limeburn to see that?

The wind changed direction and the other children under the overhang shuffled off to find somewhere drier to stand until the bell rang. Ruby was too miserable to notice.

'Why are you crying?' demanded Essie Littlejohn.

'Shut up,' said Ruby. 'I'm not.'

But Essie only tilted her head so she could look at Ruby better, and said, 'Is it because nobody likes you?'

'Shut up, *whore.*'

Ruby didn't know what the word meant.

But it shut Essie up.

After school Ruby cleaned the mud off Daddy's walking boots, gouging it from the treads with a pointed stick and scraping it off the leather with a teaspoon.

On Tuesday she spent hours sorting his fish hooks into the right little plastic boxes, even though she jabbed her thumb twice – sending tingles right up to her ears, and drawing a deep-red bubble of blood that made her shiver.

On Wednesday it stopped raining long enough for her to clean the car. First she took out all the rubbish and put it in the kitchen bin. There were receipts and sweet wrappers and one of Mummy's old earrings in the passenger-door pocket, but mostly it was empty Strongbow cans.

She had to make two trips.

Washing the car took buckets and buckets, and twice she slipped on the cobbles while trying to reach the roof and spilled freezing water all over her shoes.

Adam came out of his house and asked what she was doing.

'Washing the car for my Daddy,' she said, and then she bit her lip and turned away and went on washing, because she didn't want Adam to see her crying. But he didn't say anything else after that – just did the roof for her and helped to squeeze out the sponges.

'Thanks,' she sniffed, and squelched home.

Later, Ruby stuck the little hoop earring into her diary with clear tape. Underneath it she wrote carefully, *I found this treshure in my Daddy's car when I cleaned it for him. I also washed the outside and it took three buckets.*

On Thursday she recorded *True Grit* for him off the telly. The old film, not the new one, because Daddy didn't trust any cowboy with long hair, or who wasn't John Wayne.

Mummy and Daddy didn't speak except to say *Pass the butter*, and when Ruby came home, Daddy was often not there. Sometimes the car was gone, sometimes just he was. Sometimes he went out at night, even when Mummy was working. He told Ruby not to tell Mummy and she didn't – partly because she was on his side and partly because she was ashamed to admit to anyone that Daddy would go out and leave her alone. What if she burned the house down? Ruby didn't like the feeling it gave her – that something bad could happen and she was too small and weak to do anything to stop it.

Mummy did a lot of extra shifts, and often had to walk

up the hill to catch the bus, but Ruby reckoned it served her right. This was all her fault. Her and her fancy man. What if *Mummy* wanted a divorce? What if Daddy left? What if they moved? What if she got a new Daddy she didn't like?

At night she lay awake for hours, straining to decipher the voices from the next room. The soft bitterness that made her understand all the anger and all the fear, and none of the meaning, while the wind squealed and howled through the bathroom window, in a ghostly soundtrack to her misery.

School was seven hours a day when she didn't know where Daddy was, so Ruby tried her very best not to go.

She had a belly ache; she had a broken foot; she couldn't see out of one eye.

Mummy had all the answers. She gave Ruby peppermint cordial for her stomach, she rubbed Deep Heat on to her toes and threw a pair of balled-up socks at her.

'There,' she said. 'You couldn't catch those if you were blind in one eye, because of depth perception.'

But Ruby was dogged. 'My chest hurts,' she said. It didn't right then, but it did quite often, so Ruby didn't think of this as a lie. More like a postponement of the truth.

Mummy said nothing. She drew back the curtains, although it hardly made the room any lighter, the leaves and branches were that thick around the window. Then she sat down on the edge of the bed and took Ruby's hand, but Ruby took it back.

'Are you happy at school, Ruby?'

Ruby said yes, even though saying yes to that question was silly. Who was happy at school? Nobody, apart from Miss Sharpe, as far as she could see. But if she said no, then Mummy would know her chest wasn't really hurting.

'Nobody's bullying you, are they?'

'No,' said Ruby, because if she said yes, Mummy might come up to the school and give Essie Littlejohn or the kids on the bus a row, or ask to speak to their parents. And then Ruby would be an even bigger target than she already was.

'Let's have a look at your chest then . . .'

Ruby pulled her Mickey Mouse T-shirt up to her armpits and Mummy peered down.

'Why are you mean to Daddy?' said Ruby.

Mummy looked surprised. She didn't say anything for a little while – just pulled the T-shirt back down and patted Ruby's tummy.

'You know, Ruby, sometimes grown-ups have arguments, just like children do. It doesn't mean they don't love each other.'

Ruby thought about that for a moment, then said, 'Daddy says he used to be your hero.'

Mummy nodded. 'He was,' she said. 'He came along just when I needed him most.'

'Don't you need him now he hasn't got a job?'

'I—'

Mummy started and then stopped.

'What?'

'Nothing,' said Mummy. 'Listen. These are grown-up things, Ruby. I don't want you worrying about them. Worrying is a mummy's job!' She was trying to make a funny joke of it, but Ruby didn't smile back.

'Up you get now,' said Mummy.

'But my *tummy* hurts.'

'A minute ago it was your chest,' said Mummy, and Ruby realized she'd blown it.

'You have to go to school, Ruby,' said Mummy. 'You don't want to grow up stupid, do you?'

'I don't care,' said Ruby.

'Well, I care,' said Mummy. 'Up you get.'

Ruby sighed and got up.

Mummy didn't understand. *She* could get off the bus.

13

MISS SHARPE BOUGHT a *Gazette* and read the front page as she walked towards school.

> ### POLICE WARN AFTER SECOND 'ET' ATTACK
> *Police have warned that the man responsible for two assaults on lone women in North Devon could 'go too far' and commit an even more serious crime.*
>
> *In terrifying ordeals, the women were made to strip, while being threatened with violence by a man known as the ET attacker, because he makes his victims phone home.*

Miss Sharpe took a moment to snort derisively. One man and his dog in the *Gazette* office might know him as 'the ET attacker' but nobody *normal* ever said rubbish like that.

> *Neither was physically harmed, but both were left traumatized by the encounter with the man, who wore a black balaclava.*
>
> *One woman was assaulted on Westward Ho! beach, and the other in woodland near Clovelly.*
>
> *Detective Chief Inspector Kirsty King, who is leading the*

investigation, told the Gazette, '*These were disturbing and frightening attacks on young women minding their own business in broad daylight.*

'*Thankfully, neither suffered any physical harm, but we are concerned that the nature of the attacks may be escalating, and fear this individual may injure somebody.*

'*We would appeal to him to come forward so that he can receive the help he needs before he goes too far.*'

Oh yes, thought Miss Sharpe, *that'll happen*.
She read on:

'*We would also urge women alone in isolated areas to be aware of potential threats, and not to put themselves in harm's way.*'
 Police have described the man as being white, with a local accent, and about six feet tall.

Despite the newspaper hype, the story was disturbing. Miss Sharpe was relieved that she was far too busy to wander about pointlessly on beaches or in woodland, and decided that she'd take a lot more notice of whether her doors were locked at night. It was easy to become casual in the countryside, but she already had a spyhole and *never* opened the door to anyone she didn't recognize. Maybe she'd get a chain put on the front door by the local community policing team. She was overthinking things, she knew, but Miss Sharpe's motto had always been *Better safe than sorry*.
 EEEEEE-ee-ee!
The car screeched to a halt less than two feet from her

hip. The yellow bonnet with two broad black stripes running down it sprang back up from the sudden harsh braking.

She'd walked straight out in front of it. Hadn't even realized she was in the road.

'Sorry!' she mouthed. 'Sorry!' But the reflection of the sky in the windscreen made it impossible to see whether she was forgiven or not.

She finished crossing and the yellow car swerved noisily around her.

Not forgiven.

Nerves fizzed all over Miss Sharpe's body. She'd almost been killed! While she was planning her own safe passage through life. One split second of inattention and she could be dead now, or paralysed, seriously injured, lying in the road with two broken legs and tarmac under her cheek.

She started to shake.

It was shock, certainly. But it was also anger at herself. How could she have been so *stupid*? That wasn't like her. That was the kind of thing other people did. People who weren't as cautious; weren't as clever.

Those were the people who were alive one second and dead the next.

And in the *Gazette* the day after that.

14

'LOOK!' RUBY SAID triumphantly from the triangle behind the sofa.

'What's that?' said Daddy.

'The back off the remote control.'

Ruby clambered over the back of the sofa with the bit of plastic and the glove.

'Clever you,' said Daddy.

Daddy fixed the remote and pressed Play on *True Grit* and for a bit they watched a one-eyed fat man help a little girl find the killers of her father.

Ruby over-laughed in all the good places, but Daddy didn't. He toyed with the glove and tried it on, but it was too big for him.

'This was behind the sofa?' he said.

'Uh-huh. There's a pen lid too. Shall I get it?'

'No,' said Daddy. 'Leave it.'

Ruby snuggled up under his arm, but Daddy was restless. In the middle of the shoot-out, he made her stand up so he could move the sofa to look for the other glove.

It wasn't there.

He stood for a moment, staring down at the carpet, then looked at the door and said, 'Back soon.'

'How long is soon?'

'Not long,' he said. 'Be a good girl.'

He closed the door behind him and Ruby heard him picking up his fishing gear from the porch. She switched off the TV by pressing the remote-control button as hard as she could.

She'd *been* a good girl and it hadn't worked.

So she went upstairs and messed with Daddy's cowboy things.

The cowboy drawer always swelled in the damp, and Ruby got red and sweaty in the wrestle.

Once she'd got it open far enough to reach inside, she put the gunbelt on first, hitching it all the way round to the final hole, which was small and stiff. It was too big for her, but not *too* too big, and if she spread her legs a bit, it would stay on her hips. The holster hung to her knee.

Then the hat.

She lifted out the black Stetson and placed it on her own head like a crown.

The Jingle Bobs were complicated. She couldn't work them out. She spun the little wheels to make them ring, and decided she'd try them on another time.

Holding the gunbelt up all the way with a casual hand, Ruby waddled splay-legged the few paces to the mirror on the back of the door.

She looked *exactly* like a cowboy. Her bunny slippers spoiled it a bit, so Ruby chose not to look at them.

Her right hand fell naturally to the holster and she felt a jag of disappointment that there was no gun to play with. Sticks were just fine until there was something real to measure them by. In this holster they would have been just sticks. A real holster needed a real gun.

Ruby drew her finger at the mirror. 'Pow! Pow-pow!'

The hat fell over her eyes with the recoil.

Ruby pushed it back, then tried to catch sight of herself while she wasn't looking, so she could see how she *really* looked.

Still amazing.

The tip of the fishing rod dipped and danced, but John Trick didn't see it. He saw *past* it – across the pale-grey sea to the vague hump of Lundy Island on the fuzzy horizon, and beyond that to a more distant place, while the crabs made merry with his bait . . .

As a child, John had rarely gone to primary school, where he'd been relentlessly teased about the scars on his face. And when he had gone, he'd learned to lash out first and let the other kids ask questions afterwards – if they still had teeth that weren't a-wobble in their heads.

But then – on his first day at big school – he had seen Alison Jewell.

She had hit him like measles.

He hadn't stopped fighting, but he had gone to school every possible day for the next four years just to see her – just to occupy the same space. Now and then, he and the other boys would shout inappropriate things at her in a bid to make contact, but he never had the courage to say anything *real*, because she came from Clovelly, and he'd heard that her mother was a doctor.

Her *mother*!

Even though he'd barely spoken to Alison in all the time they shared a classroom, just enough of that unexpected schooling rubbed off on John Trick that by the time he left he was taken on as an apprentice welder at the shipyard.

John remembered the early mornings when he got up in the dark and felt like a man. Riding his scooter through the lanes, the indicator clicking loudly in the night, to join the other men. They'd start with nothing but their hands and a plan and they'd build a ship. Every day they welded and moulded and fabricated their own lives; their own pride; their own futures. They talked and they shouted above the noise and they told dirty jokes and laughed whether they were funny or not. They arrived together and they left together, bonded by clocks and hard labour.

With his first pay packet he'd got just drunk enough that he'd caught a bus to Clovelly, banged on doors until he'd found Alison Jewell's home, and asked her to marry him.

She'd laughed.

'I didn't even know you liked me,' she'd said.

'I don't like you,' he'd told her. 'I *love* you.'

Alison had frowned – as if she couldn't understand how someone who looked like him could ever love someone who looked like her – and so he'd leaned in and kissed her with tongues, and then pushed her down on to her bed under her Take That poster. Her parents were downstairs, so she'd tried to shove him off, but she hadn't tried *that* hard, and he wasn't so drunk that they couldn't seal the deal.

Happy days.

He'd wanted to tell the whole world, but Alison said it was more fun if they kept it a secret, and was careful not to let on at school or anywhere else. She'd barely even let him *see* her, let alone have sex again – that's how much fun she thought their secret would be – but they couldn't keep it a secret for ever.

Ruby had seen to that.

At first John couldn't believe his bad luck. Getting Ali pregnant on their very first time! But, as it turned out, a baby on the way was like a proof of purchase for a girl he would otherwise never have been able to afford.

Alison's father had hit the roof. Gone *through* the roof. He'd actually cried. It would have been funny if it hadn't been so insulting. And the more pissed off Malcolm Jewell got, the more obstinate *he*'d become. Mr Jewell had demanded an abortion – what he called 'Taking care of it so we can all get back to normal' – but Alison had refused point blank. Even John had been surprised by how vehement she'd been about wanting to marry him – and moved by how much she loved him.

For the first time in his life, he'd felt he had the upper hand. Alison was *his* now. She was having *his* baby and *he* would call the shots – and if that meant a register office and a suit from Oxfam, then so be it. Her father could rage and her hoity-toity mother could cry and moan all she liked, but John had taken pleasure in telling them both that he was not one for charity.

'It's not about *charity*,' Rosemary Jewell had said in her squeaky, sneaky, pop-eyed way. 'It's about *tradition*.'

John Trick snorted and snapped open another can. Tradition, bollocks; it was about *possession*.

Nine-tenths of the law.

They'd married in Barnstaple register office, with Alison in a plain blue dress and her mother sobbing throughout. He hadn't even told *his* mother. She'd made her own choice years before, and it wasn't him.

When he'd kissed the bride, she'd cried and whispered into his mouth, 'Thank you.'

It seemed a long, long time ago, and lately, even nine-tenths didn't feel like enough.

In the slow drizzle of the beach, John stared into the shimmering gold of his cider and thought about possession. Possessions were difficult things. Other people liked them too, and would take them from you if they could.

Alison's parents would like to take her from him, for starters. They *still* thought she was too good for him. He tried only to see them at Christmas, but he could tell that was true in Malcolm's stiff handshake and the way Rosemary touched his good cheek with hers – dry and distant despite the contact. They gave Ali money in secret – he knew that. Not just for her birthday and Christmas, but at other times too. She tried to hide it from him, but he had eyes. He'd found the receipt for the groceries they could not afford; noticed the new jeans Ruby was wearing before her old ones had even gone through at the knees. They were trying to buy Alison back, to control her with money, to loosen his hold. They must have thought they had a shot at it, ever since he'd lost his job.

As if losing his job had made him less entitled to his own wife.

And they tried to buy Ruby too, even though she was more *his* than anything had ever been. Last birthday they'd bought her a bicycle – pink, tassled, and the silliest gift you could buy for a child who lived squeezed between a hill and a cliff. Malcolm Jewell had spent hours puffing up and down the hill behind Ruby, holding on to the saddle, and with his face as red as his thinning hair. Ruby never rode the bicycle now, John was pleased to note, but buying it had been disrespectful to him.

And the worst of it was, Alison *let* them disrespect him and then *lied* to him about it. He could always tell – the way she tucked her hair behind her ear.

And now something strange was going on too. Something to do with the big glove, and those new shoes that were too high for either of them.

Alison lied to him about money. Now – for the first time ever – he wondered what else his wife might lie about.

And he wondered who the shoes might *really* be from. Or for.

15

THERE WERE TWO things Donald Moon hated above all – liberals and litterbugs. They were the same thing, really. Without liberals there would *be* no littering. Nor much crime at all, Donald figured, because without liberals, those found guilty of any crime would be locked up so fast that their feet would barely touch the ground.

And at the head of that queue, if Donald had his way, would be the litterbugs.

Donald had once owned seventy acres of clifftop along the coastal path, and had spent half his life picking up plastic bags and bottles so that his lambs wouldn't choke on them, and the other half glaring through binoculars, hoping to catch someone red-handed in the act of dropping contraband. He never did – the stuff seemed to drop itself! – but he never gave up.

Donald and his wife Marion had kept a hundred endangered sheep until he'd finally had to admit that he had become that most endangered breed of all – a small farmer in a world where livestock was just another product, like cardboard or biscuits. Each year it got harder and harder, and when his income finally became an outcome, Donald sold sixty-five acres to a neighbour and ninety-seven sheep to other doomed enthusiasts. He turned his remaining five acres over to vegetables and fruit to save on the shopping bill, and used his last three Leicester Longwools to lever his way into a part-time job at The Big Sheep in Bideford. Tourists flocked there to watch sheep shows and sheep shearing and even sheep races, where sheep competed in the Sheep Grand National, with straw-bale jumps and little knitted jockeys on their backs – all as though sheep were exotic beasts in a woolly circus.

Once his sheep and his land were gone, there was nothing to stop litter becoming Donald's primary focus. He would roust the stout Marion every weekend to traipse across North Devon armed with pointed sticks for spearing paper or hooking Tesco bags out of hedges. They wore matching Day-Glo vests for safety, and carried big green waste sacks for the cans and the plastic that people flung randomly around the countryside, and the disposable nappies laid carefully in lay-bys – as if they would soon be dealt with by some kind of state-funded poo patrol.

Donald was on his way home from work that Saturday when he saw the newspaper in the lay-by into Abbotsham.

Newspapers were Donald's *bête noire*. An entire village could be ruined by a copy of the *Sun* and a stiff breeze. Lurid headlines flapping in gutters, flattened against hedges, fluttering up trees. Paper tits dissolving to porridge in the rain.

So, even though the light was almost gone from the

sky, and even though it had rained all day and his overalls were damp against his thighs, Donald Moon did a U-turn and pulled over.

This newspaper was the *Daily Mail*, which was even thicker than the *Sun* and, therefore, potentially even worse. Already the *Coffee Break* insert had escaped and spread itself across a field gate twenty yards away.

Donald picked up the main section, then went after the rest. When he got to the gate, he could see in the dim light that *Coffee Break* had already come apart, and that several pale pages were now dotted about the wet grass of the field beyond.

There was nothing for it. Now he had seen it, he had to do something about it. Donald muttered under his breath and climbed the gate.

In the half-dark he dropped to the ground on the other side and landed on something that rolled under his boot. He slipped to one knee, while the other leg twisted away from him at an angle that made his eyes water.

Donald was not a swearer by nature, but he couldn't help himself, and he was surprised to find that – contrary to what he'd always claimed in company – it actually *did* make him feel better.

Finally he got his breath back and blew tears out of his nose between his finger and thumb.

Then he peered down through the gloom to see what it was that he had trodden on.

It was a woman's face.

16

WOMAN'S BODY DUMPED IN LAY-BY.

Miss Sharpe had read the *Gazette* right there, outside the newsagent's.

The meagre report underneath the giant font consisted mostly of caution and police-speak. The police wouldn't say who she was or how she'd died. They wouldn't even call it murder. Yet. All they were doing was asking anyone who'd seen a woman hitching a lift between Bideford and Northam to contact this number. There was a photo of a five-bar gate and a field beyond it.

Now Miss Sharpe stood at the staffroom window with a cup in one hand, a saucer in the other, and felt a wave of melancholy wash over her.

The thought of some poor woman lying in that lay-by – maybe for days – undiscovered in the rain, had disturbed her deeply.

Without a face or a name for the victim, it could be anyone.

With a hitch in her chest, she almost felt that it could be *her*.

After all, who would miss her? Who would call the

school and let them know she hadn't come home the night before? She had only moved here three months ago; she didn't have a husband or a boyfriend. Her father was across the other side of the country and her colleagues were friendly, but only as far as the car park. Her badminton partner at the club was a sixty-year-old man called Edward, whose dentures had once fallen out during an exuberant rally, and who only ever spoke to her to shout things like 'Mine!' and 'Down at the net!' He might miss her drop shot, but he wouldn't miss *her*.

Only Harvey would miss her if she disappeared – and then only when the Bugsy Supreme ran out.

A loud wooden squeal interrupted her thoughts. Behind her, Dave Marshall was making his usual noise. He was the PE teacher, and so used to shifting the gym equipment around the school hall that he couldn't even sit down for a cup of tea without a great scraping of furniture. He was the only male member of staff, and treated everyone – even the headmistress – like girlish underlings.

Now – without even turning her head – Miss Sharpe could tell he was picking up the *Gazette*. Flapping it open like a tarp in a typhoon.

It took him a nanosecond to form an opinion.

'Silly cow,' he pronounced, expecting to be listened to, as always.

Usually Miss Sharpe wouldn't indulge his masculine nonsense, but today she was rattled by death, so she turned a cool eye on him. 'Excuse me?'

He held up the newspaper for her to see. 'Hitchhiking. What does she expect?'

A couple of the other teachers tittered nervously. Not Miss Sharpe. If Miss Sharpe ever caught herself tittering, she'd give herself a good smack.

'I imagine,' she said icily, 'that she expected someone to pick her up and drop her off closer to home.'

Marshall gave a snort of laughter.

'Why, what would *you* expect?' she demanded.

'What I expect and what *she* can expect are not the same thing,' he smiled.

'What do you mean?'

'I'm a man,' he pointed out, in case she hadn't noticed his lack of deodorant. 'Everyone knows women shouldn't hitch.'

Miss Sharpe knew that too, but she still bristled like a hog. 'That's as good as saying she deserved to get murdered. I suppose women shouldn't wear short skirts either? Or show off their ankles.'

Marshall snorted again. 'Don't get your knickers in a twist, Emily Pankhurst.'

'Emme*line*,' she snapped.

'Christ, I'm only joking,' he said – then raised his brows and rolled his eyes meaningfully.

Miss Sharpe was *this close* to tipping her tea over his big stupid head. She knew that look. Her father used to do it too – more and more after her mother had died. It was a look that said she was acting irrationally, but that he wasn't going to argue with her because acting irrationally was what women *did*, and that sanity would only be wasted on her.

Miss Sharpe controlled her urges, and turned her back on Dave Marshall.

She wasn't being irrational. A young woman – just like her – had been murdered and dumped in a lay-by like a fast-food wrapper, and a grown man thought she had it coming.

Wasn't that reason enough to be angry?

17

THE WOMAN WHOSE face Donald Moon had found under his size-ten boot turned out to be Frannie Hatton, a twenty-two-year-old addict-slash-barmaid, who had been reported missing after failing to show up for a shift at the Patch & Parrot in Bideford.

And the police – who hadn't been that interested in a missing junkie – were *very* interested in a dead one . . .

Detective Constable Calvin Bridge checked the rearview mirror to make sure he looked like a policeman.

Because he never felt like one.

Take this morning. This morning, any *real* policeman would have been happy. Here he was, driving Detective Chief Inspector Kirsty King to Old Town to speak to Frannie Hatton's mother. It was quite the coup for a young constable with only six months in plainclothes under his belt; DCI King was an impressive woman and right now everybody was trying to impress her back, because there was a promotion in the offing. Detective Sergeant Franklin had taken early retirement due to ill health. And that thing about filling up his wife's car with police petrol. Anyway, it was quite possible that now he had gone, a couple of people at Bideford would move up a rung of the ladder without much effort – which had been Calvin's preferred method of advancement ever since kindergarten.

He'd only applied for plainclothes because keeping his uniform clean and pressed and shiny had been an awful lot of work.

So driving DCI King around on a murder investigation was a feather in his cap, even if it was really only because he had known Frannie personally, though marginally. She'd been a few years behind him at school, and light years ahead of him at everything else.

Calvin Bridge knew he should be on cloud nine.

So why did he feel like a man in a wool suit on a hot day?

The car behind theirs tooted and DCI King looked up from the pathology report on her lap and said, 'Green light.'

'Sorry,' said Calvin, and raised his hand in apology before pulling away, barely fast enough to keep up with his frantic windscreen wipers.

All up Meddon Street he gave himself a good talking to. *Don't be so bloody ungrateful, Calvin. You're young and solvent and you've got your health. Look at Frannie Hatton! Dead in a ditch! You think she wouldn't change places with you? Pull yourself together!*

Calvin always heard his mother's voice in his head when he was giving himself a good talking to, because she always knew best.

Just like his girlfriend, Shirley.

Shirley wore the pants in their relationship. Calvin didn't mind; he was too lazy to wear the pants. Shirley was a stolid, no-nonsense girl who, at twenty-nine, was five years his senior – and she was used to having things her own way.

Calvin was happy to have things her way too.

Most of the time.

But this weekend she'd taken pants-wearing to a whole new level.

She'd caught him off-guard while he was watching Formula 1 at her flat. Cuddled up to him on the sofa just as the red lights went out and said, 'Why don't we get married?'

'Hmm?' Hamilton was on pole but Vettel darted up the inside and the two of them went into the first turn a bare inch from each other at 180mph. Bloody brilliant.

'Why don't we get married?' she'd said again.

Calvin had had to think fast. If he'd said no – or even hesitated – there'd have been a row or a terrible silence, and he'd have had to leave her flat and drive to his flat, which would have meant missing twenty critical laps. Thirty if he got stuck behind a tractor.

So he'd said, 'Good idea,' and hoped that would be non-committal enough to take the pressure off until the end of the race at the very least.

Instead Shirley had gone into an uncharacteristic frenzy of squealing and kissing his ear and calling her mother and each of her sisters in turn, then her mother again.

Apparently he'd proposed.

Calvin had felt a bit uneasy at first, but by lap thirty-two he was getting used to the idea. Why *not* marry Shirley? He might as well. They'd been going out for three years and they got along fine. He loved her, he supposed, although he had nothing much to gauge it by.

Shirley was big boned, but she was clean, self-financing and happy to sleep with him, all of which Calvin liked in a woman. They never rowed because he always gave in, and whatever it was she wanted to do usually turned out to be pleasant enough. They went out three times a week to the pub or the pictures, and they had sex once a week, either in bed or on his leather sofa – but never on her corduroy one, because it was harder to get clean.

Anyway, by the time Vettel took the chequered flag, Calvin had decided that marriage would probably just be more of the same but without all the hassle on Valentine's Day. Last year he'd bought Shirley a cheese grater and they hadn't had sex for a fortnight – even after he'd shown her the receipt! It wasn't *any* old cheese grater – it was one endorsed by her favourite TV chef and had cost a ridiculous sum for a piece of metal with holes in it.

Marriage had suddenly seemed like the simpler option, and Calvin almost wondered why he hadn't thought of it before.

'You've gone past it,' said DCI King.

'Huh?'

'You've gone past it,' she said, tapping the window. 'It's back there.'

Calvin said, 'Sorry, Ma'am,' and started looking for a place to do a U-turn.

Mrs Hatton lived in a run-down terrace with a cracked-concrete front garden. Calvin reckoned she couldn't be more than fifty, but she looked seventy. She wore a long porridge-coloured cardigan and maroon carpet slippers. One of her big toes was showing through at the end.

He made the tea. There was no milk but he pressed on bravely. Tea was vital to the investigation. People told you things over a cup of tea that they wouldn't under torture.

The tiny kitchen smelled of drains, and the mugs were chipped and charity-shop random. RGB Building Supplies, the Little Mermaid and a Smurf. Obviously he would have the RGB mug, but he dithered over the allocation of the other two. Neither seemed appropriate to either a senior investigating officer or a bereaved mother.

He put them all on a tray to let Fate decide.

'She was crying,' said Mrs Hatton flatly, as Calvin came in with the mugs. 'She kept saying goodbye and I love you.'

'And this was on the phone?' said DCI King.

Mrs Hatton nodded and took the Smurf.

'Was Frannie alone when she called you?'

'There was a man's voice.'

Kelly Bradley and Katie Squire popped into Calvin's head. It was inevitable. Most police work in these little country towns was as uncomplicated as Calvin had hoped it would be – and often revolved around the three Ds –

drink, drugs and debt. So two women forced to strip naked and phone home was a bit different and was sure to stick in the mind – even *his* mind, which could be like a Teflon butterfly unless it was about sport.

DCI King reached over the Little Mermaid and took his RGB mug. 'Was it Mark?' she asked.

Mark Spade was Frannie's boyfriend. They already had him in custody and were making him cry. Mostly because he couldn't get his next fix.

'I don't know,' said Mrs Hatton. 'The reception was very bad. And I'm a bit deaf.'

'You couldn't see anyone?'

'It was on the phone.'

'You don't have a smartphone?' said Calvin.

'What's that?'

DCI King raised her eyebrows at him. Calvin looked around the dingy front room with its dirty carpet, its glued-together china ornaments and its smell of wet dog, and realized how silly the question had been. Mrs Hatton only just had a television set – a big old thing in a wooden case, like something out of the ark. *Like* an ark.

He should probably just shut up.

'Could I possibly see your phone, Mrs Hatton?'

Mrs Hatton handed King the oldest of Nokias and King handed it to Calvin.

'Find her call, will you?'

Calvin had never seen a phone as big as this one; it was like a brick in a plastic case. It had an *aerial*. He ran through the received-calls menu, but Mrs Hatton apparently didn't know how to assign names to each contact.

With some fiddling, and with a break for Mrs Hatton to find her glasses – which were around her neck on a chain all along – Calvin identified Frannie's number.

'There are two calls here from her,' he said. 'Right after each other.'

'I didn't get another call. Didn't answer it, anyway.'

'Why not?' said King.

The grey-faced woman shrugged at the wall over the mantelpiece, where a square of clean wallpaper spoke of an absent painting. Or maybe a mirror.

'Did Frannie say anything else?' King asked.

'She said he was going to kill her.'

DCI tilted her head and said, 'Pardon me?'

Mrs Hatton cleared her throat. 'She said he was going to kill her.'

There was a pregnant silence before King asked, 'Did you call the police?'

'No,' said Mrs Hatton, and sighed as though she'd forgotten to pick up washing powder at the shops.

Calvin felt cold. Frannie Hatton had called her mother and said she was about to be murdered, and her mother hadn't called the police. Hadn't even picked up the phone to her second call. And had only mentioned it now as an afterthought! Calvin didn't have kids of his own – didn't really *want* kids of his own – but even to him that sounded just . . . *wrong*.

He looked around the room with new eyes. What had to happen that a young girl who'd started out right here in this little house had ended up dead in a lay-by – her last desperate plea ignored by her own mother? Did Mrs Hatton have a personality disorder? A habit of her own?

A boyfriend who hadn't been able to keep his dirty hands to himself?

So many forks in the road where things had gone wrong when they should have gone right.

Calvin sighed inwardly. They'd probably never know. Only Frannie knew and Frannie was dead, and the only question to be answered about her now was who had killed her.

There was no excuse – *could* be no excuse – for Mrs Hatton's inaction. Calvin felt that anger deep in his core.

DCI King cleared her throat and modulated her tone to take all the judgement out of it. Calvin recognized what she was doing and admired her. Along with the tea thing, it was one of the most useful things he'd learned on the force. He used it all the time.

'Why didn't you call the police, Mrs Hatton? When she said this man was going to kill her?'

'I don't know.'

They both knew she must know, and neither of them spoke in the long tea-filled silence that followed.

Finally Mrs Hatton went on, 'She'd say anything, you see? To get money out of me. To get clean, she always said, but I knew it was for drugs. Even if she *meant* it, I knew she wouldn't *do* it. And even if she *did* it, I knew it wouldn't last.'

The anger left Calvin Bridge and instead he felt naive. What had seemed unjustifiable was obvious. What had seemed monstrous was mundane. The ghastly roller-coaster of addiction. Hopes raised a little and dashed a lot. Again and again and again, until all the hope was gone and all that was left in its place were broken hearts and suspicious minds.

'Had you given Frannie money in the past?' DCI King asked Mrs Hatton cautiously.

'Of course!' she said with sudden fire. 'I'm her mother. I gave her everything I had!' She gestured roughly at the room. It looked as if someone had moved out and this was all they'd left behind.

'I'm sorry,' said King. 'I didn't mean to—'

But the outburst had exhausted Mrs Hatton's tiny reserve of energy. She flapped the apology away, then rested her hand on the head of the faded little terrier on the sofa beside her.

'Makes no difference,' she said. 'She'd only have stolen it.'

Missing, presumed run off with her smackhead boyfriend, had been the local consensus about the disappearance of Frannie Hatton, but now that she was dead, people had nothing but good things to say about her.

Poor girl.

Pretty little thing.

Wouldn't hurt a fly.

'Her was a right skinny maid,' said Shiny Steele the next time the Gunslingers met. 'But her had a proper pair on her regardless.'

'What a waste,' said Scratch, speaking for them all.

Shiny drank at the Patch & Parrot, and Razor Riddle

claimed to have known Frannie Hatton 'for years'. Both of them – bald and thick respectively – had been bought drinks all evening on the strength of it.

'Her'd shake 'em in yer face for a good tip,' Shiny added. Then he sighed like he was missing an old dog, and all the Gunslingers felt the loss of Frannie Hatton just that bit more personally. If *they*'d been in the Patch & Parrot, she might have shaken her proper pair in *their* faces. Now that would never happen, and they called for another round to drown this new sorrow.

Then another.

'To Fannie,' slurred Razor, slopping his latest cider into the air, and there was an immediate outcry.

'*Frannie*, not Fannie, yur wazzack!'

'Thought you an' her was like *this*!'

'Owe me a bloody pint, you do, Razor!'

'No, boys,' said Hick Trick, holding up a hand for quiet. 'I'm with Razor on this.' And when they all looked at him in bewilderment he raised his pint and said, 'To Fannie!'

The men whooped with laughter and echoed his toast, and Daisy mooed enthusiastically until Jim Maxwell came over and told them all to keep it down or they'd be out. He was nice enough about it, because he knew which side his economic bread was buttered, but he'd barred them for a week after the Pussy Willows fight, so they knew he'd do it again, and let their laughter tail off into a series of snorts and exaggerated sighs.

'Ah well,' said Scratch in the new quiet. 'It's a shame.' There were grunts of agreement all round.

'Wouldn't happen in the West,' said Blacky, and even

though they were *in* the West, they all knew he meant the *wild* one.

'That's right,' said Chip Fryer. 'A man who was thinking of doing something like that *didn't*, 'cos he knew he'd be strung up.'

There were enthusiastic nods all round. Lynching was a well-worn trail the Gunslingers rode down whenever a crime had particularly offended them. It didn't have to be murder; often it was child abuse, sometimes it was the mugging of an old lady, and just two weeks back, they'd agreed that it should be imposed for whatever bastard had keyed Blacky's car in the car park of the George.

'Young girl murdered right under our noses,' sighed Whippy Hocking, 'and there's nothing we can do about it.'

All the men muttered now, their anger warming them just the way their laughter had.

'Short of a posse,' said Scratch, to nods and grunts all round.

'And a gun,' said Whippy.

His words hung there in the sudden silence of the bar. They were so self-evident that they didn't even *have* to be agreed with out loud.

Instead, the Gunslingers nodded sombrely into their glasses and looked almost as wistful for a gun as they had for Frannie Hatton's boobs.

The police made Donald Moon cry too. They searched his house three times that first week, they questioned him hard and often, and they only bought his story about stopping to pick up the *Daily Mail* when his terrified wife showed them the his 'n' hers Day-Glo vests and pointy sticks.

They did meticulous forensic sweeps of the lay-by and of the victim's flat in Northam, and at a press conference they launched an appeal to find Frannie's missing bag, which had contained various personal items and a week's wages.

The *Gazette*'s in-depth investigation revealed the contents of Frannie Hatton's Facebook page, and they printed the only photo that did not feature an obscene gesture or an illegal substance. It was an old picture of Frannie as a blurry bridesmaid, in a dress so pink and sleeves so puffed that she looked like a gay quarterback.

The same photo appeared on posters that the police put up in public places and on lamp posts, so that people who'd never known the victim almost felt as though they had, and started to refer to her as 'Frannie' instead of 'that girl'.

People left bouquets and little teddy bears in the lay-by, and the regulars at the Patch & Parrot, who felt guilty that none of them had ever offered her a ride home, started a collection on the bar to help her mother with the funeral expenses.

All in all, dying was very improving for Frannie Hatton.

18

RUBY COULD TELL Daddy was in a good mood, just by the way he opened the front door.

'That's a twenty-quid fish!' he said as he dropped the dogfish on the draining board.

'It's like a *whale*,' she enthused. She'd seen bigger, but having Daddy in a good mood again changed everything: everything *did* seem better than it was before.

The dogfish had bitten Daddy as he took it off the hook, but he didn't even care. 'Been bitten by worse!' he said and put some salt on it so it wouldn't go manky. Then they measured the fish with Ruby's school ruler. Twenty-seven inches! A lot of that was tail, but even so. Then he let her feel its skin – smooth one way, rough the other – and touch its sharky little teeth with her finger until she shivered with dread, and they both laughed.

She got a chair to kneel on so she could watch him gut the fish. The insides were such a dark red they were almost black. Daddy scooped them down the cut-off foot of one of Mummy's old tights, all the way to the toe, then knotted the top and put it in the freezer. Ruby knew that the next time he went out on the Gore, he would dangle it in the water and, as it thawed, blood and juice would leak from it and attract more dogfish, and eels too.

Daddy wrapped the rest of the fish in plastic and put it in the fridge. Then he started to wash down the drainer and the sink. Without looking at her, he said, 'Can you keep a secret, Rubes?'

'Yes,' she said instantly, because she wanted to hear one.

'Cross your heart?'

She crossed her heart. 'And hope to die,' she said. 'What *is* it?'

Daddy stood very still. He glanced towards the kitchen door as if someone might be there, spying on them. Ruby looked too, as the atmosphere thickened in the dingy little kitchen, and she drew closer to Daddy to hear the secret.

When he spoke it was in a low voice, only just above a whisper.

'The Gunslingers are getting up a posse.'

That was all he needed to say. Ruby's mouth fell open and she felt almost dizzy, as foreign-familiar images flooded her brain. A hot place, with a wide sky that smelled like summer. Cowboys firing their guns in the air, legs flapping, spurs digging, manes flying; dust clouds and small boys swirling in their wake. A posse was fearless and fast. A posse was the law. When a bad man came to town, a posse hunted him down and made him pay. A posse never gave up. The thought of Daddy on a posse was completely thrilling.

'We're going to catch the man who killed that girl,' Daddy went on in hushed tones.

'What girl?' said Ruby, matching his whisper.

'That girl. Frannie something.'

'Oh yeah.' Ruby remembered vaguely; there was a poster on the shop door next to the one about the Leper Parade. 'What will you do when you catch him?'

'Well, we're *supposed* to call the police.' Daddy shrugged. 'But who knows?' He did the cowboy accent. 'Blood's running pretty high, Miss Ruby.' He made a finger gun and drew a bead on her with narrowed eyes, then blew the tip.

She stared at his fingertip, enthralled – as if she could actually see the smoke curling off it.

'Can I come with you?' she whispered. 'On the posse.'

'It's not a game, Rubes. This is serious work. *Man*'s work.

'I *know*.'

Ruby frowned. She was the wrong sex – again.

'But I could help you,' she suggested. 'I could look out for him.'

Daddy wrung out the cloth. Bloody water squeezed out between his knuckles. 'Mummy will be home soon.'

Ruby could tell he was trying to change the subject and she was determined not to let him. 'Please, Daddy? You can look one way and I'll look the other way. Then we're looking *all* the ways. I'm *really* good at looking for things. Even out of the very corners of my eyes. Watch this!' To demonstrate, she looked away from Daddy and slid her eyes right to their very corners. 'See?' she said. 'I can see you really well.'

'I don't know, Rubes . . .' The water ran clear through the cloth now.

BELINDA BAUER

Ruby rushed, 'Please, Daddy – I want to go on the posse! I'll be really, really good and quiet. I *promise*.'

There was a chink of silence and Ruby held her breath.

'You'll get bored.'

'I won't!' said Ruby vehemently. 'I *won't* get bored! I'll be too excited!'

'You'll whine to come home.'

'I won't! I won't whine!'

'Well, we'll be out really late and what if it's a school night? Mummy will be cross with us if she finds out.'

'She'll be at work! And I won't tell her! I won't!'

'What if she sneaks in to kiss you goodnight and you're not there? Then I'll get it in the ear.'

That could be a problem. Mummy did come in and kiss her when she got home from work. Sometimes Ruby woke up and grumbled at her.

Ruby frowned. She felt the approach of crushing disappointment. Mummy was such a spoilsport!

'Can't we get home before her?'

Daddy shrugged as he wiped down the sink. 'We can *try*,' he said. 'But maybe there's some way we could fool her into thinking you're *in* bed when you're really not.'

Ruby had a flash of inspiration. 'I'll put Panda in my bed so he looks like me! I'll put him under the blankets. Mummy won't even know I'm gone!' It was a ruse they'd seen in more than one TV Western – the baddie emptying his gun into the hero as he lay by the campfire, then picking up the bedroll full of rocks that he'd mistaken for a man. Panda was quite big. It would definitely work.

Daddy laughed. 'That's pretty clever, Rubes.'

122

'Can I come then?'

He put up his hands in cowboy surrender. 'You got me, Deputy.'

Ruby squealed with delight and buried her face in his old blue jersey that smelled of salt and smoke.

19

D C CALVIN BRIDGE looked down at Frannie Hatton and thought that she was just his type.

If she'd been alive, of course – he wasn't sick.

Dark-haired, petite, but with nice tits – if you ignored the Y-incision – and with a neatly tended ladygarden.

He stared at the dead girl's crotch and thought that Shirley could really take better care down there. She had when they'd first started to go out together three years ago, but nowadays he was lucky if she shaved her legs, let alone her bits. Calvin never mentioned it. But now, seeing Frannie Hatton's wasted Brazilian made him wonder if maybe things with Shirley weren't happening a bit quick. He didn't object in *principle* to marrying her – just to the *speed* of it all.

But how to raise the subject without Shirley mistaking one for the other?

He couldn't.

Could anyone?

He sighed.

'Hard day, Calvin?' said DCI King sarcastically.

'Excuse me, Ma'am,' said Calvin. 'I was miles away.'

'Well, don't be,' said King sharply. 'Be right here.'

Calvin blushed. He had a tendency to drift off, and knew he *must* try to concentrate if he was going to be even slightly impressive.

'Was she sexually assaulted?' asked King.

'No indication of that,' said Dr Shortland. He had a manila case file in one hand and a cheese and coleslaw sandwich in the other. Calvin could smell formaldehyde and mayonnaise and there was a piece of cabbage in Dr Shortland's beard.

'And yet she was naked,' mused King. Then she bent over Frannie Hatton's face and pointed at a tiny dark mark on the side of her nose. 'What's that?'

'Aaah,' said the pathologist. 'Watch this!' He handed King the file, picked up a needle and casually slid it straight through the tiny hole.

Calvin swallowed sudden sick.

'Stud?' said King. She handed back the file and bent to have a good look at the hole.

'I assume so,' said Shortland. 'It's not new.'

Calvin regained his equilibrium. 'She was wearing a nose ring on Facebook.'

They both turned to look at him.

'We haven't found a ring,' said King. 'We'll do another sweep of the scene.' She turned away and studied the woman's face again, then asked, 'She was suffocated?'

'Indeed.' Dr Shortland took a messy bite of his sandwich. 'Although she was found face-up, there's bruising consistent with finger marks on the back of the head and neck, upper arms, shoulders, contusion of the nose and lips, and mud in her teeth, eyes and nostrils.' He didn't open the slim folder, because his other hand was full of

125

sandwich, but he waggled it as he spoke – apparently to indicate that what he was telling them was all in there, if they didn't believe him.

'So someone held her face-down in mud until she died,' said King.

'That's my conclusion.'

'After quite a struggle, from the look of the other bruises.'

'She certainly put up a fight.'

King bent again to examine Frannie's face. Under the stark bulbs of the path lab, her skin looked almost translucent. She had a ring in one eyebrow, another in her belly button, and a tattoo cuff around one bicep.

Calvin pondered whether Frannie Hatton's death had been an accident, or whether the killer had always known that this was how his obsession was going to end.

King looked around and then took what appeared to be a long-handled spoon from a row of instruments on a nearby counter, and prised open Frannie Hatton's lips. The dead girl's teeth had dark bits between them, like brown spinach.

'Is this mud from the crime scene?'

Good question, thought Calvin.

'Good question,' said Shortland. 'And the answer is, I don't know.'

'So she could have been killed somewhere else and then dumped.'

'Possibly.'

'Shit,' sighed King, and straightened up.

'Indeed,' said Shortland.

Half a minute later, Calvin caught up. Two crime

scenes – one unknown. The body wasn't helping them narrow their options.

'Any idea where the mud in her teeth came from?'

'No.'

All three of them stood in silent contemplation of the body.

DCI King sighed. Then she held up the spoon thing. Its bowl was pierced, making it look like a little metal squash racquet. 'What is this?'

'A gall-stone scoop.'

'Can I keep it?' she asked.

Dr Shortland looked a little surprised. 'If you think it will be useful.'

'Thank you.' DCI King tucked it into one of the several pockets of the belted Barbour jacket she wore over everything – skirts, dresses, slacks, jeans. She looked good in all of them, Calvin thought, with a very nice bottom for jeans.

'What do you think, Calvin?'

He blinked. 'About what, Ma'am?'

'Life, the universe and everything,' said King so flatly that, for the smallest of seconds, Calvin Bridge almost told her that he didn't believe in God but that he *did* hope for an afterlife, and some system of spiritual checks and balances, dependent upon his actions as a corporeal being.

Then he realized she'd just caught him looking at her arse.

A phone rang somewhere and Dr Shortland excused himself and the rest of his sandwich.

'Here, help me turn her over,' said DCI King.

Calvin looked cautiously at the door through which the pathologist had disappeared.

'Oi,' said King. 'I'm the senior investigating officer. If I want to turn the body over, I don't need a note from my mummy.'

Calvin blushed and helped turn Frannie over. From the back she looked like a child, and Calvin was sorry he'd ever looked at her front disrespectfully.

King started to walk around the table, bent a little at the waist so that her eyes were good and close to the corpse. Now and then she stopped and parted Frannie's hair, or changed her angle of vision. Touched a mark or a mole with a latex finger. Stood and thought.

'What are those?' she said. Calvin followed her finger to one of Frannie's waxy white shoulder blades, where there were two small blurred marks, maybe three-quarters of a centimetre long.

'Bruises?' he said.

'That's right.' She checked the map of the body that Dr Shortland had put in the file and read from his notes: '*Two small curved contusions to right shoulder blade. Possibly caused by contact with a hard, undetermined material immediately ante mortem.*'

There were plentiful bruises down Frannie's arms, but only a few on her back – one large one on her left shoulder and these two small ones.

'So,' said Calvin, 'during the struggle. Or when she was in transit. Maybe little stones or something that were under her back at some stage?'

'Maybe,' nodded King. 'And now look at this one.'

Calvin leaned in to her and peered at the Celtic cuff tattooed around Frannie's right arm.

'Where?' he said.

King put her finger on a mark that was easily missed, hidden in the ink. Even now Calvin had spotted it, it was hard to make it out, but it looked similar to those on her shoulder blade, although the edges were a little more distinct.

'They look as though they've been made by the same object, wouldn't you say?'

'Yes,' agreed Calvin.

'Curved. Maybe a fingernail?' King put her hands around Frannie's bicep – first the left and then the right – and tried several different ways to make her nails fit the bruise, but nothing seemed quite natural.

'This one's more distinct,' she mused. 'Sharper.'

'Because she wasn't wearing sleeves,' said Calvin, surprising himself by remembering. 'Didn't the witnesses at the Patch & Parrot say she was wearing some top that was all . . .' he mimed a big pair of breasts before he could stop himself, then quickly tucked his hands into his armpits and finished the sentence with 'revealing?'

But King just gave him a serious look and said, 'That makes sense.'

They both looked again at the tiny mark disguised within the indigo design.

'So,' said King, 'assuming that this case is connected to, and followed the pattern of, the earlier assaults, these bruises could have been made before she was naked.'

Calvin nodded eagerly. 'What would that mean?'

'Who knows?' said King. 'But every little helps.'

DCI King had taken over the driving duties, which Calvin Bridge found refreshing rather than insulting. In his short experience, senior officers loved the idea that they had a driver, rather than a colleague, and rarely dirtied their hands behind the wheel.

She drove well, too. At Tiverton they came off the dual carriageway and, to his surprise, King turned away from the link road and chose instead to take the old road to Bideford, which was little more than a lane in some places, and forty miles long.

Within minutes, Calvin understood why she'd chosen the old road. There wasn't much traffic, and he could tell she was enjoying the corners. They weren't *breaking* the speed limit between the high hedges, but they were testing it, and every now and then, Calvin resisted the temptation to put his hand on the dash. DCI King's own hands were at ten and two and there was a little frown of concentration on her face, as if she was defying the world to slow her down.

'When we get back,' she said, 'I want you to call Professor Mike Crew at the university in Falmouth. He's in the geology department.'

Calvin wrote it in his notebook. *Mike Crew. Geology. Falmouth.*

'He knows all about mud,' King continued. 'What it's made of, where it's from, how it got there.'

'Very interesting,' said Calvin, although he didn't think so.

'Most boring man on the planet,' said King. 'And I've

130

known some corkers. But we'll pick a sample out of Frannie Hatton's teeth and send it to him. See what he can tell us about where she might have been killed.'

'Yes, Ma'am.'

She glanced at him and said, 'Always be honest with me, Calvin. Don't bullshit me or tell me what you think I want to hear.'

'Yes, Ma'am,' he said.

'It's not a crime to say you don't know something,' she went on. 'You're a constable in the Devon and Cornwall police, not Stephen bloody Hawking.'

'Yes, Ma'am.'

'And if you've got a hunch, let me know. Hunches are fine, as long as they're part and parcel of good police work, not a replacement.'

'Yes, Ma'am.'

'Good. Any questions?'

Actually he *did* have a question. He wasn't sure how important it was, but on the basis that he wasn't Stephen Hawking, he decided to ask it anyway.

'There is one thing, Ma'am,' he said cautiously. 'What's the significance of the gall-stone scoop?'

DCI King just gave a short laugh, then changed down to a much louder gear.

Calvin sighed. He'd obviously already missed something critical. He was starting to wonder whether he was really cut out to be a detective.

Maybe just taking better care of his uniform would have been easier.

20

I T WAS COWBOY NIGHT AND Mummy and Daddy were both out, and so was the sea. Ruby couldn't see it from the house because the big limekiln on the beach blocked the view between the cottages, but she knew in her gut that the tide was low. It made her feel calmer to know that it was far away, and not pounding the cliff or surging up the slipway.

Once, when she was little, a storm had driven water all the way into the square between the cottages. The limekilns had been waist-deep, and she'd held on to Daddy's trouser leg at the garden gate and watched the sea sigh across the cobbles towards them. She remembered the stink, and the rat that had been washed from its nest in one of the kilns, scuttling frantically about at the water's new edge, sitting up now and then to stare anxiously out to sea for its lost babies. Daddy had crept up behind it and Ruby had tensed almost unbearably, but the rat hadn't seemed to care – even when he'd hit it with a spade.

Ruby rolled on to her side on the spider rug.

Her chest hurt. It could be cancer or something, but Mummy still didn't care because of the letter from the headmistress.

Daddy wouldn't make her go to school.

'*I* wouldn't make you go,' he'd said. 'But women always stick together. Like your Mum and Miss Bossybritches.'

'Miss *Bryant*,' Ruby had giggled, and Daddy had winked. 'That's what I said.'

She rolled back on to her elbows and sighed down at *Pony & Rider*. Despite the big, exciting headline PLAITING MADE EASY! the article made plaiting look incredibly difficult. Ruby had triple-checked the numbered photos, but there still seemed to be one missing. One minute the pony's mane was all tufts and fingers and dangling thread, and the next it was a perfect little hair rosette, with all the ends tucked in. Instead of reassuring her, the article had only increased Ruby's anxiety that when the time came, she would be found wanting in the plaits department.

Somebody knocked at the front door, and Ruby's head snapped up.

Mummy and Daddy had keys. They never knocked. *Nobody* ever knocked because strangers never came to Limeburn – not even Jehovah's Witnesses.

A pedlar had passed through once.

A goose walked over Ruby's grave.

She tiptoed carefully across the room. She pressed her ear against the door. There was a knock right on it, and she squeaked in surprise.

'Ruby?'

She stared at the door. The person who was knocking knew her name. Was that a good thing or a bad thing?

'Ruby?'

'Yes?' she whispered.

'It's me.'

She frowned. 'Adam?'

'I have something for you.' he said. 'Open the door.'

Ruby hesitated. She wasn't supposed to let anyone into the house when her parents weren't there. But they didn't mean Adam, she was sure. And he had something for her. So she fumbled the key into the lock and let him in, along with a faceful of rain.

Adam was wearing the same red hoodie he'd lent her that day in the haunted house.

'All right?' he said.

'Hi.'

They stood and looked at each other for a moment.

'You OK?' he said. He seemed nervous.

'Fine,' she said. Ruby was nervous too. She didn't know why. They talked all the time when they were up on the swing or in the haunted house. She didn't know why this was different, but it was. Maybe because it was night and she was alone, and because Adam had never been in her house before, and this seemed like a strange time to start.

'It's raining *really* hard.'

'I know.'

Adam looked around the room and Ruby was acutely aware of its every shortcoming – the old stained sofa, the threadbare carpet, the dark patch of damp in the corner of the ceiling. Adam's house was fresh and clean, and had one chair so old and precious that no one was allowed to sit on it.

'Your house smells of fish,' said Adam.

'Yes,' she said. 'Daddy catches them in the Gut.'

He nodded.

'Sometimes he sells them to the hotel,' she continued, just to fill the air. 'They're worth loads but he only gets ten pounds.'

'That's bad business,' said Adam sagely. 'He should speak to my dad. He knows how to make money for people. That's what he does.'

'That's a really good job,' she said.

'Yeah,' he said, 'but he's away a lot.'

Ruby already knew that. Mr Braund was a tall, well-fed man who wore suits and drove up and down to London every week, in a different car each year.

There was a longish silence.

'Do you want a custard cream?' Ruby said.

'No thanks.'

'OK,' said Ruby, then she asked, 'What have you got for me then?'

'Oh. Yeah.' Adam handed her a smallish packet wrapped in blue tissue paper. He kept his other hand in his jeans pocket, as if he didn't care.

'What is it?' she said.

'Open it,' he shrugged, 'and find out.'

Ruby parted the tissue cautiously. Inside was a little plastic donkey. It was covered with grey flock, with beige around its eyes and muzzle, and hitched to a small wooden sledge that had *Clovelly* painted on the side.

Ruby felt a wave of something so warm and special flood through her that she almost cried.

'Wow!' she breathed. 'It's . . . *amazing.*'

'It's nothing really,' said Adam.

It wasn't nothing. It was *something*. *More* than something.

'Did you get it in Clovelly?'

'Yeah. I remember you said you wanted a donkey, so . . .' Adam tailed off. Then added, 'I walked all the way there and all the way back. It rained the whole time.'

'I'm sorry,' she said.

'That's OK,' he said.

'But it's not even my birthday.'

'It's not a birthday present. It's just . . . you know, for *any* old day.'

'It's the best present I ever had.' Ruby meant it; she couldn't think of a better one right at that moment.

Adam went red but he looked very pleased.

'I'm going to call him Lucky,' said Ruby.

Adam moved closer so that their heads almost bumped. He touched the sledge. 'I thought it would be pretty funny to put some carrots in here; like, *behind* the donkey.'

'Yeah,' nodded Ruby. 'That *would* be pretty funny.' She didn't know why, but she totally agreed.

'Thank you,' she added.

'No problem.'

They stood together for a moment, looking at the donkey. Then Adam said, 'Anyway, I'd better go. Got tons of homework.'

'Me too,' she said.

'Mine's Roman roads and aqueducts,' he said.

'Mine's a diary,' said Ruby. 'We have to write something every day.'

'That's harsh.'

'I know. I usually just do it all on one day.'

He nodded at the donkey. 'Well, today you can write about that.'

'I will,' said Ruby.

'Night,' he said.

'Night.'

She closed the door behind Adam and locked it, then took the key out.

Ruby went upstairs to bed, even though it wasn't even nine thirty. She made a space on her bedside table, carefully sweeping a spot clear between the mugs and the sweet wrappers and the books, and put the donkey there.

They didn't have any carrots so she got a potato from the sack in the kitchen and put that in the sledge for now, like a big pale-brown boulder.

She wrote FRIDAY in her diary.

Adam brought me a donkey from Clovelly. It's the best present I ever got. He walked there and back in the rain. He has a slej and his name is Lucky. I am going to put carrots in the slej because that will be pretty funny.

Ruby tried to stay awake, straining to hear Daddy's car pull up on the cobbles, but instead she fell asleep, looking at Lucky.

John Trick was late home because someone had cut off Tonto's tail.

Most of the Gunslingers had already meandered their

way down Irsha Street by the time he and Shiny and Nellie helped Whippy outside to his steed.

The old horse was tied to the drainpipe where Whippy had left him, chewing on a complimentary sachet of Heinz Salad Cream.

They got a chair for Whippy to sway on, and guided his boot into the stirrup, then Hick and Nellie pushed, while Shiny ran round the back to stop Whippy tumbling straight off the other side. It had happened before.

'Hey,' said Shiny, but the other three were puffing and grunting too hard to hear him.

'Hey!' he said again, and rejoined them. 'Tonto's tail's gone.'

'Bollocks,' said Nellie.

But it was true.

They helped Whippy out of the stirrup and off the chair and then the Gunslingers stood and stared at the rough bob, which was all that was left of Tonto's wavy white tail.

Sometimes people shouted that they were wankers. Sometimes kids threw pebbles at them. But this was much worse.

'Bastards!' shouted Whippy. '*Bastards!*'

Hick Trick shook his head. 'First Blacky's car gets keyed, and now this.'

They peered under wooden tables and even crawled about between chair legs – as if finding the missing tail would rectify the situation.

But Tonto's tail was gone for good.

21

M IKE CREW *was* the most boring man on the planet. Calvin Bridge had only been in his company for half an hour, and yet he had already mentally moved him to the top of that chart in the face of tough competition from his old European History teacher, Mr Branch, and the desk sergeant, Tony Coral, who had an extensive collection of railway memorabilia and didn't care who knew it.

'People think mud is just mud. They could not. Be. More. *Wrong*,' said Professor Crew, with all the excitement of a member of the Magic Circle who has decided to blab.

Calvin glanced at DCI King from the corner of his eye and saw the same glazed look on her face which spoke of a monumental effort to give a shit. He was going to have to work very hard not to drift off.

Or laugh.

Would that be so bad? Calvin hadn't laughed for ages. Last week he'd tried to make a joke about the bridesmaids' dresses, but it had backfired. Then he'd committed the cardinal sin of not knowing what frangipani was. He'd thought it was a kind of cake, but

Shirley told him he was just being 'difficult'. He realized that the few minutes when DCI King had forced him to engage with her over Frannie Hatton's corpse had been the most fun he'd had all week.

That couldn't be right, could it?

'These are your two samples.' Crew was holding up two glass slides. 'I have taken the liberty of labelling them OS 2425 by 1265 Interdental 45, identifying the geographical location according to the Ordnance Survey, and the physiological area from where the sample has been extracted – in this case interdentally – and finally a code relating to my own files and order of work, which is really just for my personal reference—'

'And what did you find?' said King, rubbing her hands together and leaning forward a little in the universal body language of 'Let's cut to the chase.'

Crew stuck his hand in front of her face and said imperiously, 'Culm down, dear!'

King looked coldly at his palm.

'Old pedology joke!' Mike Crew laughed all by himself while King and Calvin exchanged strained looks. Then he continued, '*So*, the other sample has been labelled OS 2425 by 1265 Gateway 46.'

He stopped – almost daring King to try to hurry him up, but Calvin could see her mentally biting her lip. You couldn't hurry some people. Professor Crew was going to say what he wanted to say and any attempt to curtail him would only result in prolonging the agony. It was like talking about seating plans, which was fast becoming the Rubik's Cube of the wedding. Everyone had a back to be got up, an offence to be taken; everyone bore a grudge.

Shirley assured him that there *would* be a way to make it work, but they just hadn't found it yet.

God forbid people should just sit down and shut up and be grateful for a free lunch.

'*So*,' said Crew, 'sample OS 2425 by 1265 Interdental 45 is basically a Capers series soil of heavy clay with particulate inclusions. How*ever*, sample OS 2425 by 1265 Gateway 46 consists of Manod soils, which are typically Brown Podzolic, which is a silty loam most prevalent over rock typical of the area between Bideford and the village of Abbotsham.'

He stopped again and they both waited for the next bit, but Crew just got a disappointed look on his face, and said a little tetchily, 'That's it.'

Apparently they'd missed the punchline.

'Oh!' said King. 'Sorry, I was just . . . engrossed.'

That placated him. 'I *know*!' he enthused. 'We walk on it every day, build our homes on it, grow our food in it, bury our dead in it, and yet how many people really *think* about soil? How many people really *care*?'

Calvin had to turn his head so he wouldn't catch King's eye.

'So these are two different soils?' she said.

'The fine earth fractions are entirely incompatible,' nodded Crew.

'So you're saying that Frannie Hatton was killed somewhere else?'

'Of course,' said Crew. 'As we say in the business – mud don't lie.' He affected a bad Al Jolson voice and matching racist hand-waggle, but King remained utterly straight-faced. She was a better man than Calvin. She cleared her throat. 'And do you have any idea where that somewhere else might be?'

Crew milked it, of course. He made a great show of finding an Ordnance Survey map of North Devon, which was in his desk drawer all along. Then he spread it across the pens and books and in-trays on his desk so that it was almost as bumped and hilly as its printed surface swore it should be.

Finally he hummed and hawed and waved a pencil over it like Harry Potter, until he settled on an area between Westward Ho! and Appledore.

'Around there,' he said.

'That's the Burrows,' said Calvin.

'What's the Burrows?' said King.

'It's this sort of . . . flat bit. Behind the pebble ridge.'

'What's the pebble ridge?' said King.

'It's a ridge, Ma'am,' said Calvin. 'Made of pebbles.'

'Aah,' King smiled. 'The clue was in the name.'

Crew hurried to regain the lead role in this play. 'If you could send me a sample, I could be more specific. Close to the sea, given the presence in OS 2425 by 1265 Interdental 45 of particulate glucosamine.'

'Sugar?' said Calvin.

'Shells,' said King.

'That's right!' Crew rushed to expand. 'Tiny particles of crustacea, either fragmentary or granulated, interspersed with the parent pedogenic structure.'

'Ground-up shells,' King translated firmly. She had her message; apparently she no longer needed to massage the messenger.

'Have a look,' said Crew, and at his urging, Calvin

stepped over to the microscope and peered through the eyepiece while the professor twiddled things.

The smear of mud they'd collected from Frannie Hatton's front teeth blurred and unblurred and was suddenly in focus – and unexpectedly beautiful, with a thousand tiny fragments which Calvin assumed had once been shells, glittering like mother-of-pearl stars in a chocolate sky.

Even though he was looking at a blob of mud down a microscope, Calvin suddenly felt very small. He wished he could be that tiny, that insignificant.

That hard to find.

'Are the Burrows near the sea?' asked King.

Calvin straightened up. 'Without the pebble ridge, Ma'am, the Burrows *are* the sea.'

DCI King glanced over as she swung the Volvo out of the car park and said, 'Don't say I didn't warn you.'

'You *did* warn me,' admitted Calvin. 'But I still wasn't ready.'

King laughed. 'The mud lets the boyfriend off the hook, wouldn't you say?'

Calvin looked at her blankly. He had no idea why she was asking him or what the right answer might be.

'They lived together . . .' said King encouragingly, and then stopped speaking to allow him to pick up the thread.

'Yes,' he agreed. 'So . . . that . . . means . . .' he went on, speaking slowly to give himself time to think.

She helped him out. 'If you lived with someone and you wanted to kill them, where would you be most likely to do it?'

Calvin thought about killing Shirley. He'd have to avoid the corduroy sofa.

'In the bath?' he said. 'With a knife?'

King raised her eyebrows. 'I wasn't thinking of specifics,' she said. 'But you'd kill them at home, right?'

'Probably,' he agreed.

'You wouldn't take her out to a field and push her face into mud until she died, and then load her body into your car and drive it somewhere else and dump it, would you?'

'Probably not,' said Calvin again. He wasn't crazy about mud in his car.

'That would be too much like hard work,' King went on. 'Too organized.'

'Yes, it would,' he agreed.

'Especially for a junkie who doesn't own a car,' she said, and Calvin finally caught a glimpse of how her mind worked.

It was apparently quite different from the way *his* worked.

In fact, Calvin was starting to worry that his mind worked differently from everybody else's.

For instance, he had gone out last Saturday and bought Shirley an engagement ring, but instead of postponing everything for a couple of years the way he'd imagined it would, the ring had only seemed to make her worse. Suddenly there was a church booked, and he was being bombarded by wedding-invitation designs and something called *swatches*, and he was expected to pore over *The Big Book of Baby Names* on date nights, instead of watching Korean gangster movies and having sex on the sofa.

Calvin had committed to a ring; he hadn't realized that the ring had committed *him* to pretty much everything Shirley claimed it did – including three children, because 'It's a nice round number.' He'd wanted to point out that in fact three was uneven and also a prime, but was afraid that Shirley would actually agree with him – and push for four instead of dropping back to two.

Calvin sighed and wondered what having kids would be like. Better or worse than puppies? Probably very similar, he thought. Messy and tiring to start with, and then after a few months they learned your routine and things got a lot easier.

He could always do extra shifts at work until then.

'Calvin!'

Calvin blinked at DCI King. He had the distinct feeling she'd said his name more than once.

'Are you *deaf*?'

That confirmed it. 'No, Ma'am,' he said.

'Well then, try to pay attention, will you? I don't want to keep repeating myself like those idiots you see calling their dogs in the park.'

'Sorry, Ma'am.'

Calvin touched his sleeve to his brow. Trying to keep up with life was making him sweat.

22

J UST AFTER MUMMY went to work, Daddy appeared at
Ruby's bedroom door in his cowboy clothes even
though it wasn't Friday.

'Want to go catch a killer, Deputy?'

Ruby gasped in excitement and Daddy held up a
warning finger. 'Don't tell Mummy.'

'Cross my heart and hope to die,' said Ruby, and
bounced off the bed

Ruby kept craning forward on her seat, even though it
wanted to tilt her backwards. She wanted to see the killer
first; wanted to be the one to spot him; wanted to shout,
'There he is!' and point her finger, and feel the car swing
around hard in pursuit.

If they didn't catch him tonight, next time she would
bring a cushion.

She looked at Daddy. 'You should have a badge,' she
said. And then immediately, 'Can *I* have a badge?'

'What kind of badge?'

'A deputy's badge. And you can have a sheriff's.'

'We'll see how it goes, Rubes. I don't think the Gunslingers would want me to give out badges until they knew you were going to stick at it.'

'I *am* going to stick at it,' Ruby assured him.

'We'll see then.'

Ruby perched on the edge of her seat, even though they weren't in Bideford yet. They passed tiny hamlets, no more than a house or three, but she glared at them all with raw suspicion.

They reached the outskirts of the town – the supermarket and the discount shops and the little industrial estates where little industry happened.

Here they saw people, out and about, walking their dogs, waiting at bus stops, eating chips from paper cones.

'What does a murderer look like?' Ruby eventually thought to ask.

'The news said white and about six foot tall.'

'How tall is six foot?'

Daddy showed her a few inches between the tips of his thumb and forefinger. 'About yea much taller than me.'

'What colour is his hair?'

'Don't know.'

'What colour are his eyes?'

'Don't know that too.'

Ruby screwed up her face. 'It's *difficult*.'

Daddy laughed. 'If it wasn't, the police would have caught him, I reckon. That's why we got up the posse, see? To keep an eye open.'

'I thought we were on the posse to hunt him down?'

'We are,' said Daddy. 'But that's *how* we hunt him

147

down. You keep an eye open and when you spot him you hunt him down. These things take time, Rubes. I told you it weren't a game, didn't I?'

Ruby nodded.

They drove through Bideford in a zigzag, and then went on towards Westward Ho!, slowly up the long hill, and quickly down the other side as if they were surfing a wave to the beach.

'Where are the other Gunslingers?' she asked.

'Round and about,' he said. 'We split up so we can cover more area. Some of us on this side of the water and some on the other, off towards Barnstaple. Chip's covering Torrington. Nobody knows where he'll strike next, see, Rubes? That's why he's hard to catch.'

She nodded. That made sense, although she was disappointed that they weren't all riding in convoy, the way she'd imagined they'd be. Of course, she was even more disappointed that they weren't all on horses, but even she knew that that was unrealistic.

Now and then Daddy did flash his lights at another Gunslinger, or raised a hand as they passed. When he did, he'd murmur their names.

'Shiny,' he'd go. Or 'Whippy.'

Just that. No more.

Ruby watched the men's silhouettes pass and longed to ask questions about Shiny and Whippy and Blacky and Daisy. Wanted to know why they had those names; wanted to say hi and show them that she was a deputy, even though she was only a girl and only ten. But the Gunslingers didn't stop to talk, just drove on – all hunting for the same killer.

It was very grown-up.

They looped through Westward Ho! and then went through the lanes to Appledore, past the shipyard, and back up to Northam.

They slowed a few times as they passed men walking alone, or sitting in parked cars, and Ruby peered from the window with her heart thudding in her ears.

What would she see? What would a killer look like? Would she be able to spot him? And if she did, would he *know* he'd been spotted? The idea made her shiver, and at those moments when Daddy took his foot off the pedal and they coasted past a stranger, Ruby wished she'd brought her guns. Even if they were sticks, somehow she'd feel safer with them in her pockets.

'Any good, Rubes?' Daddy would say.

'No good,' she'd say.

Some were too short to be the killer. Some were too tall. Some were too fat or had dogs, or umbrellas, or were laughing, or holding hands with a girl.

'Everyone looks just . . . *normal*,' she said.

'Well, everyone is,' said Daddy. 'But even normal people do bad things.'

Ruby didn't like that idea. If *that* was true, then *anyone* might be the killer – and that made her feel a bit weird inside.

As they drove back along Bideford Quay, with the shops and pubs on one side of the road, and the masts and rigging and wheelhouses of little ships on the other, Ruby started to sing 'Red River Valley', and Daddy joined in.

Then he sang 'Mama, Don't Let Your Babies Grow Up

To Be Cowboys', and by the time they were halfway to Westward Ho! they were both singing 'Stand By Your Man' at the top of their voices. Daddy did the '*boom boom BOOM*' in a funny deep voice that made Ruby laugh so hard she could barely catch her breath.

Then Daddy stopped singing.

'Dad-*deee*!' giggled Ruby. 'You missed your booms!'

But he was looking at a young woman, who was walking back towards Northam with her thumb stuck out.

'Look at this,' he murmured, and shook his head.

He checked his mirrors, then swung the car around in the road.

'What are you going to do?' asked Ruby.

'Take care of her,' he said. 'Before anybody *else* does.'

'Where am *I* going to sit?'

'In the back.'

Ruby made a face. 'But I don't *want* to. I can't see the killer so well from the back!'

'Taking care of people is part of the job, Ruby,' said Daddy sharply. 'Don't spoil the whole night now.'

Ruby pursed her lips and crossed her arms. She didn't want to spoil the whole night, but she also didn't want to sit in the back. It wasn't *right*. The back was where she sat when she was a little girl going to school with her Mummy and Daddy, not when she was a deputy on a cowboy posse.

The woman looked around with a frown as the car stopped beside her, then bent as the window squealed down slowly. It was electric but it didn't work that well.

'Hi,' she said warily. She was younger than she'd looked from behind – maybe eighteen, and with hair

150

pulled so tightly into a knot on top of her head that her eyebrows were miles above her eyes.

Daddy leaned across Ruby. 'You shouldn't be hitch-hiking. We'll take you anywhere you need to go.'

The girl looked at him, then up and then down the road, then at Ruby.

'This your little girl?'

'Yes,' said Daddy. 'She'll get in the back if you want a ride home.'

The girl looked at Ruby, then smiled and said, 'Yeah, OK. Thanks.'

Ruby huffed and puffed and squeezed between the seats so that the girl could sit in the front, and they set off.

The girl's name was Becks. She was coming from her grandmother's in Appledore, and walking the three miles home to Bideford.

'Why don't you catch the bus?' said Daddy.

'I do if it's raining.'

Daddy leaned forward and made a show of peering up at the black sky through the windscreen wipers.

'And it's three quid each way,' the girl amended.

'Still,' he said. 'That Frannie girl got herself murdered around here, you know.'

'Yeah,' shrugged the girl, as if she doubted the relevance of that. 'But everyone knows that were her druggie boyfriend, and six quid's six quid, innit?'

'It is,' said Daddy. 'Are you going to call your grand-mother to let her know you're safe?'

'I don't have a phone.'

'You want to use mine?'

'Nah, it's fine. She'll be in bed by now. Thanks.'

They slowed for a roundabout and Ruby hung between the front seats. She couldn't resist telling the girl, 'We're going to catch the murderer.'

'Yeah?' said Becks, looking at John Trick with new eyes. 'Are you a policeman?'

'We're just helping out,' said Daddy. 'The police haven't got the manpower these days.'

'I'm a deputy,' said Ruby. 'I'm getting a badge soon.'

'What's a deputy?'

Ruby rolled her eyes. 'It's like a sheriff, but his assistant.'

'That's nice of you,' said Becks. 'More people should take care of each other like that.'

Ruby tickled the back of Daddy's neck. It was an apology, and she was rewarded with a smile.

Then they drove down into Bideford in silence until Becks pointed and said, 'Right here.'

They turned right into the lane that ran behind Blackmore's Coal, and let her out halfway down.

'Hold on,' said Daddy. 'It's raining. I've got an umbrella in the boot.'

'No need,' said the girl, but Daddy insisted on going round to the boot and getting a big golf umbrella Ruby had never seen before and walking the girl to her door. While he did, Ruby clambered into the front seat once more with a sense of relief.

Daddy came back and opened the boot again, and Ruby could see a tiny strip of him shaking out the white and green umbrella before putting it in and slamming the boot shut. Then he got in and turned the car around and set out on another long, winding circuit.

'She was a nice girl,' said Ruby.

'She was a very stupid girl,' said Daddy. '*Anyone* could have picked her up and done anything they wanted to her. Women are just asking for it if they hitchhike, Rubes. I want you to promise me you'll never *ever* do it.'

'OK, I won't.' Ruby started to sing 'Red River Valley' again, but Daddy cut her off sharply.

'*Promise me!*'

'I promise,' said Ruby in surprise. She was a little cowed. Daddy didn't often shout at her.

He glanced over her way and softened. 'It's only because I love you hundreds, Rubes. You're my little cowboy and I want you to be safe, that's all.'

'I know.' Ruby nodded and hugged his arm. 'I love you hundreds too.'

It was gone ten o'clock when Daddy pulled up outside the Blue Dolphin and bought them both chips. Just the smell was like heaven – the actual explosion of oil and salt and vinegar on Ruby's tongue was almost too much. Mummy never made chips at home; she called them artery plugs.

They drove down to the end of the quay and parked on the corner near the statue with the road cone for a hat. There was a small gang of learner motorcyclists there too, admiring each other's bikes in the drizzle, and an old yellow sports car with black stripes down the front. Now and then the driver tooted the horn and it played the first few bars of 'Dixie'. Ruby laughed at first, but Daddy said

153

'*That arsehole*' and after that she agreed that it was very irritating.

She finished her chips before Daddy was halfway through his, and so he gave his to her, and reached into the back to get a can of cider instead.

He handed her a bottle of Ribena. Not *real* Ribena, but blackcurrant squash in a water bottle.

'Brought that for you,' he said.

'Thanks!' She drank half of it in one go, she was so salty.

'Yum!' she said, and wiped her mouth just the way Daddy always did. 'This is the best posse *ever*.'

Daddy laughed.

Ruby ate, but she never took her eyes off the people passing by. Small groups of drunken girls or shouting boys; old men with small dogs, fumbling poo into black bags; two teenagers peeing against the Arts Centre wall; a man alone, staggering a little and singing loudly as he emerged from Rope Walk, taking advantage of the flattering echoes from the high warehouse walls.

When Ruby had finished her chips, Daddy got out to throw away the chip paper. He walked back, wiping his hands on his jeans.

'You're doing a great job, Deputy. Ready for round three?'

Ruby yawned loudly but nodded and said, 'Mmm.' She was tired, but she didn't want him thinking she was too young to be on the posse.

She didn't want to be Em.

But round three of the posse turned out to be more like being a free taxi service than a posse. The pubs were coming out, and they picked up two more women and took them home. One from a bus stop in Northam to East-the-Water, and another from Bideford to Abbotsham. Each time Daddy made sure they got home safe and dry under the umbrella; each time Ruby had to get in the back. For a while she did her best to look for the killer, but it *was* much harder from there, especially when her eyes kept closing.

The last time someone got out of the car, Ruby didn't even say goodbye. She was curled up in the back, fast asleep.

Posses were exhausting.

23

THE SECOND MURDER was textbook.
Murder for Dummies.

A twenty-five-year-old woman named Jody Reeves put out her thumb and thought, a little tipsily, 'Mum would *kill* me if she saw me doing this.'

She wouldn't have done it at all, except that she'd had a row with her boyfriend at the pub, made a bit of a scene and stomped off.

Her mother had always told her, never *ever* hitchhike. And she never ever would have . . . if only it hadn't kept raining and if only the buses hadn't stopped running, and if only two miles wasn't such a long way in those stupid heels that lengthened her legs while they shortened her stride.

Jody was blonde but she wasn't dumb; she knew all about the dangers. But she also knew what a weirdo-slash-mad-axeman looked like – and how to say *Thanks, but no thanks* and to wait for a woman, or a family, or some-one she knew.

She heard a car approaching from behind and turned to look over her shoulder.

Jody Reeves wasn't about to take any chances, but

with a bit of luck she'd be home in five minutes, her boyfriend would still be worrying about her, and her mother would never know a thing.

Ann Reeves was watching *You've Been Framed* when her daughter called her for the very last time. Children hitting each other at weddings seemed to be the theme of the show, because all the little girl combatants were in party dresses, and all the little boys wore cummerbunds. Ann had had two glasses of red wine during the course of the evening, which made toddlers pushing each other down church steps even more hilarious.

So she was still laughing when she answered the phone to Jody.

'Hi, darling! It's *You've Been Framed* and these little kids are knocking seven bells out of – *oh*!' she chortled. 'Right in the eye! What, darling? I can't hear you.'

Ann reached for the mute button. The room was suddenly very quiet.

'Say again, sweetie?' She smiled.

'What do you mean?' she said, turning to look at the photo of her daughter that sat on top of the piano. Not a grand piano – just an old upright her mother had left her. She'd learned by ear and Jody had the same talent, right from when she was little. Sometimes they still sat there together and played 'Heart And Soul' or 'Bridge Over Troubled Water'.

'What do you *mean*, Jo? I don't understand . . .' Ann frowned at the photo as if it could translate for her, from the muffled, sobbing, cracked voice that the caller ID claimed to be her daughter's.

'*Mummy. He's going to kill me.*'

Ann Reeves stood with the phone to her ear and felt real life drop away from her like a silk cape sliding from her shoulders.

She walked on without it.

Crumpled in her wake, she left behind her the night Jody was born; the smell of her head, the childhood illnesses, the pink eyes, the clammy hair, the spots – each with a dab of camomile lotion crusted around it – the mumps, the colds, the tonsillitis ice cream; the first day at school in an Alice band and long white socks; the sports-day beanbags; the homework tears; tadpoles in a jar and bringing home the hamster for the holidays. The first disco, first date, first period, first teenage row.

I hate you!

I hate you too!

It was all behind her now.

Ann flinched at a new voice on the phone, then slowly put it back to her ear and whispered, 'Who are you and what do you want?'

She listened to the answers without the life left inside her even to beg. She was defenceless, but she had nothing left to defend anyway.

The sounds of a struggle flowed into her head, grunting and harsh.

'*Mummy! Help me!*'

Ann dropped the phone. Horror ran amok in her with no outlet. She couldn't scream. She couldn't cry. She couldn't move. She was a closed circuit – a super-collider where the only conscious thought particle whirring endlessly in her head was, *There's nothing I can do.*

When Jody needed her most. The only time it really counted. She couldn't do a thing to help her.

Bile boiled in her throat and she turned her head as it sprayed from her mouth and nose – across the sideboard, the fruit bowl, the scented candle.

It was a vent. A breach.

A release.

For a long, clouded moment she stood and watched pink-tinged bile drip off an apple. Golden Delicious – Jody's favourite.

Ann had fallen in love with Jody the very first moment she'd seen her. Heart and soul. The thought of Jody being frightened and hurt and alone was unbearable. *Unbearable.*

Then she knew that there was something she *could* do.

Ann Reeves breathed.

She bent.

Her numb fingers found the phone and finally managed to pick it up and put it to her ear. The struggle was still going on. Her little girl was still fighting for her life.

Ann croaked and stopped. Then she cleared her throat and said loudly and clearly, 'I'm here, Jody.'

'*Mummy! Mummy!*'

Ann swayed. She put out a hand and held on to the sideboard for support. 'I'm right here, Jody. Don't worry about anything. I won't leave you. I won't ever leave you.'

There was a small shriek, an angry grunt, the sound of something heavy hitting the ground.

'Mummy! I love you!'
'I love you too, my beautiful baby girl.'
Ann Reeves let go of the sideboard.

Then she stood up straight on her own two feet –
pinned there by love alone – and stayed with her
daughter while she died.

At the end of the day, only one car had slowed down
beside Jody Reeves.

That was the one she'd climbed into.

That was the one that had driven her to her death –
and from there to a place where no human being would
ever find her.

Textbook.

24

PEOPLE WERE STRANGE and obsessive beings. This much Calvin Bridge had learned since joining the police force.

Some of them spent their life savings on toys they never touched; others had secret wives who only ever met at their husband's funeral. Some paid other people good money to smack them on the bottom with a ping-pong paddle. Calvin's own twin brother shaved until he bled, and his body was as hairless as a squid's. They'd been camping in the Peak District last summer and Louis had plucked his own shins by the light of the campfire, with a pair of machine-edged pink tweezers.

Basically, Calvin had learned that people who were *without* kinks and quirks were the exception, rather than the rule.

But forcing a woman to call her mother while she was being murdered was a kink that his heart couldn't fathom.

They hadn't found the body yet, but nobody expected to find Jody Reeves alive – not the *Gazette* or the police, or even her mother.

Especially not her mother.

'He'll kill again,' Calvin told Shirley as they watched Jeremy Kyle.

'Shush!' she said. 'It's the results of the lie-detector test.'

Calvin shushed, but he knew he was right.

The death of Jody Reeves was nothing like the death of Frannie Hatton. With Frannie there had been an undercurrent of excitement at the station at the thought of a *serious* crime – the kind of crime most of them had joined the force to solve. And Frannie herself – well, it was a shame, of course, but junkies weren't expected to die of old age.

But Jody Reeves was no junkie – she was a bright, hard-working young woman, and suddenly the under-current at the station was one of fear. While Calvin and his colleagues did their jobs and went about their business and followed procedure, there was a disturbing sense that they weren't the ones in control. And the worst of it was that the where and the when, and the who and the how were already out of their hands. The only real question left was 'How many?'

Shirley turned to him so suddenly that he flinched. 'Did you order the hotel brochures?'

'Yes,' said Calvin. He'd started saying yes before he'd properly processed any question. It was safer that way. There was a list of hotels that Shirley and her mother wanted to hire for the reception. It was his job to order the brochures and price lists. He hadn't done it yet, but there was plenty of time.

'Thanks, Pookie!'

Pookie was her affectionate name for him. He didn't know why.

Jeremy Kyle's audience booed. 'I knew it!' said Shirley. 'I can always tell when they're lying.'

She leaned against his arm, which was often a sign that she was open to offers, and they were on the leather couch too . . .

But Calvin wasn't in the mood.

There was a killer on the loose. Not the one-off, fumbling, accidental killer they'd all hoped for, but a killer who had started small and was escalating, and whose trajectory could be charted and predicted along psychological x and y axes.

Ever rising.

The school was abuzz with murder.

Miss Sharpe was a little appalled to discover that a class of ten-year-olds were quicker to lurid speculation than a tabloid journalist. Wide-eyed children told each other the story of Jody Reeves, even though they all knew it already and almost none of it was true. Then they told it again a different way – to even greater effect.

Their diaries testified that several of them had heard screams in the dead of night. Shawn Loosemore had patrolled with a torch and a pellet gun. *Its for rabbits*, he wrote, *but it would blow a hole in your face if you put it rite up close.* Craig Hunter had hitched a ride home with *a weerd man with half a beerd*, Essie Littlejohn said she'd found the dead woman's shoes in a hedge, and even Ruby Trick had entered the fray . . .

If she was hichiking then she was just asking for it.

It was straight out of the Dave Marshall school of sexual liberation.

Even in the staffroom, the teachers crowded around Melanie Franklin, whose husband was Jody Reeves' cousin. From her they gleaned every possible detail about the deathly phone call – using tea and digestive biscuits as sly leverage – while Dave Marshall himself stood on the fringes and said loud, pointless things like 'I know what *I*'d do to the bastard,' and 'Just give me five minutes alone in a room with him,' which guaranteed a no-risk return on his empty machismo.

Miss Sharpe would love to have granted Marshall his wish of five minutes alone in a room with a serial killer. She believed she could have sold tickets.

She sighed and turned to the window to watch the children at play. In the tarmac yard beyond the staffroom window, games of tag and football and hopscotch were in full flow. Kids bickered and laughed, and a black and white ball rang against the brick-wall goal. Ruby Trick's red hair drew her eye. She was alone, as usual, but as Miss Sharpe watched her crouch on the tarmac to re-draw the blue chalk squares melting in the drizzle, her reflection relaxed into a more familiar smile.

She had done the same thing when she was that age. In identical long white socks.

Things changed, but things stayed the same.

Feeling encouraged, her eyes drifted across the playground. She became aware of a pattern emerging in a group of children near the school gate. It was mostly 5B, she noticed – all playing some rough game of pushing and pulling and running away screaming, then back in, laughing. A boy would grab a shrieking girl around the neck and hold her, while the others scattered. Then one of them would speak urgently with their fist at their ear, then the others would rush in, release the girl from the boy's grip and wrestle him roughly to the ground with his hands behind his back.

Then the whole thing would start again.

For a moment Miss Sharpe just stood there, trying to make sense of it. Then gooseflesh skittered up her arms as she realized that they were playing murder.

She put down her mug with a sloppy bang and elbowed her way past the ghouls. She stormed out of the staffroom, down the short corridor and out into the rain.

The playground air was filled with the shrieks and chatter of a giant aviary, and although Miss Sharpe shouted 'Stop!' three times, she was almost on top of the children before they looked up. Connor quickly dropped his arm from around Essie's neck and the giggling child hitched her coat back into place.

Miss Sharpe was shaking. 'What do you think you're doing?' she demanded. 'What are you playing?'

Nobody answered. Her eyes drilled into them one by one. 'This game is *sick*. Do you understand?'

Their faces said they sort of did, sort of didn't.

'Two young women are dead,' she snapped at them. 'And that's not something you laugh about in a playground and tell lies about in your diaries! It's something very, very serious!'

Connor laughed and then stopped. The other children stood and looked uneasy and didn't make eye contact. Essie and Amanda Fitch started to cry. *Good*, thought Miss Sharpe. *Teacher's pets, the pair of them, and not used to being yelled at.*

'If I see *anyone* playing this game again, you'll be coming to Miss Bryant's office with me. The whole lot of you. And your parents will get a letter. Do you understand?'

Rose Featherstone, who was on playground duty, wandered over and said, 'What's going on here then?'

'Nothing,' said Miss Sharpe, and brushed past her to walk briskly back inside. As she did, she felt tears start to spill from her eyes. She'd been wrong: things *did* change; they got worse. And there *was* no innocence. Not any more.

'All right?' said Dave Marshall as she passed the staffroom doorway.

'Fine,' she said curtly, then shut herself in the staff toilet and cried until the bell rang for the end of break.

Little children playing murder.

Ruby Trick's well out of it, she thought.

Nanna and Granpa came round with a copy of the paper and a bunch of bananas for Ruby, as if she were a pet chimp.

'What do you say, Ruby?' said Mummy.

'Thank you, Nanna and Granpa,' said Ruby, appalled.

'Full of potassium,' said Nanna to Mummy. 'And

at least it's *good* sugar. She's still a bit tubby, isn't she?'

She said it right in front of her! Like she was deaf or something. Ruby hated Nanna, with her high voice and her chicken neck and her poppy eyes. She was glad Mummy always said *No, thanks* when Nanna and Granpa offered to take care of Ruby on the nights Daddy was out and she had to work – even if it *did* mean she was alone.

'It's puppy fat,' said Mummy. 'She'll grow out of it.'

Nanna made very high eyebrows, then she shook the paper at Mummy. 'Did you see about this other poor girl?'

'Yes,' said Mummy, glancing at Ruby.

'He made her call her mother while he did it!'

'Ruby,' said Mummy, 'go and put the bananas in the bowl in the kitchen.'

Ruby knew Mummy didn't want her to hear about the murder, but she knew anyway, because of school and Mr Preece's headlines. It was scary, but it was exciting too.

Ruby went through to the kitchen and put the bananas in the fruit bowl. The bowl was always full of keys and old pens and shrivelled-up apples, and the bananas looked too bright in there.

'You want me to cut one of those up for you?' said Granpa behind her.

'No, thank you,' said Ruby.

'You sure, maid? Chopped-up banana with a little bit of cream on it?'

That didn't sound much better. A banana was a banana. But Ruby pretended to think about it for a while so as not to hurt Granpa's feelings.

'No thanks, Granpa.'

He winked at her and lowered his voice. 'I know. Bananas. Ugh.'

Ruby laughed.

'But they're full of potassium,' he said in a high whisper with an exaggerated shrug.

He was being Nanna. It was pretty funny.

Then he said, 'Is there any cake?'

'No,' said Ruby wistfully. She looked at the door to make sure nobody could hear them. 'But there *are* biscuits.'

'Good,' said Granpa. 'Where are they?'

'I don't know. Mummy hides them.'

'Your Mummy can't hide anything from me.' He winked.

They looked through all the cupboards together. He even looked in the pedal bin, which made her giggle.

'What about on top of the cupboards?' he said, stepping back to see.

'Maybe.'

'You want to see what's up there, maid?'

'OK,' she said and reached for a kitchen chair, but Granpa said, 'Don't bother with that—' and picked her up under the arms.

'No!' Ruby hadn't been picked up for years and she didn't like it. She stiffened and Granpa's fingers dug into her armpits, and Granpa regretted it too, because he muttered '*Jesus!*' and almost dropped her before plonking her down on the kitchen counter with a huge puff of air from his red cheeks.

'I'm not as young as I was,' he chuckled, but his whole head had gone so red that Ruby could see it through his ginger hair. She went red too, at the embarrassment of nearly killing Granpa from being fat. But it was his own fault; she *told* him not to pick her up.

He stood for a moment, getting his breath back, and Ruby checked the doorway to make sure nobody had heard them. While they were quiet Ruby could hear Nanna, still talking about the dead girls.

'What that poor woman must be going through. Not being there when her daughter needed her most . . .'

'Get up there then,' Granpa said, and Ruby got to her knees and then her sock-clad feet on the counter so she could feel along the top of the cabinets. Granpa put both his hands on her bottom in case she fell.

'Careful now, baby girl,' he whispered as she shuffled along. He gripped her a bit tighter to hold her steady.

'There's nothing up he—'

'What are you doing?'

They both jumped and Ruby nearly fell off with fright. Mummy was in the doorway.

'Nothing,' said Granpa.

'Granpa wanted a biscuit,' said Ruby.

'Get *down* from there.' Mummy came over, took her hand roughly and made her clamber down quickly on to the floor.

Nanna tutted and said, 'The last thing she needs is biscuits.'

'Just *leave* it will you, Mum!' said Mummy, and Ruby knew it was serious. Her face was all tight and her lips had gone white. About *biscuits*!

'Go to your room,' she said.

'What did I *do*?' said Ruby.

'I said go to your *room*! *Now!*'

'It's not fair,' said Ruby. 'I only—'

'NOW!'

Ruby made as much noise as she possibly could going upstairs to show everyone it wasn't fair. Then she got out last week's *Pony & Rider* and flicked through it angrily.

Nanna and Granpa left soon afterwards, and she heard their big fancy car start up on the cobbles and drive slowly up the road. Their car was red and in the boot there was a carpet that was nicer than the one she had in her room. In the *boot*.

She listened to Mummy clearing up downstairs and then the creaking of the wooden steps. If Mummy was still cross with her she was going to be rude. She was going to tell her it was all *their* fault. Nanna with her stupid bananas and Granpa wanting a biscuit.

But instead Mummy came into her room with a glass of milk and a custard cream and said, 'I'm sorry I shouted at you, Rubes.'

It took all the angry wind out of Ruby's sails and she said, 'OK.'

Mummy sighed. 'Nanna really winds me up sometimes.'

'I know,' said Ruby. 'She winds me up too.' She put down her magazine and nibbled the end of the biscuit.

Mummy smiled and touched Lucky on the head. 'Where did you get this?'

'Adam gave him to me. His name's Lucky.'

Mummy picked Lucky up carefully and touched the lettering on the sledge. 'I thought Granpa might have given it to you. You know, as it comes from Clovelly.'

'No,' said Ruby. 'Adam walked all the way there and all the way back and it rained the whole time.'

'Well, that's nice,' Mummy said. 'Why is he pulling a potato?'

'Because we didn't have carrots.'

'Aah,' said Mummy, and laughed. Then she went over to the little window, where the tree outside pressed right up against the glass.

'Daddy should cut back these branches,' said Mummy.

'I don't mind. Except for the scratching.'

'Wouldn't you like to see out properly?'

'I don't really care.'

Mummy stared between the leaves at the dense forest beyond. 'I'd like to be able to see out,' she said, but then she drew the curtains anyway.

The few Gunslingers who had bothered dressing up and coming out that Friday night were in a sombre mood.

A second murder had knocked all the swagger out of them – as though their disapproval alone should have been enough to stop it happening twice. A photo of Jody Reeves stared at them accusingly until Daisy Yeo turned the *Gazette* face-down with a short, disgruntled moo.

A posse was a joke, a rope was not enough.

There had been some vague notion that they might find a watering hole of normality together, but it had dried up in the face of their own impotence, and staring into the dust of their failure was no help.

They didn't have much to drink or much to say. Chip

and Shiny played a desultory game of cribbage where they lost score halfway through and didn't care. Nobody even thought to put money in the jukebox, and they sipped their ciders and nursed their shorts to the upbeat jangle of 'Barbie Girl'.

They didn't stay late, and when Hick Trick said he was off, they all left together.

Which was how they all discovered at the same time that some son-of-a-bitch had kicked in the front right headlight of each of their cars.

25

THE HEADLIGHT WAS only a bit of old plastic, but when Daddy told Mummy about it over breakfast, she cried.

Ruby had seen Mummy cry before, but never so openly. Before, she'd always tried to hide it; this time she cried like David Leather had cried when Shawn threw his violin on the toilet-block roof – with the tears running out of her eyes and down her face in shiny rivers, and making a proper boo-hoo noise, and the air going all wobbly whenever she took a deep breath.

It made Ruby uneasy.

'Stop it, Mummy,' she said, but Mummy didn't.

'Come on, now,' said Daddy. 'It's only an old headlight. I'll get one from the scrappy. And it's just the one. I can still drive it.'

'You *can't*,' sobbed Mummy. 'The police will pull you over and give you a ticket and then I'll have to pay for that *and* the headlight!'

Ruby looked anxiously at Daddy, who pursed his lips and spread out his palms. 'It's not my fault,' he said. 'Someone did all the boys' cars while we were in the George.'

'I *know*,' said Mummy. 'I *know* it's not your fault. But it's always *somebody*'s fault and *I*'m the one who always has to pay for it!'

Daddy got up angrily. 'It's always about the bloody money with you!' He picked up his keys, then strode through the house to the front door and Mummy didn't even try to stop him, so Ruby ran after him.

'Can I come?'

'No,' he said and slammed the door behind him.

Ruby stared at it for a long moment, waiting for him to come back and say she could really.

When he didn't, her nose tingled with hurt and anger. Why did Mummy always have to make Daddy feel so bad?

She started to pull on her coat and boots.

Mummy darted out of the kitchen, wiping her eyes and nose on a piece of screwed-up tissue.

'Ruby! Where are you going?'

'To the swing.'

'Why don't you play indoors today?' Mummy was trying to stop crying fast. Trying to smile. 'There are lots of fun things you could do right here,' she went on. 'Maggie can come round for tea if you want. I'll do fish fingers. You could make a den in the garden.'

Ruby was suspicious. Usually her mother couldn't wait to get her out of the house. She was always going on about fresh air and exercise and things being *good* for her. And the *garden*? She hadn't played in the garden since she'd learned to walk.

'Why?' she demanded.

'I just don't want you running about in the woods all

the time. It's so wet and muddy, Rubes. Wouldn't you rather be indoors? Where it's s— dry?'

She'd been going to say *safe*.

Now Ruby understood: Mummy was scared of the killer. She wanted Ruby to be safe. She wanted something *from* her – and Ruby sensed an opportunity.

'If I play indoors, can I have a biscuit?'

Her mother hesitated. Ruby knew what she was thinking – they'd only just had breakfast, and she wasn't supposed to eat biscuits at all before teatime . . .

'Just the one,' said Mummy.

Ruby ate her biscuit while she tried out cushions for the next posse. She chose the blue tapestry one on the easy chair. It was small and hard, and would give her lots of extra height.

Then, when Mummy went upstairs to strip the beds, she sneaked out anyway.

Ruby sat on the damp bench next to the swing, and picked the bark off two new guns.

Beside her, Maggie painted her fingernails bright red. She had already done her toes, and now she sat with her dirty bare feet tucked up on the bench, spotted with scarlet, while her flip-flops lay empty in the mud.

'You going to the Leper Parade?' Ruby asked, even though Maggie was only seven, so it didn't make any difference to Ruby *what* she did.

'Yeah.'

'I've got a sack to wear,' said Ruby. 'And I'm going to have bloody scabs all over.'

'I'm going to be a fairy,' said Maggie.

Ruby screwed up her face. 'You can't be a fairy. You have to be a leper.'

'I don't care,' said Maggie. 'I got the costume. It has wings and everything.'

Ruby made a noise that meant that Maggie was an idiot, just like all the girls at school with their secret lipstick and their pop-star crushes and their pencils topped with pink fluff. She must remember to tell Mummy to get Rice Krispies to make the scabs.

'Look!' said Maggie, and spread her left hand for Ruby to see. 'Like a lady.'

Ruby grunted.

'Mine,' said Em, snatching at the nail polish. 'Mine.' She had only just started to talk but had already mastered all the useful words. *No. Shut up.* And, just lately, *Mine.*

'No!' said Maggie and slapped Em's hand away. 'You want me to do yours, Ruby?'

'Nah. My Daddy says girls who paint their nails are slags.'

Maggie shrugged. 'Just a thumb then?'

Ruby shook her head and Maggie started on her other hand. This one wasn't even as good as the first. Out of the corner of her eye, Ruby watched Maggie's left hand bend and twist awkwardly as she tried to control the little brush. The polish splodged over the edges of her nails and smeared down her fingers. Some even dropped on to her dress.

'Shit,' said Maggie.

'*Shi*',' said Em. '*Shi*' *shi*' *shi*'.'

Maggie laughed as she painted. 'Listen to her! She only knows bad words, don't you, Em? Shit and fuck. Shit and fuck.'

'Shi' an' fuh!' said Em, and then shoved a finger so far up her nose that Ruby had to look away.

She finished taking the bark off the second stick and held them both out like a gunslinger, twitching with recoil. *Pow. Pow-pow.* One was better than the other.

Voices floated up through the woods, and soon Adam and Chris followed them.

Ruby hadn't spoken to Adam since he'd given her Lucky and wasn't sure what to say.

'Hi,' he said, so she said hi back.

'What are you doing?' said Chris.

'Painting our nails,' said Maggie.

'*I*'m not,' said Ruby scornfully. 'I'm making guns.'

Adam came over and she handed him the sticks. 'This one's good,' he said.

'I know,' said Ruby. 'The other one's just the best I could find.'

It didn't feel any different from the last time they'd spoken, and Ruby was relieved.

He handed both of the sticks back to her. 'I'll see if I can find a better one in the woods,' he said, nodding his head towards the avenue of trees beyond the stile.

'Are you going to Clovelly?' asked Ruby.

'Not today.' He smiled, and Ruby blushed.

'Look!' Maggie waggled her red fingers at the boys and Adam laughed and said, 'Very grown up.'

'She's going to do mine in a minute,' said Ruby quickly. *She* was the eldest, not Maggie!

'Mine,' said Em, and snatched one of the guns. Ruby held on to it and didn't let go, and then did – and Em fell backwards on to her bottom, squirting an invisible cloud of noxious fumes from her nappy.

'Oh my God, it's a stink bomb,' said Chris, and both boys jogged away, laughing, and vaulted over the stile.

Ruby watched them until they disappeared around the turn in the path.

'Ready?' said Maggie.

Ruby turned. Maggie had the little brush out, ready for action. Ruby looked at it warily. It was so *red*!

'Just a thumb then. And don't go over the edges.'

Maggie did go over the edges, but only a little bit. Ruby held up her thumb. It shone like a sucked sweet. It was so gorgeous that it made her other nails look pale and naked.

'D'you like it?' said Maggie.

'Sort of,' said Ruby. She didn't want Maggie to think she'd been right all along.

'You wave it around like *this* and it will dry. This is the stuff that dries really fast.'

Ruby started to wave her hand.

'You want them all done?'

Ruby screwed up her face. 'How long does it last?'

'Not long,' said Maggie. 'And it's easy to get off.'

'Yeah?'

'Yeah. You just rub it with cotton wool. I seen my mummy do it.'

Ruby hesitated for ages, then said, 'OK then.'

She held her right hand steady while Maggie leaned over it.

When Maggie lifted her head away, Ruby regretted her decision. Five fingers was *way* too many to paint – especially badly. Instead of her single thumbnail looking like a marvellous and exotic jewel, her hand now looked as though she needed first aid.

'You went over the edges!'

'Only a little tiny bit.'

'I don't like it. Take it off.'

'You have to rub it with cotton wool.'

'Go on then.'

'I don't have any.'

'Well how am I going to get it off then?'

'Your mummy can get it off when you go home.' Maggie got up and hung over the rope swing on her belly. 'Don't blame me,' she croaked. 'You wanted it done.' Then she looked at the stile and wheezed, 'They're coming back.'

Ruby got up and walked over to the stile, but she couldn't see Chris or Adam.

'No they're not,' she said.

Maggie got off the swing and joined her. 'I heard them.'

The path led away from the stile for thirty yards before curving sharply inland to skirt a gouge in the cliff. It was made of a narrow strip of compacted earth that softened at the first hint of rain.

Ruby leaned against the slab of slate that made the stile; it was cold against her ribs.

'Hey!' she shouted, and there was the sudden sense of something *stopping*. To listen?

'They're sneaking up on us,' whispered Maggie.

'Then I'm going to go sneak up on them,' Ruby decided suddenly, and felt a dangerous thrill as she heard her own words.

She wasn't allowed over the stile, but who cared what Mummy said? She'd been on a cowboy posse, hadn't she? Hunting a *killer*. She could climb over a *stile*. She would hide and jump out at the boys right at that corner thirty yards off, before she even had to lose sight of the stile and the bench and rope swing. She'd give them a fright, and Adam would see how grown up she was, and they'd all walk back together.

'You're not allowed,' said Maggie.

'Shut up, slag,' said Ruby. She swung a leg over the top of the slate.

'I'm going to tell my mummy on you,' said Maggie.

'See if I care.'

'Shut up.'

'Shut up times a *zillion* times and no returns.'

There was no answer to that, so Maggie took Em's hand and yanked her off down the path. Em started bawling – as usual – waddling after her sister with her muddy nappy showing under her dirty pink skirt.

As she watched them go, Ruby felt a flutter of excitement in her tummy. She clambered awkwardly over the stile and dropped down on the other – new – side.

She looked over her shoulder. She was only inches beyond the stile, but the little clearing already looked much smaller.

She turned and walked away from it.

With every step her confidence grew. She was doing it! She was over the stile and walking on the coastal path. If she kept going she would end up in Clovelly! If she wanted to she could go and find Granpa and Nanna's door. They'd be so impressed by how she'd walked all the way by herself. They'd have tea and biscuits – not fruit – and then she'd walk back again and Mummy would never even *know*.

Ruby steadied the guns in her pockets and started to swagger. Up ahead she heard twigs and small branches snapping, but her own footsteps were silent in the mud.

The curve up ahead was the perfect place for an ambush.

She jogged towards it on tiptoe, careful not to make a sound. Then she dropped to her knees and inched forward until she could see around the thick hazel and ferns.

After the corner, the path straightened out and ran for another fifteen yards before turning to the right again.

Nobody was on it.

Ruby stood up, a little confused. But she had heard someone coming! Maggie had too. And the path was the only—

The back of her neck prickled as she saw a brief flash through the trees to her left. Heard the rustle of undergrowth.

Ruby held her breath and her right hand dropped to her gun.

There was no path there. Nothing but close-grown forest and ferns, and brambles that sent out runners in long, tripping loops. But something was moving through the dark woods – down the hill towards the village. Towards her.

The killer.

Ruby's mouth went dry.

She turned and looked back at the stile and the clearing beyond. It seemed to be a lot further than thirty yards now. Could she make it?

Her legs decided for her.

She ran.

She almost wished she hadn't. Running made everything more frightening. The thirty-yard dash; the scramble over the stile, banging her knees and falling on her hands; slipping and sliding down the muddy track into the village, now on her feet, now on her bottom. Ruby's ears were filled with the sound of her own heart and lungs. Once she turned and saw something big between the trees. Not the boys, and not on the path. Something big was very close to catching her.

She thought she could hear it breathing.

Ruby's chest burned for air. She wasn't going to make it home. She wasn't going to make it into the village.

The Bear Den!

She tumbled inside, headfirst and frantic, then reached up awkwardly and slammed the little door shut behind her.

It was utterly black and instantly cold. The dirt floor was lower than the pathway, and had turned to mud.

Shock hit Ruby hard and she started to shake and then sob. The dark took the sound and wrapped it around her like a thick marshmallow echo.

She had to stay quiet. She had to hold on.

She put her hands to her guns, but they had fallen out of her pockets, so instead she drew her knees up and clenched her fists at her chest, shivering.

It smelled. It smelled so bad.

Something brushed against her leg and she slapped it away. What was in here with her? She told herself: *Nothing, don't be silly.*

She froze as she heard footsteps outside. Someone approaching, breathing in short, angry bursts. A chain rattled and she thought of the pedlar under the hearth, all bones and revenge.

Something stopped – right outside the door.

Ruby clamped her hand over her mouth. Her hot tears pooled along the edge of her finger as she looked up at the blackness where she knew the door to be. She had nowhere to go – nowhere else to hide. If she made a sound now, she'd be found. The something touched her leg again, and the smallest shriek escaped her.

Then there was an endless silence where she couldn't even hear the beating of her own heart.

The door opened.

And a bear lunged through it. Lunged at the child who had invaded its home. Huge and snarling, its white teeth shining against its blood-red tongue—

Ruby screamed and screamed and screamed.

Long after she knew it was a dog.

Long after she could see it was attached to a policeman.

There were four dogs searching for the body of Jody Reeves. Two big German shepherds and two brown and white spaniels.

Ruby watched them from the front window, wrapped in a blanket and drinking sweet tea with a custard-cream chaser. Mummy had left the tin on the wide sill, so she could have as many as she wanted, but she'd been on this one for ages.

The dog that had scared her so badly was called Sabre. His handler had tried to get Ruby to shake his paw, to show her what a nice dog he was. Sabre had waved his paw again and again, but she had only cried and clutched at Mummy's waist, while Maggie and Em and Chris and Adam stood in a worried knot along with the rest of the village, who'd run to see the hoo-ha.

She could see Sabre now, coming up the slipway, head down, ears pricked, bushy tail swinging. She hated him for scaring her so. She shivered for the hundredth time as she recaptured the fear for just a split second. That was plenty.

Once they'd come out of the forest, the dogs had moved through the village like panting, wagging pin-balls, zigzagging their way up and down the lane and along the banks of the stream, and between the houses and around the cars. The men had told Mummy they were heading towards Westward Ho! and meeting another team that had started from there.

Now they passed the front gate and Mummy and Ruby went to the kitchen window to watch them clamber up the slippery steps of the Peppercombe path.

Just as the last dog and handler disappeared, the front

door burst open and Daddy shouted 'Ruby!' and Ruby cried all over again while he hugged her and asked if she was OK and checked her hands, as if for injury. Then he hugged her again while Mummy rubbed her back.

And even through the crying, Ruby thought: *This is how it used to be. All of us together.* And she stayed there as long as she could, feeling loved and safe.

Mummy ruined it by saying, 'What's that *smell*?'

'What smell?'

They stepped away from each other and Ruby sniffed. There *was* a smell. It burned the back of her throat and made her eyes water, the way the limekilns did.

Mummy gasped at the muck on the carpet.

'Where the hell have you *been*, John?'

'Must've been tar on the beach,' Daddy said. 'Sorry.'

'Take your shoes off! It's all over the carpet!'

Mummy got the bucket from outside the back door, making a lot of angry noise with it. She started scrubbing, then she looked at the clock. 'I have to be at work in twenty minutes!'

'I said I'm sorry, didn't I?' said Daddy. 'I was worried about Ruby. That idiot Tim Braund told me she'd had her hand ripped half off!'

'I thought it was a bear,' said Ruby, welling up at just the memory, but nobody looked at her.

Mummy threw the sponge in the bucket and dumped them both in the kitchen sink with a clatter. 'He's not an idiot. She wasn't bitten, but she was very frightened.'

'What do you mean?'

'What do you mean, what do I mean?'

'You said he's not an idiot.' Daddy followed her to the kitchen. 'What do you mean by that?'

'Nothing! I just meant he was mistaken. That doesn't mean he's an idiot. That's all. It's not important.'

'It's important to me.'

Ruby watched them anxiously.

She knew why Mr Braund wasn't an idiot. As Mummy had led her home, shaking and crying, Mr Braund had seen her fingers, stained bright red with nail polish.

Did it bite her? he'd yelled.

She's OK, Mummy had called as they'd hurried up the hill. *She's OK.*

Then, while Ruby had stood and sobbed, Mummy had got cotton wool and something from under the sink and scrubbed her fingers and nails until they were clean and sore and smelled like decorating.

Mummy tried to leave the kitchen, but Daddy filled the doorway.

'Just tell me what you meant,' he said. 'That's all I'm asking.'

'*Nothing!* I just *said* it.' Mummy ran her hands through her hair and then put them on her hips. She looked at the wall. 'John. Please. I need to get changed and I need a lift to work or I'm going to be late.'

He stared at her. She stared at the wall. And Ruby stared at both of them.

Finally Daddy stepped aside.

Mummy brushed past him, then opened the little white door and ran upstairs.

Daddy glared at the door as if he could still see her through the yellowing paint.

Ruby stood on the spider rug, unsure of what to do. She hugged the blanket closer to her. She'd like to go upstairs to bed, but following Mummy upstairs might look like she was taking her side.

Daddy turned to her. 'You all right, Rubes?'

She nodded.

'Good,' he said, then he whispered, 'I'll get some biscuits and something to drink. Why don't you go and put Panda to bed?'

They were going on a posse.

Ruby screwed up her face. The fear of the Bear Den was still fresh in her mind. It was too easy to revisit. To relive how quickly she'd turned from a swaggering cowboy into a scared little girl – and from that to a screaming baby, unable to stop crying even when Adam was standing right there with his father, watching her.

She wasn't in the mood to hunt down a killer.

'I'm so tired,' she said. 'Because of the dog and all the running and everything. Can you go? And I'll come the next time?'

She was letting him down, she could see it on his face.

'You scared, Rubes?'

'No!'

'It's OK if you're scared. You can tell me.'

'I'm *not*. I'm *tired*.' She'd battled so hard to get Daddy to allow her to go with him. What if he thought she was just a silly scaredy-cat girl now? He might never take her on another posse.

Or anywhere.

Daddy sat on the sofa and patted the cushion beside

him. She sat down and leaned into the space under his arm that seemed to fit her so well.

'You know how I got these scars, Rubes?'

'You were bit by a dog,' said Ruby. 'Mummy told me.'

'Did she?' said Daddy. He stroked the scar that ran through his eyebrow and stared thoughtfully at the table.

'Did it hurt?' she breathed.

'Hurt like billy-o,' said Daddy.

'Did you cry?'

'Like a baby. Much harder than you cried today. And I was *scared*.'

'Did the police take the dog away?'

'No.'

'Why not?'

'Well, it was my own fault. I was always winding the dog up. My mother always said it would bite me one day.'

'Oh.' Ruby nodded. 'But I didn't do *anything* to the police dog.'

He laughed without smiling. 'You can't trust the police, Rubes! They're always out to get you – even the dogs.'

Daddy took her hand. There was a tiny speck of red at the base of her left thumbnail, but he didn't notice.

'The point is, I *understand* about being scared, you see, Rubes? But when that dog bit me, you know what I did?'

'What?'

'I got back on the horse.'

Ruby pricked up her ears. 'What horse?'

'When you fall off a horse, you have to get straight back on, or else you might start worrying about falling off again, and then you'd *never* get back on. See?'

Ruby nodded.

She could hear Mummy starting down the stairs.

'So,' Daddy said in his cowboy voice, 'you all set for the posse, Deputy?'

Ruby hesitated.

'Next time,' she said. 'I'll get back on the horse next time.'

26

IT WAS A DARK and stormy night and the last bus was late. Or Becky Cobb had missed it. She was so drunk she kept forgetting which was most likely.

She frowned at the watch Jordan had given her for her eighteenth birthday, and saw that it had stopped. She shook her wrist and it started again. It really was a piece of shit, but how could she not wear it? He'd only want to know where it was if she didn't. It was a fake Rolex he'd got in Morocco for *Asda price* and it looked great – apart from the green mark it left around her wrist – but when it came to telling the time it was as useful as a chocolate teapot.

Becky shivered. Seizures Palace was always hot – warmed by the sheer number of bodies on the dance floor and crowding the bar – so Becky was wearing long black boots, a micro-miniskirt and a pink polo-neck sweater that was all neck and barely any sweater, because it showed off her belly ring. It was her latest acquisition and therefore demanded to be displayed, whatever the cost to her health. Now the warmth of other bodies was wearing off fast and she rubbed her arms and looked up and down Bideford Quay, as though she could conjure a bus out of thin air.

She decided to call Jordan. He'd be cross that she'd woken him, because he worked shifts, but it was his fault for buying her a fake watch, so she didn't feel too bad.

For a moment she thought she *had* already called him, and wondered how long he would be and did she have time to nip behind a car for a wee? Then she remembered that she *hadn't* called him, and needed her phone if she was going to.

Becky staggered a little with the effort of peering into her handbag. Why didn't they make them white inside, so a person had a bloody chance? Especially in the dark.

'Sorry to wake you, Jordy, but my watch stopped and I've missed the last bus home.' That's what she would say when he answered.

When he answered.

The phone went to voicemail, so she hung up and tried again.

Still Jordan didn't answer.

'Bastard,' she said.

'Pardon me?' said a man walking his dog.

'You too,' said Becky.

The man shook his head and walked on.

Becky dialled again. Jordan was a deep sleeper. She'd once had a ten-minute shouting match with that old cow next door right under their bedroom window, and he hadn't stirred. And now he couldn't hear his phone. Becky had imagined it on the bedside table, but now she adjusted her mental picture to it being on the kitchen counter, or in his jacket pocket in the hall cupboard. All those things were just as likely.

'Come *on*, Jordy, pick up the *phone*.'

He didn't.

Becky left a message, then hung up and shivered again.

A car pulled up alongside her and the window went down.

'Need a ride?'

She put one hand on the roof of the car to steady herself, and peered through the window at the man. She couldn't really see him in the dark, but he sounded nice enough. She was half tempted. But he was a man alone in a car and she was a girl alone on a dark and stormy night, and she still had options. Jordy might call her any minute now, and she could probably get a cab.

'Naah,' she mused. 'Better not.'

'You sure?' said the man. 'You've been waiting a while.'

'You been watching me?' said Becky. 'That's fucking *creepy*! My boyfriend'll smash your face in.'

'Be like that,' said the man, and drove off, leaving Becky without the car to keep her upright. She stumbled and would have fallen into the road if it weren't for the lamp post.

Of course, as soon as he drove off, Becky realized that the driver wasn't a mad axeman, that she'd have been perfectly safe in his company, and wished he'd come back.

'Come back!' she shouted. 'Oi!'

He didn't, and she was back to square one.

Jordan didn't call and finally Becky hitched up her tits and wobbled her way across the road to Key Cabs. She knew she didn't have enough money in her purse for the fare, but she was sure they'd take her home on a promise of payment at the other end. Becky wasn't quite so sure that Jordan would have the cash when they got there, but by then it would be the cabbie's problem, not hers.

'Can't do it,' said the big man behind the Formica counter in the tiny Key Cabs office.

'Oh, come on,' said Becky flirtatiously. 'I bet you do it all the time!'

The man was immune. He took a bite of kebab and shook his head.

'*Never* do it,' he said, letting Becky see lamb and lettuce swirl in his mouth. 'Been conned too many times.'

Becky wasn't used to being refused when she was wearing this skirt. 'Can't you do me a favour? I've missed the last bus.'

'Get a watch,' he shrugged.

'I've *got* a watch.' She showed him and then pouted. 'But it stopped.'

The man glanced at it and said, 'Get a *proper* watch.' Then he took a more ambitious bite. This time the shredded lettuce hung from between his lips like barbels, and some kind of thin orange sauce trickled down his chin. He sucked in the lettuce noisily and cleared the sauce with the back of his hand, which he then wiped down the side of his leg, somewhere below the level of the counter.

'Fat pig,' said Becky, even though she knew it sealed her fate.

He shrugged again and said, 'Enjoy the walk, slut.'

Becky headed back towards the bus stop because she didn't know where else to go.

She tried Jordan again and mentally cursed him to hell and back for his deep sleep and his lousy gift. She should get a new boyfriend; one who would come and fetch her from a girls' night out. When she got home, she might break up with Jordan.

Becky waited another few minutes. She hoped for the last bus; she hoped the man in Key Cabs would relent and wave her back across the road; she hoped Jordan would wake up and wonder where she was, and call her back.

When none of those things happened, she put up her umbrella and started to walk. What the hell – she was young and healthy and more than capable of walking the four miles to Weare Gifford any day of the week. It was on an unlit, tree-lined country road without pavements, but she'd just have to be careful, that was all. She wasn't *that* drunk. She'd be fine.

By the time she passed the police station four hundred yards up the road, she was feeling less confident. She *was* that drunk, and kept veering off the pavement and perilously close to the road. Once she hit a dog-mess bin and had a little cry because she'd touched it with her bare hands. Also, her boots weren't made for walking. They'd cost her thirty-five quid in the New Look sale, but they were starting to leak, and squelched coldly with every step.

She had almost left the lights of Bideford behind when a car pulled over and rolled slowly to a halt right in front of her.

Brilliant. Becky almost cried with gratitude.

The door opened and the driver stepped out and

walked towards her, and Becky Cobb felt her whole body prickle in fear.

The man didn't have a head!

For a ghastly, free-falling moment Becky thought she would faint with the horror of it. Then she realized he was wearing a balaclava. Black and woollen, with holes for his eyes and mouth. That was hardly any better. She was transfixed by it; she couldn't move – couldn't even look away.

He pointed at her face. 'When I say get in the car, you get in the car,' he said firmly. 'It's easier for everyone.'

She hit him with her umbrella. It didn't hurt him, because the umbrella was open and the drag slowed it through the air, but it hit his arms and stopped him being able to grab hold of her properly, so Becky turned and ran back down the middle of the dark road, towards the lights. 'Help me!' she screamed, horrified by how small the noise sounded. 'Help me!'

The man yanked her off her feet so fast that all the breath left her as she hit the ground, and she was dragged away from the lights and towards the car, the wet road grazing the small of her back and rolling her micro-mini down around her hips as she kicked and struggled and flailed about for something to grab on to.

They were at the car. The back wheel passed her peripheral vision and she twisted and grabbed hold of it, hugging the tyre like a long-lost lover while the headless man yanked at her arms and prised her fingers open.

'Let go, bitch!' He picked her up so that her body and legs were completely off the ground, but Becky didn't let go. She clung on to the wheel, screaming and shrieking, with her cheek pressed to the tyre.

'Hey!' someone shouted. 'Hey!'

She twisted her head. There was a person running towards them – silhouetted gloriously against the last streetlight in Bideford, like Jesus in a sunbeam.

The man dropped her.

Just like that.

One minute Becky Cobb was being kidnapped by a maniac and the next the car door slammed, the engine gunned and she was lying face-down in the road – wet, filthy, and sobbing like a helpless child.

Within minutes Becky Cobb was at Bideford police station, waiting for the doctor and DCI King to arrive, and telling the desk sergeant, Tony Coral, everything she remembered.

It was remarkable how much Becky *did* remember, given how drunk she still was.

Tony Coral took down everything she told him methodically and accurately. He couldn't remember hearing a more detailed description in all his thirty-one years on the force.

Sadly, it was a description not of a kidnapper, but of a wheel. Four bare bolts, the black cable tie holding the hubcap in place, the crack in the plastic shaped like a dolphin, the metal valve cap and the zigzag pattern of treads on the tyre.

'I'd know that wheel anywhere,' Becky slurred vehemently every time she woke up. '*Anywhere.*'

27

Miss Sharpe picked Ruby Trick's diary off the top of the pile. The title on the cover was written so wrongly, and yet so carefully, that Miss Sharpe didn't have the heart to correct it.

She skimmed the latest entries, corrected a few spelling errors, made a few ticks. She smiled to herself as she wondered whether the childish pleasure of a red pen would ever wear off.

The last line in the book made her gasp.

She had to read it twice to make sure she wasn't imagining it.

And when she had, Miss Sharpe closed the little blue book and sat for a very long time, just staring at the words: *My Dairy*.

Then she picked up the phone to call Ruby Trick's mother.

Just as Calvin Bridge had promised, the Burrows was a thousand acres of flat land that would have been a lagoon if it weren't for the pebble ridge that ran for over a mile and was as high as a house.

These were not any old pebbles. Not pebbles that would sit snug in the hand or skip across a pond. These were kings among pebbles. Emperors of smooth grey sandstone – each one as rounded and as beautiful as the next, and ranging in size from palm to prize-winning pumpkin.

And the irony was that the sea itself had built the ridge that now kept it at bay. For a hundred thousand years, the tide had picked up and pounded jagged rocks from the foot of cliffs as far away as Clovelly. It had rubbed them and washed them and shaped them and rolled them along ten miles of beach, until each rock was worn to a smooth piece of perfection. Finally the ocean had piled them into this natural wall – slowly cheating itself out of the Burrows, which were instead annexed by locals for their sheep and their ponies and, later, their golf.

Twice a day, the angry sea came back for the Burrows. It slunk about the foot of the ridge, casing the joint. Then, with the full weight of the Atlantic behind it, it threw itself at the pebbles, clawing and snarling and roaring its intent to take back its rightful property. Once a month, General Moon ordered it over the top, where it sometimes caught a tantalizing glimpse of what it had lost, and hurled insults and froth, but rarely managed more.

Every year, the Potwallopers walked the tattered edges of the ridge by torchlight and heaved giant pebbles that had been dragged on to the sand back up to the top of the magnificent ridge. Then they feasted on the beach – taunting the sea, and daring it to try again, if it thought it was hard enough.

In sunshine the pebbles were a tasteful pale grey, some with elegant white crystalline pinstripes. But today it was raining, and they were slate-grey and shiny.

On *any* day, Calvin knew they would break your ankle as soon as look at you.

'Remarkable,' said DCI King as they drove along behind the ridge, and Calvin felt a swell of proprietorial pride at this most prominent feature of his home town – as if he'd built it himself.

King yawned.

Calvin didn't take it personally. He knew she'd been up half the night with some girl who'd been dragged down the Torrington road on her arse.

'Any luck with that girl, Ma'am?' he asked.

'She's not going to be any help,' said King, and yawned again. 'Even sober.'

They left the Volvo on a patch of gravel at the foot of the ridge and started walking. The grass underfoot was as smooth as lino. Any blade that dared put its head above the parapet was immediately cropped by sheep or ponies. Now and then there was a ditch for drainage, or a stand of spiky marsh grass to remind them that they should have been underwater. Calvin held out a hand to a passing pony. It stretched its neck and lips, but lost interest when it found that all he had to offer was fingers.

They stopped at a shallow pan of mud and Calvin bent down to scoop a sample into a small plastic jar.

'Keep your eye open for Frannie's nose ring,' DCI King reminded him.

'Will do, Ma'am,' said Calvin, although they both knew it was a hopeless task.

'So,' said King, 'when's the big day?'

'What big day?'

'The wedding.'

'Oh. Next year. March thirteenth.'

'Lucky for some.' She shrugged. 'Looking forward to it?'

'Sure,' said Calvin, putting the lid on the little jar.

'What's her name?'

'Who?'

'Your fiancée.'

'Oh! Shirley. She's a really nice girl.'

'You make her sound like a spaniel,' said King.

Someone shouted 'Fore!' and they hunched their shoulders. A dozen yards away, a golf ball thudded softly into the turf beside an uninterested sheep.

Pans were a feature of the Burrows. They took mud samples from two more before it started to rain hard and King decided they had enough for Mike Crew to make a reasonable comparison with the soil between Frannie Hatton's teeth.

They got back in the car.

'You can take those samples down to Mike Crew tomorrow,' said King.

Calvin made the outraged face of a fourteen-year-old boy and she added cheerfully, 'Isn't the chain of command wonderful?'

She put the car into gear and pulled off the gravel on to the narrow road.

Calvin looked out of the window at the wet grass and mud-pans slowly filling with sandy brown rainwater, and sighed deeply.

'Getting cold feet about the wedding?' said King, not unkindly.

'No, no, no,' Calvin said. 'Yes.'

King laughed, but he didn't, and she stopped.

'It's just that it's all happening very fast.' He made what felt like a ridiculous face and waved his hands to show he was totally OK with it all. 'Very *exciting*, you know? Bit of a blur.'

He laughed awkwardly. King cleared her throat but said nothing. That was his invitation to say nothing too.

But instead, after a minute or so, he said something.

'It's just that everything feels different. People aren't the same.'

'You mean Shirley's not the same?'

'Yeah. Suddenly she's not about *us* any more. She's all about the wedding and the honeymoon and all the children we're going to have.'

King raised her eyebrows and said, '*All* the children?'

Calvin nodded. 'Three. Rosie, Charlotte and Digby.'

'*Digby?*' laughed King. 'Bloody hell, Calvin! Get out now, while you still can!'

Calvin opened his mouth to tell her that Shirley had wanted Algie, and he'd got it reduced to Digby on appeal, but he was suddenly flung forward so hard in his seat that the inertia reel belt jammed against his shoulder and he braced his hands against the dashboard.

The Volvo fishtailed a little, then lurched to a stop.

'Get out!' said King.

'What?'

'Get out of the car! Out!' And she poked him in the arm.

Confused and a little worried, Calvin opened his door. He didn't move fast enough for King. She poked him twice more in the back as he went, shouting, 'Out! Out!'

He did, then took a few paces before turning to face the car.

King got out of the driver's side, looking flushed. 'That's it!' she said. 'Those marks on Frannie Hatton's arm and back – they're in the places they'd be if someone was poking her to get her out of a car!'

Calvin frowned and touched his arm where her forefinger had first landed. There would be a little bruise there, for sure – even through his jacket. And the two on his back were lower than the marks on Frannie, but then, he was a lot taller.

'*Get out!*' said King. 'That's what made me think of it. But Frannie didn't want to get out – she must've known that something bad was going to happen. So he poked her with his finger and the nails left those short, curved bruises.'

She was pacing with excitement.

Calvin frowned.

'What's wrong?' she said instantly.

'Well,' he said, 'a man doesn't *poke*. A man *pushes*.'

King stared at him, then jerked a thumb at the car. 'OK, you get in the driver's seat and push me out. Let me see.'

He did, and she saw. He sat behind the wheel and shoved her out with his spread fingertips and the heel of his hand. He didn't poke.

'And even if he did poke,' he said, staring at his forefinger, 'men don't have nails long enough to leave marks like the ones on Frannie Hatton.'

King grimaced and said, 'You're right.'

'And Katie Squire noticed that his nails were quite bitten,' said Calvin. 'It's in the report.'

'You're right again. Bollocks.' She sat back down in the passenger seat.

That made three times Calvin had been right in the past two minutes. He was *never* right about swatches.

'Maybe it was a gun,' said King.

'Seriously?' said Calvin. This was Devon; now and then a farmer sawed his granddad's shotgun in half so that he could put the end of it in his mouth, but criminal guns – handguns – were still mercifully few and far between.

But King said, 'Yes, seriously. The bit at the front. The barrel—'

'The muzzle,' he supplied.

'Yes, the muzzle. That would leave a little curved bruise.' She made her fingers into a gun and poked him slowly three times in the shoulder. 'Would – 'nt – it?'

'Yes,' he said, 'it would.' Then he paused cautiously and added, 'But none of the girls who escaped mentioned a gun.'

'I know,' said King. 'Although he could've had a Howitzer and Becky Cobb probably wouldn't have noticed.'

'And if he *did* have a gun, why didn't he just shoot Frannie Hatton?'

'Noise?' shrugged King. 'Or maybe she tried to run and he caught her and lost control of the situation or himself. Or he dropped the gun. Or she knocked it out of his hand and he had to improvise. Maybe it jammed. Or it's traceable. Or he only needed it as a threat and never intended to use it. Could have been lots of reasons.'

Calvin nodded. They all seemed obvious now that DCI King had said them.

'Or maybe he just likes the intimacy of suffocation,' she added more slowly.

Calvin frowned at her.

'You imagine it,' King went on. 'Putting your hands around somebody's throat or holding them face-down in mud or sand or water. Feeling them fight and then weaken and finally give up and die.'

Calvin did imagine it.

'You'd literally hold a life in your hands,' said the DCI bleakly.

'Yeah,' nodded Calvin, and – almost unconsciously – his hands gripped the steering wheel in front of him, and squeezed so tight that his knuckles went white. 'You'd really have everything under *control.*'

DCI King gave him a serious look.

'Jesus, Calvin. Just tell Shirley to slow the fuck down, will you? Nobody has to die.'

28

RUBY WATCHED THE sea a hundred feet below. The tide was on the turn and the deep green water slid quietly up against the cliffs and then just hung around with nothing to do until the next swell came along.

She hadn't been to the haunted house since that last time with Adam. She'd been nervous of the flagstone in the hearth. But now the thought of the swing and the stile and the dark woods that hemmed the Clovelly pathway made her *more* nervous.

Her nose was pressed against the floorboard. It smelled of rot. Now and then she moved her eye and put her nose to the hole instead, to breathe the sea air. Now and then she got a whiff of kelp and dankness that reminded her of the muddy paddock, devoid of horses.

She thought of the horseshoe on Miss Sharpe's charm bracelet tinkling as she tapped her finger on the page of her diary.

Where did you hear that word, Ruby?
I don't know, Miss. On the bus, I think.
Do you know what it means?
No, Miss.
Well, it's not a nice word, Ruby. Don't use it, OK?

I wasn't going to, Miss.

Good.

Ruby was a bit confused. She'd heard Daddy use that word, and it couldn't be *that* bad because then she'd been asked to wait after class, and then Miss Sharpe hadn't been angry with her at all. She had asked her about the swing and the paddock and Adam, and if everything was all right at home. Ruby had said, *Yes, Miss* because the house was fine apart from the damp patches and the bathroom window. She hadn't got a clue why Miss Sharpe wanted to know about their home. Grown-ups often said confusing stuff.

Then Miss Sharpe had said, *You know you can always come and tell me things, Ruby.*

Yes, Miss.

Even secret things.

Yes, Miss.

Miss Sharpe had put her head on one side as if she was waiting for something. Ruby didn't know what.

I have a secret. Do you want to hear it?

OK, Miss.

Well . . . I have a pet rabbit called Harvey, and sometimes I talk to him just like he's another person!

Ruby had smiled because Miss Sharpe had smiled, but she didn't see why talking to a rabbit like a person was such a big deal. She talked to Lucky all the time and he was made of plastic. It was like some grown-ups didn't know the difference between games and reality.

Do you have any secrets, Ruby?

No, Miss.

That was a lie, too. But what was the point of *having*

secrets if you were going to tell them to the first person who asked? Then they weren't secrets any more.

She did wish she had a rabbit though.

A sharp crack close to her ear made Ruby jump.

'Shit,' said Adam. 'I was trying to creep up on you.' He lifted his foot carefully and the floor creaked back into place.

They both made the same alarmed face, and then laughed.

Adam sat cross-legged beside his own hole, like an Eskimo going fishing.

'You OK?' he said.

He meant after yesterday, Ruby knew, but for some reason she didn't feel embarrassed, even though he'd seen her cry.

'Yeah,' she said.

'It didn't bite you, did it?'

'No.'

'They're trained not to bite,' he said. 'Not until the policeman says so. We had a demonstration at school.'

'Yeah?' Ruby was surprised. The only demonstration *her* school ever had was a policewoman with ladders in her tights showing them how to ride a bicycle.

'Yeah, this bloke had a big padded suit on and when the policeman told the dog to bite his arm, he bit his arm, and when he said to bite his leg, he bit his leg. But the dog only did that when he was told. Otherwise he just barked. Those dogs are so well trained.'

'I hate them,' said Ruby.

Adam nodded. 'Yeah, I'd hate them too if one trapped me in the Bear Den.'

He leaned sideways on to his elbow, and then rolled on to his tummy beside Ruby and put his eye to the hole.

There were hardly any waves, and no foam at all.

'It's rubbish today,' said Adam against the wood.

'I know.'

But they watched it anyway.

'How's Lucky?' said Adam.

'He's fine,' said Ruby.

'Did you get carrots?'

'No, a potato.'

'A potato?'

'Mmm.' Ruby was sorry she hadn't got carrots now. Adam had told her to and it would have been funny. 'It's like a boulder,' she explained.

'That's funny too,' said Adam.

Their feet touched.

'Sorry,' said Adam.

''s OK,' said Ruby. Then she giggled and nudged him back.

'Hey!'

They wrestled gently with their ankles for a bit, never taking their eyes from the holes in the planking. Then Adam leaned over and nudged her shoulder with his.

'Ow!'

He looked up. 'Did I hurt you?'

She looked up too. 'No.'

They laughed.

When they put their eyes back to the floor, their shoulders remained touching. Ruby's eyes were on the sea but her whole mind seemed to be thinking about

Adam's shoulder touching hers. She could feel his warmth right through their T-shirts.

The sea was dead dull but they kept looking at it anyway.

Ruby wanted to thank Adam. She wasn't sure why. For Lucky, or for saying he'd have been afraid of the dog too, or just for lying beside her so they could watch the sea together.

But talking would have been too loud, so she didn't.

Her elbows started to hurt. She should get up and give them a rest. But she lay there instead, pressing Adam's shoulder with hers.

'My dad's got a girlfriend,' said Adam.

Ruby looked over at him. 'What?'

Adam didn't take his eye from the hole in the floor. 'My dad's got a girlfriend. I heard my mum telling my gran on the phone.'

Ruby stared at Adam's ear. The outer edge of it was very red. Was it always so red? She wasn't sure.

'Who's his girlfriend?' she said, dreading the answer.

Adam rolled on to his side so they were facing each other, but he stared at the floor between them, picking at it with his fingernail. There was a crack there where he'd trodden just now, and a jagged edge. 'Somebody in London, I think. He's always there.'

Ruby wasn't sure what to say. She was relieved to hear that it wasn't Mummy, but she felt sorry for Adam.

'That's horrible,' she said.

'Yeah,' nodded Adam. 'He's a bastard.'

Ruby was shocked to hear Adam use that word about his own father. He must *really* hate him.

'Is he going to leave you?'

'I don't know,' sighed Adam. 'I'm not even supposed to know about it. Nobody knows I know.'

'Does Chris know?'

'I don't think so.'

Ruby picked at the crack too, so they were doing it together. The wood was so rotten it was easy to pull bits off, even with their fingers.

'Who will you live with if they get a divorce?'

'I don't know.' Adam shrugged. 'With my mum, probably.'

'Yes, mostly the kids stay with the mummies,' said Ruby with some authority. 'That's what all the kids at school do.'

Adam nodded and said, 'Yeah.'

He worried the wood angrily with his fingernail until Ruby touched his hand.

He looked up at her.

Then he kissed her.

It took her by surprise, but she only drew back a little tiny bit. She kept her eyes open and so did Adam as his mouth touched hers like electricity. For a second she saw herself reflected in his pupils.

Then they heard Chris banging into the haunted house, crunching something underfoot and saying, 'Shitting bollocks to *that*,' and Adam rolled over and put his eye to the floor once again.

'Adam!'

'What?'

'Tea.'

'OK.'

He sighed and knelt up and said, 'Bye, Ruby.'

Ruby got up and went to the window and watched Adam and Chris and the dogs all the way down the hill to their house.

29

CALVIN BRIDGE WAS exhausted.

Somehow he had imagined that getting married would mean more of the same, but it was turning into *none* of the same. In fact it seemed to be a process of *chucking out* the same, and filling the same's space with a whole bunch of new stuff that wasn't the same at all. Stuff he really had no interest in. Organization. Commitment. Babies.

Swatches.

How had it happened? Was he overreacting? Was this just the way things went? And was it temporary? After the trauma of the wedding, would he have the old Shirley back? Or was the Shirley that was morphing into a completely different person in front of his very eyes the *real* Shirley? The one he'd be married to for the *rest of his life*.

Calvin actually shivered at the thought.

He longed for drink, drugs and debt. He longed for a Korean gangster flick and a meat-feast pizza all to himself.

He longed for another life. But, between them, Shirley and the Devon and Cornwall Police had him running through *this* life like a hamster in a wheel.

As well as trying to catch a serial killer, on Tuesday

night Calvin had held Shirley's hand through a tablecloth crisis. The choices were Ivory, Buttermilk and Vanilla. They were all the same, but it had taken three hours hunched over the huge and hideous books of swatches, and two long, weepy interludes, to reach a decision.

And the swatches were only part of it. Shirley had turned Calvin's flat into her own little incident room, swirling with a thousand paper samples and cloth samples and cake samples and favours and flavours, and infinite lists that Calvin was supposed to have memorized. It was a glittery tide of wedding porn – all of which cost a thousand times more than *real* porn. The invitations were impregnated with bits of lavender and had edges that were 'hand-torn' – presumably by experts, given the price. And the centrepieces – which were only made of *flowers* – were each the same price as a crate of reasonable beer. The cake was costing more than Calvin's first car.

'Is it made of *gold*?' he'd said, and Shirley had cried for the four millionth time since the Italian Grand Prix.

'Do you know what I'm thinking?' said Kirsty King.

'No,' sighed Calvin. 'I don't know what *any* woman's thinking. Ever.'

DCI King gave him a quizzical look. They were eating lunch in the incident room, which doubled as the staffroom. There were vending machines containing curly sandwiches and warm chocolate bars, and a frieze of evidence around the wall. Photos of Jody Reeves and the Burrows and the lay-by, and of Frannie Hatton's body – still the only one they had.

Most of the major-incident team had gone out for

213

chips, but Calvin was eating a sandwich from the machine that was so tasteless he had to keep looking at it to make sure it was still prawn. DCI King brought the same lunch from home every day – a pork pie and olives, which she fished out of their tall glass jar with Dr Shortland's gall-stone scoop.

It was perfect for the job.

Now DCI King popped one in her mouth, ignored his lament, and carried on where she left off. 'I'm thinking, maybe the women weren't the targets.'

Calvin raised an eyebrow. 'Frannie Hatton would probably disagree with you.'

'Touché,' said King. 'They were target*ed*, of course, but what if they weren't the people he was really aiming to *hurt*?'

Calvin wasn't quite sure what King was getting at, but he was happy to go along with her, if only because she wasn't talking about renting an owl as a ring-bearer.

'We have so little to go on,' King continued. 'But, taking the assaults on Kelly and Katie into account, what we *do* have to go on is a consistent m.o.'

She started to count the modi operandi off on her fingers, using the gall-stone scoop as an aid. 'One: he covers his face. Two: he makes them take their clothes off, but he doesn't sexually assault them. Three: he makes them phone their mothers.'

She paused and Calvin looked at her expectantly for 'four'.

'That's it,' said King. 'Those are the only three things we know for sure. Everything else is just extrapolation or assumption.'

'OK,' he agreed.

'So, covering his face is obvious. But you tell me, Calvin, why does he make them strip and then not touch them?'

Calvin did try to think, but it seemed counter-intuitive. Once a woman took her clothes off, the whole *point* was to touch them. Otherwise you might as well just read a magazine. He had to admit, 'I don't know.'

'Neither do I,' said King. 'I mean, I know it's going to turn out to be some weird screwed-up reason because of some sexual dysfunction or some shit that happened when he was a kid or something. But what it does do is speak to *motive*, and it tells us that – for the first three assaults at the very least – the motive was *not* to sexually assault these women. Even if he'd been working up to it, then I reckon he would have got there by Frannie Hatton, don't you? I mean, if you can murder someone, you can sexually assault them, surely?'

'Right,' Calvin assumed. 'That makes sense.'

Did it? He wondered. What made sense to a killer might not be what made sense to DCI King and him, eating their lunch in Bideford police station.

King went on, 'But *call your mother*. That's bizarre and it's consistent and it's very specific. And he's been saying it right from the start, so it must be an important element in whatever sick game he's playing. It makes me think, why are they all *young*? And that makes me think – they're all young enough to have mothers to call, so maybe the mothers are the key.'

'But there are no links between the families,' said Calvin. 'The mothers don't know each other, they don't share the same interests or incomes or lifestyles, they don't go to the same places or know the same people.'

'Right,' said King. 'And that's why I started thinking, maybe the mothers have been the targets all along. Not because of *who* they are, but because of *what* they are.'

'And what *are* they?' said Calvin.

King stared at him. 'They're mothers, Calvin.'

Calvin frowned. 'But how can *they* be the targets if he's killing someone else?'

'Think about it,' said King. 'Who suffers more – the victims or their mothers?'

'The victims,' shrugged Calvin. 'They die.'

King tapped her teeth with the scoop. 'You don't have children, right?'

'Not yet.'

'Nor me,' said King. She drummed the scoop on the table a few times, thinking, and then looked over her shoulder to the desk sergeant, Tony Coral, who was eating a cheese and onion pasty at the table behind her. 'Tony, you have kids, don't you?'

'Two boys,' nodded Sergeant Coral, with flaky pastry down his front.

'What are their names?'

'Ivor and Martin.'

'Would you rather die yourself or watch Ivor and Martin die?'

'Bloody hell!' He coughed, but King just kept waiting for an answer, so he croaked, 'How are they dying?'

'Horribly,' said King.

Coral brushed flaky pastry off his tunic and shook his

head. 'Jesus, I couldn't watch that. Don't even like thinking about it.'

'So you'd rather be dead yourself than watch your children die?'

'Yup,' he said, and put his pasty down with a look that said he wouldn't be picking it up again.

'Cheers,' said King, and turned back to Calvin. 'See? What if the killing's just part of the whole *thing*? The stripping and the calling the mothers, and forcing them to witness the murder? The girls suffer and die, but the mothers have to suffer and go on *living*.'

Calvin frowned. 'It seems a bit of a roundabout way of hurting someone.'

'Maybe he can't hurt his own mother – or maybe he doesn't even know he *wants* to – and so he's taking it out on other people's mothers.'

'Acting out,' said Calvin. 'I think that's what Americans call it. Shirley watches those shows where people blame their parents for everything. Acting out. Or is it acting up?'

'No, that's the kids on *Supernanny*,' said King. 'But whatever the Americans call it, it makes sense, don't you think?'

Calvin shrugged. 'As much sense as any other bloody thing.'

DCI King nodded and sat back in her chair. Then she said, 'You're shedding cherubs.'

'Huh?' Calvin followed her gaze under the table to his feet, where a light sprinkling of tiny silver and gold foil cherubs had escaped his turn-ups.

That *fucking wedding*.

30

*E*XTREME *FISHING* WAS on TV because Daddy liked to
tell the men on there where they were going wrong.
A fat man in a red baseball cap was up to his hips in a river.
He looked like a marker buoy.

Daddy was busy checking Mummy's phone while she
was in the shower. The shower always made the whole
back wall of the house shudder like someone driving
over a cattle grid.

Daddy thumbed through the messages and Ruby
watched, glazed, as the words on the little screen rolled
by in time to clicks from his thumb. Now and then he
would stop and open a message and then close it again
and keep clicking.

It was boring. He never found anything good.

The man in the red cap didn't catch a thing, just like
Daddy said he wouldn't.

'He didn't catch one,' said Ruby.

Daddy said nothing.

Mummy came downstairs. She was dressed for work,
but her hair was still wet.

'When were you going to tell me about this?' said
Daddy, tapping the phone.

'What's that?'

'This meeting with Ruby's teacher.'

'Is that my phone?' said Mummy.

'What meeting?' said Ruby.

'Are you checking my phone?' said Mummy.

'Don't you think I'd want to know about it?'

'*What* meeting?' said Ruby again. Why did Miss Sharpe want a meeting? She'd been *going* to school, hadn't she?

They both ignored her. 'You never come to school things,' said Mummy.

He shrugged. 'I'm coming now.'

'Good,' said Mummy, and made a half-hearted grab for the phone, but Daddy laughed and snatched it away and held her wrist while he kept thumbing through the messages.

'Why are you checking my phone?'

'Is there any reason I shouldn't?'

'Maybe!' Mummy tried to break free, but Ruby could tell she wasn't trying too hard. She was half laughing, and so was Daddy. It made her feel like laughing too.

'Who's T?' said Daddy.

'Who?'

He read the text: '*Call you later. T.* Who's T?'

Mummy stuck out her tongue. 'None of your beeswax.'

But Ruby could tell Daddy had stopped playing. 'Tim Braund?' he said.

'Don't be daft. It's Tina on reception. She told me about a book and said she'd call me later with the title.'

'What book?' said Daddy.

'How should I know? She hasn't *called* me yet.'

'I don't believe you,' he said. Ruby didn't believe her either.

'Don't believe me then,' laughed Mummy. 'Let me *go*.'

'I won't,' said Daddy. 'Not either of you.'

But he did let her go, and she rubbed the red mark on her wrist and said, 'Ow. That hurt.'

'Sorry,' said Daddy. 'You want me to kiss it better?'

Mummy just held out her hand for the phone. Daddy gave it to her, then he winked at Ruby and whispered against her ear, 'Go upstairs and put Panda to bed.'

Ruby's heart skipped a beat. She was going on another posse! She ran up the narrow stairs on her hands and feet for added speed.

She'd had Panda all her life – Granpa and Nanna had bought him for her as a nought-birthday present. For years Panda was bigger than she was, but he'd shrunk now, and one of his arms had fallen off from too much hugging. It was still somewhere in her sock drawer, but Mummy never had time to sew it back on. It didn't make any difference to his latest role, which required him to lie in bed and pretend to be Ruby. Aided and abetted by a pillow, he did a grand job.

Ruby put Panda in her bed and arranged the covers over him so that just the tip of one ear was showing. Then she went to the window.

Outside the trees cut out all but a ragged strip of sky that she had to peer upwards to see. It was still getting dark, but it was already night in the forest – a dense, brooding wall of leaf and trunk that rose up to its full height barely twenty feet behind The Retreat. Now and then Ruby saw a squirrel or a bird in the trees, but mostly it was dead and silent.

She drew the curtains so that the room was even murkier than usual.

Mummy would never guess it was Panda and not her in the bed.

Alison Trick waited until they heard the creak of Ruby's bedroom floor before she said quietly, 'I don't think you should take her out.'

'What?' John looked at his wife in surprise. 'Why?'

'I don't think she should be driving all over the countryside on a school night.'

'You're the one who's always going on about her watching too much TV.'

'This is different.'

'How is it different? We go fishing together. We watch telly together. We go driving together. How's that different?'

Alison shrugged. 'I just don't think it's healthy. She's ten. She should be tucked up in bed, not gallivanting around with a bunch of idiots dressed as cowboys.'

'She's not with a bunch of idiots. She's with me.'

Alison shrugged.

'You're just jealous,' said John Trick.

'No, I'm not.'

'Yes, you are.' He nodded. 'She loves it. It's a big adventure. We have a great time. We talk and we sing and we eat chips. We have fun together. We have fun without *you*, and you don't like it.'

Alison shrugged. 'I *am* a bit jealous. What mother wouldn't be? I'm missing out on so much of her growing up. But this isn't about me, John. I don't want to stop her having fun – I just want her to get enough sleep. It's not rocket science.'

'What's that supposed to mean?'

Alison sighed. 'What?'

'*It's not rocket science*. Are you saying I'm stupid?'

'No!'

'Just 'cos I haven't got a big fancy job and a big fancy car like Tim fucking Braund.'

Alison Trick looked down at the china dog on the window sill. 'Why are you always trying to pick a fight with me? I can't say anything any more.'

'You can say whatever you like. Nobody's stopping you.'

Alison picked up her bag and dropped her phone into it.

'Can we just go?' she said. 'Please.'

John Trick picked up his keys.

When he'd dropped Mummy at the bus stop, Daddy called upstairs and clapped his hands. 'Ready, Rubes?'

She came to the top of the stairs. 'I haven't had any tea.'

'I've got some squash for you. Grab some biscuits and let's go.'

Ruby couldn't believe her luck.

She followed Daddy downstairs and they searched

for the biscuits. They weren't in any of the cupboards.

'Have some bread or something.'

'But you said I could have biscuits.'

Daddy got impatient. 'Maybe there *are* none.'

'There are. There's a whole tin of custard creams.'

'Then why the *hell* does the stupid cow hide them?'

'She doesn't want me to have nice things to eat,' explained Ruby. 'Only vegetables.'

'I'll buy you chips,' said Daddy. 'Let's go.'

Daddy didn't get any chips for himself, because he had cider.

As they sat outside the Blue Dolphin, a gaggle of giggling women came up Bridgeland Street, all dressed in fishnet stockings and pink T-shirts that read HANNAH'S HENS LOOKING FOR COCKS.

'Look at this lot,' said Daddy, shaking his head.

Ruby knew they were slags, and was suddenly deeply grateful to Mummy for cleaning the nail polish off her hands before Daddy had had a chance to see it.

The rain dwindled to nothing, and made it easier for Ruby to keep watch as they started off again, but the only people they passed were a boy pushing a broken-down motorbike and a man walking a white dog.

'Can we get a dog?' she asked.

'No.'

Ruby bit her lip. Stupid. Now she'd asked and been told no and so she couldn't ask again for ages. She wondered whether Daddy would say yes to a rabbit, like

Miss Sharpe's, but that was a question she'd store up for when he was in a better mood. Maybe when Daddy wasn't on his third can of Strongbow. She didn't understand why he bothered spending money on something that only made him cross. At least Mars bars and *Pony & Rider* made her happy.

They swooped down the hill back into Bideford twice before they saw anyone who needed help.

It was a young woman waiting for a bus. She had short blonde hair and jeans and her name was Steffi. She was only going across the river to Instow, and asked to be dropped off outside Paul's Deli on the seafront.

'I'll take you to your door,' said Daddy. 'Don't want to leave you somewhere that's not safe.'

'Thanks,' said Steffi, 'but I work there and need to pick up my wages. I walk home from there all the time. It's not far.'

'You should be more careful, you know,' said Daddy seriously. 'Taking lifts from strangers. You know there's a nutter about.'

'Well,' shrugged the girl, 'you have your little girl with you, and I've been walking to Paul's and back for yonks, so . . . y'know . . .'

'I wish I could work in a sweetshop,' said Ruby. 'Do you eat all the sweets?'

Steffi laughed. 'They don't let you. You get fired if you eat the sweets *or* read the magazines.'

Ruby frowned. 'Even *Pony & Rider*?'

'Oooh,' said Steffi. 'I used to read that all the time!'

'Did you?' said Ruby excitedly. 'Do you have a pony?'

'When I was little I did. His name was Lundy Lad, but we called him Laddie.'

'I wish I had one,' said Ruby wistfully, 'but it's too expensive.'

'It's not just the money,' snapped Daddy. 'It's a lot of work, a horse. It's not just the money, Ruby – you're just like your mother, you are.'

Ruby sat back. She was stung. She wasn't like Mummy; she was like Daddy!

They drove the rest of the way in silence.

They dropped Steffi outside Paul's. She said thank you and waved Ruby goodbye, before going into the shop.

'Here, Rubes,' said Daddy after a moment. 'Go and get yourself an ice cream.'

He held out a pound coin. Ruby knew it would only buy a lolly, not a proper ice cream, but she also knew it was a pound's worth of sorry, so she took it and squeezed between the seats, and followed Steffi inside.

From the outside, Paul's looked like it was going to be rubbish, but inside it was much bigger and brightly lit, with a deli counter and sweets and a huge wall of magazines and comics. There were even ice creams in the ice-cream freezer.

Ruby was hanging over it to ponder the lollies when Steffi stopped beside her.

'You OK?' she said.

'Yes, thanks,' said Ruby.

'I didn't mean to make your dad cross.'

Ruby shrugged. 'He's only cross because he hasn't got a job.'

'Oh,' nodded Steffi. 'Sorry.'

'That's OK.' Ruby picked out a Fab.

'Hey,' said Steffi suddenly. 'Put this towards your pony.' She dug a five-pound note out of her jeans pocket and handed it to Ruby, then walked out of the shop.

Ruby was so stunned that she couldn't even say thank you. She'd had three quid once off Granpa for a birthday kiss, but she'd never had a five-pound note in her hand that actually belonged to her.

Five pounds!

She spent every penny. Mostly on chocolate bars and crisps, but, because it was free money, she got a magazine as well. She already had the latest *Pony & Rider*, so she bought something called *TeenBeatz*. On the cover it said SIX WAYS TO TELL IF HE REALLY LOVES YOU and GET KISSING RIGHT FIRST TIME, and it had a free pencil sharpener stuck to the front. Ruby added everything up in her head and made up the last few pennies with aniseed balls from a box by the till.

'Where'd you get all that?' said Daddy in the car.

'She gave me five pounds!'

'Who did?'

'That girl. Steffi.'

'Why?'

'Dunno,' said Ruby. 'But I saved your pound for you.'

He took it without a word.

They drove down the seafront, with the lights of Appledore on their left, reflected in the still river between them, and the big fancy houses on their right. Long gardens and glass balconies, and the Commodore hotel all low and white, and lit up by spotlights on the sweeping lawns.

'Hey!' said Ruby. 'There's that car with the funny horn.' They cruised slowly past the yellow car with the black stripes parked on the seafront, and Ruby could see the dark silhouette of the driver at the wheel.

'Arsehole,' said Daddy, and Ruby giggled.

Daddy needed the loo, which was in the car park next to the dunes, where the road curved away from the sea.

The car park was just a flat piece of ground sandwiched between the dunes, the beach and the road. It had been tarmac once, but now was almost covered with shifting sand that made a crunchy little noise as Daddy swung the car round and reversed it neatly against the looming banks of sand.

'Wait here, Rubes,' said Daddy.

''K,' she said. Not that there was anywhere to go.

As soon as he was out of the car, Ruby got in the back where she could stretch out on the seat, and started on a Mars bar and *TeenBeatz*. She had to squint in the low yellow interior light, but reading a magazine about kissing, while eating a free Mars bar washed down with blackcurrant squash, made her feel like a grown-up.

Ruby woke on a bang and a scream.

Her heart bumped and her breath felt like she'd been running; she sucked in blackcurrant spittle that had collected at the corner of her mouth as she lay on the back seat.

The end of the scream sighed away and stopped, and there was only silence.

The car wasn't driving but it was *tilting*, and she sat up slowly, expecting to see that they were home and parked on the uneven cobbles. They weren't. They were still by the dunes.

'Daddy?'

Daddy wasn't there. Ruby rubbed her eyes and looked around her, then twisted and got to her knees so she could look out of the window.

Someone was crouching down beside the car.

'Daddy?'

The someone stood up and stepped backwards and looked around the car park. There was a streetlight behind him so his face was in shadow, and for a second she thought it was Daddy because he was wearing a cowboy hat, but it wasn't Daddy – he was a lot fatter, and the streetlight silhouetted the fluffy mutton-chop side-burns on his cheeks.

Ruby held her breath.

What was he doing?

And what would he do next?

Something in his hand caught the moonlight and glittered.

A knife?

He came towards her – straight at her! Ruby shrank away from the window and squeezed down into the footwell. He must surely see her! And when he did, he would open the door and reach in and murder her. Stab her in the heart. Cut her into little pieces.

She hadn't found the killer, but the killer had found her.

He was inches away. He reached the back window. But instead of smashing it and diving through it and grabbing her and slitting her throat, he bent and dropped almost out of sight.

Ruby found her voice. 'Daddy!' she screamed. Then she crawled up and along the seat and hammered on the window over the man's head. 'Daddy! Daddy! Daddy!'

The man staggered upright and stumbled backwards and for a second their eyes met through the glass. Then he threw up his arm to hide his face.

'Oi! *Oi!*'

Then suddenly the man was running and Daddy was running after him. Out of the darkness, past the car and after the stranger, their feet hitting the ground with a rhythmic ring, across the road and between the houses, where the night swallowed them both as if they'd never been.

Ruby sat, stunned, her hands and forehead pressed against the glass like something forgotten. Abandoned.

Then she wriggled between the front seats and locked both the doors, panting with fear.

She waited.

She waited.

She should get out and cross the car park and knock at one of the houses and asked them to call the police, but she was too scared to get out; too worried that the man might already have killed Daddy, and circled back through the dunes that squeezed the car park, and might even now be waiting for her to lose her nerve and make a run from the relative safety of the car.

Her heart caught up with her head.

He might have killed Daddy.

Ruby bit her lip hard, trying not to cry, but fear escaped her in a long thin whine she didn't even know she was making.

She tugged open the glovebox in search of a weapon, but there was only rubbish – cigarette papers, pens, a Bic lighter, a roll of black plastic tape, and a brown medicine bottle with a sticky lid.

Nothing she could use to fight off the stranger.

She even looked through the rear window at the dunes looming over the car. If she saw the man coming back along the road, she would run into the dunes and hide. The thought of leaving the car was terrifying, but she would do it if she had to.

From the tunnel of black that was the lane between the houses, a shadowy figure emerged, and Ruby's nerves sang like reeds.

She fumbled with the door handle and fell out of the car on her knees. Then she scrambled to her feet and ran into her father's arms.

'I thought you were never coming back,' she wept. 'I thought you were *dead*.'

He held her tight. 'I'm fine,' he said. 'Sssshh. I'm fine, Rubes.'

'I thought he was going to kill me,' sniffed Ruby against his ribs.

He laughed. 'He's not killing anyone. Specially not my best Deputy!'

They started towards the car.

'Was he the killer?'

Daddy shook his head. 'That wazzack? Nah, Rubes.

See how he run off? A killer doesn't run off like a big bloody baby. A killer stands and fights!'

'But what was he *doing*?' said Ruby.

'Shit.' Daddy stopped dead and pointed at the car. '*That*.'

Ruby didn't look.

She couldn't. She couldn't take her eyes off Daddy. Her breath went funny in her chest and she felt the damp sea air fill her mouth in shallow sips.

Daddy's arm was outstretched. His hand was pointing at the car.

And in his hand was a gun.

31

THE GUN WAS a beautiful thing. Made for the hand of a real cowboy, and the colour of a stormy sky.

Ruby and Daddy sat together in the car that had been made lopsided by the flat tyre and studied it by the sick yellow of the interior light.

'Is it *real*?' she whispered.

'No,' said Daddy, and a little of the magic left the gun. 'But it *looks* real, right?'

'Yeah! *Really* real.'

'It's called a Colt,' he said.

'*Wow!*' said Ruby. 'Like the horse!' That made it even better! Her tears and her fears were forgotten before the salt had even dried on her cheeks. All thought of danger had been chased away as quickly as Daddy had chased the stranger into the darkness. She was too enthralled to be scared any more.

'Where'd you get it?'

Daddy tapped the side of his nose to show that that was Top Secret.

'But what about the government?'

'What they don't know won't hurt 'em,' said Daddy.

'Can I see it?' Ruby reached out, but he pulled the gun away.

'You see with your eyes, not your hands.'

'Why not?' she said. 'If it's not real?'

Daddy looked serious. 'A gun's a dangerous thing, Rubes, even if it's not real.'

She wrinkled her nose. 'Why?'

'It's real enough to give you a good scare. And real enough to give you bad thoughts. And if anyone saw you with it, it's real enough to get you shot or arrested by some idiot policeman.'

Ruby nodded. All of that made sense.

But she still wanted to touch it.

'It's *amazing*,' she said dreamily.

But Daddy looked at her intently. 'Promise me you'll never touch it, Rubes.'

'*Never?*' That seemed like a big ask.

'Never. Promise?'

Ruby struggled and then pouted. 'I promise.'

'And promise me you'll never tell.'

'I promise.'

'This is the biggest secret of *all*, Deputy. I could get into proper trouble if anyone knew I'd got this. Don't tell Mummy. Don't tell *anyone*. Cross your heart?'

'And hope to die,' said Ruby.

'Good,' he said. 'Now I got to change the wheel. You stay in the car and keep a lookout down the road.'

Ruby looked around warily. 'Is the man coming back?'

'I doubt it,' said Daddy.

He got out of the car – and took the gun with him.

Daddy took for ever to change the wheel. First he had to go and find stones in the dunes to put under the other wheels. Then he banged and bumped about with the boot open, grunting and muttering and jacking the car up and then down again. When he dropped the wheel into the boot, the whole car tilted backwards.

And all the time Ruby kept nervous watch, perched on the tapestry cushion, riding the car up and down – scanning the road in case the bastard returned.

So she was the first to see the blue lights of police cars.

'Daddy!' She opened the door. 'Dad—'

'Stay there, Ruby! What did I say?'

She nervously pulled her foot back in and said, 'But Daddy, it's the police!'

'Shit!'

Daddy slammed the boot and wiped his hands on his jeans and squinted at the approaching lights. There were three cars. Two went up between the houses. The third came slowly closer until it drew up outside the car park, and then it turned in and came slowly towards them. Ruby could hear the sand grinding under its wheels, grain by grain.

The police car stopped thirty feet away, facing the front of their car, lights on.

Nothing happened.

'Daddy—'

'Shh,' said Daddy. 'Stay in the car and don't say *anything*.'

'But—'

He pushed her door shut.

Ruby was anxious. If she wasn't supposed to *say* anything, she hoped the police didn't *ask* her anything. The police were always out to get you, even if you hadn't done anything wrong.

For what felt like ages, nothing happened. She sat, Daddy stood and the police car stayed right there.

Finally a policeman got out of the car and came towards them.

'Evening, sir,' he said.

'All right?' said Daddy.

'Car trouble?'

'Got a flat,' said Daddy.

'Want a hand?'

'Sorted it now. Must've been this sharp gravel.' He kicked at the ground with his boot.

Ruby wondered why Daddy was lying. It wasn't *his* fault a bastard had popped the tyre. He should tell the police so they could catch him!

'Would you mind putting the tyre iron down, please, sir?'

John Trick looked at his hand as if he'd forgotten he was still holding it.

'Course,' he said. 'Sorry.' He bent and put it on the ground beside the car.

When they talked, it sounded like it did when Ruby's head was underwater in the bath. Sort of a long way off, even though they were right there.

'Can I ask your name, please, sir?'

'John Trick.'

The policeman nodded, then looked past Daddy

235

and straight at her. Ruby shrank back against the seat.

'And who's this?'

'My little girl.'

'And what's her name?'

'Ruby.'

'You mind if I have a quick word with her?'

'Why?'

The policeman smiled at Daddy. 'You mind if I have a quick word with her, sir?'

'Course not,' said Daddy. 'No bother.'

'Thanks. Would you mind waiting over by my car, sir?'

Daddy looked at him for a moment, then walked away. Ruby felt panicky to see him go. He stopped halfway between the two cars and turned round, silhouetted by the headlights.

The policeman came over and tapped on the window.

'Hi, Ruby. Can you open the door for me?'

She opened the door a crack.

The policeman opened it a bit more and squatted down on his haunches next to her. 'Hi,' he said. 'My name's Calvin. What's yours?'

Daddy had told her not to say anything, but how could she not tell a policeman her name? It was against the law.

'Ruby Trick.'

'Hello, Ruby,' said Calvin. 'Been anywhere nice tonight?'

'We went to get chips,' said Ruby. 'Then I got sweets and a magazine at the shop.' She held up *TeenBeatz*.

'That's nice,' he said. 'So that's your dad, is it?'

Ruby nodded.

'And where's your mummy?'

'At work.'

'Where's work?'

'The hotel.'

'Do you know the name of the hotel?'

Ruby thought about it, then screwed up her face. 'Something manor.'

'That's OK,' said Calvin. 'Do you know your address, Ruby?'

'The Retreat, Limeburn, North Devon.'

'I'm impressed,' said Calvin, writing it down.

'I know my phone number, too,' said Ruby proudly. 'I've known it for yonks. Since I was young.'

He laughed and said, 'And what's your mum's name?'

'Alison Trick.'

'And your dad?'

'John Trick.'

'Very good.' The policeman stood up and tucked his notebook into his pocket. 'Thanks, Ruby.'

'OK,' she said, basking in the warm glow of his approval. She'd got all the questions right and hadn't said anything about the posse or the broken headlight or the cowboy with the knife in his hand.

The policeman walked back towards John Trick. 'That's fine, thanks, Mr Trick,' he said. 'We've had a missing-person report, you see.'

'No problem.'

They both looked across the road. The police cars had parked somewhere in the narrow streets behind the houses, and their flickering lights lit up the tiled roofs like a school disco.

'Hope you find her,' said John Trick.

237

'Me too,' said the policeman.

The road came at them fast in a gritty black sheet, lit by their single headlight.

'Is the gun in the boot?' said Ruby.

Daddy said nothing.

'When we get home, can I see it again?'

'Leave it now, Rubes. When we get home you're going straight to bed.'

Daddy put on the radio and whistled along through his teeth, the way Ruby loved to hear. When she was little and they used to go on holiday to Cornwall, she would drowse on the back seat and listen to Daddy whistle along with Kenny Rogers and his four hundred children and his crop and his fields.

But tonight she couldn't stop thinking about the gun. She imagined touching it. Not that she was *going* to touch it. She'd promised Daddy and she was good at promises. But she could *imagine*, couldn't she? She could imagine how she'd look in the mirror, wearing the hat and the holster *with a gun* in it. She'd look like John Wayne. 'Specially if she took her bunny slippers off.

She imagined pointing the gun at Essie Littlejohn and watching her mean little face crumple in terror. Making her run. She imagined pulling the trigger. Pow! Pow-pow!

Not *at* Essie.

But not that far from her either.

Ruby grinned at the mental picture, then suddenly frowned at a dull bang from the back of the car.

'What's that?' said Ruby.

'What?' said Daddy.

Thud. Thud.

Ruby twisted in her seat to look behind them. There was nothing to see, of course, except the hedges glowing dull red in their tail lights.

Thud.

'What's that noise?' she said.

'I don't hear it,' said Daddy.

Ruby was nervous. The car had to break down one day. Why did it have to happen now when it was so late already and she was so tired? What if Mummy got home and found Panda instead of her?

Bang-bang.

'*There!*' she said.

Daddy shrugged into the rear-view mirror. 'The jack's come loose,' he said. 'I didn't put it back right and it's come loose.'

'Maybe it's the gun.'

'Will you shut up about the fucking *gun*? Jesus Christ, Ruby!'

Ruby flinched in shock and Daddy braked hard and swung into a farm gateway. He got out of the car and slammed the door and went round to the back and opened the boot.

Ruby twisted in her seat and watched him through the small strip of space between the boot and the back of the car. An inch of forearms, pushing down to make the jack fit.

It was her fault. He'd told her to leave it and she hadn't left it. She should have left it.

Daddy got back in and slammed the door again and blew out his cheeks like he'd just run up the slipway.

She eyed him nervously.

'I'm sorry I shouted, Rubes. It's just that sometimes you really wind me up.'

She nodded. 'Sorry, Daddy.'

He shook his head and stared out of the side window for a moment, then snorted in what might have been a laugh.

'You must get it from me. I was the same when I was your age. I used to wind up my mother's boyfriends all the time.'

Ruby was pleased to hear that she and Daddy were the same. 'How did you wind them up?' she said carefully.

'All sorts. I'd dance about in front of the telly. Or I'd get between them and Mum on the sofa. Or put mud in the bed. Just little things to make 'em mazed.'

'And what did *they* do?'

'Mostly nothing. Mostly just a whack here and there. But this one time I got out of the bath and peed in the water before he got in.'

Ruby laughed heartily, and Daddy gave a little smile. 'It *was* funny to start with. He chased me all through the house, bare-arse naked.

Ruby giggled. 'Were you scared?'

'You bet I was! I was only seven and he was so angry! He caught me in the kitchen,' said Daddy. He stopped for a moment, and adjusted his hands on the steering wheel and looked in the rear-view mirror. Ruby waited eagerly for him to go on, a smile near her lips.

'He caught me in the kitchen,' said Daddy again, 'and held my face down on the hot stove.'

Ruby's smile froze.

'Really?'

'Really.'

Slowly she looked up at Daddy's face. For the first time she read the scars not as random puckers, but as three rough pink rings. She thought of the heat coming off the spiral plate, and shuddered.

'I thought a dog bit you,' she whispered.

He shook his head. 'We just told people that because we didn't want the police coming round. Still, I got a month off school, so it wasn't all bad.'

He winked at Ruby, but she didn't feel like smiling.

'What was his name?'

'Kevin,' said Daddy. Then he frowned and said, 'Or Steve. Or Dave. One of them. They all had hands.' He laughed again, but Ruby didn't.

'Did your Mummy break up with him?'

'No.'

'Why not?'

'I told you!' said Daddy impatiently. 'It was *my* fault. I was always winding them up. That's all I'm saying, Rubes – don't wind people up. When people say leave it, then just *leave* it, OK?'

'OK,' said Ruby quickly, even though her brain was bursting with questions. She glanced at him every few seconds, gauging his mood, waiting for a thaw. But Daddy kept staring at the road ahead, his hands tight on the wheel.

Then – after a mile or two – Daddy went on talking, as if they'd never stopped.

'We needed him to stay, see? Because we didn't have anything and he took care of us.'

Ruby nodded, although she didn't understand. Not one little bit.

'Women can't help it,' shrugged Daddy.

Women can't help it.

Daddy had said the same thing about Mummy, the night they'd fought over the Jingle Bobs and the job and the fancy man.

Ruby nodded. She still remembered what it was that women couldn't help.

Being whores.

～

By the time the car bobbled to a halt on the square, Ruby was asleep again.

Daddy got out and came round to her side. He took her hand and tugged gently, and she followed her arm out of the car and on to unsteady legs. It had stopped raining and the wind had dropped, and Ruby could taste the sea. If she kept her eyes shut, then maybe she could make it all the way to bed without really waking up.

To her surprise, Daddy picked her up, with one arm under her back and the other behind her knees. Ruby let it happen. She turned her face into his shoulder and put an arm around his neck, and couldn't remember the last time she'd been carried like this. She wished it could last for ever, this swaying, jogging feeling of being lifted and held like a baby again.

He carried her across the cobbles and up the short hill to The Retreat.

When they got to the step, he put her down carefully and opened the door.

'Don't wake Mummy,' he whispered.

She nodded sleepily and whispered back, 'Where are you going?'

'Just to clean out the car.'

Ruby hugged him. 'Love you hundreds, Daddy.'

'Love you hundreds, Rubes.'

He closed the front door behind him.

Ruby hauled herself up the narrow, curved stairs. Her legs were heavy and her arms swung like wet ropes. She didn't do her teeth; she didn't have a pee. She didn't even touch Lucky for luck.

In the few seconds before she fell asleep, Ruby only had one thought.

I have to hold the gun.

32

STEFFI COLE WAS almost home when she stopped being a person and became a means to an end.

Just past the Boat House restaurant, something hard jabbed her in the back, and when she turned to be cross with some joker, a man with no face hissed, 'Keep walking. This is a gun.'

So Steffi kept walking. She tried to keep thinking, too, but she had to keep walking while she was thinking, because of the gun.

Was it robbery? She could cope with robbery. She had sixty-five quid in her jeans. She wouldn't volunteer it, but if he found it, he could have it.

Was it rape? She braced herself mentally. If she had to, she would cope with a rape. As long as the man didn't hurt her, she could cope with anything, she realized.

Funny how your perspective changed as fast as the circumstances.

The man kept jabbing her in the middle of her back. She tried to decide whether it felt like a gun. As if she would know! It was probably a lie. Nobody had a gun. Nobody in Instow, anyway.

But could she take that chance? Steffi thought about

the possible consequences of failing to outrun the man. Of him shooting her in the spine before she'd gone five paces.

Life in a wheelchair, peeing in a bag.

She thought of falling, of being caught, of making him angry. She thought of the *embarrassment* of running in terror – in case it *was* a joke after all and she looked like an idiot.

Even as part of her mind was screaming at her to slow down and stay close to the houses and pubs, so the alleged gun forced Steffi away from them. An obedient, self-destructive auto-pilot had been switched on inside, and she had lost manual override. And before she came up with any practical way to escape, she simply ran out of time.

'In here.'

Another sharp jab in her back, between the shoulder blades, and Steffi turned left and stepped on to the fine sand of the dunes.

She went up the first of them, her feet sinking deep into the white sand.

'Where are we going?' she said.

He didn't answer for a few strides, and then he said, 'We're going to call your mother.'

Steffi's stomach lurched as if she were on a roller-coaster.

She knew exactly what he meant.

Not robbery. Not rape. She felt hollow and dis-believing. Not ten minutes ago she'd picked up her wages and told her boss she'd see him tomorrow, and now here she was, with a gun in her back and being prodded towards what the *Gazette* promised was 'unspeakable horror'.

She also couldn't believe she'd kept walking along the sea front as if everything was normal. She should have just run. *That* was an escape plan. *That*'s what might have saved her. But she'd thought too hard about it.

Thinking hard was natural to Steffi. Putting sweets in bags and scooping ice cream at Paul's was just a casual job for her. Her real life was studying for a B.Sc. in computer science. She was in her second year at Bristol, absolutely nailing modules in ethical hacking and counter-measures.

Counter-measures. The word mocked her now as she stumbled in the soft sand and hauled herself up the slope by a tuft of tough beachgrass. She'd never taken self-defence classes; never watched a Jackie Chan film. Not even ironically. And she'd refused a ride all the way home when she was offered one – out of sheer complacency. She could *kick* herself. Her whole future was about outsmarting the opposition and yet here she was, on a dark and deserted dune with what was probably a murderer.

If he *wasn't* a murderer, she'd be fucking furious. If this was some sick ruse to get her to a beach party with her friends, then this guy was a dead man. The second he pulled off that silly balaclava and said 'Surprise' she'd punch his bloody lights out.

Scream.

That was *another* thing she could've done while she was still close to the houses, Steffi realized too late.

Run. Scream. Both required instinct, not logic.

Her logic might cost her her life, and Steffi filled up momentarily at the unfairness of that.

Then she got a grip. She mustn't stop thinking, just because she was playing catch-up on her animal instincts. Logic dictated that she could still find a way out of this. They were almost at the top of the dune. Steffi knew these dunes like the back of her hand. She'd played here as a child, walked the family dog here, had her first kiss here. It was with Barry Stoodley. He'd been too spitty, and she'd been too worried about being seen.

Another five or six awkward strides and she'd be at the top.

That would be the time to run. When she could get up some instant acceleration down the other side, while the *arsehole* behind her was still struggling on the ascent. Steffi felt excitement confirm that it was the right thing to do. She visualized it, the way she did with her tennis serve. That was the secret to sporting success – visualization. So she knew the exact moment when she would attain the peak of the dune. At that very second she would run down the slope of sand. She would have thirty feet on him before he could even reach the ridge and start down after her. That would be enough. Even if he *did* have a gun. It was dark and the sand gave no good footing, and she recalled reading somewhere that most people couldn't hit a barn door at ten paces with a handgun; it was harder than it looked, apparently.

If she could just get that first run down the dune . . .

She knew all the paths and shortcuts – the sharp right turn and then the little dogleg that would look as though she was heading back to safety – back to the lights of the

Boat House. But then there was the clever little loop that would let her double back through a narrow gorge in the dunes and come out a hundred yards away on flat, hard sand, which was so good for running.

And this time she *would* run—

'Stop here.'

'What?'

'I said stop.'

Steffi stopped, staring up at the dune's dark horizon, jagged with grass and tantalizingly close.

He wasn't going to let her reach the top.

'Take off your clothes.'

'What do you want?'

'Take off your clothes.'

Steffi's fear made her angry and her anger made her brave. She decided to take control and put a stop to this before she became inert with terror. It wasn't nipping it in the bud – the bud had already opened so it was too late for that – but calling a halt could be done at any time, and she needed to use her calm, scientific brain if she was going to change this situation to her advantage. She needed to act like a B.Sc. undergrad, not some disposable extra in a murderous teen flick.

She mustered all the calm confidence that she could.

'I'm just going to turn round, OK?'

'No you're not.'

'I'm going to do it very, very slowly,' she said reassuringly.

She started to turn and he hit her hard in the face.

Steffi fell down, although because the slope was so

steep, she didn't have far to go, and landed sitting in soft sand, facing the man.

'Now give me your phone and take off your clothes.'

She looked up at him in a weird, jerky daze. He did have a gun – he hadn't lied about that. But was this the same man who had killed that Frannie girl? She hadn't been *shot*. She'd been strangled or something like that, hadn't she? Something manual. Through the pain in her cheek and nose, Steffi wondered which was worse – to be shot or to be strangled. Logically, she'd rather be shot because it was over in a second and there was a quick end to the fear – but with manual there was always a chance you'd find a way out of it. Something might happen to come and rescue you. There was more chance of rescue or a miracle.

Manual *must* be better.

Steffi was starting to realize that logic had no place when it came to murder.

It was too late now anyway. The gun was what had kept her walking like a sheep when she should have been running and screaming and getting away. And that was all that mattered.

She gave him her phone and she took off her clothes. As she folded her green and white striped blouse, she wondered whether someone would soon be identifying her by that awful photo on her Students' Union card. That would be as humiliating in death as it was in life.

Taking off her jeans in front of a stranger felt like a point of no return. There was no miracle: no knight in shining armour; no swooping Hollywood rescue; no beach-bum wino stumbling into view to scare the man away. Nothing happened to stop Steffi sliding the rough denim down her thighs and wobbling as she stood on one leg to step out of them.

Nothing to stop her crying.

She tried to stop stripping at her knickers, but the man stared at her until she was naked. She shivered and sobbed and tried to cover her privates and her breasts, but he didn't seem that interested in them anyway, so she hugged her arms instead.

'I'm cold,' she whispered.

He laughed. 'Not as cold as you're going to be.'

Steffi felt a whirring panic in her head and belly. She still didn't believe that *this* was how her life was going to end, but she needed to do something fast and she didn't know what. She had a future. She had *plans*. She was only twenty. She had a sister called Maggie, and a cat called Mouse, and she hadn't bought her father a birthday present yet. She'd been a bit short last month and had put an IOU in a card.

IOU One Birthday Pressie (when I get my student loan). Kiss Kiss Kiss.

She'd thought it was cute. *He*'d thought it was cute. It wasn't cute, she realized now; it was selfish. She had money for cigarettes, didn't she? She had money for a bus to Barnstaple to see the latest Johnny Depp film. But she didn't have money for a birthday present for her own father.

Where was the logic in *that*? There was none. She sobbed harder.

He made Steffi sit down.

He made her call her mother.

It was a blur. A numb blur of horror. Her mother was *so close*. If Steffi hadn't been crying so hard, she could have picked out the porch light from the electric kaleidoscope that Instow had become. Steffi could barely speak; she was one big shake. Her teeth chattered and her hands trembled so badly that the man had to hold the phone.

'Say goodbye now,' he said.

Steffi's mother was pixellated by hysterics. Steffi tried to calm her. Tried to calm herself. Still thinking there would be a way out. Still not believing.

But then the man gripped her hair in his left hand and started to force her face down towards the sand.

Frannie Hatton had been *suffocated*. It came back to Steffi in a jagged flash. The word conjured a pillow, but it could have been anything; it could have been sand.

This *was* the man. This *was* the killer.

She stuck out her arms and tried to brace herself away from the beach, but the man kicked the inside of her elbow and it collapsed like a hinge.

He bent her almost double, pressing her nose and mouth into the choking sand, his knee in her back, one relentless hand in her hair, the other holding the phone so her mother could see what she'd done.

'You see?' he kept saying. 'You see?'

Steffi finally believed it was possible for her to die here in the dunes, with the beach in her teeth, not a hundred yards from her home.

Her bladder surrendered, and so did she.

With the last strength she had left, she twisted her

head so that her mouth could draw one final breath . . .

'Tell Daddy I'm sorry about the present.'

Then she drowned in the sand.

And nobody would ever find her.

33

STEFFI COLE WAS lighter than Jody Reeves, but not as light as Frannie Hatton.

For the hundredth time, John Trick was grateful that he hadn't killed that first girl on the beach. He'd never been a big man, and the thought of picking his way across the precarious pebbles with Kelly Bradley's fat arse slung over his shoulder was comical to him now.

A stone shifted under his left foot and he stopped and adjusted his balance. It was hard enough to walk across the beach in the daylight. At night and with a weight, it required great care and patience.

He'd learned patience. His lack of it had almost blown it for him right at the start . . .

He'd stopped the car beside Frannie Hatton on the road between Bideford and Westward Ho! At first she'd been grateful to him for the offer of a ride. And then, for some reason he couldn't work out, she'd changed her mind. Just straightened up and backed away and said, 'Actually, thanks, but I think I'll walk.'

Cheeky little slut. With her stringy junkie arms and her nose ring and her tattoos. Saying no – like she was better than him.

Like *she* was calling the shots.

So he'd got out to show her who was really in charge. Right there under the streetlights that made everything orange and weird.

Frannie Hatton had just stood there, watching him come around the front of the car, with her mouth open like a fish. She couldn't believe what was happening. He could hardly believe it himself.

Too late, she'd turned to run . . . And he'd grabbed her arm.

The moment his fingers had closed on her bicep, John Trick had known he was going to kill her. There was no going back, even if he'd wanted to go back. Which he didn't.

So he'd gone on.

He'd gone too far and it had felt so good.

She had fought him, mind. She was only a skinny little thing, but Frannie had fought like two rats in a bag. She'd even bitten his hand as he'd bundled her into the car. If another car had passed it would all have been over. He'd just got lucky. He'd learn from that, too.

He'd driven erratically to the Burrows. He'd forced her out of the car at gunpoint. What choice did she have? And then he'd led her away from the car and over the golf course to a shallow bunker of mud.

It hadn't stopped raining all summer and mud was easy to come by.

She'd had a phone, of course. Everybody had a phone nowadays, even if they didn't have a job.

'Call your mother.'

Her mother had hung up the phone before he'd got

started, which was gutting, and then had ignored the second call – the uncaring whore. But when he'd finally got Frannie Hatton face-down, and his fingers had got a good grip on her hair, and he'd pressed down, down, down . . .

He'd felt all the control leave her body and pass up his arm to his own. Filling him with power, making him *mighty*.

Just thinking of it now made him feel like a man.

John Trick put Steffi down with a grunt, and looked at the naked bodies already laid out at his feet. A rat ran out of the stinking darkness and between Jody Reeves' small, firm breasts.

Trick hadn't felt this good about himself since he'd started work at the shipyard when he was sixteen years old. Something inside him swelled a little. If he remembered correctly, it felt a lot like pride. Pride in himself and pride in Ruby. He'd been wary about taking her with him, but it had paid off in spades. Killing was much easier when his daughter was with him.

It was his little cowboy who'd shown him how it should be done in the first place. Picking up her teacher at the bus stop was a stroke of genius. The way the woman's suspicion had changed to grateful acceptance as soon as she saw a little girl out for a drive with her daddy.

Who *wouldn't* get into the car?

It'd be rude *not* to.

The wind snatched the laugh from John Trick's mouth.

Ruby was the key. Sometimes he wondered whether

she knew all along what she was doing. How she was teaching him, just as he taught her.

Like tonight – he should have made sure Steffi was dead in the dunes – but the terror in Ruby's voice had been like an alarm going off inside him. She was in danger. His own flesh and blood needed him. He didn't want to make excuses, but it was *biological*.

As long as he learned from his mistakes – that was the important thing. It was like starting a new job. Nobody could be expected to know everything to begin with, but when you got it right – when it was *textbook* – the sense of achievement was overwhelming.

Addictive.

Murder was a learning curve. But he was getting better at it all the time.

34

MARK SPADE HAD sworn off heroin the day his girl-friend Frannie had been found murdered, so it was no surprise to find him serenely high when Calvin and King arrived with a search warrant.

They didn't even need to show him the warrant; he was totally cool with anything they wanted to do. He let them into the dingy, cluttered bedsit and then stood with his back to the door while Calvin and King stared around at the clothing and garbage, scattered knee-deep in places, and hoped they could avoid an actual search with a simple question.

'We're looking for Frannie's nose ring, Mark,' said DCI King. 'Have you come across it?'

Mark Spade didn't answer, and when Calvin looked more closely he realized why.

'He's asleep,' he said.

'You're kidding,' said King. 'He's standing up!'

'Oi, Mark,' said Calvin. He tapped the man's shoulder and Spade opened his eyes and said, 'Ask my probation officer if you don't believe me.'

King and Calvin both laughed and Spade's eyes cleared a tiny bit and he said, 'What?'

'We're looking for Frannie's nose ring, Mark,' King tried again. 'Remember? The ring she always had in her nose?'

'Oh yeah,' he nodded. 'Her nose ring.'

'That's the one,' said King. 'Do you know where it is?'

'In her nose.'

'No it's not, Mark. Remember? It wasn't in her nose when we found her.'

'She never takes it out.'

'Well, she took it out this time, Mark. Or someone else did. Or maybe she took it out here, so that's what we want to make sure of. If it's not here then it might be a good clue for us, see? To try and find the man who killed her.'

'Oh yeah.'

'So can we look around then?'

'Her nose?'

'The flat. Can we look round the flat?'

'This flat?'

'Yes, this one.'

'OK.'

'Thanks,' said King. 'Can you remember what it looks like, Mark?'

'The flat?'

'The nose ring.'

'It's a ring. In her nose.'

'OK, good. What colour?'

'Colour?'

'Was it silver or gold?'

'Yes.'

'Which one?'

Mark Spade frowned and closed his eyes in an effort to recall the nose ring.

After a minute, Calvin nudged him again and he woke up and said, 'Silver.'

'Do you use needles, Mark?'

'No needles,' he said. 'Spoons.'

'So we're not going to get stuck, are we? Because if DC Bridge or I get stuck, we're going to be very pissed off.'

'No no no,' he insisted, shoving up his sleeves to show off his arms. 'Only spoons.'

Calvin opened a drawer in the ramshackle area that looked most like a kitchen, and held up a bent and buckled spoon, scraps of foil and a selection of Bic lighters.

'He's a smoker, not a poker.'

'Right then,' sighed King, snapping on a latex glove. 'I suppose we'll get started.'

They spent all day in the bedsit. Mark Spade slept on the sofa throughout, and so they decided to simply pile everything they'd searched on one side of the room, and then move it all back again and do the same to the other half.

It was disgusting, even with the gloves.

Among the clothing and debris on the floor they uncovered a selection of paper plates covered in what looked like bean juice, dozens of unopened packets of supernoodles and the various scattered components of what looked like a hamster cage, including a broken plastic wheel and wood shavings. Everything in the room was sprinkled with small pellets of shit, as if someone had spilled a big carton of chocolate Tic-Tacs.

Around lunchtime, Mark Spade woke up and demanded spaghetti hoops on toast. There was no bread or spaghetti, or even a pan that Calvin could see, so he went out and got three portions of fish and chips. But by the time he got back, Mark was asleep again.

King and Calvin ate standing up. Mark was on the sofa, and the only other chair was piled high with egg cartons and three Jack Daniels bottles filled with urine.

After lunch, they put on new gloves and worked their way methodically through the mountains of stinking trash and unwashed clothing and droppings, and there was no nose ring, although nose *plugs* would not have gone amiss.

'It's all glamour,' sighed King.

They searched the bathroom and toilet during an hour of overtime Calvin knew they wouldn't get paid for, and they finally felt reasonably confident that there was no square inch of the filthy bedsit that hadn't been checked.

Except the sofa, where Mark Spade was now snoring loudly.

'We should look down the back of the sofa,' said King. 'In fact, when I think about it, we should really have looked there first.'

Calvin shuddered. 'Can't we just wake him up and tell *him* to do it?'

'C'mon! Where's your sense of adventure?'

'*My* sense of adventure?'

'Yes,' said King. 'Obviously I'm going to pull rank on you.'

'Can't we toss for it?'

'No,' said King. Then added more encouragingly, 'Go on. Anything you find, you can keep.'

Calvin sighed and went over to the sofa and shook Mark Spade until it was clear he wasn't going to wake up. Then he and King dragged the sleeping man carefully on to the poo-strewn carpet, and Calvin dug his hand down the side of the cushions. The sofa was corduroy, he noticed, and now he knew why Shirley wouldn't have sex on hers. It was a smorgasbord of suspicious stains, flaky lumps and congealed spaghetti hoops.

He dug his hand down the first side and moved it carefully around, removing anything solid. He found three ballpoint pens, a Bourbon biscuit, eighty-eight pence in small change, countless salt sachets, and a ticket to a Killers concert.

He dived in again.

'Ha!' He held up a five-pound note, folded into a small, thick triangle. 'Mine!'

'You can't keep anything *valuable*,' King qualified.

Calvin muttered darkly and went back in.

He was almost done when he said, 'What the *shit*?' and withdrew his hand with a look of disgust on his face.

King came over and peered at the dark, sticky chunk of *something* impaled on the tips of Calvin's fingers. At one end of it was a ragged piece of fuzzy string.

Calvin sniffed it and almost choked. 'What. The fuck. Is that?'

'Tampon!'

They both jumped and turned to look at Mark Spade, who was suddenly awake, alert and cheerful as hell.

261

'A tampon?' said King, aghast.

'Not *a* tampon! Just Tampon. Frannie's mouse. He went AWOL ages ago.'

Calvin's fingers were in a dead mouse.

He cried out and flicked his hand in horror and the corpse arced across the room and stuck to the wall above the television.

'Shit!' he shouted. 'ShitshitshitshitSHIT!' He bounded off the sofa and rushed to the kitchen area, where he peeled off his glove and tossed it in the sink on top of the pile of mouldy dishes, then turned on the tap.

'There's no soap!' he yelled while DCI King giggled like a schoolgirl.

'Yeah, there is,' said Mark Spade calmly, and got up and came over to the nearly weeping Calvin. He bent and opened the oven and took out a large cardboard box, still sealed with packing tape. He slit it open with one long, dirty fingernail, and Calvin could see that the box was filled with what must have been fifty bars of designer soap, each individually presented in its own upmarket paper wrapper with – he couldn't help but notice – hand-torn edges.

Spade took a deep sniff before handing it to a desperate Calvin.

'Cinnamon and myrrh,' he breathed.

'Think you've got enough?' said King, peering into the box.

Mark Spade looked at her seriously and said, 'You can never have too much soap.'

They left the bedsit without the nose ring, but each clutching a gift of soap that had been pressed into their hands by Mark Spade, despite their protestations.

'For Frannie,' he kept saying. 'For Frannie.'

Cinnamon and myrrh filled the Volvo as Kirsty King drove back to Bideford. Even so, Calvin couldn't wait to get home, strip off, and scrub himself in a hot shower until the soap was a mere nub of scented heaven.

In a rare show of sympathy, DCI King had let him keep the fiver, but it was nowhere near enough.

35

RUBY COULDN'T STOP thinking about the gun. She wanted so badly to tell somebody about it that she thought she might burst.

From the window she saw Adam and Chris disappearing up the Clovelly pathway. Quickly she struggled into her coat and boots, but by the time she had puffed and slithered up to the clearing on the cliff, they were nowhere to be seen.

Maggie was on the swing – hung over the fraying rope like a dishcloth, with her knees dragging in the mud.

'Have you seen Adam?'

'They went over the stile,' croaked Maggie.

Ruby was almost relieved. Now she couldn't tell Adam about the gun. And telling would have been *wrong*, because it was a big secret.

So big that Daddy had kept it from *her*.

Ruby didn't even want to admit to herself how much that hurt. They were supposed to keep secrets from *Mummy* – not from each other.

It made her feel . . .

It made her feel . . .

Not *angry*, but . . .

Something.

Out of habit, she bent and picked up a stick from the forest floor. It fitted well in her hand, but she stared at the damp, gnarled wood with sudden disdain. Only a stupid little kid would think a stick was a gun. Now she'd seen the real thing she could never go back.

Something inside Ruby missed the stick, even as she hurled it into the forest.

She flopped disconsolately on to the bench. The wooden slats were damp and had little aqua flowers of lichen growing all over them. She picked at them intently, peeling them away from their home and flicking them towards the swing.

Finding stuff out wasn't all good.

The gun was good, but it had ruined the sticks for her. Having secrets was good, but keeping them was *hard*. And growing up was good, but, at the same time, she didn't want to lose that warm, safe, little-girl feeling of being carried in her daddy's arms.

She had been so impatient for everything to change, and now that it had, she had the strangest sense of wanting to reach out and slow it all down – maybe stop it altogether – just for a little while, while she decided what she thought about it all.

She sighed deeply and blew out her cheeks and stared at the dank forest.

'Hey,' she said suddenly, 'where's Em?'

'Over there,' said Maggie vaguely towards the sea.

Ruby wandered across the clearing, brushed aside the overhanging branches, and there she saw Em, sitting on the edge of the cliff, high above the beach, her bare legs and pink glittery wellington boots dangling in space, and the hem of her dress hitched up so high that Ruby could see the blue elastic of the Pampers she still wore. Em sang tunelessly under her breath, kicking her legs in time to an imagined beat.

She didn't see Ruby.

Quietly, Ruby stretched out her arm, the way Daddy had on the beach – catching Em in the sights created by her thumbnail and finger. She imagined the butt of the gun snug in her palm, her finger curled around the cool trigger, and the glimmering curve of the bullets winking at her from the fat, grooved barrel.

Real enough to give you a good scare. And real enough to give you bad thoughts.

She thought of the jolt of the shot, the high-pitched scream on the way down, of Em hitting the big black pebbles a hundred feet below.

One of the toddler's boots had worked its way down her chubby little leg, and she leaned forward to stop it falling off.

'Ruby?' Maggie called from the swing.

Ruby opened her mouth to answer . . . then closed it. And just watched.

Em teetered – trying to grasp the top edge of the plastic boot. She gripped it briefly, then her fingers slid off, and her whole body wavered back and forth with the recoil before steadying.

Ruby breathed again.

But Em leaned forward once more . . . seemingly oblivious to the drop, grunting with the effort of bending so far to reach something that had now slipped even further down her leg, a bubble of snot starting to blow in and out of her rosy nose, while with her other hand she tried to keep her tangled blonde hair out of her eyes.

Ruby suppressed a small pang of guilt. Em wasn't *her* sister. She didn't *love* Em. Em was a pain who slowed them all down, with her short legs and her socks always wrinkling into her rubber boots, and the foul stench that often wafted from her over-padded rear end. Whatever happened, it wasn't Ruby's fault. No one would blame her. She'd have something exciting to write in her diary and everyone would want to be her friend.

Nothing could beat a dead child.

Em grunted in frustration, and kicked her legs – and the boot flew off. She lunged to try to catch it, her centre of gravity tipping suddenly too far—

Ruby grabbed the hood of Em's coat and yanked her back from the edge, dragging her away, across the mud and stones, her heart thudding with how close it had come – how close she had *let* it come . . .

Her adrenalin raced. 'NO!' she shouted in Em's face and shook her too hard. 'NO!'

Em's face screwed up and she started to roar with fright.

Ruby didn't care. *She* was the one who should be roaring with fright. It served Em right if she had got a shock. It was better than falling off a cliff, wasn't it? Let her cry. Ruby almost slapped her too, just for being so stupid.

'What's wrong?' said Maggie, running from the clearing.

'Em nearly fell off the cliff,' said Ruby. 'I saved her just in time.'

Maggie stared at her and then at Em. 'Oh,' she said, 'thanks.' Then she grabbed Em roughly by the hand and shook her too, prompting new screams.

'I told you not to go close to the edge! Where's your other boot?'

'It fell over the cliff,' said Ruby.

Maggie rolled her eyes – just the way Ruby had seen Maggie's mother do.

'Come on, you,' she said, and started back down the path, pulling the bawling Em behind her with her one wrinkled sock already clotted with mud and trailing out behind her.

When they had gone, Ruby edged to the drop on her knees so she could look over. Far below on the beach, a tiny pink L was Em's boot.

Empty of a child.

Ruby stayed there for ages, just looking at it.

She couldn't help feeling disappointed.

36

MISS SHARPE SMILED at Mr and Mrs Trick. It was what she liked to call her Meet the Parents Smile: head tilted, eyebrows a little concerned, teeth not showing. It was a smile that said, *Your child is special and unique and wonderful. BUT . . .*

Mrs Sharpe sincerely wished she had time to invite parents along just to tell them that their children were well behaved and handed their homework in on time; it would have been a refreshing change. Still, it was good that both Ruby's parents had come. It was so nice when the fathers engaged.

While she'd waited, Miss Sharpe had played her personal guessing game. She had met Mr Trick already, of course. He was wiry and brown, with dark sideburns. Sideburns that were just that little bit too long, perhaps? Verging on the Elvis impersonator. Miss Sharpe liked a good Elvis, but Elvis was The King and Mr Trick was plainly not – although when they arrived he *was* dressed in black boots, black jeans and black shirt – a dusty Comeback Special.

Mr Trick looked nothing like Ruby, so Miss Sharpe had imagined that Mrs Trick would be a stout and freckled redhead to make up for it. But when Alison Trick walked in, Miss Sharpe gave herself one mark out of ten – and felt *that* was being generous. She had never been a beauty herself, but had always appreciated beauty in others, and Ruby Trick's mother had been beautiful.

Apart from the tired smudges around her eyes, she still was.

Mrs Trick's skin was flawless – that clear, pale complexion that is only achieved through good genes moisturized by rain. Her bobbed hair was the colour of ripe wheat, while her eyes were icy blue, and fringed with long, coppery lashes.

She was so far out of Mr Trick's league that Miss Sharpe wondered how he'd got so lucky. Even *she* felt a little flustered by it.

'Now I see where Ruby gets her lovely red hair,' she gushed, but Mrs Trick didn't smile. She only brushed her own hair around one ear in a nervous tic and said, 'It runs in my family.'

Mrs Trick couldn't take a compliment. She sounded dismissive – almost defensive – and Miss Sharpe decided to move swiftly on.

'Have a seat,' she said. They all sat on the children's chairs because parents were *equals*, and they quickly got on to first-name terms because this wasn't the 1950s.

Alison and John.

'Thanks so much for coming,' Miss Sharpe kicked off. 'Ruby's a wonderful little girl.'

Silence.

That was unusual. That was the point where the parents always said, *Thank you!* Or *Yes, we think she's a genius.* Or *We're glad to hear you say so, because at home she's a little shit.*

Something.

But Ruby Trick's parents said nothing. They just continued to look at Miss Sharpe with mild concern. They seemed to have no interest in the *wonderful.* Only in the *BUT . . .*

So Miss Sharpe stopped the flannel and got to the point.

'But the reason I've asked you here is because I'm just a little bit concerned about her, too. Lately she's been quite tired at school.'

Miss Sharpe noticed that Alison glanced at her husband, but he didn't return the look.

'She seems fine at home.'

'She's not complained of feeling unwell?'

Alison smiled faintly. 'Only every day. She tries it on, you know? All kids do, don't they?'

'Of course,' said Miss Sharpe. She smiled and hesitated before continuing. 'There's something else I'm a bit concerned about.' She took Ruby's diary off the table. 'Sometimes she uses inappropriate language.'

'Like swearing?' said Alison.

'No. Well, yes, but attitudes too,' said Miss Sharpe, suddenly wishing that John Trick hadn't been engaged enough to come along. 'She's started using derogatory words like "slag" and "bitch", and even more in-appropriate things . . .'

'Really?' Alison Trick looked genuinely surprised.

'Not a lot, but it seems to be getting worse.'

'Can I see?'

Feeling herself starting to redden, Miss Sharpe fumbled the book around so that Alison could read it, which she did – out loud.

'*Daddy loves Mummy, even though she is a whore.*'

There was an uncomfortable silence.

So uncomfortable.

So silent.

Alison Trick handed the book back without a word, but there were two new small rosy patches on her pale cheeks. Like a doll. She didn't look at her husband.

'I hope I haven't upset you,' said Miss Sharpe.

Alison just shook her head, so Miss Sharpe went on, 'Please don't worry unduly. Children make up all sorts of rubbish in their diaries. I'd have to be in cloud cuckoo land to believe half this stuff! I mean, I've got children in my class who would be in the circus – or in prison – if you believed everything they wrote!'

Miss Sharpe knew she was talking too much, but that was only because they weren't talking at all. She wasn't used to people who didn't know how to hold up their end of the conversational bargain, and now she couldn't stop babbling.

'Obviously I don't want the children to feel inhibited while writing their diaries, but this is a little unusual.'

Alison gave a small, brief smile. 'My mother used to say, "A bit of inhibition goes a long way."'

Miss Sharpe blushed. Alison Trick was right. She should have been more strict about the diaries. More of a grown-up.

'Can I see that?' John held out his hand for the diary.

Trick flicked blindly through the little blue book on his lap, while his brain churned. Random words skittered accusingly along the blue lines. Bitches and skanks and slags . . . his own words and thoughts bounced back to him now off the pages of a child's diary.

Only slags paint their nails.

If she was hitching she was just asking for it.

Whore.

Adam.

He stopped and read that.

Adam brought me a donkey from Clovelly. Its the best present I ever got.

Adam Braund sniffing around. Just like his father. He'd have to keep a closer eye on that little prick. You couldn't trust anyone. Everyone was—

My Daddy's got a gun.

John Trick went numb. He stared blankly at the words between his thumbs.

My Daddy's got a gun. Not a real one a play one but he won't let me touch it because its real enough to give you a good scare, he says. I promised not to tell and I'm good at promises and nobody sticks together with Daddy.

Only me.

John Trick's head spun.

She'd promised not to tell. She'd *promised*.

Just like Alison had promised to love, honour and obey.

Just like his mother had promised to kick her boyfriend out . . .

But she hadn't. Not even when he'd cried and tried to tell her how frightened he'd been; how he'd pissed down his own bare legs as the mighty hand on the back of his head pressed his face down towards the searing heat. Even then she hadn't seen. Hadn't *wanted* to see.

You don't understand, Johnny, she'd said.

But he *did* understand.

He understood every night when he heard the boyfriend fucking her.

'John?'

Alison's voice swam towards John Trick through the sea in his ears.

The rest of the meeting was a blur of nodding and agreeing and promising to speak to Ruby about things, and of thanks and goodbye.

They were almost out of the door when the teacher said, 'Oh, Ruby's diary . . .'

Trick looked down stupidly at the blue exercise book he was still holding.

'Oh,' he said. 'Sorry.'

Miss Sharpe smiled and held out her hand, and he gave it back to her.

As soon as Mummy and Daddy left to see Miss Sharpe, Ruby ran upstairs to find the gun.

The cowboy drawer squeaked and grunted like a wooden pig, and got stuck halfway at an angle. She knelt down and leaned into the deep old wooden drawer and felt as far as she could go. Her fingers nudged the gun-belt, slid over the brim of the Stetson, shifted the Texas string tie. Right at the back, her fingers closed on something soft and she took out a black woollen hat.

She'd never seen it. It must be for fishing on the beach in the winter when it got so cold.

She pulled it on and it went right over her face! Ruby giggled, then realized there was a hole in it. She yanked it off quickly, with a little tingle of fear in case *she*'d made the hole and Daddy would know she'd been messing with his stuff, but in fact there were three holes and they were *meant* to be there. One for the mouth and two for the eyes. Ruby pulled it over her face again and looked at herself in the mirror. She could see one eye, one cheek and a bit of her chin. She looked pretty funny. She giggled and kept it on while she dug her arm back into the drawer.

The Jingle Bobs clinked musically, but the gun wasn't there, and nothing else held her interest now.

Ruby frowned and sat back on her heels. The gun should be with Daddy's cowboy stuff. Where *else* would he keep it?

The hat was hot and itchy, so she yanked it off again and stuffed it back in the drawer. Then she went through Daddy's wardrobe, looking in shoes, patting pockets, lifting underpants.

Nothing.

Under the bed.

Nothing but dust bunnies the size of mice.

Ruby brushed them off her T-shirt and sat on the bed and frowned.

Then she searched the rest of the house. The gun wasn't in the wardrobe and it wasn't behind the sofa and it wasn't in any of the kitchen drawers or cupboards. It wasn't in a whole lot of other places too.

She did find the custard creams in the washing machine though, so the evening wasn't entirely wasted.

Alison Trick managed to reach the car before she spoke.

'*Mummy is a whore?*' she said

'I don't know where she got *that* from,' said John. 'Maybe that Maggie Beer. That maid's got a right dirty little mouth on her. Her *and* her mother.'

Alison didn't look at him. He reversed out of the parking space and put the car in gear.

'I don't want you taking Ruby out at night any more.'

'What?'

'You heard. She's tired in class.'

He swung the car on to the coast road. 'She's fine. You said so yourself.'

'I didn't want a row in front of her teacher.'

'Who's rowing? You're the only one who's rowing.'

'I'm not rowing. I'm just *saying*.'

'You can say whatever you like. We've been out a few times in the car, and where's the harm in that?'

'If you and your mates want to act like ten-year-olds, that's your choice. But Ruby really *is* ten and she needs more sleep.'

'That's just your opinion.'

'Well, my opinion counts because she's my daughter!'

'Yeah, well, she's my daughter too.'

John Trick glared at Alison. His wife pushed her hair behind her ear in a nervous tic he knew so well, but he felt he was seeing it for the first time. Her pale hand; her straight, strawberry-blonde hair; her delicate ear with the lobe that was like velvet.

The hand, the hair, the ear – slowed a thousand times, so he finally understood that the tic was the only truth Alison knew how to tell.

She did it when she bought shoes with other people's money. She'd done it tonight when the teacher mentioned Ruby's red hair. She did it whenever she lied.

Trick gripped the wheel in a spasm and the car swerved and almost hit the kerb.

Ruby wasn't his.

'Careful, John!'

He got it back on line and fought to stay sane. He felt sucker-punched, kicked in the balls. He'd been played for a fool and he was dizzy with shock.

But it would explain so much.

It would explain *everything*.

The lack of respect.

The glove behind the sofa.

Ruby's betrayal.

And – worst of all – the fact that Alison hadn't been a virgin.

Not that first time, in her bedroom, with her parents downstairs watching *Who Wants To Be A Millionaire?* They'd never talked about it, but John Trick had thought about it, over the years.

More than he'd wanted to.

Alison was his, and Alison was *perfect*. So perfect he'd convinced himself that she'd lost her virginity riding a bicycle, or a pony. That was the kind of shit she did before they got married. Fancy shit.

But now – at last – he saw the light.

This wasn't just about Tim Braund. This wasn't just something that had happened since he'd lost his job. This had been happening *from the very start*. Alison had fucked *him* on a first date – and how many others? How many before him and how many since? How many while they were 'keeping it a secret'? How many while he was slaving at the shipyard? How many at the hotel while she was supposed to be working? How many at the super-market? How many in their *fucking bed* while he was fishing on the Gore? How many? How many? *How many?*

They drove the rest of the way to Limeburn in gaping silence, and when the car stopped, Alison immediately got out and walked briskly up the short slope to The Retreat.

John Trick didn't follow her with anything but his eyes.

Maybe Ruby got her red hair from Alison, maybe she didn't. All he knew was that she sure as *shit* didn't get it from him.

37

THE NEXT DAY, the sun came out. Having spent the summer wasting its warmth on the backs of the clouds, there wasn't much left to scatter on Limeburn, but as soon as Ruby got home from school, she picked up her little orange fishing net and ran down the slope to make the most of it.

Not for the first time, she stopped on the cobbles and tried the doors and the boot of the car.

Locked. Locked. Locked. Always locked now. Daddy never used to lock it; he had always lived in hope that one day someone would steal it and they could get the insurance money and buy a better car.

The gun was in there. She *just knew* it.

She sighed and went on down to the slipway and looked across the beach to where she could see Daddy in his camping chair, fishing in the Gut.

'Ruby!'

It was Maggie, crossing the square towards her with Em trailing behind her. Maggie wasn't allowed to take Em on the beach any more – not since a rogue wave had knocked her off her feet so hard that it had washed the shit right out of her nappy. It had been so funny, but

Maggie had got a good thumping when they'd got home, and now they were only allowed to play on the cliff.

So Ruby went down the slipway. She didn't have to run fast to leave them behind. She wanted to be with Daddy. Wanted to remind him that she was a cowboy, and cowboys stuck together.

It took her ten careful minutes to cross the beach to the Gut, testing each pebble for wobbliness before trusting her weight to it.

'Hi, Daddy,' she said.

Daddy looked round at her with a Strongbow in his fist.

'I'm going to go fishing too,' she declared, holding up her net.

He grunted.

She'd have to be good and not wind him up.

There was a big rockpool close by, and Ruby took off her daps and rolled up her jeans and paddled about in it for a while. There were dozens of snails and deep maroon anemones that clenched their fingers and turned to soft rubber fists when you touched them. There were limpets dotted around like cats' eyes, and a whole wall of sharp purple mussels, draped over the rock and into the pool – making that end of it impassable to bare feet.

Ruby sneaked up on a limpet, banged it off the rock with a pebble and gave it to Daddy for bait, but he took it without thanks.

She went back to the pool and poked about until she disturbed a tiny fish – sending it darting under an overhang.

'There's a fish in here,' she said.

'I'm going to the Gore,' he said.

Ruby was disappointed. She'd only just got here, and Daddy knew she hated the Gore, jagged and sticking so far into the sea that the water around it was deep and dangerous.

But she wanted to stick together with Daddy. It was the only way she'd ever get to see the gun. And so when Daddy had reeled in and picked up his catch bucket and cider, and tucked his chair under his arm, she carried his bait box and followed him across the pebbles and down the long, thin spit of black rock, all the way out into the waves to the big rock at the end, where the Devil had finally abandoned his plans.

The blood leaking from Mummy's old stocking worked its magic and, just as the tide turned back towards them, the fish started to bite. Ruby put down her net and just watched Daddy haul in catch after catch. At first he put them in the big white bucket and it was her job to keep scooping out old water and putting in new, so the fish didn't die. But when there were four in there, Daddy caught a nice dogfish, so he threw all the other fish back, to make room for it.

'Wow!' said Ruby, staring into the bucket at the sinuous, shark-finned beast. 'Let's take him home!'

'Not leaving while they're biting,' said Daddy, so Ruby kept a good supply of fresh water trickling into the bucket, using an empty Strongbow can and going gingerly back and forth to the water's edge.

Daddy hooked an eel then, but lost it on the rocks and swore so hard that Ruby said nothing at all, not even sorry. She just kept on, to and fro with the can of seawater.

Slowly it dawned on her that she wasn't walking so far each time. Now she was only taking a few careful paces to the edge of the Gore.

For the first time in an hour, Ruby stopped her work and looked around her.

She felt as if a big black pebble the size of her head had dropped into her tummy.

'Daddy!'

'What?' He turned in his chair.

The tide was coming in fast. A lot of the sea was already behind them and, in places, the Gore itself had narrowed to mere inches. Bigger waves covered it completely, and in those places the black, slime-covered rock was only visible in the troughs.

'What are we going to *do*?' cried Ruby.

'We're going to hurry,' said Daddy. He started to reel in his line, but halfway through, he stopped and took a knife from his tackle box and cut it instead, then he grabbed the rod, tackle box and fish bucket and started back down the long spit.

'Bring the bait,' he shouted.

Ruby dithered. 'What about your chair?'

'Leave it. *Bollocks*.'

Ruby snatched up the bait box and her net and went after him. The path back to the beach was always treacherous with rough rocks and wobbling pebbles – all with a lethal frill of algae and weed – but nothing like this. Now it was also narrowing fast and – washed by the sea – sometimes it was even invisible. What Ruby had carefully picked her way across before, she now had to negotiate at speed, and with the tide tugging at her ankles. Every few strides a bigger wave broke right over the Gore and she was knee-deep in water. More than once she slipped and nearly fell, only the thin bamboo shaft of her little fishing net keeping her upright.

She looked up and saw that Daddy was twenty yards ahead of her now, and between them there was more water than Gore.

She froze. 'Daddy!'

He turned at her cry.

'Come *on*, Ruby! Don't just *stand* there!' he shouted.

But she couldn't move. Not even if she'd wanted to. That day of the dog in the forest, her legs had decided to run all by themselves. It had been terrifying, and the fear had only got worse and worse and worse, all the way to the blind terror of the Bear Den.

This time her legs decided *not* to run. This time her legs downed tools and told her to stay *right there*.

A swell pushed her sideways and she almost fell over. Only a quick hand on a sharp rock stopped her, and when she staggered upright again, her palm was bleeding, her jeans were wet right up to her crotch, the bait box was gone and her net was floating away from her – out of reach.

'*Daddy!*'

She looked up through the spray and saw Daddy – rod and tackle box in one hand, bucket in the other, looking at her with a strange expression on his face.

Not panic. Not worry. Not fear.

Just.

Looking.

He was going to leave her there. Ruby *just knew* it.

Her chest went tight with terror as the dirty green ocean tried to knock her down and swallow her whole.

'Daddy! Help me!' she shrieked.

He did.

Of course he did. He was her Daddy. He wouldn't leave her to drown. He took a few uneven strides towards her and then swore soundlessly and discarded the bucket. Ruby saw the dogfish spill back into the waves and wriggle away.

Daddy splashed towards her. She stretched out her arms, as if he might pick her up and carry her – the way Granpa had lifted her on to the kitchen counter – but he just grabbed her wrist and pulled her along behind him. She still stumbled; she still fell; the waves still knocked her sideways and threatened to wash her off the spit and into the hungry sea.

But now Daddy was there to take care of her.

When they were only ankle-deep, they stopped and looked back. Ruby's teeth chattered with cold and fright. She couldn't believe how close they had been to not making it. The sea had swallowed the Gore – all but the highest rock right at the end, where Daddy's chair still perched. As they watched, a large, dark wave slapped it down and dragged it off.

And then there was just the sea and the foam and the gulls laughing overhead.

'Fuck,' said Daddy. 'That was a twenty-quid fish.'

Then he squeezed her hand and said, 'Don't tell Mummy.'

Ruby nodded, shivering and blue in the lips, even though she wasn't sure what she was supposed to not tell Mummy about – the lost dogfish, or the *fuck*.

Or the way she'd nearly drowned on the Gore.

38

MARION MOON WASN'T sure Donald was ever going to get over the Frannie Hatton thing.

Stepping on a dead woman's face in the half-dark was bad enough, but the subsequent questioning and searching and suspicion had almost finished her husband off.

'It's almost finished me off,' he sighed several times a day when she least expected it. Staring at his uneaten dinner; in the ad-break of *Countdown*; waiting for the cat to come in.

The Big Sheep had been very patient with him, but after six weeks of calling in sick, they finally had to give him an ultimatum. If he didn't return to work by Monday, they'd have to find someone to replace him. Permanently. Donald told them that he understood and he'd do his very best – and then hung up the phone and cried for everything he'd lost and was going to lose.

'Come on,' said Marion after an hour or so. 'We'll go litter picking. That'll cheer you up.'

It was a universal truth that however tragic and unfair life got, nothing ever seemed so grim once it was tidied up a bit. So Donald changed out of his pyjamas for the first time in three days, and he and Marion took their pointy sticks and Day-Glo vests and their big green plastic bags over to Instow beach, which was always a safe bet for blue rope and used condoms.

And parking tickets.

Donald raised his pointy stick up to his face to examine the third one he'd found in fifty yards. And all of them unopened. Therefore unpaid. That was a lot of council revenue being denied the taxpayer right there.

'I've got one too,' said Marion.

'Cheeky monkeys,' said Donald. 'Probably think by throwing them away they won't have to pay 'em.' He speared another one, closer to the sea wall that separated the beach from the road, with its line of parked cars.

'In *fact*,' he went on, 'in *fact*, they'll have to pay *double*.'

Marion said nothing. But in a minute she'd say, 'Why's that?' and let Donald tell her that it was because of computers linked to the DVLA in Swansea.

This was how their marriage worked: this measured back-and-forth of Donald knowing all, and her requesting knowledge. It wasn't that she really didn't know things, of course; Marion knew plenty. But most importantly, she knew that Donald liked to take the lead and tell people things, and so she saw no harm in following and being told. It was a habit she'd fallen into in the early days of her marriage just to avoid petty disagreements, but which she'd have found hard to break now – even if she'd wanted to. She joked about it to her friends occasionally, but now that that back-and-forth hadn't been there for six weeks, she missed it.

They'd been the hardest six weeks of Marion Moon's

married life. It would have been easier to pull a two-headed lamb out of a virgin ewe than to cheer Donald up since he trod on Frannie Hatton. The whole affair had knocked the stuffing out of him, and had made Marion realize that the stuffing was the best bit of her husband.

But now, on Instow beach on a blustery, spitty day in late October, it felt almost like old times, and Donald already seemed perkier.

So a minute after he said that in *fact* the driver would have to pay double, Marion said, 'Why's that?' and jabbed a cigarette packet. They were a rarity nowadays because branded cigarettes were so expensive. Most people who were really devoted to getting cancer had to roll their own. Rizla packets, plastic water bottles and knotted black bags filled with dog poo – these were the litter pickers' new stock in trade.

Marion looked up, wondering why Donald hadn't said *Computers linked to the DVLA in Swansea*, but Donald was standing upright, peering at something over the sea wall.

'What's wrong?' said Marion.

'They're all off the one car,' said Donald.

'What?'

'They're all off the one car, I reckon. All these tickets. Come see.'

Marion trudged through the soft white sand to the sea wall and peered over it to the line of parked cars.

Directly opposite them was a yellow car with two broad black stripes down it.

'Mark II Capri,' said Donald. 'Duncan had one of those.'

Duncan was Donald's younger brother. He'd had one

of everything at some stage. Now he had one ex-wife, one daughter who didn't speak to him, and one stupidly big house so encumbered by negative equity that it was actually subsiding under the weight.

There were three more parking tickets under the windscreen wipers, fluttering their slow way towards freedom on the beach.

Donald tore open one of the tickets on his stick and confirmed that it did indeed come from the Capri.

'See?' he told Marion.

'I do,' she nodded. 'I do see. Well spotted, Donald.'

With a new spring in his step, Donald strode off the beach, round the sea wall and over to the Capri, with Marion in tow.

'One a day, by the looks of things,' he said. 'I should call the council.'

'What for?' said Marion dutifully.

'Well, to let them know about the car. All these bits of plastic blowing about aren't helping the situation, are they?'

Donald shook open a new green bag and stuffed all the parking tickets in it and then tied it to the aerial, where it flapped about like last place in a balloon race.

'I mean,' he went on, 'what's the point of a warden just sticking a ticket on it every day? Owner's obviously not bothered. It should be towed away. Impounded. Owner fined. But instead it's sitting here on two flat tyres, being used as a rubbish bin by some idiot in epaulettes filling his quota. No joined-up thinking, see? Bloody local-government robots.'

He'd worked himself up into a pedantic fugue, and Marion couldn't have been happier.

Donald just wasn't Donald without a bee in his bonnet.

When they got home, Marion made tea while Donald called the county council's highways department and then their environmental services department. Then he rang the district council's car-recycling department. Marion noticed that he was on the phone longer each time, over-explaining and under-listening to make sure he got best value for his council tax.

She'd made Donald's favourite – lamb chops on mashed potatoes – and when it was ready she went into the hallway to summon him to eat.

Marion stopped dead.

Donald was on the phone, talking to the Big Sheep.

Marion stood and cocked her head to hear him better, and felt a long-lost smile start to stretch her face.

He was telling them he'd be at work on Monday, come hell or high water.

39

INSTOW WAS A pretty village, but apart from the beach there wasn't much to see or do. It had no amusement arcades or fairground, or shops selling tat, or pedalos for hire. Instow was smarter than that – it had Paul's Deli, a couple of small galleries, the Commodore Hotel and three or four upmarket bistros painted fashionably dark grey or maroon.

It was nice.

But it was dull.

Which is why, when the council caved in to Donald Moon's campaign of harassment and sent a truck to tow away the illegally parked yellow Ford Capri, the operation drew the kind of crowd more usually seen under a man threatening to jump off a bridge.

Old ladies got the plum seats. They squeezed on to the benches in beige quartets, armed with their 99 ice creams and plastic rain scarves and with tissues up their sleeves, ready for dabbing.

Then came the dog-walkers – with their wet, sandy charges panting on leashes – and mothers with buggies. And once the dog-walkers and the mums had stopped to stare, it seemed the whole village got wind of something happening on the sea front, and by the time the tow-truck driver had hitched up the Capri and was ready to start winching, there must have been a hundred people waiting patiently to be mildly entertained.

The truck driver's name was Andy Shapland and he enjoyed the audience, especially the small boys, who he could see were truly impressed by his retaining straps and his road cones and his big hook – rather than the idle bystanders who simply had nothing better to do on a rainy Wednesday afternoon.

Shapland took care with the Capri. His father had had one, although not so well cared for, even in 1976. Luckily the doors were unlocked, so he hadn't had to break a window to release the handbrake. Now he lined the wheels up with the ramps, put on the steering-wheel lock, and pressed the big red button on the remote, which started the winch.

Slowly the car's nose started to rise on to the low-loader, and the small boys burst into a smattering of spontaneous applause. Andy Shapland grinned and took a little bow, and they clapped harder.

Distracted by uncommon glory, he didn't notice that the Capri was heading for disaster. It was a low-slung car, even when new, but this one had been restored and repainted and lowered again. Not a lot. Not so you'd notice unless you were used to seeing Ford Capris every day – which, of course, nobody was any more. But it had low-profile tyres on it, and shorter shocks, and – most damning of all – it had a big fat exhaust system with far fewer inches of ground clearance than was really prudent.

At maximum tilt – just as the Capri was almost home

and dry – the big fat exhaust hit the ground hard. The nasty metallic scraping noise drew an 'Oh!' from the idle bystanders and then a ripple of laughter, as the boot clicked open in response to the jolt, like a sleeper opening half an eye to see what all the fuss was.

Shit. Andy Shapland hit the big red button to stop the winch.

He could see from where he was standing that he'd broken the exhaust. He'd done that once before with a Lotus and the owner had had a meltdown on the A361, but, to be honest, cocking it up on an old Capri in front of a crowd was much more embarrassing. From the corner of his eye he saw the small boys looking disappointed. And if he knew small boys, it would only be another few seconds before their childish disappointment turned into shouts of derision. Especially as the boot popping open had lent the whole thing a comedy air.

He walked over quickly to slam the lid shut, then stopped, staring down into the black-lined interior of the Capri.

Then he said, 'Shit!' and 'Call the police!'

'What?' said an old lady on the nearest bench.

'Call the police!' shouted Andy Shapland in a panic. 'Call the police!'

Several people laughed, thinking it was part of the show.

'Call the police!' He'd do it himself. He could do it himself. He suddenly realized that *he* could call the police. Andy Shapland's fingers felt numb. His head felt numb. He put the phone to his ear and it was only when everybody laughed again that he realized he was trying to call the police on the remote for the winch, speaking into the big red button.

'There's a body in the boot!' he shouted. 'There's a body in the boot!'

A thin man with two Border collies on leads stepped off the pavement and peered into the boot and confirmed that that was true.

Lots of people called the police then, and the police came and made all the old ladies and the mums and the dog-walkers and the small boys stand far enough away so that nobody else could see anything interesting.

Killjoys.

Conveniently, there was a driver's licence in the body's wallet, and it didn't take Sherlock Holmes to match the photo of a stout middle-aged man with fluffy grey mutton-chop sideburns to the swollen, stinking body in the boot of his own Ford Capri.

His name was Leonard Willows.

Also known as Pussy.

When the Gunslingers heard about Pussy Willows they tried to be sorry, but it didn't work. Their only fond memory of him had been the fight that had got them banned from the George, and that was no basis for false regret.

Within minutes of meeting that Friday, they were deep in drink and speculation about who'd killed him.

'Ex-wife,' said Blacky. 'Sure to be.'

'Was he married?' said Shiny.

'*If* he was married,' said Blacky.

'Police haven't said it was murder yet,' said Whippy, who was always the most cautious.

'Bollocks,' said Scratch, flicking his poncho over one shoulder so it didn't dip in his cider. 'Didn't kill himself and hide himself in the boot, did he?'

The Gunslingers nodded firmly at that. The police hadn't even officially identified Pussy yet, but Scratch's wife's uncle had a boat moored at Instow and so had all the inside information, and there'd been a photo of the car in the *Gazette*.

'What was that name he wanted?' said Hick.

'What name?'

'The one we wouldn't let him have.'

'Dunno. Oi, Shiny! What was that name he wanted?'

'Deadly, I think,' said Shiny. 'No, not Deadly, Dead*eye*. That's it.'

'Well, he's got two of 'em now!' shouted Nellie, and they all laughed.

Daisy Yeo mooed for another beer from the bar, and when it arrived he raised his glass and said, 'To Pussy Willows. Couldn't have happened to a better man.'

They all laughed and sipped their drinks.

Then Hick frowned and said, 'I hope *we*'re not suspects.'

They smiled a little bit, but then realized he was being serious.

'Why would *we* be suspects?' said Razor.

Shiny rolled his eyes and said, ''Cos of the fight, innit? It's not like it was private! Everyone round here knows about it. And Pussy bore a grudge, you know. Remember that time Razor seen him in the Blue Dolphin? Cut him dead.'

'Cut me dead,' agreed Razor. 'I said, "Right, Pussy?" and he wouldn't even look at me.'

'Still,' said Whippy, 'it's a motive, innit?'

'But *he* started it,' said Chip.

'And we finished it!' said Blacky, to cheers all round.

'And that's the truth,' nodded Shiny, 'if Mr Plod comes knocking.'

'Who's Mr Plod?' said Razor.

'The police!' said Shiny. 'Don't you read?'

The Gunslingers had the best meeting they'd had for an awfully long while. They laughed and sang along to a new Lyle Lovett on the jukebox, and Jim Maxwell let them buy a final round a whole ten minutes after he'd rung the big brass bell behind the bar.

And the cherry on the cake was that when they got out to the car park at the end of the night, not one of their cars had been vandalized.

'No Pussy Willows, nobody fucking with our cars,' said Hick Trick. 'Says it all, dunnit?'– and they all agreed that it did, indeed, say it all.

40

DADDY HAD CHANGED, and Ruby didn't know why.
When they drove up the hill in the mornings, he snapped at Ruby, 'Don't hang on my seat like that!' and when she asked Mummy for more pudding he said, 'You'll get fat. Ter.'

Fat. Ter.

Fatter.

She felt fractured. Didn't he love her any more? She must've done *something* wrong – but nothing she did could make it right.

She sat with Daddy and watched *Extreme Fishing* and *Man v. Food* and brought him Mummy's phone without being asked, and fetched wood from the woodpile, even though it was full of spiders. She even brought Panda downstairs and sat him on the easy chair, to let Daddy know they were ready when he was.

But he barely spoke to her, and twice that week he went on the posse by himself, leaving her alone in the house.

And Ruby no longer felt safe in the house.

It was almost November and the forest was at its most overbearing – pendulous with leaves and seeds and dripping rainwater, and, however loud she turned up the TV, Ruby could never block out the sound of the rustling against the back wall of The Retreat; the itchy squeak of branches against the windows; the creak of beams, like the masts of an old ship. Mice scratched and scrabbled behind the damp plaster, and Mummy came down early one morning and stepped on a toad halfway down the stairs. The big spiders had moved indoors in force, and Ruby didn't even dare to sit on the rug, where their camouflage was complete.

There were cracks in the walls that Ruby had never seen before. Or if she had, she hadn't remembered them. And the crack that had always been in the corner of her room, over the bed, seemed to have got longer. And wider.

Sometimes something in the roof or the walls gave a short, sharp report, like a cap gun – as though something was snapping, letting go, breaking free. At night she would wake from blood-soaked dreams to feel her ears ringing with something they'd heard in her absence. And when she lay there waiting for a repeat performance, The Retreat held its breath and waited until she'd dropped back into a fitful sleep before cracking its knuckles and grinding its teeth.

But worst of all was the bathroom window that Daddy was too lazy to fix.

As the wind swung around to the north and picked up its winter cold and strength, the high whine became howls of pain and low groans, like somebody dying upstairs, while downstairs nobody talked about it. It was too obvious to talk about; too loud to mention – there would only be a row.

So they suffered in the opposite of silence.

The next Cowboy afternoon, Ruby went into the little shop and spent her week's pocket money on a tube of glue and a *Gazette*.

'You on a diet?' said Mr Preece, even though she noticed that he had to reach over his own belly to ring up the sale.

She passed the empty paddock with barely a glance, and hurried down the hill.

On her bedroom floor she tore the newspaper into strips and put them in a bowl full of warm water to soak.

Later, when Daddy had left, and Mummy was downstairs with Nanna and Granpa, she got to work.

They had made *pâpier mâché* once at school, but she couldn't remember the exact recipe. They'd moulded masks over balloons. Ruby's was of a mermaid, but she was much younger then.

She squeezed the water out of the soggy strips of paper until they became a pulp, which she squirted with glue and then fed into every gap she could find in the bathroom window frame.

She found plenty – some with her eyes and some just by feeling the air cooling her wet fingertips. The ghostly keening grew smaller and more distant as she worked the pulp between the wood and the glass, using her ruler to push it in and tamp it down.

She kept listening for Daddy's return. She wanted to finish before he got back. Once she thought she heard the car and panicked a bit, but it was a false alarm.

When she'd filled in all the gaps she could find, she squirted glue into them too, to seal the paper. Some glue got on the window, and when she tried to rub it off with toilet paper, the paper stuck to her fingers, and to the glass.

And to the carpet.

But the noise of the wind grew smaller and smaller until finally it ceased.

Ruby stood in the bathroom and listened to the silence. It was only now that it had stopped that she realized how that sound had become part of her life – a ghostly undercurrent that had grated through her head for years.

She shivered. How had they all put up with it for so long? The thought of hearing it ever again made her feel ill.

She decided to do the same for the crack over her bed.

Halfway through the *Gazette*, Ruby tore through the face of someone she knew. She stopped.

RING CLUE IN MURDER HUNT.

Ruby laid the two bits of newspaper back down together and adjusted them carefully so they aligned.

It was a picture of that girl who had given her the five-pound note. The caption reminded Ruby that her name was Steffi. Next to that was a photo of the girl in the big pink dress, and then one of a pretty girl with long blonde hair, whose name was Jody.

She read the story.

Police hunting the killer of Frannie Hatton say they want to find a silver nose ring she is believed to have been wearing when she disappeared.

Frannie, 22, from Northam, was killed and her body was left in a lay-by in Abbotsham seven weeks ago.

Although she always wore a nose ring, it was not on her body when it was found.

In Bideford yesterday, Detective Chief Inspector Kirsty King said, 'We believe now that Frannie was probably wearing the nose ring when she was abducted and killed.

'If anyone has found it, or knows where it is, please contact us in confidence because it might be vital to our investigation.'

Frannie's grieving boyfriend, Mark Spade, 28, said, 'She never took it out. I've looked everywhere for it but it's not in the flat.'

A neighbour said yesterday, 'She was a pretty little thing who wouldn't hurt a fly.'

Police are linking Frannie's murder with two earlier assaults and with the subsequent disappearance of two other young women from North Devon.

Jody Reeves, 25, disappeared on 3 October after a night out with her boyfriend, while Steffi Cole, 20, went missing on the walk home from her part-time job at Paul's Deli in Instow a week later.

Both women were forced to phone home before disappearing, leading police to believe they could also be victims of the masked man known as the ET Killer. They have appealed for witnesses who may have seen Jody or Steffi on the dates in question to contact the police in complete confidence.

Ruby was agog. *She* had seen Steffi! She was completely confident about *that*. She'd left the shop after giving Ruby a fiver and that man with the bushy sideboards had stabbed the tyre soon afterwards. He could have murdered Steffi!

Then she noticed something she hadn't the first time round. At the foot of the story was a small photo of a plain silver loop. The caption said: *Similar nose ring.*

Ruby's mouth popped open in surprise.

It was the earring she'd found in Daddy's car! The one she'd stuck in her diary!

With excitement buzzing in her tummy, she pulled her diary out of her pony backpack and flicked through the pages.

The earring was gone.

Ruby touched the place where it had been with her fingers. This was definitely the place. There was her writing . . . *I found this treshure* . . . but all that was left was a rough white patch on the page to show where the sticky tape had been ripped off and had taken some of the blue lines with it.

She looked in her backpack in case the ring had fallen out in there, but it was nowhere.

She remembered that Mummy had seen her diary. Maybe she'd taken the earring back. Except that Mummy never wore earrings, and the earring didn't match anything Ruby had seen in the rumpled bag of jewellery in the back of the wardrobe.

Ruby checked the newspaper photo again. She couldn't be sure without actually having the earring in her hand, but it *looked* like the one she'd found.

She went very still. If it was Frannie Hatton's nose ring, why was it in Daddy's car? Why had he lied to the policeman the night Steffi was killed? Why had he kept the gun a secret from her? And what *other* secrets did Daddy have?

Ruby had all questions and no answers.

And one was bigger and more painful than them all.

Why doesn't Daddy love me any more?

Tears scorched her eyes.

Then Ruby got up, took her diary from her pony backpack and hid it under her mattress.

She wasn't even sure why.

41

CALVIN BRIDGE BROKE up with Shirley.
He couldn't believe he had the guts to do it, and
– from the look on her face – she couldn't believe it
either.

'What do you *mean*?'

'I mean, I don't want us to be together any more.'

'But we're getting *married*!'

'I'm not.'

'What do you mean, *I'm not*?'

'I mean I'm not getting married. Sorry. I should have
told you sooner, but, y'know . . .'

'But *why*?'

'Because—' he started, and then wondered whether
he should tell her the truth or not. He had no desire to
hurt Shirley any more than he already was. But he
couldn't think quickly enough to come up with a plausi-
ble lie, so the truth it had to be.

'Because I'm just not that . . . *enthusiastic* about it.'

'About the wedding?' said Shirley, in a voice that let
him know that although she was trying to be understanding, she had no inkling of how anyone could not be
enthusiastic about a *wedding*.

'About any of it really,' he confessed. 'I'm not enthusiastic about the wedding. Or the children or the corduroy sofa or the idea of being together for the next sixty years when I haven't even *done* anything with my life yet. I mean, I'm only twenty-four.'

'What do you mean, you haven't done anything with your life?' snapped Shirley. '*This* is what we're doing with our lives! We've been together for years and we love each other and we want to share our lives and now we're getting married and that's what people *do*, Calvin! People get *married* and then they have *children* and they work together to bring them *up*. That *is* life! That's what life *is*!'

'Yeah,' said Calvin doubtfully. 'But I'm not crazy about it, that's all. I mean, it's not really what I want for *my* life. Not right now, anyway.'

'If it's not what you want, Calvin, then why did you ask me to marry you?'

'I didn't. *You* asked *me*.'

'Then why did you say yes, you *idiot*?'

Calvin paused and then figured *In for a penny, in for a pound* and said, 'Because if I'd said no you'd have been all upset, and the Italian Grand Prix had just started.'

Shirley slammed the book of swatches shut so hard and so close to his face that she nearly pressed Calvin's nose like a Victorian flower.

'You bastard!' she shouted. '*Get out!*'

'But it's—'

'GET OUT!' she shrieked, and heaved the book at his head. It landed splayed open on the floor behind him.

'But it's my flat,' Calvin pointed out cautiously.

That's when Shirley started screaming. Everything up until then had been mild by comparison. All Calvin could do was stand there and wait for it to end, while Shirley gathered up random wedding things in her arms, weeping and yelling and red in the face.

The fact that he could muster only mild concern for her heartbreak was all the proof Calvin needed that he really didn't love her after all.

At least he'd learned that.

It didn't stop the break-up being bloody awful, but when it was all over and Shirley and all the wedding things had left his flat for good, Calvin Bridge felt a lovely sense of calm.

For a few minutes he stood in the middle of his living room, just looking around him at the sheer absence of Shirley, while his banished existence crept slowly back towards him from every corner of the flat.

Then he turned on the second half of England versus San Marino and settled down on his leather sofa to live the rest of his life.

42

AFTER MUMMY WENT to work the next night, Daddy came into Ruby's bedroom.

'Panda's looking tired, Rubes.'

Ruby didn't even look up from *TeenBeatz*.

'No,' she replied. 'He's fine.'

'What?' said Daddy, cocking his head as if he'd heard her wrong.

'Panda's fine. I'm not going on the posse.'

'But you're my deputy,' said Daddy, then did his cowboy voice. 'Cain't go on no posse without my deputy.'

Ruby didn't smile. She shrugged. 'I'm not a deputy. I don't even have a badge.'

'I told you. I talked to the others about that. They said you can have a badge. But they take a while because they come from America. Because they're like *real* deputy badges, not toy ones.'

'You didn't tell me.' She shrugged again. 'But I don't care.'

Daddy leaned against the door-frame and looked at his fingernails. 'You feeling sick, Rubes?'

'No,' she said. 'I just don't want to go.' She pretended

to keep reading. *How to get a date with the cutest guy in school*. There were no cute guys in her school, but still.

'There must be a reason,' said Daddy. 'You scared?'

'No,' she said. 'I'm just not going any more.'

She turned on her side and curled her back towards the door. She waited for the creak of Daddy walking away, but it didn't come.

It was completely silent.

Completely still.

Suddenly Ruby missed the whine of the bathroom window. It masked so much bad stuff, she realized now. She wished she'd never fixed it. Daddy hadn't even *noticed*, and Mummy had just told her off about the glue on the bathroom carpet.

'You know,' Daddy said slowly, 'Whippy was talking about Tonto.'

Ruby said nothing, but her ears pricked.

'He told me he's getting too old to ride any more. He said he might be looking for a new home for Tonto.'

Ruby's tummy fluttered the way it used to when she approached the paddock. *Maybe. Maybe . . .* She pushed it down. She didn't want to give him the satisfaction.

Daddy detached himself from the door-frame and wandered towards her. 'I told him I knew an empty paddock where Tonto might be able to live. And a little girl who would be happy to look after him and ride him every day.'

Daddy stopped at the side of the bed – looming over her. 'What do you think of *that*?'

Ruby felt tears stinging her eyes and it took all her strength not to crack and throw herself into his arms and smother him with kisses. Daddy had hurt her and now she had to hurt him back, otherwise what was the point?

'I don't care,' she said flatly. 'I don't even *like* horses any more.'

There was a long, awful silence, and then Daddy snorted bitterly. 'I'm disappointed in you.'

Ruby's heart broke.

Never in a million zillion years had Ruby Trick ever thought she'd hear her Daddy say those words. After everything she'd done for him.

Her lips went all funny. '*I'*m disappointed in *you*!' she shouted, and started to sob.

'That's right,' he said. 'Cry like a girl.'

'I'm *not*!' she cried like a girl.

'Yes, you are. A stupid little girl. Look at this bollocks you're reading.' He picked *TeenBeatz* off her bed and shook it. 'Stupid slutty shite. I thought you were my little cowboy. But you're turning into a fucking slut, just like your mother.'

'Shut up!'

'*You* shut up!'

Daddy had never smacked her, but Ruby flinched as he leaned down suddenly – his face only inches from hers. She could smell the cider on his breath and see the smooth puckers of the scars around his eye, gone white in his red face.

'Now,' said Daddy, low and tight, 'put your fucking *Panda* to *bed*.'

He walked out of the room and down the stairs.

Ruby sat up, her whole world shaking around her.

She wished Mummy was here.

She wished Daddy wasn't.

But she was too scared not to do as he said.

Ruby didn't talk to Daddy. Not from the minute she sat down in the front seat and he said, 'Where's your cushion, Deputy?'

He was trying to make things normal. She wasn't going to let him. She said nothing and didn't even look at him, and he said, 'Be like that,' and then reversed off the wet cobbles and drove up the long dark hill out of Limeburn.

Ruby didn't look out of the window for the killer and Daddy didn't remind her to.

She hated him.

More than she'd ever hated Mummy. More than she'd ever hated Em or Essie Littlejohn – that's how much she hated Daddy.

Tears fizzed up her nose again and she wiped her eyes hard.

Daddy didn't care that she was crying. He didn't even look at her.

He didn't love her.

They were on their second circuit when Daddy indicated and pulled over to pick up the first woman.

The window grunted down beside Ruby and the rain came in.

'Hi,' said Daddy. 'Can we give you a ride?'

The woman looked at Ruby. Ruby was used to that now. They all did that. Ruby didn't smile.

'Umm,' said the woman, and gave a little laugh and looked up and down the road. They all did that, too. Ruby wondered what they were all looking for. A better offer?

'OK, thanks.' The woman smiled. She was about Mummy's age and was wearing jeans and an anorak. She wore glasses that went up in the corners like a cat's eyes.

'I live in Torrington,' she said. 'Are you sure that's OK?'

Torrington was nine miles away through a winding road overhung with trees.

'Yeah, fine,' said Daddy. 'You don't want to be waiting for a bus in this rain. Jump in the back, Rubes.'

Ruby was so used to jumping in the back now that her arms and legs almost moved by themselves – and when she stopped them, they tingled, as if surprised.

'In the back, Ruby. Chop-chop. The lady's getting wet.'

Ruby stayed exactly where she was.

Fuck him. That's what she thought, even though she was a little bit ashamed of using the F word, even in her head.

Fuck him.

Daddy took hold of her arm and gave it a tug to get her moving, but Ruby pulled away from his hand.

The woman's smile faltered. 'Are you OK, sweetheart?' she said to Ruby.

'She's fine,' said Daddy. 'Jump in.'

'Oh, that's OK,' the woman said, straightening up. 'Don't worry about it.'

'No, it's fine,' said Daddy. 'Ruby! Get in the back!'

She didn't budge.

'Don't worry,' said the woman. 'Really. The bus will be along soon.' She started to walk away from the car.

'She'll move,' said Daddy. 'She's just being a brat!' He grabbed at Ruby again, but she leaned against the door and folded her arms tight across her aching chest.

But the woman wasn't coming back. She walked away and crossed the road, glancing back frequently over her shoulder.

Ruby put the window up. It took ages to squeal and judder its way to the top.

She and Daddy sat there together while the engine idled and the rain drummed on the roof.

Ruby was glad she hadn't moved. It served Daddy right. The woman had been nice and maybe she was safer on the bus.

Daddy leaned in so close to her face that when she turned her head away she could feel his breath on her ear.

'You'll be sorry.'

Ruby trembled, but she didn't turn round, and eventually Daddy's breath drew off, leaving her ear damp and cold.

He drove fast towards home. So fast that Ruby clutched the sides of the seat.

A few miles from Limeburn, he jammed on the brakes next to a little wooden bus shelter, and then swung the car down a steep, narrow lane between high hedges.

At the foot of the hill was the hotel where Mummy worked.

Daddy drove slowly past the entrance, then turned around and parked close to the hedge, in the piles of wet brown leaves that had drifted there.

Ruby didn't know what they were doing and she wouldn't ask.

They were there for ages. Half an hour, at least, and Ruby's teeth were chattering by the time they saw the yellow slit of a door opening and Mummy came out.

There was a man inside, saying goodbye to her.

He was an older man, with greying hair and a beard. His ears stuck out, just like Essie Littlejohn's, so Ruby guessed that it was her father.

Mr Littlejohn raised a hand in goodbye and Mummy opened her umbrella and started walking away from the car – up the hill towards the main road and the bus stop.

Daddy started the car and they drove slowly up the lane behind her.

Mummy heard them coming and stepped close to the hedge so they could pass in the narrow lane. She didn't know it was them, of course, because they were in darkness, but she was illuminated so brightly by the headlights that Ruby felt as though she were seeing her mother for the first time – as if she were a complete stranger.

She was thin, and her skin looked very white. Her old brown coat was belted tightly around her waist, and already her jeans were wet up to the shins from walking in the wet lane. Her umbrella had one broken strut so that it dropped and flapped on one side.

Daddy didn't slow down to pick Mummy up. Instead he went faster – the car skidding in sudden protest as he changed down a gear and forced it to pick up speed up the hill.

Mummy turned and squinted.

Ruby squealed and covered her eyes.

There was no bump, no thud. No screech of brakes.

Ruby opened her eyes and twisted in her seat. By the red glow of the tail lights, she could see Mummy. Still upright and pressed against the hedge. And then she was lost on a bend in the road.

Ruby looked at Daddy, but Daddy didn't look at her.

Ruby slept badly.

She got up in the dark to go to the toilet. She didn't need the light because she knew the house so well she could do this in her sleep.

As she padded back across the dark room to her bed, she stepped on something hard and sharp that made her hop about and bite her lip.

When the pain had subsided, she turned on the lamp.

Lucky's sled was on the floor, the plastic shafts snapped off.

Under the bed she found the little donkey, all squashed and bent.

'Oh *no*,' she whispered.

She picked up Lucky and tried to bend him back into shape. She got the dent out of his belly, and three of his legs reasonably straight, but his dear little head was still squashed, and the fourth leg had been twisted so badly that when she tried to make it right, it broke off in her hand.

Ruby bit her lip to keep from letting out a sob.

The potato was still on her bedside table, letting her know that this was no accident.

43

MUMMY OPENED THE curtains before the alarm went off, and Ruby woke with a hard rock of anxiety in her belly.

The bed went all wonky as Mummy sat down on the edge of it. She didn't say anything for a minute, then she picked the potato off the chest of drawers.

'Where's your little donkey?'

'I don't know,' said Ruby quickly. Lucky was in the bottom drawer. She didn't know what to do with him. She didn't want Mummy to see what had happened to him; didn't want her to start asking questions. Ruby didn't have answers – not ones she understood.

But Mummy only stroked the potato with her thumb. There was a little bit of white root crawling out at one end, seeking the light like a worm.

'Ruby, do you know what a whore is?'

Ruby picked at the bed cover.

'Ruby?'

'What?'

'Do you know what—'

'*No*,' said Ruby rudely.

Mummy nodded. 'You use some bad words in your diary, Rubes.'

Ruby didn't look at Mummy, but she felt her ears going red. When had Mummy read her diary? Had *she* taken the nose ring?

'I don't know if you understand them, but they're all bad words about women.'

'I *know*,' said Ruby, although she didn't. Why couldn't Mummy just leave it? It wasn't even her fault. It was Daddy's fault for using bad words.

'It's OK if you *don't* know, Rubes. Life's all about learning. I just don't want you learning the wrong things, you see, because then you might end up *doing* the wrong things. Do you understand?'

'Yes.'

Go away, thought Ruby. *Go away*.

Mummy nodded and sighed and put the potato back, and Ruby thought she was going to go, but she didn't.

'How's your chest, Rubes?'

She shrugged.

'You know when it hurts sometimes?'

Ruby nodded cautiously.

'Well,' said Mummy slowly, 'there's nothing wrong with you, sweetheart, it's because you're starting to develop.'

'What's *develop*?'

'It just means you're getting little boobies.'

Ruby sat upright in shock. 'No, I'm *not*!'

'It's nothing to worry about. It's natural.'

Ruby barely heard the words. A seed of panic germinated rapidly inside her. She'd assumed that the aching in her chest would go away, but boobs were for *ever*. They *never* went away. They just got bigger and bigger and more and more in the way. Already she could hardly lie flat on the spider rug.

'I can't get boobs!' she burst out. 'How will I even *read*?'

Mummy smiled as if she'd made a joke, but she hadn't. She hoped *Mummy* was joking.

But Mummy wasn't joking. Instead Mummy said, 'If you're starting to develop them you'll probably start your periods soon too. Do you know what periods are, Rubes?'

'Are they like lessons?' frowned Ruby. There were periods at school. PE was the worst. The last thing she needed was more lessons; she was rubbish at the ones she already had. Although she couldn't think of anything worse than growing boobs!

And then Mummy told her the facts of life . . .

Ruby sat in stunned silence.

The facts of life. The *facts* of life? That couldn't be true. She'd never heard of them! Were they even *real*? Surely nobody could keep that a secret – something so disgusting, so scary? Who else knew about this? Did Miss Sharpe know? Did Adam? How *could* people know, and still walk around all day as if nothing was wrong?

The boobies and the blood and the boys and the babies.

'I don't believe you,' she said with a trembling lip.

Mummy smiled sympathetically. 'It's true, Ruby, but

don't worry about it. These things happen to all girls when they become women, so you have to know about them.'

'But I don't *want* to know about them!'

'But Ruby,' said Mummy gently, 'if girls don't know the facts of life then they won't understand about boys and sex and they can get into all kind of trouble.'

'What kind of trouble?'

'All sorts of things. Things that can ruin their lives.'

'What things?'

'Just . . . horrible things.'

Ruby's mind boggled. How could anything be more horrible than the things Mummy had just promised were going to happen to her?

And soon!

It seemed her body had played a mean trick on her. It had started out as one thing and now it was going to change into another thing without even asking.

In the back of her mind, Ruby knew that girls grew up to be women. But for some reason she'd always assumed that *she*'d grow up to be a cowboy.

Daddy had warned her. He'd warned her about growing up and she hadn't understood.

Tears pricked at the backs of Ruby's eyes. She understood now.

She understood that she was never going to ride a bucking bronco, or hitch her pony up outside school, or keep wolves at bay with a fire and a six-gun. Instead she understood that she was going to get boobs and have to sit in a chair to read a book, and paint her nails and kiss boys, and have babies and blood come out of her front bottom.

'No!' she said firmly. '*No!*'

Mummy tried to put her arms around her, but Ruby pushed her away.

She didn't want it. She didn't want *any* of it. She didn't want to be a slut and a slag and a whore. She *hated* women and she hated Mummy for telling her about it.

No wonder Daddy didn't love her any more.

Ruby burst into tears.

Alison Trick was stunned.

She'd been nervous about 'the talk' for a while now. Her own mother had left it far too late, and she hadn't wanted to repeat that mistake.

She'd expected Ruby to be embarrassed. Confused. Maybe a bit apprehensive.

But she hadn't expected hysteria.

She tried to console Ruby, but she wouldn't stop crying. The little girl wept with every bit of her being, doubling over, holding her tummy in her fists, while tears ran off her face and on to the bed, like rain off old gutters.

Alison felt her own throat ache. 'Ruby, what's wrong?' She rubbed her back and stroked her hair, and bent down so she could peer up into her daughter's hot little face.

'Tell me what's wrong, sweetheart. *Please*. You're starting to scare me.'

Ruby shook her head. A couple of times she tried to speak, but she couldn't. She cried and cried and cried in her mother's arms, and when she finally got words out, they were so tiny and feeble, and so clotted with snot, that Alison Trick had to put her ear close to Ruby's lips, to hear what it was that her little girl was trying to say.

'*Don't tell Daddy.*'

44

O<small>N</small> T<small>HURSDAY</small>, R<small>UBY</small> rode the bus to school, deaf to the yells and the insults and the dirty names and the hair-pulling. The bus no longer registered on the scale of turmoil that her life had become.

As they passed through Fairy Cross, she thought of Miss Sharpe.

A bigger boy stamped on her foot and ran the sole of his other shoe down her leg, pushing the white sock down her shin and leaving a long scrape of mud and red skin behind it.

Ruby stared at him with unseeing eyes until he got up and moved to the back of the bus.

You can always come and tell me things, Ruby. Even secret things.

It was time to ask a grown-up for help.

Miss Sharpe was off sick.

The supply teacher's name was Mr Brains and he didn't want any jokes about his name because he'd HEARD THEM ALL BEFORE.

Still, 5B tested him on that claim from nine thirty when he introduced himself until the final bell rang at three thirty. Mr Brains couldn't win. If he knew a fact the children laughed because his name was Mr Brains, and if he didn't know a fact, or a face, or what happened after the next bell, or where the staffroom was, the children laughed because his name was Mr Brains.

Ruby didn't laugh. Ruby nearly cried. She had to *tell* someone. She wasn't sure *what* to tell them, but now that she'd decided to tell, she just had to tell *somebody something* and let a grown-up decide what to do.

But who *was* there?

She couldn't tell Mummy because she'd lied to her about the posses. Adam was just a kid like her – and if he told his father then Mr Braund might come round and there'd be a fight.

Who else could she trust?

There was nobody.

Ruby went through the school day in a haze of anxiety and on the way home on the bus she leaned her head against the glass and felt every bump through her temple as she worried about what to do.

Before she was really aware of it, Ruby had got off the bus in the wrong place. She got off in Fairy Cross, along with three children she hardly knew. They all looked at her funny, and then walked away, giggling.

She walked in the other direction – towards the pub.

It had been dark when she and Daddy had been here before, and raining then too, and she took a couple of wrong turns. But Fairy Cross was so small that even if you took *every* turn wrong, you'd find the right one quite soon, and it wasn't long before Ruby found herself outside Miss Sharpe's house.

She opened the little wooden gate and closed it behind her, then went up the path and knocked on the door.

She was nervous. But the longer Miss Sharpe took to answer the door, the less nervous she got, until she realized Miss Sharpe wasn't home, so she didn't need to be nervous at all.

When she stopped being nervous, she got a bit annoyed, and also worried. She'd got off the bus and now she wasn't sure how to get on another one. She'd only ever caught that one school bus from the stop at the top of the Limeburn road. She didn't even have any money, she realized, and got even *more* annoyed with Miss Sharpe for not being at school, even if she *was* sick.

Suddenly Ruby wondered whether Miss Sharpe might be so sick she couldn't get out of bed to answer the door. Maybe she was so sick that she needed a doctor.

Or an ambulance! Ruby might have to dial 999, which would be so *exciting*! Everyone at school would be so jealous! She hoped Fairy Cross had a phone box. She didn't want to knock on a neighbour's door for help and for *them* to make the 999 call and get all the glory.

She tried the door handle, because a lot of people never locked their houses or cars.

Miss Sharpe did.

She went round the house and knocked on the back door.

'Miss Sharpe!' she shouted. 'Miss Sharpe!'

The back door had little glass windows in it, although one was cracked and one was missing altogether, and the room Ruby could see through her cupped hands was the kitchen. There was stuff all over the floor – little pellets of something. Ruby frowned, trying to make out what they were. While she stared at the pellets, a large grey rabbit suddenly bobbed across the floor and started eating them.

'Harvey!' said Ruby. The pellets must be rabbit food.

Well, if Harvey was home then Miss Sharpe must be too. In bed. Sick. Needing blue flashing lights and a siren and a saviour.

Ruby tried the door and found it unlocked. Feeling like a burglar, she went inside.

It was scary being in somebody else's empty house, even if it was Miss Sharpe's. It was very, very quiet, and smelled a bit funny, like dinner, but there was nothing on the stove.

'Miss Sharpe!' she called out.

The rabbit came over and Ruby crouched down to stroke him. She was very gentle but he wasn't scared at all, and let her stroke him all over as much as she wanted. As she stroked him, Ruby felt better. It was like touching Lucky for luck, but nicer and warmer. The longer she stroked Harvey, the better she felt. He was so soft that she had to watch her own hand in places, to make sure she was actually touching him.

His ears were brilliant.

'Good boy,' said Ruby. 'Wait here.'

Harvey did wait, while Ruby crept quietly into the front room. 'Miss Sharpe!'

No one was there, so she went slowly upstairs. Halfway up she heard a sound and spun round to look behind her.

Harvey was at the foot of the stairs, sniffing her footprints.

'Good boy, stay there.'

She stood on the landing. 'Miss Sharpe? It's me. Ruby Trick.'

There were three bedrooms, and Miss Sharpe wasn't in any of them. The beds were neatly made, and on a chair in the biggest room was Miss Sharpe's handbag. Ruby recognized it because it had a little leather tag shaped like a Scottie dog.

Ruby went downstairs again and Harvey was there to meet her. He followed her into the kitchen, too.

She saw that the rabbit food strewn across the floor had rolled out of a big bag in the corner that had fallen on to its side, so she righted it. It was called Bugsy Supreme.

Near the back door were two bowls. One had more Bugsy Supreme in it and the other was empty. Ruby picked it up and filled it with water.

The second she put it back on the floor, Harvey hopped over and started to drink.

'Awwww, poor boy!' she said. 'You were so thirsty!' She crouched down and stroked the rabbit while he drank, and when he'd finished, he sat up straight and pulled his own ears down around his face, one by one, to clean them, which made Ruby laugh out loud because he looked like a toy rabbit or one in a cartoon.

She was cross with Miss Sharpe for not being there when she was supposed to be sick, but she was even crosser that Miss Sharpe had gone out and left Harvey without any water. If *she* hadn't come by he might have died!

She should take him home.

The idea came to her fully formed. She would take him home. It wouldn't be stealing; she would just keep Harvey safe and fed and watered until Miss Sharpe came back. Then she would give him back. Miss Sharpe would probably be *grateful* that Ruby had rescued Harvey. Ruby bet she *would* be.

She could always tell someone, of course. She didn't *have* to take the rabbit home. Ruby frowned at *that* fully formed thought. She could go next door and ask them to look after Harvey until Miss Sharpe came back. She could tell the school and they would call Miss Sharpe's mobile phone and see how long she'd be away. She could call the RSPCA and they would send a man in a van to take Harvey to a rescue centre.

If she did *any* of those things, then she wouldn't have to take the rabbit home.

So she didn't do any of those things.

Instead she found a carrier bag and scooped plenty of Bugsy Supreme into it, then knotted it at the top. There was no kind of cage that she could see, so she emptied her backpack on to the kitchen counter and put Harvey in there. She pulled the zips up high, so that only his head was poking out of the top of the bag, right beside the plush pony's head, which looked pretty funny, like she had a rabbit *and* a pony in her bag! She'd have to show Adam.

Then she picked up the food and left, closing the back door behind her.

Ruby waited for a bus for almost an hour. When she

got on she told the driver she didn't have any money.

'I got off the school bus at the wrong stop,' she said.

He looked Ruby up and down. 'Are you new?'

'No, I was just thinking about something else.'

The driver sighed and said, 'How far are you going?'

'Limeburn.'

'All right then,' he said. 'Just this once.'

When she got home, Mummy was there and Ruby was relieved to see her.

She told Mummy she'd been chosen to bring the school rabbit home.

'I didn't know you *had* a school rabbit.'

'Yes. His name's Harvey. He's Miss Sharpe's really, but she's off sick so they said I can look after him.'

'Didn't they give you a cage?'

'I couldn't carry it on the bus.'

'Did they give you some food for him?'

'Yes,' said Ruby, and showed it to her.

'He's very cute,' said Mummy. 'We'll make him a bed outside.'

'Harvey lives inside,' said Ruby.

'Well, here Harvey lives outside. You can let him out every day and play with him in the garden, but he'll poo on the carpet indoors and that's not on.'

'OK,' said Ruby reluctantly.

Mummy made a really good house for Harvey out of an old metal dustbin on its side and steadied with bricks. They filled it with sawdust from the shed next to the wood store where Daddy sawed up the logs, and they made a door from chicken wire.

Ruby played with Harvey for a while before tea – even after it started to rain – and Adam leaned over the gate and couldn't believe how lucky she was.

And, for a short while, Ruby couldn't either.

It was dusk before John Trick noticed he was drenched, and when he reeled in his line, there was a small, exhausted whiting on the hook.

He took his priest from his pocket and knocked the fish on the head, but he'd had four cans of Strongbow and he missed. The glancing blow only seemed to revive the fish, and it leapt from his hand and started to slap across the jagged rocks towards the sea.

Trick went after it, lurching and slipping. He missed it twice as it flashed and shimmered. On the first miss he dropped the priest between two rocks; on the second he ripped his jeans and skinned his knee.

The whiting was a flip-flop from safety when Trick finally grabbed it and pressed it hard against the slime-covered rock. Panting, he groped about and his hand closed on a smooth pebble the size of two fists.

He hit the fish twice, caving in its gills and popping out a silvery eye.

Then he hit it again and again and again – until the rock was coated with blood and guts, and scales were scattered around him like glittering confetti.

45

THE DAY OF the Leper Parade dawned grey and unseasonably sultry. The air was so heavy that it had pressed the sea into submission, and – even though the spring tide was due – the water lay flat and grey all the way to Lundy Island. Or where Lundy Island should be. There was no sign of it on the pale horizon.

> *Lundy high, sign of dry,*
> *Lundy low, sign of snow.*

Lundy wasn't low. It just wasn't there.

Ruby stood at the top of the slipway and stared out past the Gut and the Gore. She'd always felt the sea in her belly, and even though the tide was low and the water a long way off, today she felt it more than ever. *There's a storm coming*, she thought. But that was ridiculous. She'd never seen the sea more calm, or felt the air more still.

By lunchtime the air was like breathing water. The sky was giving her a headache. She could feel it pressing on her face, right under her eyes, and as soon as she pulled the potato sack over her head, it stuck to her skin.

Mummy got ash from the fireplace in the front room

and smeared it all over her face and arms, but it didn't stay as ash – it turned to paste and rolled up in the damp.

'Can I have scabs?' said Ruby.

'How do we do scabs?' said Mummy.

'Rice Krispies and tomato sauce.'

'We don't have Rice Krispies.'

Ruby had forgotten to ask for them. There'd been so many other things to think about lately. She sighed. She'd never win best leper under fourteen with just a sack and some ash. Any old leper could do that.

'I'm sorry, Rubes,' said Mummy.

'It doesn't matter,' said Ruby.

Suddenly she wanted to give Mummy a hug. It had been so long since the last one that she wondered whether she even should, but then she did anyway.

She was glad she had. Mummy's arms were warm and kind, and didn't seem surprised at all that Ruby had finally come home to them, even if she'd surprised herself.

'Love you hundreds,' Ruby said.

'I love you too, Rubes.'

Ruby nearly told her then. She nearly did. About the posses and the gun and the slashed tyre and Daddy not loving her, the feeling of dread in her tummy.

But if Daddy left them now, it would be her fault, because she'd made him so angry.

And then Mummy's arms might not be so warm and welcoming.

So instead she just stood there on the spider rug and rested her head on Mummy's chest and hugged and hugged and hugged.

Ching-ching.
They both looked up at the ceiling.
Ching-creak. Ching-creak.
'Daddy's coming.'

~

Taddiport was teeming with lepers that evening. Hardly anyone had come to watch – they were all taking part.

Daddy wasn't the only one who hadn't come as a leper – several people were in fancy dress. Crusaders and pirates spilled out of the pub and into the narrow road to mix with beggars and cripples and both halves of a pantomime horse: the front rearing up with his head flung backwards down his neck and holding a pint in his hoof; the back, red-faced and sweating, in hairy brown trousers and a tail.

Ruby kept a firm grip of Mummy's hand, and they followed Daddy through the crowds. Now and then they lost sight of him for a few strides, but they could always find him again by listening for the Jingle Bobs, which cut through the hubbub.

The crush was so great and the air so thick that every handshake was damp and every face red and shiny. Ruby was clammy and itchy, and, under the fried onions from the burger van, she could smell the bodies of the other people in the crowd.

They went along the row of little stalls selling all things for lepers. There were anti-leprosy crystals, leper begging bowls, and one-armed, one-eyed rag dolls. Mummy had given Ruby two pounds to spend and they stopped so she could buy fifty pence' worth of pus fudge, which was green with red swirls.

The man with one leg from the King's Arms swung past them on a rough wooden crutch, ringing a bell.

'Unclean!' he called every few strides. 'Unclean!'

'Look at his stump,' whispered Ruby, wide-eyed.

'Show-off,' said Daddy.

The sun set, although nobody could tell – the clouds on the horizon were so thick and black.

46

IT WAS UNCOMMONLY quiet for a Saturday at Bideford police station and the night-shift were playing canasta in the incident room.

Calvin wasn't. He was just enjoying the peace and quiet. Not only was it quiet here, but when he got home it would be quiet there, too. Or as noisy as he wanted to make it. The choice was his – that was the point. If he wanted to, he could spend the whole night watching porn and listening to Motörhead and eating all the crisps in the flat, which – after yesterday's demob-happy supermarket sweep – was a *lot*. He'd got to the checkout feeling as high as a kite, and watched in cocky rebellion as the checkout girl had put through the beer and the snacks and the frozen pizzas and the DVDs with guns on their covers. He'd thrown in a Fifa soccer game from the bargain bin and he didn't even have a PlayStation! He'd get one though. And an Xbox too, if he wanted it. All around him, Calvin had felt the envious eyes of married men burning into him and he'd felt like beating his own chest at the dearth of vegetables in his trolley.

How had he let that wedding nonsense go on for so

long? He could see everything so clearly now. He felt as though he'd escaped a cult.

'You're very happy,' King had said suspiciously.

'Yes,' he'd told her. 'I broke up with Shirley.'

'Oh dear. Was it awful?'

'Yeah. But I don't think she was my type.'

'What's your type?'

'I'm not sure I have one.'

King had laughed and said, *Very wise*, and that was all they'd said on the matter.

Calvin looked up. Tony Coral was at the door of the incident room. He'd never mastered the phone system, even though it was the most basic version money could lease. Instead he liked to put the caller on hold and then get out of his chair with a creak and a sigh and wander about the building looking for the caller's target recipient.

Now he put one hand against the door-frame and tilted, standing on one leg with the other extended behind him, as if he were about to glide into the incident room on ice skates.

'Got a bloke here with a missing person.'

Calvin was the youngest at the station and the card players all looked at him, so he went out to the desk, to save Tony Coral the trouble of cutting the caller off.

'I want to report someone missing,' said the man on the phone.

'Right, sir. Can I take your name, please?'

'Marshall. David Marshall.'

'And what's the name of the person you believe to be missing?'

'Georgia Sharpe.'

'Sharpe with an *e*?'

'I think so. On the end.'

Calvin took all the details the form demanded. Georgia Sharpe was a teacher at Westmead Junior School. She was only twenty-something and he wondered out loud why her family weren't reporting her missing.

'I'm not sure,' said Dave Marshall. 'I think it's just her and her father, and he lives miles off. Scotland or somewhere like that.'

'Is she Scottish?' said Calvin. An accent would be helpful on a missing-persons report.

'No.'

'Oh.'

'Look,' said Dave Marshall, 'I hope I'm not wasting anyone's time. I don't know Georgia that well. She only started here in the summer. But she's a nice person and very good at her job and I don't think she'd miss work unless she was sick, and if she were sick then I think she's the type who'd definitely call in, and she didn't, and I couldn't get an answer on her phone.'

'OK, Mr Marshall,' said Calvin. 'We'll send someone round to check whether she's there and then if necessary we can take things further.'

Calvin would bet a pound to a pinch of dog shit that they'd find Georgia Sharpe in bed with flu or a boyfriend, but he liked saying *We'll send someone round*. It was the kind of thing they said in American cop shows, even though he knew it would probably end up being just *him* going round and tapping on a window like an elf.

They'd give it twenty-four hours, of course. They always gave a missing person twenty-four hours to show

336

up unless it was a child or someone had seen them bundled into a van.

Or they'd called their mother.

But that hadn't happened in this case. This sounded far more straightforward.

Calvin was typing up the report to leave for whoever was on tomorrow night when Tony Coral came back again. He lowered his voice to a stage whisper.

'Got a maid here with a box of pornographic videos.'

'Good for her,' said Calvin.

Coral jerked a thumb over his shoulder and back towards the front desk.

'Name's Sheila. She wants to talk to you.'

As the youngest, Calvin knew to be on his guard against pranks – especially on a Saturday night – so he followed Tony Coral with a frown of caution fixed firmly on his face.

But it wasn't a prank.

It was *much* worse than that.

It was Shirley.

Shirley, with a cardboard box full of junk he'd left at her flat. Including three or four DVDs they'd watched together right at the start of their relationship, when they were still making an effort. It wasn't hard-core porn – just Milfs and Big Boobs – but it still wasn't the kind of thing Calvin wanted to assume ownership of across a police-station counter – especially from an ex-girlfriend who had obviously been drinking and crying in equal measure, from what he could see through the crack in the door.

He stopped dead and signalled Tony Coral back towards him.

'That's my girlfriend,' he hissed.

'Oh yes?' said Tony Coral. He leaned again – backwards this time – to get a better view of Shirley. 'Pretty maid,' he said approvingly.

'My *ex*-girlfriend,' Calvin added.

'Quite *sturdy*, in't she?'

Calvin ignored that out of old loyalty. 'We just broke up a week ago.'

'Ah,' said Coral, nodding as if he understood everything. Then he added, 'I don't understand.'

'I don't want to see her.'

'Aah,' nodded Coral. This time he obviously *did* understand.

'Can you say I'm out on a job?'

'I already said you were here.'

'Can you say you were wrong?'

Tony Coral looked offended. 'That would be lying.'

Calvin sighed. He knew Coral wasn't joking; he really was a stickler for the truth, however inconvenient.

'Then I'll go out,' he said. 'Right now. Give me five minutes and then tell her I'm on a job and by then it'll be the truth.'

'Righto,' said Coral. 'What job?'

Calvin thought for a second. 'That missing person that just came in. I'll go out to Fairy Cross and knock on a few doors, OK?'

'No problem,' said Coral. 'Shall I tell Sheila to come back another time?'

'No! Jesus!' Calvin hated this. The one true path was the one of least resistance and he desperately wanted never to have to see or speak to Shirley again. He

338

realized that that was unrealistic, both living in the same smallish area of North Devon as they did, but the *last* thing he wanted was for Shirley to keep bringing his box of porn to him at work. Which he had no doubt she would do – otherwise she would have just dropped it off at his flat, or thrown it in the bin in the first place.

She wanted to embarrass him.

Calvin sighed.

He owed her that, really. He'd hurt Shirley; he'd broken her heart and ruined her wedding with the hand-torn invitations and the fucking owl. The *least* he could do was to go out there and let her embarrass the socks off him with a box of Milfs and an engagement ring in the face.

Then he had a better idea.

'Can't you confiscate it?' he said. 'It is porn, after all.'

Five minutes later, Shirley was walking home without the pornography, and Calvin Bridge was driving a pool car to Fairy Cross.

Dave Marshall hadn't had a specific address, but Calvin thought that it wouldn't take much knocking on doors to track down Georgia Sharpe's home. Everyone knew everyone in little places like that, even if they were new. Sometimes *especially* if they were new.

He felt bad about Shirley, but really, she'd brought it on herself.

47

I T GOT DARK.

Ruby's headache had gone, along with the warmth. A sharp breeze had picked up and she wished she were wearing a jumper over her potato sack.

There was much cheering as the torches were lit and the flags were brought out and the parade started, led by the town crier and two ragged lepers on towering stilts.

Ruby felt the thrill of being part of something that felt crazy and ancient, and squeezed Mummy's hand in excitement.

They were part of a great river of people that wended its way down the hill to the old hospital. There were so few people left over to watch and clap the parade that they clapped and cheered themselves as they walked, and rang their leper bells.

As Ruby passed the grim, grey house that was once home to the lepers of the parish, thunder cracked so hard that they all jumped, and then embarrassed laughter rippled through the parade.

Ruby looked up.

There were no stars at all, and the last dim glow of

daylight showed her that this morning's flat white sky had now blossomed into dark-purple clouds.

'It's going to rain,' she said.

'What a surprise,' said an old beggar lady beside her and then cackled and rang her bell in Ruby's face.

The fields by the river were muddy, but nobody cared. They walked a path of churned mud to where a hog was being turned on a spit, and Superman and Captain Hook queued up among the lepers, all with their paper plates and bread rolls and apple sauce at the ready.

They met the Braunds in the queue. They had brought Maggie with them in her pink fairy costume with glittery wings and a wand that was tipped with a silvery five-pointed star. The perfect deputy's badge, if Ruby had still wanted to be a deputy.

Which she didn't.

Mr Braund was much taller than Daddy and he and his wife were both dressed in brown sacking, very like Ruby's. Except Mr Braund was too big and well fed to be a convincing leper; with his thick black hair, he had more of the Fred Flintstone about him. Adam and Chris were in ragged old clothes and had proper scabs. Chris had a bell, which he kept ringing right next to Maggie's ear. She kept saying, 'Stop it, Chris,' and rubbing her ear, and he kept doing it again.

The Braunds were full of jolly *hello*s. Mummy said hello to them but Daddy only grunted, and Ruby's tummy tightened the way it did on a school day.

'Hi,' said Adam.

'You look like a real leper,' Ruby said.

'Thanks,' he said. 'So do you.'

341

'I don't have scabs,' said Ruby. 'We only had Weetabix.'

'Still,' he said, 'your ashes are good.'

'There's Nanna and Granpa!' said Mummy.

Ruby giggled. Nanna wasn't in a costume, but Granpa was dressed like a pirate *with* leprosy. He had a big ginger beard to match his hair, and a fake hand that came off when you shook it.

Everybody laughed.

Granpa offered his fake hand to Daddy, but Daddy didn't shake it – just looked at him so hard that Granpa stopped laughing.

'There were trout jumping in the river earlier,' said Adam. 'You want to go and look?'

'OK,' said Ruby.

'No,' said Daddy.

'It's only over there,' said Mummy.

'Not with him,' said Daddy, nodding at Adam.

There was a surprised silence. Then Mr Braund said, 'What do you mean, not with him?'

'Just that,' said Daddy. 'Not with him. The leaf don't fall far from the tree.'

Ruby looked at Adam, who looked confused.

'John,' said Mummy quickly, 'don't be silly.'

'Who's silly?'

'No one,' said Mummy. 'We're all having a nice time. That's all.'

'And I'm spoiling it? Is that what you're saying? I'm spoiling your nice time?'

Ruby felt the other people in the queue getting quiet to listen to them.

342

'Take it easy, John,' said Mr Braund. 'She—'

'Fuck you,' said Daddy.

Mummy touched Daddy's arm. 'John— '

Daddy shoved his paper plate into Mummy's face, making her head twist sharply to the side, and she took a couple of surprised steps backwards. When the plate dropped to the ground, the bread roll was stuck for a moment on her cheek with apple sauce. Then that fell to the ground as well.

'Whore!' spat Daddy. Then he turned and punched Granpa in the tummy. Just once, but so hard that his teeth fell out.

'Stop!' said Ruby. 'Daddy, stop!' Even though she knew there were some things you could never stop, and she was afraid this might be one of them.

But Mr Braund stepped swiftly between Mummy and Daddy, and Superman and the back end of the horse were suddenly right there too, and Daddy said *Fuck you all* and walked off into the night.

'Come away, children,' said Mrs Braund, and started to try to gather them up and usher them away, but none of them went.

People were helping Granpa, and Nanna was fussing around, brushing mud off his dentures.

Ruby was shaking. And when she took Mummy's hand, Mummy was shaking too.

'Are you all right, Alison?' said Mrs Braund.

Mummy nodded and tried to smile, but it didn't work. 'I think we should go home, Ruby,' she said in a wobbly voice. 'I'm not hungry, are you?'

'No,' said Ruby. 'I'm not hungry.'

'Let Tim take you home, Alison,' said Mrs Braund.

'No, that's fine,' said Mummy. 'I'm sure John will be at the car waiting for us.'

'I'll take you,' said Mr Braund firmly. 'I'll be back in half an hour. The queue probably won't even have moved.'

So that's what they did. Ruby said bye to Adam and he said bye to her and they followed Mr Braund all the way to the car park at the top of the village, as the first big drops of rain began to fall.

Where Daddy's car had been parked was now just an empty patch of grass.

The rain hammered down on the windscreen and the roof, and the wind jostled the Range Rover all the way home.

Mummy and Mr Braund didn't talk. Mummy chewed her thumbnail. Ruby sat on the pale-cream leather back seat, and pushed her feet under the driver's seat again, the way she had that day when Mrs Braund had picked her up near the empty paddock.

Her foot touched something and she ducked her head to look, then reached down and took hold of the thing under the seat.

It was the matching glove. The left hand that belonged with the right hand she'd found under the sofa.

And now she knew they both belonged to Mr Braund.

She stared at it, holding it loosely in her lap. Adam had said his daddy had a girlfriend. He'd said it was someone in London. But was he right? Or was it Mummy all along?

Call you later. T.

Ruby didn't know what to do. Ask? Or push the glove back under the seat with her toe?

How much did she want to know?

'Look what I found,' she said, before the decision had been consciously made in her mouth. She leaned forward and waggled the glove between Mummy and Mr Braund.

'Been looking for those,' said Mr Braund. 'Well done, Ruby. Where did you find them?'

'Under the seat,' said Ruby suspiciously. 'But there's only one. I found the other one in our house, behind the sofa.'

'Wonder how it got there,' said Mr Braund. 'I'll run over and get it sometime.'

'Ruby will bring it down tomorrow,' said Mummy. 'Won't you, Rubes?'

Ruby nodded slowly. Neither Mummy nor Mr Braund looked guilty about the glove behind the sofa. Maybe he really *did* have a girlfriend in London. And did it really matter any more? Ruby wouldn't even blame Mummy for having a fancy man. Not after what just happened.

They were almost home. The forest that whipped and waved over the steep road to Limeburn gave some shelter from the wind, but when they parked on the cobbles and Ruby got out, she was blown sideways.

Even though it was night, she could see the white tops of the waves hurling themselves at the cliffs.

They thanked Mr Braund and Mummy grabbed Ruby's hand and together they ran up to The Retreat, past the stream that was swollen anew by the downpour and by the thousands of muddy rivulets running out of the forest and off the surrounding cliffs.

Daddy wasn't home and Ruby was grateful.

They went upstairs and got ready for bed. Ruby hadn't been in hers for five minutes before Mummy came in and sat beside her.

'I'm so sorry about today, Rubes. Are you OK?'

Ruby twiddled her bed cover while the tree outside clawed at the window. 'Why was Daddy so cross?'

Mummy sighed. 'I don't know, sweetheart. Daddy's had a hard time, you know? Losing a job is very difficult for a man, and sometimes they can get upset for no real reason.'

'But why did he punch Granpa?' said Ruby.

Mummy shook her head and bit her lip and started to cry big tears that tipped out of her eyes and down her cheeks in shiny rills.

She held out her arms and Ruby reached up and let herself be gathered up in them and pressed against her mother's shoulder.

Mummy rocked her and Ruby let herself be rocked. 'Everything's going to be OK, Rubes,' said Mummy. 'Everything's going to be OK.'

Ruby didn't think Mummy was lying.

But she also didn't think it was true.

48

CALVIN TOOK LESS than five minutes knocking on doors to establish where Georgia Sharpe lived, but five minutes was long enough to get thoroughly soaked. He'd lived in North Devon all his life and he couldn't remember a storm like it. The wind drove rain deep into his ear as he hunched his shoulders and ran up the narrow path to the cottage on the end of the row.

Everybody knew Georgia Sharpe, as he'd suspected. Mostly because she had a pet rabbit. 'In the house!' said more than one neighbour. Calvin understood. Around here, rabbits were pests and vermin, not cuddly pets that you paid to feed while they shat on your floor.

He knocked and got no answer and immediately ran round to the back door and knocked there too. He wasn't messing about in this typhoon.

Calvin noticed the small pane of glass missing in the door and tried the handle. It was unlocked, and he stepped out of the wild elements and into the calm of a well-ordered kitchen. Only a scattering of what he assumed was rabbit food on the floor and a small but untidy pile of books and stationery on the counter interrupted his eye. And the smell of burned meat made him wrinkle his nose.

'Hello?'

Just the way the word distributed itself through the air told Calvin that the house was empty.

He wouldn't find Georgia Sharpe here.

Still, he couldn't put that on any kind of official documentation, so he searched the house, just to rubber-stamp his instincts.

For some reason, the house creeped him out. There was no logic to it. There was nothing out of place, nothing disturbed, no nasty surprises. And yet he felt his hackles tingle on several occasions.

When he found the handbag on the chair in what he assumed was Georgia Sharpe's bedroom, his heart sank. This wasn't good. Calvin didn't know much about women, but he did know that women and their handbags were like conjoined twins. If they had been separated, then *anything* might have happened.

After he found the handbag, he put on a pair of blue latex gloves and went through the house again – this time opening all the wardrobes.

Nothing.

Back down in the kitchen, he noticed the bag of Bugsy Supreme was upright next to the dustbin. If the rabbit had pulled the bag over to get at the food, it certainly hadn't righted it. And where *was* the rabbit? There was a full litter tray in the utility room and a bowl filled with water near the back door, but no sign of the rabbit itself.

'Here, Bugs!' he called. 'Here, Bunny!'

The bunny didn't show itself.

Calvin sifted through the pile of random items on the counter. Three blue exercise books, a red card covered with gold stars with the handwritten heading *For Good Attendance*, and a pencil case in the shape of a banana with googly eyes. Inside the banana were two ballpoint pens, a pencil sharpener and the shoe from a Monopoly set. Georgia Sharpe was a teacher, but these were not the contents of a teacher's bag, but a child's.

It was puzzling. Something was definitely amiss. Calvin wished Kirsty King were here to work it out, but she wasn't, so he'd have to do his best.

Calvin picked up the first of the exercise books and smiled. In the top-right corner of the cover, in sloping, uneven handwriting, were the words *My Dairy*. And then – underneath that – the book's apparent owner: *Ruby Trick*.

He knew that name!

He wound back through his memory. He was young and he got there fast. Ruby Trick was the child he'd spoken to in her father's car. In Instow, on the same night that Steffi Cole had made her last, traumatic phone call home.

Calvin's neck prickled again and he laughed out loud. Ridiculous! Getting a chill from a child's diary. There was no connection, only coincidence.

But his hackles wouldn't let him off the hook so easily.

Feeling pretty stupid – and glad that nobody else was here to laugh at him – Calvin Bridge flicked through Ruby Trick's diary.

He stopped near the end, and this time the ripple of unease raised every hair on his body.

My Daddy's got a gun . . .

Calvin told himself not to be stupid. Not to overreact.

This was a ten-year-old girl's diary, not a treasure map in a pirate film. He needed to be objective. He needed to be cautious. He needed to be *modern* – because his ancient body was tingling and fluttering with warning.

He read the entry again, then put the diary down with a hand that shook a little. Fuck modern – this was important. This was *something* – even though he didn't know what. Yet. Right now he could only see a jumble of fleeting images that skittered about in his head while he tried desperately to grab them and make them fit together.

Kirsty King tapping her teeth with the gall-stone scoop.

Jody Reeves sticking out her thumb for a short ride to death.

Lips moving through the slit in a black balaclava. *Call your mother.*

Mother-of-pearl stars in a chocolate sky.

Ruby Trick's father at the boot of his car – squinting into the headlights.

My Daddy's got a gun.

Frannie Hatton's bruises.

Frannie Hatton's bruises.

Frannie Hatton's bruises.

Maybe they only needed one body, after all . . .

Calvin felt two pieces fit together like a puzzle, and reached for his phone.

When Kirsty King answered, he didn't even say hello.

'I know why he doesn't shoot them!' he shouted. 'The gun's not real!'

49

THE STORM CAME.

The forest around Limeburn had stood for five hundred years and seen few like it.

The wind and the rain combined to bring more water off the surrounding hills than ever before. Instead of raindrops falling on to leaves and weighing down the branches of the trees, they were immediately dashed from their resting place to the ground, where they gathered together and rushed downhill towards the sea.

The stream broke its mossy banks and flooded the road and the cobbles three inches deep. It filled the Bear Den.

In the clearing on the top of the cliff, the wind was even more punishing. Small things bent double to get out of its way.

Big things fared less well.

The giant oak that bore the swing was alone on the bluff. Unlike the forest behind it, where each tree sheltered its neighbour, this oak had stood on the cliff above Limeburn in splendid isolation for over two centuries – a lookout and a landmark – facing down nature.

But this night would be its last.

It swayed and it creaked and it strained under the assault that was a north wind coming straight off the ocean, sweeping all before it. The frayed rope whipped about until it swung so hard and so high that it got tangled in the branches. The oak started to moan, and then to squeal. If any human being had been crazy enough to be sitting on the nearby bench at the time, they would have felt the ground move beneath them as the mighty roots strained to hold on to Mother Earth. Rising and falling, rising and falling, as if the land itself were gasping for breath.

Some time just after midnight, a sound like a gunshot fired through the forest and the bench was tilted, then tossed aside by a great upheaval of soil and roots that rose vertically in the sky for ten, twenty feet. They hung there like witches' fingers, as the tree they'd nourished for so long clung to the only home it had ever known.

With a horrible shriek, the mighty oak tipped slowly forward and peered over the edge at the raging waters below and then – with a final rending sound – it tumbled off the cliff and into the ocean.

The storm was so loud and the sea so wild that when the giant tree hit the waves, it barely made a splash.

Ruby woke at the sound of a gun.

She lay there for a moment, the sweat that was cooling fast on her body the only evidence of a bad, bad dream.

But even though she was awake, something was still very wrong.

The wind and the rain outside were momentous and the branches squealed and banged at her window, but something *else* was wrong. Something closer.

She frowned in the dark and realized what it was.

She had wet herself.

Ruby sat up in slow disgust and switched on the lamp. Then she pushed her bedsheets down. She hadn't wet herself in bed for years. Not since she was tiny. She couldn't believe it had happened now.

It hadn't.

In the middle of the bed was a small patch of blood.

Ruby slithered out of bed as if she'd found a spider there, then stood and stared at the red spot on the white sheet for a very long time.

She knew what it meant.

Tears rushed up her nose and into her eyes.

She was becoming a woman, and there was nothing she could do about it. It was one of those things you just couldn't stop.

She finished crying and stood and shivered for a moment in her Mickey Mouse nightshirt. Then she went to the bathroom and took one of the little pads Mummy had shown her and peeled off the strip and stuck it in a fresh pair of knickers. She didn't know what to do with her old ones so she decided to throw them away. Not here in the little bathroom bin where anyone might see them, but downstairs in the bigger kitchen bin. Maybe even outside in the proper dustbin – although the storm howled so loud around the house that she thought maybe the kitchen bin would be enough, if she pushed them down among the rubbish so nobody knew.

Ruby crept down the stairs and opened the little white door at the bottom. *Tried* to open it. But something was pressing against it from the other side.

She stopped and frowned. She could hear something on the other side of the door. Something alive.

Something *breathing*.

'Daddy?' she whispered warily. 'Daddy?'

There was no answer but the trees trying to break in through the roof, and that strange in-out sound of deep, slumbering inhales and exhales.

It made her shiver again – and not because she was cold.

If she hadn't had the knickers balled up in her hand, Ruby would have gone back upstairs to bed and waited till morning.

Instead she pushed on the door again – hard. This time there was far less resistance. The door to the front room opened suddenly, and Ruby stepped down into the sea.

50

T HE STORM AND the highest tide of the year had joined forces with the rain-sodden forest to finally wipe Limeburn off the map.

The rats had come first. Washed out of their nests in the kilns, and dashed against the cottages and cars by the storm. The waves that crossed the cobbles were fringed with the black, seething beasts, some squealing and terrified, some sodden and limp and already dead.

Then the sea came up the slipway too. Further than it had ever been before.

It met the broken stream coming the other way and together they filled the square with three feet of water – preparing the way for the *real* onslaught.

That final assault came in the shape of the great oak. In this magnificent tree, the sea had found a true weapon of war. It heaved the oak against the bigger of the limekilns like a battering ram. Again and again and again, until – at last – the thick stone walls fell and the kiln burst apart like a bomb, spilling its dark secrets into the ocean.

Ten thousand years from now, the grey stones that once made up the limekiln walls would be smoothed and rolled for miles up the coast to fortify the pebble ridge, in protection of another place entirely.

But their work here was done; there was no barrier remaining between Limeburn and the sea.

And the sea knew it.

It had crossed the square in a single sweep of breaker, leaving only the top windows of the cottages peeping out of the waves. It had set Maggie's mother's twenty-year-old Nissan adrift, and – because John Trick's old piece of junk still wasn't between them – crashed it into Mr Braund's new Range Rover.

Then the sea had surged up the shallow hill to The Retreat, funnelled white water through the garden gate and smashed the front door clean off its hinges.

The sea!

The sea was in their house!

It was nearly up to Ruby's knees and she staggered sideways with shock and almost fell, and got wet all the way up one thigh too.

It didn't seem real. Everything else was the same: the lamps were on double – in the room and in the water. The front door was part open – hanging drunkenly on its top hinge alone. The spider rug floated gently off the floor and followed the water back outside as it retreated.

Then the sea exhaled and came again. When it came back this time, it came like a gunfighter into a saloon. The door flapped on its hinge and a wave crashed through the house and broke in a roil of foam, then spread itself around the room and slapped gently against the TV, which banged in a shower of sparks, along with the lamps, and everything went black.

'Mummy!' screamed Ruby. 'Mummy!'

The bitter water gripped Ruby's hips and she staggered sideways and grabbed the handle of the little white door to stay upright as the wave withdrew once more.

As her eyes adjusted to the new darkness, Ruby could see through the doorway and out into Limeburn.

The water was cold, but the chill that ran down Ruby Trick's spine was even colder.

She'd been wrong.

The sea was not in their house.

Their house was in the sea.

Through the broken front door, Ruby could see the silhouette of an enormous tree rolling backwards and forwards in the square, bashing and banging between the cars and the cottages.

Everything between here and there was water.

'Mummy!' she screamed. 'Mummy!'

All these years she'd been so scared of the woods, of the trees, of the creeping undergrowth and of the mud.

But the real danger all along had been the dark-grey ocean on their doorstep.

Ruby saw the next wave coming. She turned to run back upstairs, but it knocked her clean off her feet and washed her into the coffee table. She banged her head and her shin, and swallowed salt water, before getting to her hands and knees, choking and spluttering and unable to shout for help.

The sea sucked the wave back out of the house and Ruby knelt there and panted for a moment, too shocked to think straight, only aware of the salt in her mouth and the spongy carpet under her fingers.

'Ruby!'

'Mummy!'

She scrambled to her feet just as the next surge hit her, but it wasn't as great this time, and she stayed upright by grabbing the edge of the table, then splashed her way over to the stairs.

'Mummy!'

'Ruby! Where are you?'

'Here!'

Something bumped against Ruby's thigh. She looked down and frowned. She *recognized* the thing that was floating in the black water, but she couldn't *understand* it. It was beyond her. It was too much.

It was a body.

A woman's naked body. Face-down and tight with bloat, the shoulders and the buttocks keeping it high in the water.

Without a face it could be anyone. Mrs Braund? Maggie's mother? Old Mrs Vanstone? Ruby didn't know; couldn't think; didn't want to.

As the black ocean lapped at the walls of the living room, the body drifted slowly away from Ruby. Then it rebounded gently off the sofa and came back for another pass.

And that's when Ruby saw the bracelet. The silver chain bit into the bloated wrist, but the charms tinkled the way they always had – the elephant and the crow . . . and the little horseshoe.

Her heart beat hard in her head, and she felt sick.

She'd tried to tell Miss Sharpe her secrets, and now Miss Sharpe was dead.

Just like Frannie Hatton was dead, although her nose ring was in the car, and Steffi Cole was dead in the dunes behind the toilets.

And suddenly Ruby *just knew* that her Daddy had killed them all.

The wave turned and Ruby braced herself against the little white door as the water started to tug at her legs. The body floated away from her, the arm with the bracelet trailing behind it in goodbye. It bumped and turned slowly in the doorway, and when the tide sucked the sea out of the house, it took Miss Sharpe with it.

'Ruby!'

She turned and saw Mummy standing halfway down the stairs – her face panicky and her phone in her hand.

'Mummy! The sea's in the house!'

'Come upstairs! Quick!'

Ruby ran up to join her and they hugged on the landing. Ruby started to cry.

'Shh, baby. We're going to be fine.'

They weren't, Ruby knew. She shook her head, but she was crying too hard to explain why.

'Where's Daddy?' she said in sudden panic.

'Don't worry, sweetheart,' said Mummy soothingly. 'I already called him and he's coming straight home to take care of us.'

The storm that had come out of nowhere was so violent that water spurted up and out of drains and gushed across roads.

In Bideford it created long, axle-deep stretches that halted pedestrians and slowed sane drivers to a crawl.

John Trick was not one of those.

The dirty white car sent up great bow-waves as he defied the heavens and headed for hell.

He'd lost Alison.

She was dead to him. The filthy whore.

The worm of suspicion had turned into a python of hatred and self-pity – squeezing his guts and starting to swallow him whole. He saw it all now. He'd been blind, but he saw it all now.

He'd kill her. He'd kill them all! Her and her bitch mother and her red-headed pervert of a father.

Trick sobbed through gritted teeth and pressed his palm to his belly to feel the coils of the mighty snake. It was loose inside him and he had no control over it.

If he didn't feed it, then it would kill him.

But killing Alison was too good for her. Too quick, too painless, too kind. He needed to see her *suffer* for what she'd done to him. For taking away his strength and his power and his self-worth and his *fucking life* with her whoring and her betrayal and her lies.

He could punch her and kick her and slap her – but it wouldn't be enough. It would never be enough.

But there were other ways to hurt a mother . . .

John Trick turned his head.

A woman was pushing a buggy in the rain. Running

with it – head down, splashing through floodwater, regardless of the wet, which had already soaked her jeans, making them look almost black.

The baby was enclosed in a plastic bubble, a PVC chrysalis designed to keep it warm and dry.

Designed to keep it safe.

But the spray from the wheels and from passing cars had spattered mud all over the front of it, and condensation inside the bubble made the child invisible.

John Trick slammed on the brakes and slithered to a halt just ahead of the young woman.

He got out of the car and walked briskly around the back of it towards her.

She stopped. Lifted the drenched hood of her anorak from her eyes to stare hopefully at him. He knew how it would go. How it *could* go.

You want a ride?

Yes, please! I wouldn't normally, but have you ever seen weather like it?

He didn't give a shit what she'd *normally* do.

Five feet from her, he pointed the gun at her face.

'Whore,' he said.

'What?' The young woman frowned as if she just hadn't heard him.

'Fucking *whore*.'

She heard *that*! Her face dropped slowly into the more familiar confusion and fear.

Then she looked at the gun for the first time and gasped.

Trick kept the gun on her face as he bent to lift the plastic bubble.

'NO!' she screamed. '*NO! Leave him alone! Help! Help me!*'

The woman tried to pull him away, but he ignored her. Nobody was going to help her. There was nobody out in this weather. Nobody but her. The selfish bitch. Taking her baby out in this weather. Putting him in danger. Not caring about *him*.

He'd show her. He'd teach her a lesson she'd never forget.

Never.

The fastenings on the bubble were weird. He couldn't see how to undo them.

The woman clawed at the side of his head and he belted her with the gun. She fell backwards into a puddle. A deep puddle, a shallow pool. She lay there, dazed, with her eyes blinking, blood coming out of her nose, and water up to her ears, while cars went past them like speedboats.

He turned back to the buggy.

Ah, *that* was how you opened this fucking bubble. *That* was how you got inside . . .

His phone rang.

He straightened up and answered it.

He stood there in the rain, listening, nodding, responding, as the young woman raised herself groggily from the water. She fell twice getting up, water pouring from her hair and her clothes.

'My baby,' she kept saying. 'My baby.'

John Trick hung up the phone.

The woman ignored him. She staggered to the buggy and draped herself over it like a giant spider.

'My baby.'
'That was my wife,' Trick told her. 'I have to go.'

51

'WE HAVE TO get out,' cried Ruby. 'We can't stay here.'

'No, Ruby,' said Mummy. 'We're surrounded by water. It's too dangerous to try to leave. Daddy will come soon or the tide will turn and we'll all be fine.'

'No!' said Ruby. 'We have to go *now*. *Before* Daddy comes!'

'It's OK, Rubes, we'll be safe if we just wait here.'

'No!' Ruby yelled. 'We have to *go*! We *have to go*!'

Mummy took her wrist. 'Calm down, Ru—'

'I don't want Daddy to come!' Ruby shouted. 'I'm *scared* of Daddy!'

Mummy's fingers tightened on her wrist and she went white and very quiet and looked hard into Ruby's eyes.

'What do you mean?'

Ruby fought back tears. 'I don't want to see Daddy any more. I want to go now. Just with you. Please, Mummy. *Please?*'

Ruby expected Mummy to ask her why. She expected Mummy to try to talk her out of it. She expected Mummy to tell her she was being a silly little girl.

Instead Mummy squeezed her hand and said, 'OK. Let's go.'

Mummy didn't even change out of her pyjamas. She pulled on trainers and grabbed her phone and then helped Ruby dress.

'No jeans,' said Mummy. 'They'll get wet and too cold.' So Ruby pulled a thick jumper over her Mickey Mouse T-shirt, and put on her own trainers. Her hands shook so hard that Mummy had to tie her laces.

Ruby looked round her room. She had to take what she could. She put Lucky in her pony backpack, along with his broken leg and the sled and the potato. Maybe one day they could all be fixed, like the bathroom window.

'Come *on*,' said Mummy.

'Where are we going to go?'

'Up to the road,' said Mummy. 'I'll call Nanna to come and pick us up.'

She grabbed Ruby's hand and started down the stairs.

But then she stopped.

'Wait here,' she said, and ran back to her bedroom.

Ruby followed her. Mummy was down on her knees, pulling stuff out of the wardrobe.

'Mummy, come *on*!'

'Wait!' She opened the bag with the jewellery in it and started to put it on, twisting her head and wincing as she forced the earrings through half-healed lobes, her hands shaking as she unclasped the fish brooch.

Mummy had gone mad.

'What are you *doing*?' Ruby yelled. 'Daddy's coming!'

'Here,' said Mummy. 'Do this up. We mustn't lose it.'

Ruby struggled with the clasp on the necklace, but finally found the clip. Then Mummy got to her feet and they rushed out of the room.

Ruby followed her downstairs. The water was coming up to meet them. In the lounge it was thigh-deep now, and freezing cold.

Hand-in-hand, they waded past the blue tapestry cushion and the tilting TV to the front door, and took their coats off the pegs.

On the way out, Mummy reached down and picked up the little china dog from the front window sill and slipped it into her pocket.

When they passed through the flooded doorway and into the ocean of their garden, Mummy and Ruby stood for a moment in shock.

They couldn't see much, but what they could see was terrible. A vast, alien expanse of sea where the village was supposed to be. The cottages down the hill were half under water and their windows were dark. The giant tree was still trapped between them, and they could hear the crashing and the tinkling of broken windows and smashed cars as it wallowed on the cobbles.

Mrs Braund's best chair floated past them – its only occupant a large wet rat digging its claws into the yellow silk upholstery.

'What about Adam?' said Ruby.

'They'll be OK, Rubes. They'll all wait upstairs until the tide turns.'

'What about Mrs Vanstone? She can't get upstairs.'

Mummy bit her lip. 'Come on, Ruby,' she said. 'We have to go.'

'We have to get Harvey,' said Ruby.

'We can't!' said Mummy. 'We have to hurry!'

'We *have* to! He'll *drown*.'

She broke free from Mummy and splashed round to the back garden. Twice a wave knocked her off her feet and the second time Harvey's dustbin washed right over her with a clunk on her head. It was bobbing about at an angle, but he was still in there, crouched in the bottom, looking twitchy.

Ruby got to her feet and shrugged off her pony backpack. She emptied Lucky and the sled and the potato into the sea. Then Mummy joined her and carefully scooped Harvey out of the bin and put him in the backpack instead. On Ruby's instructions, Mummy zipped the bag up so that just his head was poking out, the way she'd done on the bus from Fairy Cross. It seemed a thousand years ago, but it was only two days.

Then they headed back towards the front garden gate, but it was under water and they couldn't find it and kept bumping into the stone wall, until eventually Mummy helped Ruby over that instead, and they headed to where the road used to be. The water was up to Ruby's waist, and when waves came, her feet actually left the ground, and she could feel Harvey scrabbling about in fear in her backpack, but at least it meant he hadn't drowned yet.

Mummy shrieked and Ruby turned and saw a black rat run up her arm, spiky and terrified. Mummy flailed and sent it flying back into the water.

'Shit!' she said. 'I dropped the phone.'

Ruby said nothing, because there was nothing to say.

Something big splashed towards them in the darkness, from the direction of the cottages.

'Hello?' said Mummy nervously, but it didn't answer back. Within seconds they saw it was one of the Labradoodles. Ruby saw his blue collar and called, 'Tony!' but the dog just kept swimming past them, head jutting, towards the road.

They followed in his wake.

The headlights of a car flickered between the trees.

'Someone's coming,' said Ruby.

They stood and shivered, and watched the lights approach. As the car came round the last turn into the village, it narrowly missed the terrified dog running blindly up the lane. The car swerved hard, then continued almost to the water's edge before stopping.

'It's Daddy,' Ruby said. 'We have to go back.'

They both turned and looked behind them at the black, raging sea and the flooded village, then back at the lights of the car, parked between them and safety.

'We can't, Ruby,' said Mummy firmly. 'We have to get up high, and we have to get *safe*. And even if it *is* Daddy, right now he's safer than this.'

'No, Mummy! He's not! He killed Miss Sharpe!'

'What?'

'My teacher. He killed her. He killed her and all the others too!'

Ruby knew she was babbling and she could see Mummy's confusion and disbelief, but she carried on in a rush, 'Before – when you were still upstairs – Miss

Sharpe's body came in the house and I knew it was her because of her charm bracelet and then the sea took it out again.'

'What are you talking about, Rubes? You didn't say anything.'

'There was *too much* to say.'

It was true, and Ruby felt the weight of all the things she hadn't told Mummy or anyone else. There'd been a point where she might have said something to somebody – but once that point had been passed in silence, there was simply too much to say.

'Shh!' Mummy flinched and gripped Ruby's arm as the car door opened and the driver got out. Even silhouetted in the headlights, they could tell it was Daddy, wearing his Stetson and his Jingle Bobs. And in his holster, Ruby could see the outline of the gun.

Just like a real cowboy.

Ching. Ching.

The sea around them was dark and rough and Daddy couldn't possibly have seen them, but he never broke stride. He walked into the waves as if they weren't there, and headed straight towards The Retreat. Towards *them*. There was something so relentless – so *dangerous* – about it that Ruby gasped in terror.

Mummy felt it too. She must have, because without a word she turned and took Ruby's hand and led her back into the rising water.

'The haunted house,' said Ruby. 'That's highest up of all.'

52

K IRSTY KING MET Calvin Bridge at Georgia Sharpe's
house.

He drove on from there, while she read the diary.

'It's hardly damning evidence,' she said.

'I know,' he said.

'But it feels right,' she said.

'I know.'

King put the little blue exercise book on the dash and
added, 'But it doesn't feel good.'

Calvin nodded sombrely. 'I know.'

Running made everything more scary. But Ruby knew
from the Gore that standing still could be even worse.

They tried not to splash, not because of the noise,
which was negligible in the howling wind and thrashing
forest and crashing waves, but because of the white
marks it made on the surface of the oily black brine.
There was nowhere to hide but the dark and
the waves.

Twice, submerged branches knocked them off their

feet, but Mummy kept hold of Ruby's hand so hard that it hurt, and they always stuck together.

Once Ruby turned around and saw Daddy was closer, so she didn't turn around again.

The water was terrifying – the dark and the depth and the strength of it – but the idea of Daddy seeing them was even worse.

They passed The Retreat. The temptation to run into their home and cuddle up there in their warm beds was huge, but Ruby knew that Daddy would reach the house soon, and she didn't want to be there when he did.

So they waded past the place where the front gate probably still was, and instead went through the narrow gap between the noisy, swaying rhododendrons, to the Peppercombe pathway.

It was a waterfall of muddy water, shot through with debris washed out of the forest. The first part of the path was cut through thick undergrowth, and was slow going, with debris and brambles trying to stop them, trying to hold them there for Daddy to find. Mummy went ahead to deflect the worst of the muck, but Ruby was scratched and caught by a hundred thorns and prickles, and smacked by sticks and branches being washed down the path.

Twenty feet up – above the worst of the brambles – they turned to look down at The Retreat.

Ruby's fingers gripped her mother's leg. Daddy had reached the front gate already. He was so close! They were almost straight over his head! For a terrible second she thought he was going to look up and see them and start up the path behind them. If that happened, he would catch them for sure.

But he didn't look up, and even if he had, he'd never have seen them against the dark forest. He went through the gateway – moving much faster through the black seawater than they had – and disappeared into the house.

Without saying a word, Mummy led them upwards again.

Ruby slipped and fell to her knees, but Mummy was there to pull her up again. Harvey didn't like the rough ride. He squealed and scrabbled to be free.

'Shh, Harvey,' said Ruby. 'Good boy.'

It didn't help.

Ruby fixed her eyes on where Mummy was placing her feet, and followed in her footsteps.

John Trick searched The Retreat. It didn't take long because the ground floor was flooded and the upstairs was only three rooms big. Even so, he opened the wardrobes, just in case they were hiding in there.

The house was empty. Alison had called him for help and he'd told her he was coming home, and then the fucking bitch had fucked off somewhere else.

Tim Braund's, most likely. She'd probably used this as an excuse to go whoring.

When he caught her, he'd make her suffer.

He'd make her see what she'd done to him.

He glared through the bedroom window. From there he could usually see the lights in the little white cottages closer to the sea, but under the murderous sky, the homes on the square were only vague blobs of grey in the inky sea.

He looked until his eyes ached, but he could see no sign of his wife and her bastard child.

He would just have to go out there and hunt them down.

John Trick was three steps down the stairwell when he came back up and went into Ruby's bedroom. Her window was tiny and overgrown and was hard to see out of at the best of times, so he didn't expect much.

And he didn't get much.

The forest raged and loomed and flailed at The Retreat, and he wouldn't have seen a white elephant standing ten yards into the trees, it was that dense.

He almost turned away, and then he blinked and looked again.

Nothing. Nothing.

There!

What was that?

John Trick squinted.

Through the trees and the rain – about halfway up the Peppercombe pathway – a red light flickered.

Harvey didn't like being in the pony backpack.

It hadn't been too bad the first time, because that journey had been gentle and he'd just eaten a whole lot of Bugsy Supreme, which had made him sleepy.

But this journey was not gentle. It was wet and it was

cold and it was noisy and bumpy, and after one sudden drop that left him frantic and on his back, he decided that the snare around his neck had to go.

He started to claw at the zip. It didn't take him long to get one front paw through the tiny gap he managed to make, but then things came to a halt.

Having one paw and his head out of the bag was even more unbalancing, and Harvey twisted his head and tried to chew his way out of the backpack.

He chewed on the pony's ear and then on the loop for hanging the backpack on a hook, and then on the pony's other ear.

Finally Harvey chewed on the LED light that Ruby had got free off the front of *Pony & Rider*.

All you had to do was press the button on the back.

It was only a matter of time.

53

THE HOUSE WAS haunted and draughty and smelly and hung off a cliff, but when Ruby reached it, it felt like stepping into a safe haven.

But the moment she followed Mummy inside, a pulsing red light bounced off the walls.

Mummy cried, '*Ruby!* Oh my *God*! Turn it off!' She rushed over and spun Ruby round and felt for the switch on what Ruby realized must be her LED light. Harvey bit Mummy and both of them squealed.

Ruby dropped the pack off her shoulders and found the little plastic button and the room went black.

'How long was it on for?' cried Mummy. 'How long was it on for?'

'I don't know. I don't know! What if Daddy saw it?'

Mummy hurried to the glassless window. The floor there was always creaky and Mummy gasped and held the wall for support. Ruby ran over to join her.

Below them was The Retreat, still surrounded by shiny black water.

As they watched, Daddy came out of the front door and waded down the garden path, moving *fast*, as if he knew where he was going.

Ruby and Mummy held their breath.

Daddy went swiftly to the gate – and then turned and waded towards the Peppercombe path.

Mummy clutched Ruby's hand. 'He knows we're here!' She looked around the bare room and her voice cracked in desperation. 'We have to hide! There's nowhere to hide!'

'I know where,' said Ruby.

Calvin Bridge drove down the hill to Limeburn.

The normally dark, eerie lane was now treacherous too. Twice he had to steer around fallen branches, and once a branch crashed down into the ditch right beside them.

'Shit!' shouted King, and Calvin would have seconded it, but his mouth was too dry from fear.

They looked at each other, but Kirsty King wasn't the type to go back, and Calvin wasn't the type to go back if she wasn't going back.

So he went on.

They passed the little car park where visitors parked and swung round the final corner down to the village.

'Jesus Christ,' said King in amazement. 'Is that the *sea*?'

The flagstone in the hearth weighed a ton. Even with Ruby and Mummy trying to move it together. Their fingers could barely get purchase, and risked being squashed every time they lost their grip and dropped the huge slate. It wasn't a job to do in the dark.

And Ruby didn't even know what they'd find underneath.

Bare earth? Floorboards? A hole that was big but not big enough? Or a hole already occupied . . . ?

She didn't have time to care. For now, she needed Adam's ghost story to be true more than she'd ever needed anything in her life. Their lives depended on it. So she knelt and grunted alongside Mummy, while Harvey – free at last – twitched his nose at the edges of the stone, as if that would help.

Finally they got a good enough grip to lever the slab up and peer underneath, and Ruby felt her tummy flip over.

It was just as Adam had described.

The hole was not big, but it was big enough.

Who knew why it had been dug – for smuggling or family heirlooms or for hiding a priest – but Ruby no longer had any doubt that once the bones of a pedlar had been found here, curled up and grimacing and with knife-marks on his ribs.

She shivered all down her back.

'Get in,' said Mummy. 'Quick!'

Ruby didn't hesitate. She crouched down so she could slide under the flagstone.

Ching. Ching.

Mummy dropped the slab in terror and Ruby felt her heart stop.

Daddy had come to take care of them.

54

'HELLO, WHORES.'
Ruby still didn't know what the word meant, but it made her feel sick to hear him say it.

Mummy stood up. 'Ruby. Get behind me.'

She did. She was too scared not to.

'Don't hurt her,' said Mummy, and Daddy laughed a laugh that made Ruby go wobbly inside.

He started across the room towards them and Mummy backed away, with Ruby bumping behind her. She stumbled over the backpack and the red light flickered back into life.

'John, please listen to me. You're not well. I think you're not well. Please stop this and we'll see a doctor together. I promise you, I won't let you go through it alone. We'll go through it together. I *promise*.'

He laughed again. 'Cross your heart?'

'Cross my heart.'

'And hope to die?'

Mummy didn't answer. She kept moving round, pushing Ruby behind her, and Daddy kept following them. If Mummy moved left, he feinted left. If she moved right, he feinted right, and when she stood still, he kept coming. Mummy was trying to keep the room between them. Ruby understood what she was doing. But she knew it couldn't last.

And it didn't.

Daddy backed them into a corner. The corner furthest from the door. Furthest from safety.

As Ruby felt the walls on her shoulders, Daddy stopped.

He widened his stance. His arms moved away from his sides, slightly crooked at the elbows. He stretched his fingers.

He was getting ready to draw.

Mummy didn't know, because she wasn't a cowboy, so when he snapped the gun out of the holster, she screamed like in a horror movie.

Daddy laughed and laughed and laughed to see Mummy shrinking, terrified, against the wall.

'It's not real!' cried Ruby. 'Mummy, it's not real!'

But that didn't make Mummy feel better. It made her *furious*.

'You fucking bastard!' she screamed. 'Are you crazy? How could you scare us like that? How could you scare your own little girl?'

'She's not my little girl.'

Ruby frowned and looked at Mummy.

'Is she?' said Daddy.

'Of course she's yours,' said Mummy. 'She's your little girl and you're supposed to love her and take care of her, not scare the fucking *shit* out of her!'

Mummy reached for Ruby's hand and she took it, holding on as if they were hanging off a mountain together.

Daddy shook his head slowly. 'Not mine,' he said. '*Yours*. But not mine. I used to *think* she was mine, but now I know better. The way she betrayed me? The way she's started sniffing around the boys? The red hair? That's all *you*, Alison. Not me. That's all you and—'

'Shut up!' shouted Mummy. 'You shut your *mouth*. Ruby's your daughter and she loves you! Don't you, Ruby?'

Mummy jerked Ruby's hand so hard that she winced. 'You love your Daddy, don't you, Ruby?'

Mummy's terror made Ruby nod, even as tears fogged her vision. But Mummy wanted more, and shook her hard and shouted, 'Tell him you love him!'

Ruby couldn't. She was so scared she couldn't speak.

Mummy's nails dug into her hand. '*Tell him, Ruby! Tell him you love him!*'

Ruby shook her head.

No.

Daddy spun the Colt on his finger, and gave the mean, bitter little laugh that Ruby knew so well.

'You see?' he said. 'She doesn't love me any more than you do.'

Ruby felt Mummy's grip ease, and her shoulder slump a little.

'But we *used* to,' Mummy said softly, and Ruby looked up into her mother's face and saw how tired it was, and how sad.

'We *used* to love you, John. We both did. We both loved you so much . . .'

Her voice wavered and she stopped.

And then Ruby felt her mother sort of straighten up beside her before she spoke again.

'When you were worth loving.'

Daddy flinched as if he'd been smacked. He looked dazed and very young, and just for a second, Ruby saw him the way he used to be, years ago, when he still had a job and a family who loved him – and it made her feel as if her heart might burst out of her chest with grief.

Then Daddy's face changed again and he raised the gun and made an inhuman sound and came at them like an animal; like a tiger with its teeth bared, and murder in its eyes.

Mummy screamed and Ruby dropped to a helpless ball on the floor underneath her, her eyes squeezed shut and her hands over her ears, waiting to die.

There was a huge cracking, crashing sound and a frightened howl and then a weird, grunting noise.

And then only the roar of the storm.

Slowly Ruby opened her eyes.

She frowned in confusion as her brain adjusted to what she was seeing in the pulsing red glow.

Daddy was up to his waist in splintered, rotting wood, holding himself in place only by his elbows, the gun still in his hand.

He had gone through the floor.

Right in the place where she and Adam had made spyholes so that they could watch the sea.

If John Trick had done something instead of nothing at all for the past three years, he might have had the strength he needed to haul himself out of the hole in the floor with the gun in his hand. He certainly tried. He gripped and strained and cursed and spat, and on two occasions he almost made it.

But pissing in the sea like a castaway is no kind of workout. Not like scaffolding, or labouring, or fixing the windows or the roof or the walls of a crumbling little house, where a family is cold and getting colder all the time.

Only his anger kept him from falling straight through the floor and dropping silently past the dark cliffs, into the raging sea.

Only his anger and his madness.

Ruby could see it in his eyes, and when Mummy moved instinctively to help him, Ruby cried 'No!' and held tight to the sleeve of her cardigan.

They knelt and watched in numb silence as he strained and struggled to save himself. Somewhere in the sky below the house, the Jingle Bobs tinkled. Trick's head twisted from side to side and he bit his lip so hard he drew blood as he battled to lift his body on one hand and one elbow.

But because he'd done nothing at all for so long, John Trick finally needed full use of both hands.

He laid the gun down and flattened his palms against the splintered planks.

He hissed as he started to raise himself from the hole like an angry snake.

Ruby squealed. If he got out, Daddy would kill them both. He'd said, *Hello, whores*, and now Ruby knew for sure that Daddy killed whores.

That was just a fact of life.

Daddy hated women, and Mummy was a woman, and now she was a woman too.

He would kill them both.

Ruby's legs didn't want to move at first. But when she *forced* them, she moved faster than she ever had – running on her hands and feet across the floor like a giant spider.

Daddy saw her coming; knew what she was about. He snapped his bloody teeth inches from her face and roared, 'Touch it and you're *dead*!'

Ruby faltered. She'd promised. She'd *promised* not to touch the gun. Never. She stopped on all fours, mesmerized as Daddy rose slowly beside her – his arms shaking with effort as they straightened, his hips clearing the splinters, his knee starting to worm its way on to the edge of the broken boards, to lever himself out.

'Ruby, *run*!'

Her mother's cry galvanized her. But she didn't run. Not first. First she snatched up the gun, and *then* she turned to get away.

She nearly made it.

Daddy's fingers snapped shut round her ankle in an iron grip and he collapsed back into the hole in the floor – this time dragging Ruby with him.

'BITCH!' he screamed. 'FUCKING BITCH!'

He was up to his armpits, with her leg in his fist.

Life slowed like syrup.

Ruby twisted on to her back, trying to get purchase on the floor. Her Mickey Mouse T-shirt rumpled and hitched, and her bottom scraped painfully towards her father as he sank into the hole – his elbows rising like chicken wings, his teeth gritted, his throat on fire, his hand locked around her bare ankle.

Sinking. Sinking.

Slowly.

Slowly.

Ruby's heel tipped gently over the splintered edge of the hole. If she had tied her own laces, her shoe would have slipped off her foot. But because Mummy had tied them, she was following him. Following him down into the dark.

She started to cry.

'Daddy,' she sobbed. 'Daddy, please let me go.'

John Trick said nothing, but a high noise started from inside him like a kettle whistling up to the boil. Jagged splinters dug into his arms and ribs like barbs, slowing his descent and staining the perimeter of the hole with blood.

Ruby's foot twisted painfully as her ankle tore slowly over the piercing edge, and her knee lifted to keep her ankle from breaking.

'Daddy! You're *hurting* me!'

His mouth opened just enough so Ruby could see his bloody teeth. 'I'm not your Daddy,' he said. 'I'm not your Daddy.'

Then Mummy was there. Mummy smashed the china dog into his hands and arms until it shattered. Then she got Ruby under the arms and pulled.

The slide stopped.

'Let her *go*!' Mummy shouted. 'Let her *go*!'

But Daddy didn't let Ruby go.

Instead he started to climb up her leg.

Ruby shrieked. It wasn't the pain of being stretched between them; it wasn't the agony of the twisted foot or of the splinters, or of her father's nails digging into her soft flesh . . .

It was the *horror* of the thing that used to be her Daddy crawling up her wounded leg. Up her calf, her knee, her thigh.

And when it had *used* her to pull itself out of the hole in the floor, then it would kill her.

The gun was heavy in Ruby's right hand. It didn't feel like a toy – it felt real. It felt real when she raised it, and real when she pointed it with both shaking hands, and real when she squeezed the trigger so hard she thought her fingers would break.

The noise and the shock of the recoil knocked her backwards into her mother's arms and flattened them both.

Ruby opened her eyes and for a moment she stared at the sagging ceiling. Then she scrabbled backwards across the room, slapping hysterically at her own leg, as if her father's hand was still there.

It wasn't.

He wasn't.

All there was was an empty black hole in the floor, in the place where she'd once kissed Adam Braund.

55

THE SEA HAD taken the worst of Limeburn, but it left other things in its place.

First of those were hundreds of dead rats. So many that even the Labradoodles got tired of tossing them in the air, and the council had to send a bulldozer to scoop them all up.

Then there was the sand and mud and kelp and splintered wood and debris, knee-deep in every house, and the giant oak in the square that took four men nearly two weeks to cut up and haul away, until only the rope from the swing was left rotting on the cobbles.

Finally, there were the bodies.

Bodies that John Trick had hidden in the dark, stinking limekiln, and that the sea had found and returned to their families.

Miss Sharpe had not gone far after keeping her promise to help Ruby Trick. After the tide went out, she was found wedged behind the garden wall of The Retreat, her not-pretty face further uglied by unhealed, concentric burns that the pathologist later matched to the stove in her kitchen.

Old Mrs Vanstone looked out of her window the

morning after the flood to see Jody Reeves hiding near the Bear Den. Her face had been eaten by rats, but she was still wearing those stupid shoes.

And when the stream had subsided once more between its own banks, Steffi Cole was found jammed under the little stone bridge, with what Professor Mike Crew later said was 'half the Instow dunes' in her lungs.

The sea never returned John Trick to Limeburn – or to any other place, as far as anybody knew – but the police came down the hill in waves. They ebbed and flowed around The Retreat for days, but – apart from the bullet they took from Pussy Willows' dead eye – only one piece of physical evidence linking John Trick to the murders ever came to light.

Fittingly, it was Calvin Bridge who found it as they searched The Retreat. It was in a twist of toilet paper, hidden among a dead man's underwear.

When he unfurled the paper and saw Frannie Hatton's nose ring, Calvin felt an unexpected surge of emotion. He kept his back to PC Cunningham and DC Peters as sudden tears threatened to make him a laughing stock.

They were tears for Frannie Hatton, whose own beaten-down mother had ignored her last phone call, and they were also for Shirley, because he'd had to hurt her to preserve his own happiness. But most of all they were from sheer bloody relief that this case could now end, and he could be released from the shackles of serial ignorance and get back into uniform. Drink, drugs and debt awaited him and he would embrace them with new affection. After the past two months, constant ironing seemed a small price to pay.

Calvin half-laughed and wiped his nose on the back of his hand. All this from finding a little silver ring.

'Got something?' said DC Peters.

Calvin Bridge turned to show him but, before he could speak, there was a loud rumble, the floor shook – and the whole front wall of The Retreat fell into the garden.

After that, the crumbling, sea-softened house was cordoned off and nobody ever went inside it again.

Only children, of course.

And trees.

56

ALISON AND RUBY Trick left Limeburn, and never went back.

They didn't go to stay with Granpa and Nanna though – not even for a night. They stayed at the Red Lion on the curved sea wall at the foot of Clovelly until Mummy sold her earrings and necklace, and Tiffany brooch, and then they moved into their very own little cottage halfway up the hill.

Ruby loved it. She only had to look out of her bedroom window to see little grey and brown donkeys pulling sledges up the street, loaded with tourists' suitcases, and Mummy promised next summer they'd have window boxes filled with red geraniums.

The bruises on Ruby's legs faded from black to purple to brown, and finally to banana yellow. One morning, she examined her legs in bed and couldn't see a single mark. It was one of several improvements. Her chest still ached now and then, but she got used to reading in a chair, and walking up and down the hill twice a day to stroke the donkeys in their big green paddock chased away the last of her puppy fat.

For a while the police kept coming to see them to ask

them questions about Daddy and the posses. It took Ruby a little while to let go of her loyalty, but eventually she told them almost everything.

Almost.

One time a policeman asked about a gun and Ruby said, *What gun?* just like Mummy had told her to, and that worked, because they didn't ask again.

So she never told them how on the morning after the storm – when the sea had finally finished with Limeburn – Mummy had lifted up the pedlar's flagstone, and Ruby had put the gun underneath it.

Then they'd picked their way down the Peppercombe path – she in her jumper and bruised, bare legs, Mummy in muddy pyjamas and diamonds – and Mummy had told the police all that had happened, half talking, half crying.

The only bit she'd left out was the gun.

That was their little secret.

A month or so after they moved into their new home – just as the sun was making its sheepish return to North Devon – there was a knock on the door and it was Adam. He'd walked all the way from Limeburn.

It was chilly, but it was bright and dry, so he and Ruby played with Harvey for a bit, then they went up the hill to the visitor centre and bought ice creams, and ate them together next to the donkey paddock. Ruby told Adam all their names – Sarah and Eli and Peter and Jasper and all the rest. 'You can ride them and groom them and everything,' she told him. Then – in case he doubted such wonders – she added, 'I do it every time I get my pocket money.'

Adam told her about their house falling down, and the huge hole that was left in the cliff where the mighty oak used to be.

None of it mattered to Ruby now. It was as if Adam was talking about another place she'd only heard about.

'I'm cold,' she said, and Adam gave her his hoodie. It smelled just the same as before, and made her feel just as happy.

They didn't talk about Limeburn again until Adam was getting ready to walk the four miles home.

Then he asked, 'Are you ever coming back?'

'No,' she said. 'Are you?'

'It's a long way,' said Adam. 'It took me ages to walk here.'

Ruby nodded, but she felt sad. Adam was the one thing she missed about Limeburn.

She turned away and leaned over the fence. She put her palm against Eli's broad forehead with its Catherine wheel of grey hair in the middle. His heavy head relaxed and his eyelids drooped, as she rubbed him there like a magic lamp.

Adam climbed on to the fence beside her.

For a little while he just watched her.

Then he also reached out, and stroked the donkey's long, fluffy ears and said, 'Maybe I'll get a bicycle.'

∼

Ruby tried her best never to think of John Trick, because

whenever she did, it was of his bloody teeth bared as he hissed in her face, *I'm not your Daddy*.

Eventually, she hoped that that was true.

She did think a lot about Miss Sharpe and the little horseshoe on her charm bracelet. Without it, she would never have *just known* that Daddy was a killer. She might still have believed that he would come home and take care of them.

She might even have waited with Mummy for him to do just that . . .

She thought about Steffi Cole too – giving her five pounds before she was murdered, just because they both loved ponies. And about Frannie Hatton, taking her nose ring out and dropping it in the car-door pocket – hoping it might help somebody else, even though she knew that she was beyond help.

And it *had* helped, thought Ruby. It had helped *her*. They had *all* helped her in their own ways – living and dead – just the way Mummy had always helped her. She could see that now.

Slowly, slowly, slowly, Ruby Trick started to think that ending up as a woman might not be so terrible after all.

Every day, she felt a little bit better, a little bit safer. A little bit more grown up.

But at night . . .

At night the Gut swarmed with dark sharks, and the Gore loomed, black and shiny, out of the deep green sea.

At night she woke in terror from blood-soaked dreams.

At night Ruby Trick wondered where the Devil was now.

ACKNOWLEDGEMENTS

I wrote this book during a difficult year, and would not have been able to do so without the support and kindness of Jane Gregory, Bill Scott-Kerr and Larry Finlay. Many thanks, too, to Claire Ward, Kate Samano and Stephanie Glencross for their skill and hard work, and in particular to my editor, Sarah Adams, whose enthusiasm and insight gave me hope.

THE FACTS OF LIFE AND DEATH
READING GROUP GUIDE

• Early in the novel, Ruby Trick wonders what it will be like when 'the outside breaks in'. How does Belinda Bauer use the woods and the sea as part of the narrative? Can you imagine this story set elsewhere?

• Much of the story is narrated by a ten-year-old girl. Why has Bauer chosen to make Ruby the primary narrator? How do a child's insights differ from those of an adult?

• What does this story say about attitudes towards women? How have these attitudes shaped the lives of the characters?

• Why do you think the killer asks women to call their mothers before he kills them? What do you imagine his childhood was like?

• The men who have lost their jobs in this small town come together as cowboys once a week. Why do you think they do this?

• The relationship between children and their parents is at the centre of this story. How does Ruby's relationship with her mother and father change throughout the novel?

• How do corruption and manipulation play a part in the book?

• How did you feel about the ending of the novel? Do you think Ruby's mother made the right decision?

1

Valentine's Day, 2000

John Marvel looked at his watch.

It was eight thirty-seven, and he'd done the same thing less than a minute earlier. He had promised Debbie he would be home by nine. Normally it wouldn't matter, but tonight it did, although he wasn't sure why.

He felt the cold invade his lungs as he stared up into the dome of light that masked the stars. Frost hung in an ethereal ring around the streetlamp, waiting to settle, and Marvel could feel it fingering his shins through the thin material of his trousers.

He didn't like to be outdoors. It was too ... fresh. Even here, where London had sprawled south – overlapping the river and coating what used to be the Garden of England with its grime and its traffic and its smell of soot.

Marvel had started to sprawl with it: too much home cooking.

Too much home.

Comfort had always made him restless. He needed to be always moving on, moving up, otherwise he got frustrated.

Now he looked across the road to the King's Arms. It was filled with warmth and noise and booze. It had been more than a year since he'd been there – been drunk – and he still missed it like a lover, with a yearn in his chest and a dry lump in his throat. He wouldn't have gone in tonight. Or any night. It was a test – a game he played with himself. Driving past, slowing down, craning to look.

Not stopping.

But tonight he'd stopped. He didn't know why. He was no more thirsty than on any of the other four hundred days since he had had a drink.

And then he'd seen the woman.

And now it was hard to stand here, so near, and yet so far. The pub's grubby stained-glass windows were lit from behind, like Christ in a cathedral, calling all sinners.

Marvel checked his watch.

It was eight thirty-eight. The second hand arced through the quadrant in a series of cheap jerks.

'Look,' he sighed. 'Are you going to jump or not?'

The woman on the ledge flinched and her fingers pressed more tightly against the brick parapet. In the cold amber glow, Marvel could see the goose-bumps stippling her skinny arms. She was wearing indoor clothes. A thin, strappy top and skinny jeans and those stupid little ballet shoes women wore nowadays instead of high heels.

But then, she didn't strike him as a high-heels kind of girl. She had a pinched, undernourished look to her face that made her cheekbones sharp and her eyes seem huge, but in a way that was less Audrey Hepburn, more eating disorder.

Marvel guessed she was in her early twenties, but she could have been seventeen. Or forty.

She glanced at him and shrugged one bony shoulder in apology. 'I . . . I'm waiting for a train,' she said. Then she looked back down between her shoes at the tracks.

'Interesting,' said Marvel, with a sage nod of his head – as if she had explained everything.

He stepped towards her and leaned briefly over the parapet to look at the glimmering rails. While he did, she gripped harder and watched him warily – as if he might suddenly lunge at her, grab her, pull her backwards over the wall to safety.

Heroically save her life.

Despite his name, Marvel did no such thing.

Instead he gave a humourless grunt and said, 'Then you're shit out of luck. The trains don't go through here after eight.'

She said nothing for a long moment. Then, without raising her head, she said, 'Wh— what time is it now?'

Marvel lifted his watch again – tilting it so that the face was illuminated by the streetlight. 'Eight forty.'

The girl nodded slowly at the tracks, her straggly brown hair veiling everything but her brow and the red tip of her nose. She wrinkled the brow and wiped the nose on the back of her hand.

'Oh,' she said, and Marvel could tell she was crying.

Crying was not his thing, so he decided against words of comfort or a pat on the back, which might open some kind of emotional floodgate. He just stood there while she sobbed quietly.

'I can't get anything right,' she finally whispered.

'Join the club,' he snorted.

She only shook her head slowly, apparently declining to join the ranks of any club that would have him as a member – even in her desperate state.

'What's your name?' he said.

She didn't tell him and he didn't care, but he had to pretend. It was expected.

Marvel wasn't going to keep the nine-o'clock promise. He was glad. Promises were traps; shackles to be broken.

I'll be home by nine.

I'm not in the pub.

I love you.

The girl was still crying a little.

He looked at his watch again. Eight forty-three. 'Come on,' he said brusquely. 'Hop back over and I'll take you home.'

She gave a long, shuddering sigh and nodded fractionally. 'OK.'

Marvel was a little surprised. That was easy.

Too easy.

His jaw clenched with annoyance. She'd probably never meant to jump at all. He'd stood here in the freezing February night for almost thirty bloody minutes in full tortuous view of the King's Arms, and the whole time she'd just been waiting for an opportunity to climb back over the wall.

Time-waster.

His life was full of them and they made him sick.

Still, it had given him a good excuse to be late. Not that he'd really needed one. He often lied to Debbie about where he'd been and what he'd done, and it didn't change a thing. What could she say? In his line of work you could make up any old bollocks and people had to believe you. Perk of the job.

He put out a hand to steady the girl as she swung her legs over the parapet, but she swayed away from him, so he left her to it. She slid awkwardly off the wall and dropped on to the road beside him. She was almost a foot shorter than he was, and Marvel was no giant.

She shivered and hugged her own arms for warmth.

Before either of them could say anything, the eight twenty from London Victoria shook the bridge.

They both stared down at the blurry black roof, blocking out the rails as it raced under their feet and through Bickley station.

In the silence that followed, the girl gave him an accusing look, but Detective Chief Inspector Marvel only shrugged.